The Esfah Sagas:
Rise of the Champions

By
Christopher D. Schmitz

A Dragon Dice novel

CHRISTOPHER D. SCHMITZ

© 2021 by Christopher D. Schmitz
All rights reserved. No part of this book may be reproduced, stored in a retrieval system, or transmitted in any form or by any means without the prior written permission of the publishers, except by a reviewer who may quote brief passages in a review to be printed in a newspaper, magazine, or journal.
The final approval for this literary material is granted by the author.
Dragon Dice and its terms including Esfah, Coral Elf (selumari), Dwarf (vagha), Lava Elf (morehl), Goblin (trogs), Amazon, Firewalker (empyrea), Undead (bloodless), Feral (ghwereste), Swamp Stalker (sarslayan), Frostwing (Areosa), Scalder (Faeli), Treefolk (efflorah), Dragonkin, Eldarim, Eldrymetallum, Magestorm! and Dragon Dice II: Gamer's Edition are trademarks owned by SFR, Inc.
Forgotten Realms and Dragonlance are trademarks owned by Wizards of the Coast.

PUBLISHED BY TREESHAKER BOOKS

The Esfah Sagas

Rise and Fall of the Obsidian Grotto
Cast of Fate
Army of the Dead

The Relic Quests
Ashes of Ailushurai
Rise of the Champions
Drakuwar (coming 2022)

The Cyrean Songs
Chill Wind
Eye of the Storm
Secrets of the Shadowlands (coming 2022)

Christopher D. Schmitz

Stay up to date on the world of Esfah!

Get a free copy of book 1 in the Esfah Sagas by visiting:

www.subscribepage.com/getfreedragondicenovels

Subscribers who sign up for this no-spam email list will get free books, exclusive content, and more! You'll get *Rise & Fall of the Obsidian Grotto* immediately… If you would like more details or want to follow the author, you can find his details at the end of this book.

Background

Dragon Dice™ was originally created by Lester Smith and produced by TSR in 1995. It is an Origins Award winning strategy game where players create mythical armies using dice to represent each troop and is one of several collectible dice games that emerged in the 1990s. The game combines strategy and skill as well as a little luck.

After several years, TSR, now owned by Wizards of the Coast, had put Dragon Dice™ on hold to work on other projects. In October of 2000, SFR Inc. purchased the rights to Dragon Dice™.

Most of the races and monsters in original TSR Dragon Dice were created by Lester Smith and include some creatures unique to a fantasy setting and others that are familiar to the Dungeons & Dragons role-playing game. While the world of Esfah, where Dragon Dice™ takes place, has many similarities to that of Dungeons & Dragons, it is distinctly different in many respects. In some ways, there are greater unknowns and its history is both newer and older all at once.

Around the end of 1995, I was a teenager and avid board gamer who had a burger slinging job (which gave me a disposable income) and a car (that took most of my disposable income.) In addition to many other games I played as part of a regular quartet of gamers, Dragon Dice™ was one that we all enjoyed.

I fondly remember how the four of us would cut out of elective classes, study halls, and independent learning periods to meet up for gaming sessions. Dragon Dice™ came in a pocketable carrying bag which made it perfect for that.

We also had a mutual acquaintance. An older gentleman in town owned a new and used bookstore that also carried a limited supply of gaming products. Though he did not stock Dragon Dice™, he did have a copy of *Cast of Fate*, the first Dragon Dice™ novel which included a special promo die. I snatched it up right away, as the most avid reader of the foursome (which allowed me to become the dedicated DM for our role-playing game sessions and solidified my path as a story-teller). The included promotional die was our bright and shiny object for months.

Cast of Fate by Allen Varney was not the only book set in the world of Esfah, though it remains one of the few. As I write and publish more and more fiction (both Fantasy and Science Fiction), I tend to write the stories that I've always wanted to...and I've always wanted to have a voice in a shared universe. Creating a story within the Dragon Dice™ universe is something I've always wanted to do, so I give a special thanks to SFR, a company composed of true and like-minded fans who have kept alive a product that was one of the gems of the 1990s.

-- Chris

FOREWORD

In eons past, when time was young and creation malleable, the four powers of Nature -- earth, air, fire, and water -- the children of Nature, gods in their own rights, brought forth two races of being to care for their fledgling world created by the all-father, Tarvanehl. One race, the selumari or coral elves, were created to husband the fluid forces of air and water. The other race, the dwarvish vagha, embodied the stability of earth and the tempering power of fire. Together, these two peoples worked to nurture their infant world into something glorious and beautiful.

But Nature had a nemesis in Death, the spirit of entropy. In imitation of Nature, Death brought into being its own races: The morehl, or lava elves, who worshiped fire and destruction, and the trogs, a race of goblins, who sprang from earth and corruption. From the moment of their creation, the morehl and trogs sowed conflict, defiling the very world that gave them life and corrupting the other races who tended it. War sparked over land and possessions. Soon, hordes of dispossessed selumari, vagha, morehl, and trogs swept across the lands of Esfah, locked in endless battle.

In their struggles for supremacy over the fledgling world, the First Races pressed other magical beings into their service. The morehl were the first to do so, bringing up fire-breathing Hellhounds and web-casting Driders from the deepest caverns below. The trogs followed suit, leading Trolls, Harpies, and other monsters into battle. In response, the selumari called forth Coral Giants from the ocean and swarms of Sprites from the skies. The vagha enlisted Gargoyles, Androsphinxes, and other creatures of the crags.

Conflict raged across the face of Esfah and Death delighted in the carnage.

Darkness battled against light. Each side pushed harder for victory and the battles grew ever more savage and desperate. New races arose, each pressed into the fray of bloody struggle with no end in sight.

Saddened by the bloodshed, Nature, the goddess-mother Ghaeial, dealt death to preserve life. Death, or Malgrimm the bastard child, son of Ghaeial and Selurehl and the god known as Void. Malgrimm reveled in the chaos, terror, and pain that war brought.

A tide of champions arose to safeguard the realm. Wars continued and an entire age passed. Pockets of tenuous peace grew from apathy--a new trick engineered by Death to soften the resolve of Nature's troops, almost seeming to abandon his playground for the comforts of the Abyss--but his attention had never truly waned.

Esfah has never known true peace. It is not in the planet's makeup: This is why the gods' children war on their behalf. Both old and new races struggle ever onward--creatures inspired to greater ends, forever in search of either an end to the bloodshed, or carnage renewed--as each is bent towards his or her own ends.

Esfah cannot know peace. Malgrimm--the god known as Death--will not allow it. Only a few know his true name. And to speak it aloud is to court Death himself.

For a short video overview of Esfah's origins, visit
https://youtu.be/JhF8RPFkF9I

For up to date information on the world of Esfah, and all things related to the Dragon Dice universe, including products and specials, check out:

http://www.sfr-inc.com

RISE OF THE CHAMPIONS

Prologue

Avanna stared into the airless night from her perch on the surface of Rhaudian, Esfah's moon. From atop the tall stone, the goddess watched the planet as it hung overhead in the distance, glowing like a multi-colored jewel: A roiling swirl of vibrant color. She glowered, wishing it boasted more grays and muted tones.

Behind Avanna sat her sisters, Mitta and Evaquar. They'd come down from their stones and sat in the middle of the celestial triad.

Avanna clambered down and dropped to the dust. Her skeletal consort leaned forward eagerly from where he waited. The Death Bard clutched his rebab and bow, hoping to please her with a tune on the stringed instrument.

"Not now, Hielosch," she said with barely a thought, dismissing him. The creature had once been a proud eldarim. Now, he was known to mortals as the dirge player who escorted them to the afterlife. Hielosch slunk back into the shadows.

Avanna, daughter of the god Turambar, stared jealously at her sisters who watched mortal lives play out in the ether of their looking glass. They'd found some new game of interest. "It is not fair for you to play without me." She took her seat.

Evaquar shrugged. "Perhaps neither of us wishes too harsh a fate for those souls we have guided. We don't all enjoy tormenting mortals," she accused the harshest of the Daughters of Fate.

Avanna wrinkled her nose. "What are you talking about? Mitta has tortured far more than I ever have—perhaps not so fully, but her numbers are far greater."

"I do not torture for the sake of my own amusement," Mitta clarified. "I merely give folk what they deserve—what they have earned by way of a moral ledger. But if you say that I am in the lead, then so be it." Mitta smiled her challenge.

Even Evaquar offered her an askew look. "Perhaps if *we* had each birthed a new race of devoted adherents, the middle ground would not look so large?" Evaquar summoned the magic coursing through her and forced Mitta's visage to transform so that she appeared to be the morehl enchantress Roweena: The mother of the fearsome firewalker race.

Mitta scowled. They fought like sisters… but they were still family. And like many sisters, they were in constant competition. "I thought your love life was 'not to be discussed?' Are we now allowed to talk about it?"

Evaquar quibbled with her sister over the mortal who had escaped her desire so long ago. She shook her head with a glare. A warning.

Avanna grinned. Mitta and Evaquar were often in league with each other, and so she took pleasure in setting them against one another. It also brought her pleasure to know that Evaquar wanted only peace, prosperity, and pleasure for the great love of her life; a tragic figure who had fallen into *her* hands by the end. *Though my sister has not noticed that he is a game piece that was never removed from play.*

Grinning, Avanna leaned closer to the looking glass and searched out what the others had been watching.

"Could these be a new set of champions?" Avanna mumbled. Her sisters had quieted in the background and joined her.

"We will see how it plays out, and who wins," Evaquar said as they surrounded the glass and cast their gazes into it, examining the interweaving strands of silk that connected each of those souls to each other. She watched a group of friends—adventurers—whose strength grew. They appeared like a tapestry to the fate sisters. But this one frayed at the edges.

Normally, they could observe the totality of a person's

life, with all their works and deeds. "This group is difficult," said Mitta, joining Avanna's side. "They are intimately linked and we cannot discern their threads fully. They are an anomaly."

Evaquar bowed her head. "It means that at least one of them is a champion of the gods. We will not be able to determine how to count them until his or her lives are each collected."

"That is easy enough." Avanna snapped her fingers and her formerly eldarim consort hurried over on dry, rattling joints. He clutched his instrument, and it transformed into a hooked reaping blade.

"No," demanded Mitta. "You may not simply end them now. It will ruin the weave... and the game."

Avanna scowled. "Then we cannot interfere? Where is the fun in that?"

"She did not say we cannot interfere," Evaquar pointed out. "Just that you cannot send poor Hielosch to collect them before their natural time—before the threads are woven."

Mitta leaned in conspiratorially. "Sisters, a new game is on. Shall we establish the rules?" She set a playing board upon the natural table in their midst and laid out the stones. They were marked tiles of different colors.

Avanna narrowed her eyes as she glanced to the living tapestry. "Oh, look. They have father's bracelets." Avanna set her side of the board and Evaquar took the opposite seat.

Evaquar quirked her lips and pushed a stone into play. Her sister made a counter move. They traded a few positions; it was very early in the game, still.

"Remember this," Avanna said and placed her finger upon a stone. She grinned wickedly. "The moves I make early will seem insignificant, but if you lose track of them, it will yield disastrous consequences." She stared at the looking glass. "Shall we set the stakes?"

Evaquar furrowed her brow. This was no friendly game.

"That one there," Avanna said and pointed to the sharp-eared individual. "That one's fate is the prize."

CHAPTER ONE

Year 1140 of the Second Age

Nodhan slunk through the streets of Giyrnach. The Dohanese port city was a notorious hive of villainy, as was most of Dohan proper. Sixty percent of the goods on any shelf were stolen, and many shipping companies with illegitimate ties operated out of Dohan, especially the ports of Giyrnach.

The red-skinned lava elf passed a warehouse that boasted no insignia; it hung across the edges of a few wharfs where laborers pushed cargo aboard a ship with a crimson line of paint across its transom. Nodhan knew the ship's captain, and he'd bartered for passage to Giyrnach on the *Red Herring* a number of times. He knew it made regular voyages across the Talvat Sea to Innismoon or Reeflocke on Sontarra, five-hundred leagues west. Sontarra's reputation was as equally admirable as Dohan's was villainous. The crew of the *Red Herring* had a deal with a local merchant who offloaded cargo from the Dohanese vessel and onto his small fleet of Sontarran ships, which could trade in ports where the *Red Herring* was forbidden.

He tore his eyes away from the *Red Herring* and quickened his pace when he recognized the *Chariot's Wake* berthed adjacent to it. The *Chariot's Wake* was owned by the notorious pirate and former amazon warrior, Ry'ober. Nodhan had crossed paths with her in the past and didn't look forward to another meeting. Luckily, it looked as if the *Chariot's Wake* was preparing to venture out on a longer trip to parts unknown.

The red elf kept his head down and headed through an alley, out of sight. *Best not to kick a hornets' nest*, he thought, before emerging onto the broader streets of Giyrnach.

Giyrnach was filled with pickpockets and other ne'er-do-wells. The morehl thief had grown up amongst such folk and knew all the tricks of the trade. He kept one hand in his pocket and resting upon his purse. The other he rested on the hilt of the dagger sheathed at his hip. One prized item hid behind his shirt, dangling around his neck. The seed he'd stolen from the gwereste while his former traveling companions crossed the Black Glades on their mad quest to confront Melkior the lich.

Nodhan absentmindedly touched the seed to make sure it was still bound by the strap that held it around his neck. So powerful—and valuable—was the seed that he did not know if he could ever attempt to sell the thing. He certainly could not plant it, not after its former owner activated it with the Waters of Lethial. He barely knew what it was, but he had his suspicions.

For now, the morehl traveler remained content to keep it... Though he'd begun hearing strange voices in his mind. Not quite voices—echoes of unheard voices.

Nonetheless, he'd taken another item from the trove he knew he *could* sell, along with the other items he'd collected prior to being caught and imprisoned by the prince of Niamarlee. Among them was the legendary *Book of the Void*. Nodhan had seen the rising interest in cults dedicated to the god of Death. He knew this book would fetch him a fortune. He'd already stashed the *Book of the Void* at his secret home in Port Orric, on the Talvatic Coast.

Hopefully Laelysh has the tome copied before I return to collect it for whatever buyer old Grude can find me.

Nodhan nodded cautiously to an empyrean patroller who walked past. The firewalkers had invaded five years ago and took over Dohan, occupying Prodhan, the capital, with their vassal Imperium. Their presence was meant to clean up Dohan's reputation. Nodhan didn't think it would stick forever, but it had the benefit of driving some of the most unseemly folk into the shadows, which helped the elf know where to look for trouble whenever he desired it.

The firewalker gave a slight wiggle of his forefingers: A secret signal in the hand-speak language of the thieves' guild. It indicated a potential accomplice. *The patroller was on the take.* He nodded, and they walked out of sight of each other.

It's comforting to know that, as much as things change, things still stay the same.

Nodhan ducked into a slightly lopsided building with a decaying foundation. The sign identified it as *Grude's Pawn and Loan*. The shop looked small inside. Mostly assorted sundries and baubles leftover from unpaid loans adorned the shelves. Nodhan knew that the real action took place in the other rooms hidden deeper within the building. Grude was Nodhan's fence.

Two other patrons stood in the shop, talking more than browsing. Nodhan could tell by the looks of them that they were adventurers, but still green—much like that selumari and vagha he'd traveled with back on Charnock, though they did season significantly by the end of their journey. The pair of customers had the right equipment, but lacked a certain discretion true rogues adopted in order to be successful.

"I'm telling you to get it," the one hissed. "The guy said it was *magic*. A gnomish blade could come in handy if we're going to claim the relic."

"I dunno," his friend muttered, staring at the price tag as Nodhan peeked through the shelves that separated them. He saw the first adventurer roll up a small scroll.

Nodhan knew the sword in question was not a product of eldrymetallum, nor was it forged by any gremmlobahnd forge. The sword was one of hundreds of cheap knockoffs created to trick foolish buyers. In the morehl's opinion, they were not even good swords.

One of his marks fidgeted with a trinket on the counter, and Nodhan spotted a symbol cut into his flesh. It peeked out from the exposed skin where the sleeve shifted.

He had done enough jobs for The Black Forest to know

it was a cult membership symbol on the adventurer's arm. Nodhan couldn't pick up all of their chatter, but he did overhear a word he didn't think he'd hear again soon: *Kreethaln*.

Nodhan grinned. The whispers in his mind seemed to whelm for a moment once he'd decided on his plot, but he pushed them out and carried on, placing all of his smallest coins in a small pouch he let dangle from an ill-fitting clasp at his belt. He approached their part of the store and did his best to appear like a bumbling fool.

The two adventurers quickly sized him up, took him for an imbecile, and then walked past. They bumped their way through the aisle and made the slightest contact with him. Making their apologies, they left the store with haste.

Nodhan grinned. They'd taken the bait. And with the floor clear, he gave the goblin shopkeeper a pass code to grant him admission to the back room, where he found Grude leaning against a table as he examined his records. Grude ignored an irked adventurer who complained that the savvy broker had just sold a treasure map out from under him.

Grude waved him off. "They outbid you fair and square. That map was one of a kind, and if you truly thought its potential treasure was priceless, you would have bid higher."

The figure, a tall eldarim male, furrowed his brow. He crossed his arms and stood resolute. But no amount of cajoling could undo the fact that he'd missed out on an important purchase.

Grude noticed he had a new guest and slapped his books shut for privacy's sake. "Nodhan, come, come... Sit."

The fence was a twisted faeli with a shrunken left arm and leg and undersized wings. Grude's bottom jaw seemed too long for his face, and his teeth were not quite right. But he was every bit as resourceful as he was ugly. "You have something to sell?"

The elf nodded. "I do. Very high end. It will not be

cheap—it might even be one of a kind. An item of legend, perfect for the buyers in your special roster of clients."

Grude cocked his head. "Go on," he said eagerly. Grude worked on percentage, so he enjoyed the high-end items, as long as a buyer could be procured.

Nodhan shot a sidelong look at the upset eldarim. He cocked his head and the faeli and morehl moved into a private room.

"The Book of the Void," Nodhan said with his voice verging on a whisper.

"Bah. That's a legend," he laughed.

Nodhan only stared at him.

"You have a book penned by Melkior the Dread, written upon pages made of pressed vagha skin, and bound in dragon hide?" Grude shot him a look of disbelief. "Then let me see it."

"It's no myth," Nodhan said coolly. "I have the only known copy. I chanced upon it in Krierfar's vault as I plundered it in Undrakull."

"Ah yes, our mutual friend Krierfar. I heard he died... That he was eaten by a fiendish consort who now rules in his stead. How is the old spider?"

"Dead," said Nodhan. "But that had nothing to do with me."

Grude shrugged. He hadn't cared either way. "I cannot sell anything without examining it first. You know my rules."

The lava elf crossed his arms. "You will need to take my reputation on this one, Grude. Have I ever delivered you something sub-par? I can't risk moving it from its safe and hidden location. But I will arrange private delivery after verifying payment to an escrow; you may manage that entire endeavor and take an extra percentage."

Grude stroked his chin and considered the offer. Finally, he said, "Fine. I will reach out to some buyers. It will take some time to arrange. There are several parties who may be interested for different reasons."

"That is fine. I'll check back soon," the red elf said.

"Plenty of leads, my friend," Grude's voice dripped with false sincerity. *Friend.* "I know of many artifacts and rumors of treasure. The adventuring business is still booming—even if only a handful of leads have any substance. But I have ways to sift those from the bunk. You know I always give the best leads to my most *promising* prospects... and you are one of them. Even if you never did bring me those bones I sent you after."

Nodhan nodded. "Not every lead pans out. But let's at least be honest—your best leads are the ones that make you richest."

Grude smiled with teeth sticking out from his parted lips. "We understand each other perfectly."

He suddenly felt a compulsion to leave, and a warm sensation in Nodhan's chest grew near where the seed hung bound. With a final glance back, he exited the store and began walking.

Nodhan pulled out the map he'd lifted from the pockets of the unseasoned adventurer on the storeroom floor where he'd first entered. Whatever it was, the eldarim who'd lost the bidding war was anxious to have it. He could wait until Grude found a qualified buyer; until then, he'd found his next mark, an easy cash grab.

"Hey! Wait up," Nodhan called to the tall eldarim who walked the street. He was the same one who had been in Grude's shop earlier. "I think I have a deal for you... *if you still have the gold to purchase that map you wanted.*"

Mantieth waited in the hall, absentmindedly turning the bracelet in full revolutions around his wrist. The door finally opened and the coral elf prince brightened when he recognized the dwarf prince, Hy'Targ.

Stifling a cough, they walked towards the exit of the

underground halls, much to Mantieth's relief. He was a child of air and water, a follower of the gods Ailuril and Auguarehl, and was far more comfortable without the walls of a mountain pressing in against him.

"Where is Elorall?" Hy'Targ asked after Mantieth's fellow selumari: the blue-skinned elves. "I thought she'd be with you?"

Speaking of walls pressing in against me. "She's on her way," the elf said. "We were just leaving Niamarlee when she remembered she had some last minute duties on behalf of the throne. I expect she'll arrive tonight or tomorrow."

Hy'Targ arched a bushy red eyebrow. "Your father couldn't spare her a day's worth of work?"

Mantieth shrugged. "I'm a bit relieved, to be honest," he rummaged through his silvery hair.

The dwarf grinned and laughed, "Is she tiring you out?"

Mantieth shook his head. "No. No, it's not that. It's just... It feels good to be out with just the two of us for a bit," he said. "It's just too big a romance—it's so much so soon. I feel like I'm losing who I am in all of it."

"Isn't that the point?" Hy'Targ pointed out. "That's kind of the definition of marriage."

Mantieth scowled and bit his cheek.

"Well, don't look at me," said Hy'Targ as they exited the massive gates of the Irontooth Mountain keep. They meandered into the outdoor courtyard. "You're the one who proposed to the girl."

Mantieth sighed with agreement. "I guess that's true..."

Hy'Targ caught his friend's tone. "And don't you dare break her heart. Nothin' leads to more trouble than a scorned sorcerer. Especially an *angry female* sorcerer... Even more so if her heart's been broken. You love her, right?"

Mantieth nodded slowly, after a moment of thought.

The dwarf stopped him. "See, that's wrong. You can't pause. You gotta shake yer noggin' till it practically falls off.

Real or not, it's the rule of relationships."

Mantieth cracked a smile, and the mood shifted. "You know a lot about women, eh?"

"Well, I've read a lot of books." Hy'Targ laughed. Both of them knew Hy'Targ was famously inexperienced in matters of the heart. "But seriously, be good to her, for both of yer sakes. When my mother... when *Queen Sh'Ttil* disappeared... my father... " He couldn't even bring himself to speak of the heartbreak felt by her loss. "My father has not endured it well."

Mantieth bobbed his head. "The same with my father, though Queen Naemyar still lives." A gray cloud passed across his face. "I wonder if it had been better if he'd been widowed rather than estranged."

Hy'Targ clapped his friend on the back. "And have you spoken to your mother?"

Mantieth shook his head. "We don't talk. She left on unknown—and strange—terms. It feels more like apathy than anger, and both my parents are too stubborn to reach out for one another."

Hy'Targ guffawed as they walked. "Your father is anything but weak willed. I can relate to that."

A tall humanoid in robes and light armor crossed their path. "What are we laughing about, today?"

Hy'Targ grinned. "Women, Taryl."

Taryl raised his eyebrows and grinned. He laughed. "A most dangerous adversary." Taryl was a sell-sword, though he called himself a mercenary capable of keeping both friends and principles. He'd been the vaghan king's bodyguard and head of security for decades.

"Even more than dragons?" Mantieth asked.

"Infinitely worse," Taryl said and winked.

A full blooded eldarim, he was thicker and more muscular than most humans, even the amazon warrior caste. Aside from a slightly flattened nose, the eldarim people were widely regarded as handsome, physically impressive, and talented at both magic and tending draconic creatures. They were especially adept at working with the dragonkin—all the varied breeds of drakufreet.

Some eldarim, such as Taryl, were also talented enough to directly control dragons. Because the overwhelming majority of eldarim births were male, many eldarim took lovers across racial lines, and many of their kind had been labeled sluts by jealous suitors.

"I'd rather wrestle a trio of wyrms than a trio of beautiful women," Taryl joked, casting an eye aside to acknowledge the lascivious glances three selumari women gave him. Each was a part of Mantieth's royal entourage. The eldarim winked. "Well, maybe not *wrestle*... more like have tea with."

Mantieth shot a look over his shoulder and glanced at the three women who'd served as road guards since the Great Coastal Road was still plagued with trog raiders. "Hey! One of those women is married to a friend of mine."

Taryl adjusted his belt. "Apologies in advance to your friend." He called out, "Do you ladies like tea?"

Hy'Targ chuckled and gave the eldarim a mocking shove. "Leave them alone." He chuckled. "Besides, I thought you always said the sword and the dragon were your only mistresses?"

He shrugged. "Like you with your books? I've known a few women capable of changing that. I spent most of my youth in Empyreanoral amongst the firewalkers' famed Pyre Company. You've never kissed a woman until your lips have been burned by an empyrean courtesan." Taryl changed the subject, "Should I assume you are resuming the search for Brentésion?"

Hy'Targ shook his head slightly. "Something else. Word has reached me about a clue for the second Kreethaln."

Rare artifacts remained scattered around Esfah after the

famed Magestorm Wars at the end of the first age. One of those, the mysterious Kreethaln, was part of a trio of arcane objects. They'd claimed the first already and used it to keep their four-armed friend, Varanthl, alive by its power. It did more than that. It gave the giant humanoid the ability to rapidly heal. The others were each granted other magic abilities.

"Niamarlee's scouts are closing in on the bulk of the trog infestation and they are still looking for signs of the great beast," Mantieth said. His voice sounded like he was not hopeful Hy'Targ's unique mount, Brentésion, would be located soon. Reclaiming what was stolen by the goblins was imperative for the dwarves of Irontooth, but Brentésion had to be found first.

"We are on our way to notify the stable master of our trip. We'll leave in a few days, after the rest of my companions arrive," said Hy'Targ.

Taryl bent slightly at the waist. "I shall tell him on your behalf; I am headed in that direction," he said, locking eyes with Hy'Targ. "I should like a moment with the prince before you depart, however. I hope to ask you a favor when there is time."

"I've got a few spare moments..."

Before Hy'Targ could fully respond, Taryl had already departed in the opposite direction he'd come and headed back towards the stables. Hy'Targ shot him a suspicious look, but then let it go. Few folk in the Irontooth Mountains were beyond suspicion, but Hy'Targ considered Taryl as one of them.

Elorall saw Mantieth off from Niamarlee with a kiss, knowing she'd see him in a couple days after arriving in the Irontooth Kingdom.

She grinned. Kissing him was unlike what she had imagined for so many years. They'd been friends since childhood, and for some reason, he seemed aloof whenever they kissed—but then again, she had never kissed anyone else before, and had no idea what it was like to kiss another. All her life she knew that Mantieth was the boy she'd grow up to marry... It took longer than she had hoped for the prince to realize that as well.

Regardless, she never doubted their love. She'd known him too long to think it fake. *Maybe that's why things feel awkward or different than I imagined?*

She turned as soon as he was out of sight and dashed back inside the castle. Elorall silently cursed the messenger that she'd sent to Tulgesh months ago. It was a city in Cyrea, halfway across the world. Despite the distance, she'd expected him to return weeks ago. Elorall had spotted him right before Mantieth's trip to the vagha kingdom. A white lie bought her a day so she could catch up with her agent.

Elorall cornered the selumari traveler, an elf named Kareth. "You have a report?" she asked, motioning that they should walk away from the hearing of others.

Kareth blanched slightly at Elorall's appearance. Elorall had more than a keen command of Esfah's magic; she was the future queen of Niamarlee and currently an envoy of King Leidergelth. The king was not known to be a forgiving person and did not permit his affairs to be meddled with. Kareth gulped. "I do."

They walked even further from the castle for Kareth's comfort. "I did see Queen Naemyar, and I told her everything you instructed me."

"How did she respond?"

"Indifferent at first," Kareth said. "She was happy for you and Mantieth. She made no initial promises, but later agreed to return for the wedding, but only once the trouble in Tulgesh and Balgavarr has passed."

Elorall cocked her head.

"King Matrek may call upon her company, the Riechus Aqualines to help move troops," Kareth explained. "It looks like a full-scale war in the north... but not against the areosan kingdom. Some new threat is causing strange bedfellows in the Balgavarr Reaches, and Queen Naemyar has offered assistance to the great granddaughter of the dwarf hero, Zephras Thunderfist, daughter of Balgavarr's king—or what passes for it in those parts."

"Do they have some ideas what they face?" Elorall asked, both worried for the continent and also for her own future wedding plans. "Don't they have faeli nearby? Could it be scalder mischief?"

Kareth continued, "Barbaric creatures, but unlikely. The Shadowlands are home to the areosa." He shuddered. "Citizens of Tulgesh don't trust the frostwings even if the areosans helped fight back the morehl and faeli during the last war. Though that was a generation ago. The dwarves have a solid alliance with frostwings, however."

Elorall furrowed her brow. Like most people this far south, she'd never seen a frostwing, and they drove her to curiosity.

"I met one of the creatures in passing. The areosa are far different from dwarves or elves." He shrugged. "The journey is far, though, and I suspect the situation may have resolved itself by now."

Elorall nodded measuredly and recognized his underlying request for some rest.

"Queen Naemyar did invite you to write her regularly and promises to reply, provided you don't share her letters with the king. She insists that he must write to her in his own hand if they wish to communicate... She does greatly desire to see trade open up between Tulgesh and Niamarlee, and plans to be present at the wedding. Once you have given her a date."

"Of course. Thank you, Kareth," she dismissed him and leaned against a wall.

Certainly she wants open trade lines... Naemyar is not a

princess—she is the daughter of a wealthy businessman. She's a different sort of royalty, and if I know royalty, they're all too damned stubborn to just have an honest conversation—even with their spouses. At least Mantieth is different.

Elorall turned the bracelet on her wrist. It held the ring Mantieth had given her when he'd proposed on the battlefield above Ender's Gulf. *He's not like the rest... I'm sure he'd tell me if something bothered him,* she thought. *I hope I know what I'm getting into... marrying into Naemyar and Leidergelth's problems.*

Melkior walked between the rows of headstones, mausoleums, and burial mounds. Decay riddled the graveyard where so many generations of dead were interred.

The lich had once been the undead champion of Death, the firstborn of the grave. He'd commanded untold power... Until he'd been defeated by the other Champions: The heroes chosen by the gods. And then he'd been resurrected, only to be defeated again, and on the verge of reclaiming his beloved Ailushurai—the one bonded to him in both life and death.

He shifted his bandages where the dust and salt leaked through the grievous wounds he'd been dealt by the dwarven whelp, Hy'Targ, and his four-armed friend. They'd used some kind of magic artifact to inject Melkior with a dose of raw, living energy. *Life-Bringer... One of the Kreethaln relics crafted by the gremmlobahnd.* Melkior snarled. He hated gnomes.

Gnomes, the gremmlobahnd, were master tinkerers and had crafted many arcane devices throughout the early ages, though Melkior had no idea what had happened to them while he lay in his grave for these past thousand years. They had, at some point, mysteriously disappeared from the face of Esfah.

He only knew that he still preferred to wield weapons

made by the eldarim, his people. They had long pre-existed the Making of the Elder Races by the gods. The eldarim were forgotten castoffs, masters at their pursuits, and their weapons rivaled that of the gnomes—even without imbuing them with the mystic eldrymetallum: the celestial metal that fell to Esfah from the stars and which the gnomes wove into their creations.

Melkior staunched the dry leakage from his body and pulled his cloak tighter to obfuscate his appearance. Two nights ago, someone had thrown a bottle deep into his cave. Among shards of busted glass, he'd found a parchment with a crude map leading him here. It listed only today's date and had a drawing of a broken circle. An ancient symbol of Melkior's master, the god known as Death, whose name must not be spoken.

He crumpled the note and dropped it amongst the tombstones. "Malgrimm... " Melkior hissed beneath his breath. The Death god had forsaken him and left him in the cave where Melkior and his dracolich, Rahkawmn, brooded as the undead eldarim tried to recover from his wounds. The spiritual vitriol had amplified within that hole and formed a festration; a place of intense evil that could bolster Death's power. Melkior imagined some rogue cultist had been drawn to the cave because of the growing festration. Like a dowser compelled toward water the cultists had thrown in the invitation.

It is a wonder that Rahkawmn did not eat the person. The lich scanned the tombs as he walked and reached out with his senses. He felt tremors in the dark, like micro-vibrations in the air, and smelled the blood of living creatures. Something turned in his gut. A pang of longing; a hunger to devour the flesh of the living. Melkior shook it away. He was a lich and a sentient agent of the dark one, not a mindless undead drone driven by impulse. The dark magics of Malgrimm sustained him, not the nourishment of flesh.

As Melkior approached the center of the cemetery,

heads slowly raised over the low mausoleums rooflines and tombstone heads. Low hoods covered brows as the cultists stared at him.

The lich knew his coastal cave was just inside the Hadden Bay and west of Trellan, a free city home to many folk of various races. Even in the darkness, his undead eyes could tell them apart. A handful of trogs, some morehl from nearby Garnock, and a couple humans. Surprisingly, he also detected a couple dwarves and selumari among them too.

Melkior cocked his head and grinned at the revelation. The two Elder Races had long championed their kinds as the primary forces of good and the guardians of nature, but here was proof that Malgrimm's rot had taken hold amongst even these. Melkior grinned and felt the eyes of cultists upon them.

One of their number approached slowly, cautiously, and with his robe splayed open, though the hood remained down. Upon the creature's breast, his tunic had been stitched with silvery lines to depict an inverted tree with no leaves.

Melkior spoke in his raspy, low voice. "So the Black Forest has endured all this time? It was still young when I walked the face of Esfah." He pulled back his hood and revealed his face. The ratty shawl of his cloak hung open for all to see the sallow skin beneath and the distinct tattoo upon his chest: The contract which deeded him the soul of his beloved Ailushurai—upon command, the god of the Void would be forced to relinquish it to him.

A gasp ran through the gathered coven. Their leader reached out a blue-skinned hand and gently caressed the tattooed chest.

"It is you. It is truly Melkior: The herald of Lord Death." The selumari leader whirled in a circle and urged the flock to approach. "I am Nesma of the Black Forest and I lead the Cult of Trellan. We are honored that you would come to us first. Long has this sect been of the Melkite persuasion..."

"Melkite?" the lich interrupted.

"The prophecy," Nesma insisted with shock in her voice, as if Melkior himself did not know it. "Before the end of an age, the chosen one would return: The herald, a true son of Malgrimm… " a hush fell over them when the sacred name was uttered.

"A sacrifice must be made," someone called from the rear. Anytime the name was spoken, blood had to be shed.

Another spoke with an insistent tone. "We must send for Forktongue at once to test the prophecy." Nesma nodded at both ideas and waved to a hooded figure in the distance.

The cultist dragged a bound and gagged dwarf into a clearing between the tombs and slit his throat, leaving him to bleed out among the crypts.

Nesma continued once the blood toll had been paid. "Some insisted it would be Nekarthis, the Lord of the Netherwold… but others felt it was his predecessor: Melkior. Those believers are the Melkites." Nesma took a knee and then prostrated herself before him. "We are yours to command."

All around the cemetery, the mixed company bowed down in worship.

The lich smiled and basked in the adoration. *Perhaps Malgrimm has not abandoned me after all.*

CHAPTER TWO

King Leidergelth, ruler of the coral elf city Niamarlee, poured another glass of wine for Furtaevell, his top adviser. A boozy warmth spread across his face as much as the smile did.

"All those years ago, Furtaevell, when we were just boys, could you have expected that our children would someday be married?"

The high enchanter of Niamarlee shook his head slowly as he sipped his wine. He'd known Leidergelth since they were young and had long ago learned that at least one of them ought to remain sober.

"Not then, I suppose not," he responded. "Though, watching Elorall grow up alongside Mantieth, I had long harbored my suspicions."

"Well, Elorall has certainly been a valued member of my court," the king murmured, draining another glass. "I had hoped my son would have made himself eligible for a princess so we could have formed an alliance. I'd even told him as much. Any other local girl I would have objected to... any except Elorall. She has been a loyal companion to my son. Saved his life, even."

"More than once, I am told."

Leidergelth poured another glass of wine. In the momentary silence, the blue-skinned king's mood turned somber. "Let us hope that our children's' love lives fare better than our own." He held his glass aloft and Furtaevell matched it in toast.

Both drained their glasses.

Furtaevell's wife had passed when Elorall was still young, and shortly after that, Mantieth had also lost his mother. With sorrow on his face, he looked to the king and spotted Leidergelth's carefully checked anger. Lediergelth's face remained placid, distant, and with a kind of false apathy.

"Have you heard anything from her?" Furtaevell asked, taking a tentative step into a conversation about Queen Naemyar.

Leidergelth looked to Furtaevell and his countenance changed. The flint in his face melted slightly, knowing he was speaking with his eldest friend and confidant. He shook his head. "No," he said flatly. "I told Naemyar to write to me when she was ready, but so far… Nothing. It's been years."

Furtaevell bobbed his head. He knew the king to be stubborn and proud; Leidergelth would not write to her and ask for anything. "I would have thought she'd have come to Mantieth's coming of age?" Furtaevell knew Naemyar as well. She could be equally stubborn when she set her will to it.

Only Furtaevell really knew why Leidergelth had made such a big deal out of his son's celebration, much to Mantieth's discomfort. Leidergelth had hoped to catch his estranged wife's attention half way around the world. "Did you ask Mantieth to write his mother and invite her?"

"I did. But after such a long absence, he declined." The king poured more wine. "Perhaps he feels equally abandoned by her… Though I am sure that she knew about the celebration. I know some in my court are in her employ." Leidergelth caught Furtaevell's eyes over the top of his goblet. He admitted, "I've got my own spy positioned in her house in Tulgesh."

Furtaevell shook his head with a chuckle. He had suspected as much. "She likely has one of her own, here. But I do know that Naemyar is aware of the wedding and has received an invitation."

Leidergelth shot him a surprised look. "That is something General Elalamin, my Master of Subterfuge, has yet to learn."

Furtaevell smiled. "I have my own sources." He raised his glass and dared to hope with his friend. "Perhaps we will see her return to Niamarlee soon?"

"Perhaps," Leidergelth said and matched his friend's gesture. He kept his voice flat and neutral. Furtaevell knew he'd kept his expression tightly controlled, even despite the strong drink, but there was no mistaking a spark of desire in the king's eye.

For Mantieth's comfort, Hy'Targ and Varanthl met in the library tower which protruded up from the Irontooth fortress that lay half inside a mountain. From there, they could watch for Elorall's approach.

Varanthl, the four-armed humanoid, had just returned from a short trip north visiting the People of the Sun who lived on the north side of the Stonejaws. He'd gone north with Jr'Orhr.

Jr'Orhr had been the only other dwarf to survive their previous quest to keep the bones of Ailushurai away from Melkior the lich. The vagha had proven himself a true part of the team.

"We should not expect Jr'Orhr to return any time soon," Varanthl told Hy'Targ and Mantieth. *He continued north when I stayed with my uncle.* "He took Ambassador Br'Derluch with him, but he wouldn't tell me his mission—except that he was on King Hy'Mandr's business."

Hy'Targ nodded. His father sometimes played things close to the chest, especially where diplomatic missions were concerned. Br'Derluch had most recently been involved in the trade talks that brought unity between Niamarlee and the Irontooth Kingdom, although the dwarf prince truly thought that his and Mantieth's friendship had more to do with the peace than Br'Derluch who, by all accounts, had nearly triggered a war between the two kings.

"Was there any sign of..."

Varanthl cut Hy'Targ off and shook his head negatively. "The humans have seen little sign of the trogs who took Brentésion, except for occasional scouts. According to reports, most of the raiding and attacks stopped a couple months ago."

"Our rangers noticed the same things," Mantieth said. "Do you think they moved? Maybe something else killed them... a disease, perhaps?"

Hy'Targ stroked his beard. "It could be, but I don't think so. Jr'Orhr and Elorall were with me at the first attack on the Great Coastal Road. The trog leaders were blooding their young. Educating their new warriors. I think it is likely the training is almost over..."

"And now comes their actual plans?" Varanthl suggested as he absentmindedly rubbed an itch near the bald patch of skin at his chest. The Kreethaln relic, Life-Bringer, had once been woven into the homunculus's flesh. It now resided in a thick safe in Varanthl's room. Only he and Hy'Targ could access it, though it seemed inoperable, now. For the most part, the human who had been assembled out of spare parts and given new life seemed to have absorbed the relic's power and gained its regenerative abilities.

"Fear not," Varanthal said and rested one of his four arms on Hy'Targ's shoulders. He let the matching bracelet he wore dangle from his wrist. "We will find Brentésion sooner or later."

"I should hope so," the vagha said. "I know my father has hired additional eldarim to search for any sign of her... Though I find it curious that Taryl, a Dragonlord, has been unable to find Brentésion."

Mantieth screwed up his face, agreeing with the suspicion. "Brentésion is certainly unlike any of the other drakufreet. Perhaps there is some reason beyond our knowledge."

Hy'Targ nodded. He'd have to accept that answer, at

least for now.

"So you have located the next of the Kreethaln?" Varanthl asked. After the battle of the black tower, he and the dwarf had decided it best to leave the relics where they'd been hidden... that they were too powerful to return them use as they could upset the balance of Esfah. However, a couple weeks ago, Hy'Targ had abruptly changed his mind and Varanthl waited for him to explain that change of heart in the prince's own timing.

The dwarf crooked his jaw. "Maybe I found them; maybe I've only gotten rumors. I am uncertain, but wanted to put what I've learned before the group... the rest of the Gods'own."

His companions gave him inquisitive looks.

"It's what the locals have been calling us after word of Melkior's revival got out. Though the story seems to be larger than life, if you ask me."

Mantieth asked, "The *Gods'own* is what they called the Champions of old who defeated Melkior the first time. Do they really think that is what we are?"

Hy'Targ shook his head. "Not exactly, but it plays into our favor to let the title stand. A solid reputation preceding us certainly can't hurt, and a little fame might help us locate the remaining relics." He unrolled the letter that had been sent to him. "That leads me to this..."

Varanthl put a hand over the map. "Hold on. I'm still very curious about this Gods'own thing."

Hy'Targ said, "It's just a thing that the commoners are..."

"No, Varanthl is right," Mantieth said with a lopsided grin to indicate he was at least partly joking. "We should decide who gets to be in our special club. After all, there were two selumari in the group. There can't be more than one chosen Champion of the gods, can there?"

"And could I even qualify?" the homunculus asked. "I mean, I'm made of mostly human parts, but I'm still not exactly *human."*

Mantieth cocked an eyebrow. "There was also Rhyll, the treefolk—that race wasn't even around in the time of Champions. What about Nodhan? Is Nodhan one of the Gods'own?"

An awkward silence fell over the three. Varanthl and Mantieth grinned, knowing they'd gotten the better of their friend, who rolled his eyes. "Fine... *fine*. I'll make the party rules, if it will help. Any of those who joined us on our adventure can be one of the Gods'own... We don't want to be *too* exclusive, right? Multiple members from the same race are acceptable—Jr'Orhr has already seen the letter. It arrived just before he departed north with Varanthl and I sent word to Niamarlee as soon as I'd read it. Multiple members of a race are a go: We'll let the gods sort us out. And yes, I suppose that this makes Nodhan eligible *if he so chooses*. Are we satisfied?"

The two that remained grinning, both nodding their heads in approval. Though none expected they'd ever see the red-skinned elf again after he abandoned them to the mercy of the drider and Undrakull's guards. They were fairly certain he'd set Mantieth up to accidentally summon a drake. He'd proved more of a foil than an ally.

Hy'Targ displayed the letter he'd gotten recently from someone known only as the *Gray Wanderer*. "Whoever sent this letter claims that the Kreethaln has been rumored to be northwest of Xlinea, specifically on Last Rock. He also says that some kind of cult that worships Death is after it. Perhaps only so that we cannot have it."

"So we are to quest after the relics, but leave Ailushurai's bones hidden in the crypt?" Varanthl sought clarification.

"Aye," said Hy'Targ. "I think that's best for now... it's the last place anyone would look for them. But I think we must keep Melkior's followers from acquiring any of these artifacts.

Mantieth cocked his head. "Why does that name of this mysterious writer sound familiar?"

"The Gray Wanderer is the name given to the protagonist from *The Soldier's Journey*—a famous epic," Hy'Targ said.

The elf still looked confused.

Hy'Targ clarified, "Grarrha of the feral folk mentioned it when we rescued him in the Black Glades."

Mantieth nodded with a look of sudden recognition. The dwarf turned the letter to his companions, and they verified it. The letter began, *To Hy'Targ and the others of the Gods'own...*

Mantieth asked, "Any idea on the identity of our mysterious informant?"

"The letter was handed to a vaghan courier in Port Orric when their ship stopped in the Aurora Bay. That's a long journey, I know, but the courier remembered him—hard to forget a frehlasuhl, he said."

Mantieth raised his eyebrows. "Especially if one of the gray elves had coin enough to afford to hire a messenger." His prejudice was evident in the weight of his words.

Varanthl shrugged. "I've liked every frehlasuhl I've met. I have no reason to distrust one."

Hy'Targ nodded slowly. "I'm inclined to agree. Though I'm a little surprised that our story has reached as far as Port Orric."

Mantieth crossed his arms. "Not when you consider the source. Varanthl's experience with the frehlasuhl makes this the first story in a long while that does not make the grays out to be bad guys. If the Gray Wanderer is one of them, it's no surprise that they've picked it up."

The dwarf shrugged. It made a certain amount of sense. "What worries me is the insistence that we must hurry. He pointed to the line, *Time is of the essence. Several parties are actively seeking it, and none with as good intentions or abilities as this age's Gods'own.*"

"So we leave soon," Varanthl suggested.

Before the words were even spoken, the horn sounded to announce a party of incoming travelers. Hy'Targ rushed to the window and confirmed, "That's exactly what we have planned. And we can depart soon. Elorall has just arrived."

Elorall flung open the door of the library tower, knowing that it was the best place to locate Hy'Targ. And if the vaghan prince was there, she'd also find her betrothed.

She found Mantieth on the other side of the door, reaching for the handle. He looked shocked to find her there already, and she leapt into his arms. "I'm so happy to be back! Did you miss me?" she asked.

Still surprised, he stammered, "Uh, yeah," and then wrapped her in his arms.

Hy'Targ and Varanthl stood several paces behind them. "Elorall," the dwarf said, "So glad you made it. We were just saying that… "

"Whatever it is, it can wait a few hours. It's been a few days since I've seen my one true love." She winked, took Mantieth by the hand, and started leading him away.

"He's got some very interesting information about… "

Something brightly and mischievous twinkled in her eyes. "That can wait. I've missed you." She said playfully, standing to her tiptoes. She whispered something into Mantieth's long, pointed ear and let her warm breath linger on his neck.

"Um, yeah. We'll be back later," he informed the others, following her out the door with his hand still clasped in hers.

Hy'targ's brow furrowed. "Hrmph. Women. They ruin everything."

Varanthl cast him a sidelong glance. "You do not like Elorall?"

His face softened. "Okay. That's the wrong way to phrase it. Relationships—romantic ones—ruin everything. They upset a delicate dynamic." He scowled. "I'm not particularly enthusiastic about adventuring in the first place. I'd much rather stay right here with my books, but this quest for the Kreethaln came to me, and I must see it through."

Varanthl grinned. "You've never fallen for a pretty dwarven lass?"

Hy'targ barely entertained the question. "The only pretty lass able to catch my attention so far has been a well-stocked library."

"Someday," Varanthl chuckled.

"What's that? Like you have such a wealth of experience being in love?" Hy'targ fired at him. "You're like, only a couple years old."

Varanthl shrugged all four of his arms. "I get glimmers of things, sometimes. Ghosts of old memories. Lives I've lived."

Hy'targ cocked his head, curious. Before he could probe further, the door opened again. "Well, that was quick," he teased Mantieth, but it was a dwarf who entered. One that Hy'targ didn't immediately recognize.

The nameless messenger passed him a letter and then departed with a bow.

Hy'targ broke the wax seal and unfolded it.

Varanthl watched his friend's eyes scan it in silence and noted that they jumped back to the top, reading it a second time. "What is it?"

Hy'targ folded it and bit his lip. "It's from my uncle, Hy'Drunyr." He stated flatly. "He claims to be dying." The dwarf sat in his chair and slumped, passing off the letter to his friend.

Nephew, we have never been particularly close. I fear I have as much to blame for that as any other person. I am in

Xlinea with a physician I trust; he has confirmed a diagnosis of Topher's Syndrome. It pleases me to know that you have become such a scholar. As much as your father was always the adventurer, I was the bookish one of we brothers.

What transpired between Hy'Mandr and me is not something that could ever be undone. I will not entertain further efforts, but I can at least attempt reparations for my soul before journeying to the Undying Lands. No doubt, my brother will not want to hear from me and make amends, but perhaps my nephew will hear me out?

I am told you might be venturing in my direction soon and I would love to visit. Perhaps I might aide or bless you in any way I am capable. The Gods'own, I am told by locals, are searching for lost relics. Surely that's at least half true, and I hear rumors of one near Xlinea. Stop and see me if the rumors are valid and you travel this way.

Your Uncle, Hy'Drunyr

"He has confirmed the next Kreethaln lies near the human city," Varanthl said.

Hy'targ kept his face neutral. "Perhaps. But I'm a little concerned that he knows my plans. My father did not trust him, though I don't know the nature of their discord."

"Perhaps we will unravel the answers to those questions when we arrive in Xlinea?" Varanthl wondered.

Hy'targ nodded measuredly. "Aye. But we ought to keep much information close to our chest."

Kaine awoke with a start and tried to remember the details of his dream. He rubbed his temples where he knew his sage's tattoos were. The human's fingers grazed the stubble on his head and he recognized it was time to shave again. He raked out and smoothed his long, gray whiskers where his mustache drooped far below his chin, almost to chest length.

Aerie and Sniv flitted around his head. The two sprites tinkled as the sage stood and stretched in the morning sun. Many months had passed since he had left the Feylands in search of whatever force had driven him with its compulsion to find it. It felt like a child's voice, only he'd heard it in his soul, rather than with his ears.

Kaine stirred the coals of his tiny traveler's fire and focused on the dream. He spoke to his sprites, the last two faeries that remained of his master's eidolon. "My dream was so vivid. In it, there were orbs, like the spheres that moved about within Tarvanehl's earliest creation within the void… Perhaps something new is coming?"

He shook his head. "No. No, that's not quite right. They were not spheres… They were circles, more like rings. Magic rings, perhaps?"

Aerie and Sniv tinkled. They weren't even paying attention.

Kaine shrugged. *That makes sense. They had not experienced the dream.* "Maybe this voice that called to us in our home north because something is trapped within an artifact? I've not heard of magic rings doing that, but some items such as a Dawn Blade can trap the essence of a person within, stealing their soul and negating any journey into the afterlife."

His companions continued prattling in their own barely audible tongue. Kaine shook his head. Sometimes faeries were useless.

He stood and shouldered his cloak. The sprites took up their perches, one on each shoulder.

Summoning magic from the land, Kaine doused the embers and then opened the ground to swallow the dead coals. Moments later, grass shoots pushed their way up through the freshly turned soil.

The sage picked up his walking stick and turned south. "The voice is still on the move, more like a child's whispering from a hiding place," he told his companions. To this, they did pay attention.

Sages were so few upon Esfah, and it was their mission to protect the Feylands and the magic that flowed from its source. Without the source, not only would magic disappear, but life on Esfah could cease.

CHAPTER THREE

Hy'Targ and his companions had already sent their equipment and supplies down to the stable master, who prepared and loaded their mounts. The rest of the adventurers went on ahead as the dwarf prince stayed back to say goodbye. He embraced his father.

The wizened dwarf king squeezed him tight and slipped a finger inside his son's collar. He was checking that he wore the mystic, woven armor claimed during Hy'Targ's first adventure in the prison of Sshkkryyahr the Dread.

"Your mother would be so proud of you," King Hy'Mandr said. "And so am I."

Ne'Vistar, the high wizard who Hy'Targ had long been friends with, nodded his head from a few paces back.

"Now go finish yer quest," the King said, beaming.

Hy'Targ bobbed his head, shifted Glorybringer, his magic axe, onto his back, and departed. He broke into the daylight of the walled area of the outer keep, which protruded off the side of the mountain. A shadow from the few towers further up the mountain face shaded them, and the dwarf prince caught up to his companions.

Varanthl, Mantieth, and Elorall headed towards their mounted beasts, or two mammoths and two horses. Several other horses meandered on the sloped pen nearby. The other members of Mantieth and Elorall's royal escort would go on to hunt for trogs in the nearby Moorlech, southwest of Niamarlee. It had become a hot breeding spot for the enemy, and the swampy goblin nest needed culling in order to keep the Great Coastal Road safe.

Taryl waved to Hy'Targ and hurried across the courtyard. A younger man trotted after him, who looked exactly like a younger version of Taryl: Rugged and handsome with a broadly ridged nose. The younger man stood a few steps back, wearing traveling robes that obscured the fact his armor.

"I'm glad I caught you," the dragonlord said. "I wanted to introduce you to my nephew, Yarrick." He leaned closer, conspiratorially. "I would very much like if you took him on your journey. He only recently arrived and has been useful thus far, but he could benefit from additional travel. His father, my brother, is a mercenary and is away fighting in someone else's war."

Hy'Targ looked from Yarrick to his friends. It was clear that he wanted to decline, but he also knew his party could benefit from having additional companions—if it meant more sets of eyes keeping watch at night –and that gave them each longer sleeping shifts. Finally, he bobbed his head. "I only have one condition: We cannot play nursemaid. He will need to pull his own weight."

Taryl nodded enthusiastically and motioned for his nephew to approach.

"Can you fight?" Hy'Targ asked him.

Yarrick nodded. "Both my uncle and my father privately trained me. But I have many other skills."

Hy'Targ shrugged. "So long as you can fight," he groused. "Don't tell everyone else, but I'm not nearly as talented as the commoners' stories of the Gods'own have been telling."

Yarrick chuckled.

Taryl grinned and laughed. "He's not joking! The prince skipped most of his lessons with me."

Hy'Targ shrugged. "I make up for it with a really big axe." He clapped the much taller lad on the shoulder. "You are provisioned already?"

"I am." Yarrick whistled between his fingers and a large drakufreet trotted out of the stable. It was already outfitted with a riding pack.

A pang of regret burned momentarily in Hy'Targ's gut. His own journey had started much the same way, though this creature was nowhere near the size of Brentésion, who had rivaled the bulk of a mammoth.

Yarrick crawled onto his wingless mount, which stood only a hand taller than the elves' horses. Together, they exited the gates with two more horses in tow. They would haul additional supplies as they traveled towards the Great Coastal Road. Their destination lay twice the distance of Undrakull, which the party had little desire to visit again, despite assurances from the new local leadership that the old rulers had been replaced. Especially now that the morehl's drider-matron was dead.

A duke had risen up and established a new rule and even sent the Irontooth kingdom an old dwarven skeleton from among the duke's private trophy collection. That was about as good an assurance as any morehl leader could give.

They expected no trouble from the morehl… At least not from Undrakull. But they tried to plan for any potential scenario: Trog raiders, empyrean assassins, roadside traps, and more. It felt as if some mysterious force was arrayed against them, which is why the lone rider's approach in the distance set them on edge.

The Gods'own hadn't even gotten beyond Irontooth's shadow, and they already expected their first encounter.

Eucalia reached down and rubbed the flank of her mount. "Easy, Acacia. I think we have finally found them."

The unicorn snorted in response to his green-skinned passenger. Acacia wore neither saddle, bridle, nor barding. The single horn protruding from his brow scattered rainbow-like rays of Soll's light like a prism, and every place one of Acacia's hooves pressed sprouted a knot of fresh grass blades.

Slowly, the group Eucalia had learned in the last village were called the Gods'own, came to a halt on the mountain trail that eventually intersected the Great Coastal Road.

Their dwarven leader narrowed his eyes as he took stock of her. She was a green elf. A dryad, technically. And she rode upon a rare and magnificent creature.

She pulled back her mossy brown hair streaked with brambles and mustard-hued tangles, thinking to show her face and hoping the adventurers might recognize her. Eucalia's spalted skin glowed bright green, broken up by a few brown freckles. Her green ears peeked through her hair. Slightly shorter than the longer ears of either the morehl or selumari, they more resembled those of a half-elf: The product of elf and eldarim unions.

"Hail there, Prince Hy'Targ sa'Mandr Irontooth and the Gods'own," the dryad formally addressed them. She heard them mutter a few words. *"Who made the dwarf our leader?"* And, *"I'm a prince too..."*

Her determination nearly quailed, and she bit her lip, doubling down. "Do you remember me?"

Slowly, Hy'Targ nodded his head. "Aye. So you've come to kill me, then?"

Eucalia cocked her head. "You remember what I said before leaving Rhyll'ee-vrng-nrnnnvv in your care?"

Hy'Targ reached for his axe. "You said to take care of him. And I'm sorry that we failed... But I cannot let allow you to seek vengeance on my hide. I find that I'm still in need of it."

"He saved my life," the four-armed humanoid insisted. "And I went on to help stop Melkior. Rhyll's sacrifice allowed us to stop so much evil."

Eucalia's face softened. "I know. And I am not here for vengeance." Her voice was barely more than a whisper.

With her countenance changed, the adventurers drew closer.

"Why are you here, then?" Elorall asked. "Rhyll told us you came from a grove near the far seas, where you tended the efflorah?"

She nodded slowly. "They were all taken with the gray blight. Shortly after I returned, every living thing there turned to ash. Rhyll chose rightly. Had he come with me, he might have become infected and succumbed to a long, slow death. Only Acacia and I survived."

"Then why have you come here?" Elloral pressed. "Surely you could return to the sylvan of the Feylands?"

Something raged at the corner of her eyes and belied her otherwise meek demeanor. "I could have returned to the Feylands or I might have wandered for the next grove of efflorah I might find. I chose another path. Rhyll wanted desperately to stop the necralluvium, or at least find a way to counteract its effects. I wish to take up his quest in his stead... But I know not where to turn. It is only Acacia and I, and so we decided to seek out the Gods'own. Will you help?"

Hy'Targ stroked his beard and held up a finger. "I must confer with the others."

They dismounted and huddled up.

Hy'Targ muttered, "Didn't my father always say something about having at least six members in a traveling party? Or was it six other companions?"

"But even by adding Yarrick, there are only five of us total," Varanthl pointed out

"It all sounds like superstition to me," Mantieth said.

"We *are* due to rendezvous with Jr'Orhr in Xlinea," Hy'Targ noted. "And it might be superstition, but when it comes to adventuring advice, I always side with my father. They didn't call him the Adventurer King for nothing."

Elorall watched the dryad while the others talked it over. "She's coming with us in the end," the selumari sorceress declared.

The others looked at her.

She stared at the bangle on her wrist. Before Mantieth had given it to her, their treefolk companion had worn it as a ring. "You promised Rhyll we'd help him after he located the missing Nodhan for us. Rhyll may be gone, but his spirit is still with us. He is dead, but our promise is not." Elorall looked from face to face. "And as it was with Rhyll, her task cannot be our primary mission… at least not immediately. But an opportunity to help establish the will of the gods sits before us: They offer a chance to stamp out the Death god's blight."

None of the others disagreed with her and Hy'Targ called out, "We're traveling north to Xlinea. We'd be honored for you to fill Rhyll's spot in our company. He was one of us and so now are you."

Elorall smiled warmly, glad to finally have another female companion. "Welcome to the Gods'own."

Eucalia's presence actually brightened the mood as they traveled north and skirted the edge of Niamarlee. It had been a couple day's ride. The dryad offered Elorall another connection and gave Mantieth more room to breathe, though he gladly kept his fiancé close when they stopped for the night in the coral elf city. Niamarlee provided a place to rest for one more night in comfort. The royal castle and the king's table provided all the amenities they could hope for.

They took up the road again immediately after, keeping a steady but not grueling pace, to make haste in reaching Xlinea. The human city sat on the far northwest terminal of the Great Coastal Road, nearly on the upper point of Charnock's landmass, and where the Tarvenish Ocean began working its way into the chain of waterways that eventually gave way to the Far and the Talvat Seas.

As a group, they held their collective breath while passing in sight of the flat-topped plateau that was Undrakull.

They explained the reasons for the concern to Eucalia and Yarrick, but they couldn't fully understand the depths of their nervousness as they passed through the shadow of the morehl city. In Undrakull, the party had splintered. They'd lost comrades and mounts both, been betrayed, and come face-to-face with Melkior's relentless skeletal hunters. Not to mention they had nearly been devoured by the city's drider matron.

Though they breathed easier once passing beyond the smoldering mesa, the party slept only lightly along the Great Coastal Road. Along the south side of the road, the goblin-controlled Moorlech stretched from Niamarlee and past Undrakull; the Black Glades encroached upon the north side for a hundred leagues. While the same trogs who stole Brentésion had also been seen in the Black Glades, so had other terrors. The reptilian sarslayan and inky pools of black sludge that had killed many creatures and reanimated the bodies of the dead.

Traveling at a brisk ten leagues per day, Hy'Targ began to wonder if they should have gone east to Lyandrica and chartered a ship. It would have halved their travel time twice over. *Maybe we could have convinced Leidergelth to loan us an airship, ensuring we made the voyage even more quickly.* The dwarf's mouth twisted. He knew that was an unlikely scenario. Flying coral ships were too precious to loan out—even for an adventuring son.

Hy'Targ did decide that he'd try to charter a ship for the return trip. The sour, musky smell of the mammoth below him rose in the midday heat and burned his nostrils. "I'll buy the whole durned vessel and hire a crew if I have too," he muttered. He'd forgotten exactly how much he missed his books until the toil of the road caught up with him.

By the time they arrived at the outskirts of the Xlinea, the crew was saddle-worn and weary. While many tiny pockets of mixed folk dotted the Great Coastal road with settlements and villages that catered to travelers, most of their comforts weren't much better than simply unfurling bedrolls and sleeping alongside the road. They welcomed the muddled browns on the horizon where the edge of Xlinea began.

The north side of the city abutted the inlet, where the Tarvenish Ocean met the Delmarra Bay across the Great Wash. The south-eastern edge of the city rested upon the Kolaro Bay, which protected ships that berthed without the intent of sailing around the horn and into the Ocean. Ships berthed there were likely heading east through the Wash and towards the Far and Talvat Seas, or beyond.

"I see some dwarven runners ahead", Mantieth noted. "They must have spotted our approach."

Hy'Targ said little, only acknowledging him with a vaghan, *"Hrumph."*

A short while later, with the distance between them halved, they spotted Jr'Orhr approaching on the broad road. "It's about time ye arrived," the grizzled dwarf muttered once he'd fully caught up. He gave Eucalia a quizzical look and did a double-take with Yarrick, first mistaking him for the elder Taryl. He said nothing about it.

The group slackened the pace and ambled towards the human city in leisurely fashion so they could have a private conversation.

"King Hy'Mandr sent me to keep an eye on that uncle of yours," Jr'Orhr said. "The king doesn't trust him. Always suspects he's up to some scheme."

"Is he?" Hy'Targ asked.

Jr'Orhr shrugged.

"Is he really dying?"

Another shrug. "It appears so. I've kept close tabs on him, but I was sent as the escort to Br'Derluch opening some new trade deals. I'm supposed to spy, but not look like I'm spyin'."

Hy'Targ nodded. "And does he suspect you?"

"A'course. But he can't confirm it," Jr'Orhr said. "It's

all smoke and shadows," he grumbled, obviously having little taste for subterfuge. Few dwarves did. "I may have let some details of your trip slip out as I spoke with him... It's a long journey," Jr'Orhr pointed out, "but I only did so to gain his confidence."

Hy'Targ bobbed atop his mount. "I figured. He sent me a letter. By the timing of it, he must've sent it shortly after your arrival."

Jr'Orhr thought it likely. "I've got Br'Derluch covering for me. One of his bodyguards has taken my place so I could slip away. Shall we head out at once to search for the Kreethaln?"

The prince shot him back a wearied look. "Tomorrow. If I don't get a proper night's rest, I won't be any good for adventuring."

A murmur of assents agreed all around.

Jr'Orhr stroked his beard. "This many mammoths might be a give-away, and I assume you don't want to announce our presence here... not until after finding this lost relic. I know a place we can stable them for a period and take rickshaws, or carriages, to a nicer establishment."

The party heartily agreed and let their local guide lead them. Varanthl pulled a cloak about him to disguise his unique physique. The last thing they wanted was to announce that the Gods'own had arrived to hunt treasure—that would only increase scrutiny on them and send every other adventurer within a tenday to beat them to their mark.

"Oh, I almost forgot," Jr'Orhr suddenly said. He produced a wrinkled letter from his satchel and handed it to the prince.

Hy'Targ gave him a suspicious look. "Others knew of our journey?"

Jr'Orhr shrugged. "No idea. It had been delivered to the dwarven consulate by raven nearly two tendays ago."

After breaking the seal and reading that it was addressed

to him, Hy'Targ unrolled the parchment and scanned it. Finally, he told the party, "Another letter from this mysterious Gray Wanderer. And he included a crude map to the relic."

"Isn't that good news?" Jr'Orhr exclaimed, noting Hy'Targ's dour expression.

The prince chewed his lip. "I don't know. I hope so… But this mysterious benefactor knows too much about our movements for me to be comfortable."

They neared the stables in a run-down portion of the city, near its furthest inland edge. It looked like the sort of place well-accustomed to anonymous deals, and where discretion might be purchased with a few coins.

"It could be that this person wants us to succeed and has given us every tool to acquire the item," Varanthl said, still drawing on his sympathy for the gray elves. "Especially if he or she is one of the frehlasuhl."

Mantieth's lips spread thin and tight. He stated the obvious. "It's either that… or it could be a trap."

CHAPTER FOUR

The Gods'own, fully united—with the possible exception of Nodhan—rode out from Xlinea fully rested and with no fanfare. They waited to depart until the most active part of the day, when the humans and other residents of the city were fully underway with work schedules, chores, and life's mundanity. They snuck out in broad daylight and took the lesser traveled roads, heading further into the northwest.

After a half-day's travel along the wilderness road, the paths turned rugged and winding; eventually emptying in the clearing where a settlement had been erected on the edge of the continent's north-west point.

"Last Rock," Jr'Orhr told them. "Many of the folk here are those expelled from Xlinea, for some reason or another."

Dirty children, mostly humans, played in the streets. Buildings were held together with a kind of poor craftsmanship exercised by builders who lacked genuine skill for their trade. Everywhere they looked, residents wore a layer of grime and expressions of desperation… or malice.

Eucalia wilted slightly beneath their collective gaze. Elorall sidled up next to her, aware that the dryad had no real adventuring experience. The green elf perked up somewhat; her companion's empathy reinforced her confidence.

The travelers carried plenty of provisions, and easily ignored the pleas of market criers. Vendors tried to frantically reposition their wares in the hopes that the visitors were in a buying mood. They pressed through until they arrived at the shores. Across the choppy water, a gray line whelmed on the horizon.

Hy'Targ briefly consulted their map and then hid it away as soon as an unshaven man approached from the boathouse. The dwarf pointed at the darker brown mass peeking out from the fog. "That's our target, across the shoals."

The harbor master walked towards them on crooked legs. He looked as salt-weathered as old driftwood and wore thick wool to protect against the creeping chill of the mists. A broad grin spread on his face, weaving its way between cracked lips and thick whiskers. "M'name's Hoyle. You're looking for a ferry?"

His eyes lingered uncomfortably long upon Yarrick. The eldarim pretended not to notice and stared off into the distance.

"We are," Hy'Targ said. Hoyle looked them each over, as if memorizing them. Or sizing them up for caskets. "We'd prefer to take our mounts, if a large enough barge can be found."

The old man grimaced and shook his head. "Nay. But my brother can certainly stable them… for a fee."

"Of course," Mantieth muttered, rolling his eyes.

"It'll just be a short while," the harbor master insisted. "I'll go and fetch him." With that, he disappeared.

"Must we leave them *all*?" Eucalia asked. The unicorn she sat upon expressed a certain amount of attitude about it.

"I'm afraid so." Mantieth looked across the blue chop and then back at the crafts docked nearby. "It doesn't look like any of these could carry more than one of our mounts. But Acacia would be the one to bring, if any," he assured her… and himself.

Acacia stamped, irked. His pawing at the ground made a gnarl of green protrude from the stony ground.

"It'll be okay, Acacia," Eucalia cooed to her steed. "The others will need you there to protect them," she insisted. Acacia seemed to accept that reasoning and calmed.

After far too much time had elapsed, the harbor master returned with a man who might have been his twin, except his hair fell past his shoulders in thin and tangled dreadlocks. The boarder carried an armful of various harnesses and the pair came to a halt in front of the adventurers. He demanded coin for his services.

Jr'Orhr whistled at the amount. "Sounds a bit steep to me."

The boarder grimaced. "It's for protection," he spat. "Lots of hungry folk here in town will eat anything. I'll hafta hire a hand to keep the foxes out of the hen-house till ye return."

"Mine will be fine," the eldarim said. "She's fully wild." Yarrick dismounted and threw his saddlebags over his shoulder. He touched his forehead to his drakufreet mount's brow, and the thing scampered into the thicket.

Hy'Targ frowned, but paid the boarder as he began attaching harnesses. He stopped before Eucalia, whose mount had neither bridle nor saddle.

"No, sir," she insisted. "Acacia will not accept a harness. I don't suggest you try."

The man cocked his face into a smug, toothy grin, as if accepting the challenge. Hoyle's brother attempted to slip a harness over Acacia's horn, and the unicorn lowered his head and raked the jagged spike against the man's forearm. It tore a gash open with ease and the stable man cursed and grabbed his wound, quickly binding it with a rag.

"Acacia will follow the others," she said firmly. "But he will not be bound."

The wounded man grumbled, but accepted it. For the kind of coin they'd just paid, he'd have to make some adjustments.

With a yellowed, toothy smile, Hoyle grinned. "Alright, let's shove off. You'll find my fees somewhat lesser than my brother's. How long is your trip?"

"Overnight... Perhaps two days," Hy'Targ said.

The harbor master bobbed his head. "I'm outfitted for that," he mumbled, eying Elorall. "Perhaps your spell crafter here could summon a wind and we'll make quick work of the sail?"

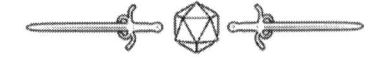

Hoyle leapt out of the boat and his boots splashed in the water. With Elorall's summoned winds pushing the sail, they were able to turn straight up a river inlet without ever having to take up an oar. The skiff coasted over the sandy, bottomed flow and straight up a landing, where Hoyle departed into the shallows.

He turned the boat's prow aside so that it missed the large stone plinth where he often tethered his vessel. Hoyle pulled the craft aground and tied it down.

Hoyle nodded towards the small shelter erected nearby, barely big enough to protect one person from the elements. "This is as far as I go," he said.

Varanthl, still wearing his cloak to conceal his second set of arms, scanned the lush rise of elevation. Stony mountain benches protruded from the green canopy where a broken ring of hillocks rose and accentuated the valleys nearest them. Many seemed to sink down to sea level, indicating likely glades beyond and all the terrors that often accompanied wilded swamps. He looked back to Hoyle; it was no wonder that the man refused to go further. "There is much danger in the swamps?"

"Not particularly. But I was paid for a ferry—not to explore a bog. And a turned ankle could lay me up as well as any goblin or sarslayan blade."

Varanthl nodded. There was logic in that. The man had his own interests to look after.

Hoyle cautioned, "If you're not back by sunrise of the day after next, I'll be leaving without you."

Hy'Targ nodded and thought of the map sent by the Gray Wanderer. "I'm certain of our location. If we can't return by then, we won't return at all... But when we *do* come back,

I'll gladly pay another full fare for each of us for the journey home."

Hoyle's eyes sparkled. He went about his work as the Gods'own retrieved their gear and departed straight away. "Smart thinking," Jr'Orhr commented. "I'd have hated to come back only to find our ferry had abandoned us."

The dwarf prince cocked his jaw in a wry smile. Even if they were running late, the ferryman would likely give them grace in hopes for the additional funds. Hy'Targ still wouldn't claim to be much of an adventurer, but he didn't lack for smarts.

Varanthl finally shrugged off his cloak and freed his remaining arms with a stretch. The Gods'own headed into the thick green of the fens.

A short while later, the party stopped near the split bedrock, where an ancient, seismic upheaval had formed one of the massive hillocks. Fresh water trickled from it freely.

Hy'Targ took a knee and retrieved the map sent by the Gray Wanderer. The party gathered around.

"I think we're right here," Hy'Targ said and jabbed a finger against a landmark scribbled on the parchment. Within the circle of hills was a swamp with a kind of shrine constructed in its center. Block letters under a drawing labeled it as *Secret Ruins*. The center had an X marked *Relic? Kreethaln?*

Mantieth looked up at the stone outcropping and mumbled, "I just wish there was a way to get up there to confirm our location."

Eucalia closed her eyes behind him, and seconds later thick vines crept from above and below to create a lattice network capable of climbing.

The coral elf smiled and then scrambled up the side of the formation. He called down, "We're right on target!" Mantieth scanned the verdant swamps ahead of them. "I see something down that way. Old stone and block work, maybe three leagues ahead—surrounded by fens. We'd be heading into the bog in short order."

Hy'Targ looked upward and noted the time as Mantieth scrambled back down. "I think we'll make camp here, then. It'll be better if we're fresh in the morning and I have no desire to sleep in the swamps."

The sounds of swamp-born insects and frogs' trilling filled the humid air, rolling off the bogs in the valley below them. Yarrick pulled a dry twig from the smoldering remains of a peat fire they'd built earlier. He tapped a cherry ember so that it fell into the cup of his pipe and sucked air until it lit his tobacco.

He'd drawn the latest watch shift, which he'd expected to fall to him since joining the party. He was something of a last minute addition and had yet to prove himself... Under normal circumstances, he might have called a cluster of drakufreet from the wilderness and convinced them to take watch for the night. That would've allowed them all to sleep well enough. But no dragonkin were present for many leagues, and Yarrick was unable to summon one.

Yarrick drew a steady breath through the stem of his pipe and the crimson glow of the dry fuel lit his face. He blinked when a set of eyes greeted him. His first instinct was to draw his blade, thinking the greenish skin belonged to a trog or some other swamp beast, until he recognized it.

Eucalia. Her figure was too angular and her frame too petite to be one of those monsters. Yarrick grinned at his error. *She is beautiful*, he recognized as the dryad sat down next to him.

"Can't sleep?" he asked.

She shook her head. "No. I'm a little uncomfortable here I've never really been away from my home *and* exposed to danger like this."

Yarrick could empathize with her somewhat. "Danger? I

don't think there will be much danger coming up from the swamp beyond a stray trog accidentally stumbling onto us."

Eucalia frowned. "I can feel it. The trees speak to me. They whisper the foul things that happen in this valley."

"What things?"

She furrowed her brow. "I... I can't quite tell. They speak a strange dialect here. The island is not connected like so many other trees. Their isolation is the likely reason for it." She turned to him. "Many foul things... Things not of the forest or swamp. They may be getting closer."

Yarrick rubbed his chin. "You're sure? The trees sound confused."

Eucalia tightened her lips and admitted, "Trees are notorious for spreading rumors. They often jump to wild conclusions and pass on bad information."

"If they're saying something is nearby that might be an enemy, we should wake the others." Yarrick turned his pipe upside down and tapped it to expel the cinders. "I just wish we could tell for certain."

A howl split the night and a white figure charged from the foliage with its blade drawn high.

"Up! *Up*—we're under attack," Yarrick yelled, rousing his companions as he swung his own blade. He hacked a nasty gash through the assailant, which turned out to be a mostly naked human. As unkempt as any wild creature he'd ever seen.

The wildling dropped his stone blade as Eucalia yelped, turning to summon defensive magic. She held her hand out as if commanding an attacker to stop. A shoot of wood sprang from the ground like a spear in time to catch the wild man. The wood spear caught him just before he plunged his blade into Yarrick's back.

A split second later, the Gods'own were on their feet with weapons drawn. A mixture of humans, morehl, and trogs poured from the trees in overwhelming numbers. Their weapons were crude, but no less deadly.

Mantieth and Elorall moved back-to-back to defend each other. Yarrick protected the dryad as she sank to her knees with her palms pressed together, summoning magic to her aide. The dwarves and Varanthl smashed any creatures that pressed too close, but it became evident that the seven Gods'own were vastly outnumbered. They feinted and positioned against each other.

The attackers' eyes burned with psychotic rage that boiled over, building up like a powder keg. They only needed someone to strike the match. In the dull light, the adventurers could see the maniacs were already bloody. Death symbols and other runes had been carved into their flesh; streams of crimson dribbled from their foreheads and cuts upon their bare chests.

Someone sparked the attack, screaming, "Kill them!"

They had just hurled themselves towards the Gods'own when vines shot up from the ground, entangling the enemy and arresting their progress. The dwarves and their companions struck back with the scales tipped in their favor.

Eucalia grit her teeth, struggling to hold the spell as the enemy thrashed against their bindings and hacked at the tendrils that wrapped their limbs. "Hurry!" she implored them.

The Gods'own fanned out and made short work of the enemy, sparing none. Snarling with bestial rage, the maddened attackers tried to wound the Gods'own rather than spare themselves—clawing and biting at them. They were beyond redemption, taken either by psychosis or zealots' fervor.

Tangled beyond hope, the Gods'own finished them off one at a time. Finally, the dryad collapsed in a sweat and the knot of vines and wild growth went limp. Ensnared corpses fell to the soil as the quiet of the night resumed.

Hy'Targ examined a few of the bodies, turning them over to access their markings.

"What do you think?" Elorall asked. "Zealots, perhaps? They must be Acolytes. Creatures who have devoted themselves to the worship of only one god. In this case, Death?"

"That's what I thought at first," Hy'Targ muttered. He wiped away the bloody leakage from one of the enemies so he could clearly read their symbol. The dwarf pointed to the previous body, which had a fresh cut in the traditional Death sigil: A broken circle appearing like a crescent moon and almost closed at the tips. The larger one on the body Hy'Targ examined looked different.

The new sigil was an embellishment upon the Death sign. The broken circle formed an inverted skull with a tree shape sprouting above a horizontal line. "I've seen this before, but I doubt any of you have," Hy'Targ said. "Except for maybe Varanthl, but I doubt he would remember it."

The others looked at him quizzically.

"I saw it in the crypt near the People of the Sun. It was carved into Melkior's sarcophagus. It's a sign of his cultists."

The seven adventurers crept through the underbrush as they approached the broken temple at the middle of the vale. They'd begun slogging towards their target after an uneasy rest that ended at first light.

Jagged rocks protruded from the crushed peat. They bore mystic engravings, and circles of binding marked various points around the site. Elorall fingered one nervously as she examined it and whispered, "The cultists may have bound elemental spirits into the area to protect it. These sigils look to have been made fairly recently."

They'd traveled unmolested thus far, but an uneasy feeling rose in the pit of Hy'Targ's gut as they entered the broken ring of ancient block work. Many of the polished, vertical edges had escaped weathering, and the dwarf ran a finger across its surface. It was made of eldari craftsmanship. Yarrick swallowed audibly behind him.

At the center of the circle rose a small tower. Its graduated steps climbed up to the peak where something glinted with light. A bog bubbled with miry stink all around, creating a natural moat.

Hy'Targ pointed to it and the others nodded. Mantieth bobbed his head towards a stone path that crossed the bog to connect with the stairs that lead to their prize. "I've got this," he said quietly.

A look of fear flashed on Elorall's face. "It looks like a trap."

"Of course it's a trap," Mantieth said, "but I'd guess I'm more nimble than either of the dwarves."

Elorall looked to both Yarrick and Varanthl. She got three shrugs in return. They were content to let Mantieth go. "Just be careful," she insisted.

The blue-skinned elf grinned and then dashed off as stealthily as possible.

Creeping as close as they dared, the Gods'own watched as Mantieth stole up the stairs towards the thing that flashed with a metallic glint.

No sooner had Mantieth laid hands on it when some large thing leapt from the water like a coiled spring. It knocked Mantieth from his perch.

Mantieth screamed as the snake-like monster wrapped itself around the master swordsman, and together they fell to the far side of the tower and out of sight.

"Was that a python?" Elorall howled, rushing to his aid. Something roared in the distance and the monster splashed into the sludge beyond their sight.

"No! It was an ormyrr!" Hy'Targ had his axe in hand and was right on her heels when more crazed cultists leapt into view. These ones wore black robes, though splashes of faded color stained them where old blood had dried. These owners had also gashed themselves to cut their bloody sigils. Low-hanging hoods concealed their faces.

The way some stood identified them as trogs with their crooked-legged posture. Shades of red skin identified others as lava elves. One in particular seemed to be the leader. He barred their path and held a spear boasting an obsidian tip.

"The Gods'own shall die in this swamp—for the glory of the Dark One and his four faces!"

Elorall's eyes flashed with urgency. For all she knew, Mantieth was being crushed beneath the murky waters. Before the rest could even act, the selumari spell caster summoned a powerful gust of wind and threw the lead cultist vertically, flinging him so far into the sky that they lost sight of him. She turned and threw a blast of ice at the other cultists who had surrounded them, freezing their feet in place, and she sprinted towards her fiancé. Elorall shook her hand against a sudden stinging pain she felt in it, but ignored the mysterious sensation.

She'd bought her teammates a few precious seconds, and the Gods'own launched themselves towards the surprised enemies floundering with their numb feet. They found themselves battling on unsure footing. Each of the adventurers dispatched their assailants before the sky-flung body of their leader smashed against the nearby broken ruins with a sickly thud.

The body snapped into an unnatural pose and tumbled onto the stony path they'd followed. His hood fell back, revealing Hoyle's face. A surprised look was frozen to his face.

Hy'Targ had followed on Elorall's heels. She hesitated at the edge of the yellow and green pool of sludge where the ormyrr and Mantieth had fallen. A patch of brown water rippled where they'd broken the skin of sludge and watery growth that floated upon the surface.

She knew Mantieth had the genetic trait that many selumari had. It allowed him to breathe underwater, but the scum and sludge were so thick, she doubted even that would help. She dare not go in after him—unlike him, she did not possess selumari gills.

Hy'Targ gripped the haft of his axe, Glorybringer, as the huge body of the ormyrr surfaced like a crocosaur performing a death roll to finish its prey. And then they saw it: Mantieth's blade penetrating the slimy flesh of the beast. Its body rolled over and the coral elf swordsman broke the surface of the water, coughing and spluttering. Hacking, he spat out thick globs of mud and clumps of water foil.

Elorall leapt into the water and hugged him, kissing his lips despite the sludge, even while berating him for not being cautious enough.

Hy'Targ had already moved up the tower and collected the relic. He had no idea what the thing was, but it was certainly made of eldrymetallum, the rare star metal that imbued most magical items.

Descending the stairs in relative peace, Elorall shook off the last vestiges of pain from her wrist as she helped Mantieth back to solid ground. Her wound looked like a burn, though it felt cold to her touch.

The three rejoined the others as they took stock of their attackers. With all the hoods pulled back, Jr'Orhr grumbled, "They are not all the typical, crazed children of the Death god."

"What do you mean?" Mantieth asked as he wrung out his clothes.

The dwarf pulled aside the hoods of two different cultists. Blue flesh. Even some of the selumari were corrupted to worship the black god of Death.

Elorall sat on her haunches near the body of Hoyle, the harbor master. "Our ferryman is dead," she said with a hint of worry in her voice. "We're more than capable of operating his boat," she observed, "but this man's brother has Acacia."

CHAPTER FIVE

Nodhan stretched and smacked his jaws together. A mental haze like drunkenness swam about his head as he tried to right himself in a hammock. Ethereal whispers dissipated like smoke as they clouded his mind like wine-induced dreams.

He smoothed his tongue against the roof of his mouth and searched for water nearby to soothe his dry throat. He found a flask hanging from his hammock and sucked down a big gulp. Another bottle hung nearby, tethered to the bedpost. Firebrandy.

The lava elf sniffed with mild amusement as his hammock shifted with a slight lurch. He could tell by the movement and the smells that he was aboard a ship. Nodhan shook his head—this wasn't the first time he'd tied one on, had too much firebrandy, and awakened on a caravan or ship sailing to ports unknown.

He swung his legs over the edge and climbed down to the floor. Uncertain exactly how he got here, the red-skinned elf ventured out of the hold and above deck.

Nodhan found a crew of industrious humans and an odd array of other persons. A dwarf, a selumari, and a bestial gwereste worked the sails of what appeared to be a trade vessel.

Most of them refused to meet his gaze, and Nodhan assumed he had been belligerent or rude on the night prior while booking passage. He hoped he hadn't insulted anyone so egregiously that he'd have to duel his way out of the situation… or worse, issue an apology.

Finally, he approached one of the humans. "Where are we?"

The human raised an eyebrow. "About a day's travel from New Elrannin."

Nodhan stared at him, wild-eyed. "But that's four hundred leagues from Port Orric!"

The man nodded. "Well, we've been sailing for days. You've mostly kept to yourself… rambling like a gibbering mouth fiend."

"No… That can't be… " Nodhan began.

"It's true. Your bunk is above mine."

The lava elf grimaced. A drunken or debauched evening he could reconcile, but emerging from a days-long fugue?

"We're on our way to Niamarlee and making good time. It's what you booked passage for."

Nodhan detached from the conversation and retreated a few steps. The odd whispers began creeping back into his thoughts, babbling in the background of his mind and urging him to make for Niamarlee with a sense of urgency. Though he could make out the ethereal words, he somehow knew the meaning of them. Nodhan shook them out of his mind.

He clutched the seed that hung like a talisman at his neck. He suspected some kind of curse was upon him for stealing it.

What is this thing? Truly, has it perhaps planted something in me?

Eucalia sat impatiently at the prow, eager to get back and find Acacia. No sooner did they arrive in the harbor that they spotted a huddle of animals waiting for them on the shore. No one was there to tend them.

Hy'Targ left Hoyle's boat untethered on the sandy shore where they ran it aground. The cultist had tried to murder them, and the prince didn't have any particular interest in treating the dead man's property well.

The dryad leapt to the ground and ran to the unicorn, who had guided the other mounts back to wait for them. "I don't understand," Elorall said. "Why aren't they with Hoyle's brother?"

Varanthl laughed. "It looks like they got the better of him. I suspect he knew about Hoyle's plan to murder us and tried to take our mounts."

Acacia snorted. Blood coated all sides of his horn as if

he'd gored someone with it. Crimson ran in a congealing rivulet down his long face. His eyes glinted with a certain pride.

Eucalia touched it. "It seems somewhat fresh. Whatever happened must not have been long ago." She turned to her companion. "Acacia, take us back to that place."

The unicorn snorted and led the way.

Blood spatters marked the sign of a struggle at the boarder's hovel. A ruined stable lay busted wide open, where the animals had been freed by Acacia. A gruesome mess of blood led away from the site. Red hand prints had dried where Hoyle's brother escaped and the blood flow had staunched to a trickle along the ground leading to town. It slowed to a few intermittent drips, and they tracked the man like a wounded animal. Eventually, the trail disappeared.

Yarrick grimaced, looking over the last few blood splats. Like most of the eldarim, he excelled at tracking and other nature-craft. He shook his head. "The trail is dead. It looks like he managed to bound his wound and here, it stops completely. I'd guess someone rendered aid."

Hy'Targ grimaced and snorted through his nostrils, scattering his gold and red whiskers. "Then it's safe to say this village is unsafe." He stuffed his hands inside his satchel and clutched the strange object they'd acquired off the point of Last Rock. "Bah. Let Melkior have a village. We have the prize."

Jr'Orhr chuffed, "But what is it?"

Hy'Targ didn't dare bring it out in view of the village lest the lich's spies see it. "I have no idea. But I think it was there coincidentally—or else Melkior and his followers had no idea what it was, either. I think they were just there to kill us. Maybe it was nothing more than bait and it's possible the thing is little more than a hunk of painted steel."

Varanthl shook his head. "No. Whatever it is, it is certainly made of eldrymetallum. I should know; I wore a huge chunk of it in my chest for all my life until well, my second life."

Hy'Targ nodded. His friend was certainly qualified to identify the substance, but its actual purpose remained a mystery.

The dwarf scratched his head and turned his mammoth east. "Back to Xlinea, then. Surely they have a library or some experts who we can consult about it. Perhaps a little research will shed some light on this mystery." He smiled wistfully; the dwarf did love a good library.

Hy'Targ ignored the dull murmur of voices outside the Irontooth Kingdom's consulate, which was little more than a hostel near the center of Xlinea. Folk of various races paused outside, hoping to get a glimpse of the Gods'own.

Outside, a street vendor took an opportunity to hawk a briefly printed story pamphlet, telling a wildly inaccurate tale of their previous deeds.

The dwarf prince stared at the hunk of metal on the table. Only Jr'Orhr and Varanthl were with him. The elves from Niamarlee had other obligations, and Br'Derluch entertained the dryad and eldarim elsewhere in the building.

"It's got too smooth of lines for it to be a break," Hy'Targ muttered. "See how this part sticks out? It must connect to something... Some other kind of interlocking mechanism."

His companions mumbled their assents. It looked like some kind of three-dimensional puzzle piece. There was a receptacle area on the opposite side where another piece just like it might plug into this one. Foreign runes engraved the outer edges of it, written in a language that Hy'Targ did not know. And he was widely regarded as an expert on languages.

"They're ancient symbols," Jr'Orhr said. "But Yarrick already said they can't be eldari."

Hy'Targ cocked his jaw and pushed his finger into the

receptacle where the similar unit might connect. It had a kind of hinged door, with a spring to keep it closed when not under pressure. "Wait a moment... There's something in here!"

The discovery drew his peers in closer. Hy'Targ made Varanthl hold it upside down and tap on it while the dwarf held the door flap open. A very old and tightly rolled scroll fell out.

They carefully unfurled the parchment and stared at something that looked like total gibberish. It had a certain logical layout, though. "I think it's a letter written in gnomish," Hy'Targ observed.

The others nodded but could offer no insight. Quickly, they each made as accurate of a copy as they could, just in case it was ever needed, and so they would not be lost if the ancient document was damaged or stolen.

Hy'Targ hid the original back inside the relic and stashed another copy in their hostel before the three adventurers sneaked into the crowd. After a short walk, they'd dodged any of their would-be fans and arrived at the local library.

A disinterested human male at the front desk cataloged returns. "How can I help you?" he practically sighed.

"I need every book you have about the gremmlobahnd," Hy'Targ demanded.

The man raised his eyebrows, but began pulling volumes from a shelf in the back. "It will take me a while to collect them all. Perhaps I can get you some of the more popular texts while you wait?"

"Are books about the gnomes popular?" Varanthl asked.

The librarian scoffed. "Hardly... with the exception of an expert who has occasionally been by to study the topic in recent years." He blew off a layer of dust and passed two books over the desk. "I heard he may be in town. Though rumors say it may not be for long... and then, who knows if he will return."

Hy'Targ cracked the spine with an inquisitive look. The human droned on. "He's the only person to have opened some of these books in the last century."

The dwarven academic worked his jaw when he turned to the inside cover flap where the "expert" had made his borrower's mark. Only one name was inscribed: Hy'Drunyr sa'Meril… Hy'Targ's uncle.

"What has 'yer father said to you about your uncle?" Jr'Orhr asked the dwarven prince.

Hy'Targ tightened his lips. "Not much. Mainly just that he doesn't want me to get anywhere near him." The two dwarves and Varanthl loitered beneath the eave of an unmarked building where Hy'Drunyr, brother of the Adventurer King, was staying. "When I was younger, I'd always assumed Hy'Drunyr was dangerous. Like some kind of shadowy figure plotting against the throne. Maybe because my father always left a contingent of loyal soldiers behind to guard against that very purpose."

Jr'Orhr shrugged. "Maybe that was just conventional wisdom. Regardless, if Hy'Mandr didn't want you to have contact, and if you insist on making it, perhaps it's best if I keep my plausible deniability."

The prince nodded with a smile. "Perhaps so. My father sent you here for a reason—best if I let you get back to it."

Jr'Orhr shook his head with a laugh. "My charge was to keep a record of Hy'Drunyr's movements and whom he spoke to." He looked at Hy'Targ and flashed him a wink. He turned towards the front door. "I think I'll take a walk. I can't be expected to keep *constant* surveillance, after all, and some visitors are bound to slip through my net."

Hy'Targ nodded and watched Jr'Orhr stroll around the corner and into the market. He turned to his four-armed friend. "Ready?"

Varanthl grimaced. "I'm not sure. This is all new to me. I've seen Hy'Drunyr around the mountain, but never understood why folk always kept their distance. It's hard for me to understand why anyone would keep family away." He looked down, the confusion clear on his face.

The dwarf knew his friend struggled with certain concepts. Varanthl's background was so radically different from those of other folk. He'd lived two lives and met two deaths, not counting his short deactivation when the Kreethaln had failed in the battle against Melkior. As a flesh construct, the homunculus was really only a couple years old, and he possessed only glimmers of his past. Like memories of hazy dreams.

"I really only know that his crimes against my father were related to my mother, Queen Sh'Ttil, and her... *disappearance.*"

"I was told she was dead?"

Hy'Targ set his jaw and knocked on the door. "Her body was never found. My father has never given up the idea she may be out there... somewhere... "

The door opened slowly to reveal a dwarf with dark, longish hair, and a short beard. For a vagha, he appeared gaunt and his manicured beard gave him an almost effeminate look compared with the wild style popular among the males of Irontooth. Wearing only a cotton shift, he appeared unready for guests, though his eyes brightened at their sight.

"You invited me, Uncle?"

Hy'Drunyr grabbed Hy'Targ and wrapped him in a hug, standing a little straighter to do so. "You came! I am so glad you did—please, please come in." He escorted them in.

An earthy, spicy kind of odor permeated the rented building, and he walked ahead of them to close a pocket door, where the odor emanated. "My treatment," he explained. "I've been unwell and all conventional medicine is useless, but a doctor in Xlinea promises I can manage the disease by bathing in smoke from dragons' weed incense. Direct inhalation also works."

Hy'Targ raised an eyebrow. "Vapors of that weed are

toxic, 'ye know? It's in the name."

Hy'Drunyr grinned sloppily. "I'm aware. It's also mildly euphoric. I feel quite better in fact... My physician claims that I may return home soon. I'm looking forward to it." He rang a bell and a frehlasuhl aide hurried into the room.

Varanthl perked up when he saw the scullion and rubbed his wrist, turning the bangle there, to remember where he'd acquired it.

"Bring us a fresh tea service, please," Hy'Drunyr requested. The gray elf nodded curtly and disappeared. "Please, sit." Hy'Drunyr took a seat at the main table of the tea room.

The servant left his tray and departed in silence.

"I just wanted to tell you that I am so sorry... I regret my part in what passed between your father and I hope that it might not prevent you and I from some sort of relationship?"

Hy'Targ kept his face neutral but nodded measuredly in response.

"I'm not even sure what happened, to be honest... Only the end result. Your mother's absence."

The prince looked away. He'd heard the stories before, all the different versions of them, in fact, and he had no desire to rehash the past. "I'm not here for that. Whatever your quarrel with my father is between you and him. I may never know the truth of it, and I long stopped trying to unravel the mystery. It's not mine to solve."

Hy'Drunyr sat back, mildly surprised, but also looking somewhat relieved. "Then what brings you by, nephew?"

"I need your help," Hy'Targ said. He set the mysterious metal object from beyond Last Rock on the table. It made contact with a weighty thud.

"Is... Is that what I think it is?" Hy'Drunyr asked breathlessly.

"You will have to tell me," Hy'Targ said. "By library accounts, you're the local expert on all things gremmlobahnd."

Mantieth and Elorall walked towards the center of Xlinea, where an observation tower rose above the rest of the city. There were several similar structures scattered throughout, but none quite as grand as their destination. With an eyrie perched atop the spire, there would surely be selumari eagle riders passing through with regularity, and surely they could get news from Niamarlee.

Elorall bumped into her prince clumsily and intentionally. She reached for his hand and intertwined her fingers with his. She smiled, still not quite free from the thoughts of how she'd almost lost him to an ormyrr.

Mantieth smiled and squeezed her hand, but then released it.

She looked as if she might pout.

"We must keep our hands free in case there are dangers about the city," he insisted.

Elorall frowned, but saw his threadbare logic. She followed him into the shadow of the tower.

They did not even get to the door before being recognized. A messenger hurried out to meet them. The younger coral elf bowed. "Prince Mantieth, I was instructed to summon you, should you check in."

Mantieth cocked an eyebrow, but followed the blue-skinned soldier. He led them up three flights of stairs and to his commander's office. The commander stood, bowed when Mantieth entered, then took his seat.

"I'm Commander Trulamon," he introduced himself. "I have some news you may be interested in, Lord Mantieth."

"Do tell," Mantieth insisted.

"Trogs," Trulamon said.

Elorall's fists tightened. "Here? In Xlinea?"

"Well, yes... but also no," he said. "There are a few who

live peacefully here in Xlinea. It is a free city, after all. That means that even trogs—at least the ones who renounce devotion to the Death god and agree to abide by Xlinea's laws—are allowed to do as they please." Trulamon winked, "The amazons keep a watch on them just in case... As do we."

"The trogs," Mantieth reminded him to get back on topic.

"Ahem, yes. We've received word of goblin movement in the south." Trulamon pointed to a map showing the upper section of Charnock. "Our scouts reported massive movement from the Black Glades across the Great Coastal Road and en route to the Raithlan Plains."

Mantieth stroked his chin and narrowed his eyes. He already knew that the forces in the Black Glades had migrated there from the Moorlech, the swamp due west of Niamarlee. They'd been unable to root them out, and now their cancer was spreading with a young force of warriors who were still very fresh. Their numbers made them no less dangerous.

"Did they see any drakufreet with them?" Elorall asked.

Trulamon shrugged. "Uncertain. Our information was very limited and our scouts didn't know to look for any. I suspect there may have been a few wild dragonkin bound to goblin service."

"You wouldn't have missed this one," Mantieth said. "Champion-sized agamid; the kind with wings. But its color is off. More metal than elemental. It's so big that it looks almost like a young dragon."

"Sorry," Trulamon said. "I only know I was supposed to notify you and tell you that Niamarlee has dispatched an army to try to deal with the threat... If only they could find it."

"How do you lose an entire army?" Mantieth asked.

Trulamon worked his jaw for a moment, and then said somberly, "We sent out eagle riders to scout the plains and swamps by air. None of them ever returned."

Mantieth thanked him and quickly departed with Elorall rushing to keep up.

"Wait up, Mantieth," she yelped, nearly losing him in the crowd. "Where are you going?"

"Back," he said, pausing for her to get close enough to hear. "We've got to figure out what's happening with these trogs. It sounds like they're on the move for war."

Elorall shot him a skeptical look.

Mantieth explained. "I can understand their expansion from Moorlech into the glades," he said. "But they're getting nearer to the plains. Why would they abandon the safety of the swamp unless they have some real aspiration?" He furrowed his brow and turned his thoughts inward.

Elorall read him before Mantieth even realized the gravity of his conclusions. "You think they're digging in for position? That they may be hoping to broaden their borders?"

The prince blasted a hot breath through his nostrils. "If that's the play, they could easily cut off Xlinea from the rest of Charnock, but that's the humans' problem. I think they may do an end run to blockade Niamarlee, cutting the city off from Irontooth. If the dwarves can't get help, my father's kingdom would fall. But I can't see goblin troop projections being correct."

Elorall interjected, "But there's a whole kingdom to the north that..." she trailed off. Undrakull would not likely come to Niamarlee's aid. Especially if they shared the same aspirations as the Moorlech trogs. "We should send spies immediately to ascertain their allegiances."

Mantieth nodded. "The drider queen was one of these same cultists we found past Last Rock and turned many in the city into acolytes. They even desecrated Undrakull's Firiel temple. If the local sentiment hasn't changed, it means they're likely to join the trogs and make a play for Niamarlee. I know their ambassadors have made claims, but talk is cheap... and that's all ambassadors do, it seems."

"Without Niamarlee, the dwarves would fall next," Elorall said.

"What about we dwarves?" a voice interrupted them.

They turned to find Jr'Orhr approaching.

"Movement from the trogs," Mantieth explained. "Elorall and I are riding out immediately to consult with the army. Tell the others that we'll meet them in Niamarlee when they return by the Great Coral Road."

"Is there word of Brentésion?" the dwarf asked.

"None could tell," the elven prince responded. "Hopefully I'll have more word for you in a few tenday." With that, the two selumari departed.

Chapter Six

Hy'Drunyr turned the object over in his hands with a kind of special reverence. He sucked the air through his teeth as if giddy. "It is definitely gnomish in origin."

"Like the Kreethaln?" Varanthl asked.

The dwarf raised his eyes and peered over the item. "Yes... but no. I never had a chance to examine that particular item," Hy'Drunyr said.

"That is a shame, when it has been so close," Varanthl rambled. "It has been a part of me for most of my life and I have kept it in a vault in Irontooth."

Hy'Targ shot his friend a severe look, intending to silence him. Hy'Drunyr seemed to have paid the comment no mind, as if he hadn't even heard it, and the glance had gone unnoticed.

"No, I'm quite certain this is something different, though it may be related in some way," Hy'Drunyr said.

Hy'Targ pointed out the engravings etched upon the piece. "I assume that is some form of gnomish script?"

His uncle nodded measuredly. "It is a form of it, yes. The gremmlobahnd had many written modes and it was a complicated language."

"Is there anywhere I could learn to speak or read gnomish?" Hy'Targ asked.

Hy'Drunyr stroked the beard at his chin. "None use the language, but there is a cypher and a limited dictionary of sorts available. I would guess the archives might have a copy of it—if for no other reason than that the gremmlobahnd once possessed a stronghold in the southern part of Charnock. It is interesting for archaeological purposes."

"Funny that the library keeper did not offer it when we visited previously," Jr'Orhr said and leaned forward.

Hy'Drunyr shrugged. "It is a rare text and quite valuable because of its historical significance, though not for its contents. Very little interest remains in the gnomes these days." He raised his finger as if he just had an idea. "The head librarian does know me as an authority on the matter, and if you gave him my name, he would likely give you access to the book. Though it might be better to commission a copy. The information is not protected, just largely forgotten about."

Hy'Targ raked his fingers through his whiskers and admitted, "That might be the best advice. Who knows how that could come in handy?"

Jr'Orhr stood to his feet. "Let's get on with it straight away, then." He and Varanthl headed for the door when Hy'Drunyr caught his nephew by the arm.

Something in his face convinced him of the truth in his words. "I am very happy to connect," he said, "but perhaps you should keep our meeting secret from your father?"

Hy'Targ nodded solemnly. "That may be for the best."

Hy'Drunyr placed the gnomish artifact into his nephew's hand. "Certainly keep me informed as to what you discover. I likely know more about the gremmlobahnd than any other person in this whole durned continent… but *this* thing's purpose is a total mystery." He grinned, "A mystery who's secrets I would very much like to uncover before I die."

Hy'Targ clapped his uncle on the arm and nodded. "We will talk again soon." He departed to meet the others in his party.

Melkior smelled the churning, inky mass of wild necralluvium in the fetid waters of a lagoon, near the cave where he and his dracolich resided. Some offshoot of the Kendall River had gotten land-locked before emptying into the Hadden Bay, creating the listless pool.

Things died in the muck of the fen, contributing to the black odor that hung in the damp air. Melkior sniffed again, catching the familiar scent. "This way," he urged Rahkawmn and they rode deeper through the swamps. "It lies ahead... I can smell it with more than just my nose." Melkior sat upon the sickly white beast.

Rahkawmn rumbled his assent, and it vibrated through his neck and torso. He smelled it too, though the dragon was not drawn to it like his master; Rahkawmn wanted to *avoid* the deathly elixir. Something had awakened the undead drake's will – freed him - in the aftermath of the battle for Ailushurai's bones but Rahkawmn knew better than to reveal that fact too soon.

He remained ever loyal to his friend of old, Melkior. But something had changed. When Rahkawmn's mind had reemerged, it was as if waking from a bad dream. Only he discovered that the dream was real.

Melkior grumbled about feeling pain. His skin felt aflame and his insides writhed as if contaminated by insect larvae. "The necralluvium is all that keeps me together after being wounded by that damnable contraption," he hissed.

"There it is." The lich pointed to a wriggling mass the size and shape of a wasp hive, clinging to a withered tree. He slid down and approached it. His knee buckled and audibly broke within his paper skin; the dust within grated between the contact points of his patella. Melkior growled, but continued onward. He shook the tree where it hung like moss on a bald cypress.

Smacking down with a wet thud, the splotch of black death would kill any living thing that encountered it. Melkior had other things in mind. He picked it up like a ripe melon and eagerly bit into it.

Inky fluid dripped from his teeth and dribbled down his jaws as he chewed up the soft, spongy mass. His eyes rolled back part way, and he already felt its effects. Bones within the lich's body cracked and snapped back into place, restored for the time being. He took a deep gasp as the wounds that refused to otherwise heal finally closed.

Melkior unwrapped the bandages that earlier held his skin together. Whenever he went too long without devouring the strange substance, he had to bind his limbs or risk losing them entirely. Eventually, the flesh would burst again and what remained of him would leak out like sand until he staunched the flow and found more of the ichor.

The lich flexed his hand proudly. He took another bite, put the remnants into a jar, and sealed it.

Melkior climbed aboard Rahkawmn again and nudged him back towards their cave. "Soon, my friend. Soon we may begin again. We still must find my beloved's bones… Then, nothing will stop us. I am certain that I can hold myself together once I have them in my possession. And then… Then we shall rule as Malgrimm intended."

They traveled in silence for a few moments. "And then I can find a way to free myself from the god of Death. Ailushurai and I both." He patted his beast's shoulder, "And you, of course, my friend."

Rahkawmn angled his head to glance at Melkior. Dragons were fully sentient, even though not all could speak, and dracolichs were not much different. Even if he could have spoken, he would not have admitted to his friend that he had considered abandoning him.

He did not believe Melkior yearned to be an evil overlord—rather, he yearned to be reunited with his beloved. Rahkawmn did not know how Melkior could free them from the Lord of Death, even if he reclaimed Ailushurai's remains. He wanted to believe in his intentions, though concern had lodged itself in Rahkawmn's mind ever since his reawakening.

For now, he would stick close to his friend. They had power and they would wield it. It had had always been this way.

Eventually, they would succeed. Eventually, they would throw off Death's yoke and be free.

Mantieth and Elorall trotted into the encampment upon horseback and spotted familiar faces. He did not know the names of the soldiers, but he knew he'd passed them before. As the prince of Niamarlee, he did not often fraternize with the lower ranks of the selumari military, but he had a way with faces.

This group had set up camp outside a village in the north-most section of the Raithlan Plains. A ragtag collection of coral elves and dwarves worked together to ascertain the threat level of the elusive Moorlech trogs who had merged with the enemy from the Black Glades. They had formed a sort of triage unit and healers on the outskirts of the village, who plied their craft while scouts hurried to a fro.

A blue-skinned elf paused long enough to salute the prince and his fiancé. "Is it just you or are the rest of the Gods'own coming?" the soldier asked.

"They will meet us east of the Stonejaws," Elorall answered. "Who is in charge here?"

"Someone else." The soldier bowed. "Not all of us citizens of Niamarlee are comfortable taking orders from the vagha," he admitted. "Tensions quelled when the eldarim took charge…"

"Someone you know," Taryl said, nudging his way into view. "At least in passing," he greeted Mantieth. He bowed courteously, but not quite so low as a peasant or coral elf soldier might.

"Taryl," Mantieth grinned. "Hopefully you're out searching for goblins and not preying upon the single women of…" he looked around, looking for some indicator of the name of this poor village, and then shrugged.

"I promise you, we've been hard at work," the eldarim stated.

"We heard that there had been word of trog invasions in these parts," Elorall interjected. "You know as well as any that my fiancé and I have been searching for any sign of Brentésion, the strange mount belonging to Hy'Targ."

"The king, actually," Taryl stated.

"Of course," Elorall said. She was well versed in diplomacy. "I was there when the dwarf prince lost Brentésion to the trogs. He saved me from trolls and trogs that day, and we would like nothing more than to see Brentésion returned before Mantieth and I are wed."

Taryl shot the selumari prince a side-long look and caught him leaning slightly away from the enchantress. He stiffened. "Yes, we'd like that very much," Mantieth fumbled.

The eldarim winked and then led them through their camp, pointing out the devastation. "We've been canvassing the area for concrete signs of the missing creature," Taryl stated. "But I'm afraid we're most interested in self-preservation at the moment."

He pointed to a huddled mass of dirty citizens from the nameless hamlet. They were mostly an equal mix of human, dwarf, and coral elf, though a flash of red skin identified a couple individuals as morehl, and at least one gwereste in the mix. Their number was barely a hundred survivors. Soot stained their faces and frazzled hair, and many of them owned obvious injuries peeking out from their torn and damaged clothing.

Elorall's face softened when she looked at them. "I understand," she said.

"Did you catch sight of the enemy?" Mantieth asked.

"Niamarlee's scouts spied them out just as the last of the trogs were slinking away." Taryl motioned them to follow, and the trio walked into the mix of refugees.

The stink of body odor and smoke clogged the

encampment. The displaced persons milled about the area. A few had blank looks of catatonia plastered to their faces, frozen by battle horrors which they could never unsee.

Taryl tapped a young human on the shoulder, a scrawny boy of maybe fourteen years. "What is your name?"

"J-Jareth," he stuttered. "Please sir... my parents..."

The eldarim frowned. "I'm sorry. If they're not here, they're most likely dead."

Elorall scowled at Taryl's harsh delivery and offered the youth a handful of nuts. She guessed he hadn't eaten in quite some time.

Jareth greedily accepted them, though they did little to quench the despair growing in his eyes.

"Can we ask you some questions?" she asked.

He nodded reluctantly, chewing the nuts quickly to keep his eyes dry..

"Did you see what happened in your village?"

Jareth nodded. "I saw it all. My parents told me to hide. It was the last I'd seen of them."

"What did you see?" Mantieth jumped in and clarified. "Goblins?"

"And monsters, too," Jareth said. "Trogs and trolls. They came so close I could smell their stink."

"What else?" Mantieth asked. "Was there a bronze creature, almost as big as a dragon? It would have looked like an over-sized dragonkin."

Jareth scrunched his face. "I—I'm not sure. There was a creature they had captured. It was tied to a wheeled sled, like a wagon, but rough built. I could not see it well. It must have been heavy. Trolls were pulling it."

Mantieth rubbed his chin and smiled. "It certainly *sounds* like Brentésion."

Elorall asked, "We—the Gods'own—heard the trogs refer to their warlord once before... that fiend, Ratargul the Smotherer."

The survivor perked up at Elorall's mention of the Gods'own, but then shot her a confused look. "The—the Smotherer?"

Mantieth explained, "He's a 'shambling mound,' an ancient monster made from earth and death magic; a lump of clay and plant matter brought to life by Malgr—by Death himself," he stated, taking care not to speak the forbidden name of the wicked god.

"I know what a shambling mound is," Jareth responded. "I've seen them in picture books when I was a child. And I heard the name Ratargul when the trogs were attacking—I was hiding beneath the floorboards of my house." He pointed to the husky building with a stone foundation. It was adjacent to the area, rutted up by the footprints of the vast army that had passed through. He had been in an excellent position to spy on the enemy.

"So Ratargul was here?" Mantieth confirmed.

The youth nodded. "But he took orders from another—a goblin. The shambler didn't seem happy about it. A trog with red and white paint all over his body. He was called Tsut and was obviously the underling of someone they called *the Dreaded One*, but I couldn't make out his name." He cocked his jaw. "I don't speak goblin very well and there was so much noise… screams… " Jareth trailed off, his thoughts turning inward as he revisited the horrors.

Elorall thanked him as they meandered away from the boy.

"I think you've found the first step on the path to reclaiming Brentésion," Taryl stated.

"But why?" Elorall asked. "It makes no sense. Why would they keep him if they could not ride him? Normally, trogs would have killed anything they couldn't use… or eat."

Taryl guessed, "Maybe Brentésion isn't edible? I could speculate… "

"Please do," Mantieth insisted. He knew Taryl was well traveled and vastly more experienced with trogs than he was. Goblins tended to be openly hostile to most Esfahn races that did not originate from Malgrimm's twisted mind... Except the eldarim, who they viewed with a sort of neutrality. Most free towns that had a goblin population only did so because they had been built by eldarim or one of the shara, what pure-blooded eldarim called each other, and had invited them to trade or settle there.

"They might view Brentésion as a trophy, if their leader is incredibly vain. I've seen that before. A token or prisoner of great power claimed to keep challengers at bay by the warlord's legacy. It is also possible that they are trying to break or tame him, hoping to eventually turn him to their purposes or for future use." He shrugged.

Elorall studied Taryl. "There's more... What else do you suspect?"

Taryl said, "Maybe they're not idiots. Trogs have a reputation for stupidity, and rightfully so... Most of them *are* idiots. But what do you expect from a culture that recognizes adulthood at age six and reaches sexual maturity a little after? They are stupid because they are barely more than toddlers by the time they spawn their own litter. That makes their mortality rate high and keeps their experience and intelligence quotient low. But sometimes—sometimes you get a *genius*. Maybe their leader is an idiot savant, or just a trog who managed to reach a healthy, long age far removed from the normally stupid thrall of the subculture and pressures of living in such a culture?"

"What are you saying?" Mantieth asked.

"Sometimes, even the muck of the swamp produces a calculating, intelligent enemy. I think this 'Dreaded One' could be such an enemy. I think he may be examining Brentésion—freed from the regular, goblinoid impulse to kill and eat."

The coral elves frowned at the idea. Facing Ratargul again had been a somber enough thought. Whoever held the

Smotherer's leash must have been imposing, indeed. That gave them pause for thought.

Taryl handed the selumari prince a sealed scroll. "I assumed I would run into you before long, at least before returning to Irontooth or Niamarlee. Please give this to Yarrick when you see him next?"

Mantieth nodded. "We have plans to see him again soon."

Hy'Targ's mammoth slowed and halted outside the archives of Xlinea. He slid down the creature's furry back as it used its trunk to playfully accept fistfuls of greenery that human children offered it.

The vaghan prince smirked and then stepped towards the building. The library keeper exited and offered Hy'Targ a wrapped bundle in exchange for some coins.

"Our small corps of copyists worked nonstop to get this done on your shortened time-line," The librarian said, looking down his narrow nose at the dwarf.

Hy'Targ huffed and added a few more coins.

The librarian relaxed his posture and bowed. "Hopefully it holds all the answers you seek, good dwarf."

Hy'Targ nodded curtly, stowed his newly bound manuscript in his saddlebags, and then grabbed a fistful of thick mammoth hair. He crawled up his mount's side and took his position, urging the creature back down the road and into a brisk lope.

Beyond the edge of town, he spotted tiny blooms and shoots creeping through the packed earth of the road. Hy'Targ spotted the unicorn Acacia first, with Eucalia riding it. The other Gods'own had slowed considerably and lagged behind.

After catching up, he understood why. The dwarf caught sight of Jr'Orhr at the front of the entourage. Given the orders he had received from Hy'Targ's father, it meant...

"Hello, Nephew," Hy'Drunyr called from his wagon seat.

Hy'Targ nodded to him. Jr'Orhr gave the prince an almost imperceptible shrug; he'd been tasked with keeping tabs on King Hy'Mandyr's brother and had little choice in the matter. Hy'Targ didn't know if the change of plans was good or bad... Yet.

"I thought I could be of some service to you," Hy'Drunyr said. "Perhaps I can help speed up your study of the gremmlobahnd's linguistics?" He nodded to the empty seat in the carriage.

"I thought you'd stay in Xlinea for your treatments?"

Hy'Drunyr showed him a kind of bottle system where a stoppered jar collected vapors from another jar containing a smoldering hunk of bark: The source of dragons' weed incense. They were connected by a thin tube. "I just need to take a sniff o'these collected fumes every morning and evening."

Hy'Targ nodded slowly. His uncle *was* the regional expert. "I don't suppose it will hurt," the dwarf said, and he certainly wanted to learn the language as quickly as possible. Study would help speed their travel.

Nodhan felt his head pounding like he'd drank far too much bloodwine. The earlier blackout fugue had not been his only instance; he may have been losing control of his body in his sleep, or *cursed,* or been manipulated by magic, gods, and dispossessed souls. Nodhan had heard of all these things happening, but did not know which one afflicted him.

His eyes focused on the familiar gray line on the horizon. Dohan.

After a brief lay-over in Reeflocke, the eastern Sontarran coast, the vessel he'd boarded in his previous fugue made the return voyage full circle. Giyrnach lay in the distance.

Nodhan scowled at it when he remembered Reeflocke… Actually, he *hadn't* remembered Reeflocke. He only had snippets of memory, as if images drawn from a drunken haze. But Nodhan had already decided he would not imbibe any substance that could tamper with his thinking; he'd set his mind as an experiment.

Something was wrong with him, Nodhan knew, and he was beginning to eliminate potential suspects. The lava elf sniffed the salty sea air and scowled.

He had always fancied himself a scientific sort. Another test would be possible soon.

He thought back to Sontarra. Before he'd blacked out in Reeflocke, Nodhan had possessed the good sense to count his coins and write down the amount before sending word to Laelysh in Port Orric. She'd been expecting him weeks ago.

Nodhan gritted his teeth as he thought of her worrying for him. He sighed. *Either I paid double for my letter, or I sent a second note after I blacked out again.*

Sea dogs barked as he stared into the distance. A sharp pain lodged in his forehead; Nodhan recognized the pain above his eyes and remembered that it always came before a blackout. It felt like *the Strange*, a kind of psychological state that came over many morehl youths, especially males, but most grew out of it with only a few encounters. A side effect of the Strange was often a sense of detachment and brief memory loss, but he'd outgrown the fits with the onset of puberty, and *his* memories covered entire missing days.

He blinked against the ebbing light of Soll and its reflection against the water. Fell whispers murmured in his mind like some kind of back-alley skullduggery.

Nodhan attempted another test. He walked towards the forward mast where none of the ship's crew currently were. He slipped his hands into his pockets and squeezed his fingers over a smooth object, felt its texture, and concentrated on it. It was a trick he'd learned from another orphaned morehl and his oldest friend, Oren Sr. The sensation helped him focus his mind and overcome the mental state brought on by the Strange.

He squeezed the change in his pocket with one hand, and his only other object in the other.

"Are you trying to force me back to Dohan? You have some errand you are trying to steer me into?"

Nodhan sneered in the silence that followed. Even the whispers ceased. "Well, I thought you could speak? Whispers at least..."

And then it suddenly spoke with words he could understand. But Nodhan did not like what the voice confessed.

CHAPTER SEVEN

The return voyage from Xlinea had proved tedious and taken longer than the Gods'own had anticipated. They encountered few other travelers, but that was part of the problem. Nothing broke the monotony. Seeing the sparse travel along the Great Coastal Road reinforced the terror the locals felt; they feared being caught in the open with rumors of a goblin army on the prowl.

But the silence, tense though it was, improved Hy'Targ's ability to study and his uncle proved a reasonable teacher. By the time they'd passed the Black Glades and entered Undrakull's domain, he had a reasonable grasp of the gnomish language's basics; with the help of a lexicon, he could parse sentences with reasonable talent.

Hy'Targ was good at those sorts of skills; the kinds based around book smarts. Even as much as his newfound role forced him into the path of an adventurer, he still much preferred a book to the saddle. The dwarf prince assumed that would always be.

As the amount of distance between the road and the edge of Niamarlee dwindled, the Gods'own breathed a collective sigh of relief. The selumari city's curtain wall rose large before the adventurers and Jr'Orhr chuckled. "T'wasn't so long ago we fled this city with burned skeletons on our heels and a hoard of coral elves in pursuit."

Mantieth grinned, thinking of the night they absconded with their morehl captive. "Apparently, kidnapping prisoners of the crown is frowned upon... "

Elorall squinted and stared into the distance. "Speaking of lava elves... "

As they neared, a solitary morehl stood in the road with his back to the city gate.

Hy'Targ sat on his mammoth instead of riding with his uncle. He rose tall in the saddle and urged his beast to the front. *That can't be Nodhan, can it?* He closed the gap and saw that it was not.

The red-skinned elf was dressed as a world traveler, but his features clearly differed from those of their former traveling companion. He waved a tube that was shut with a rotating dial-lock as he called out, "Gods'own? You are the renowned adventurers, yes? You fit their description."

Hy'Targ grimaced, but nodded. "Is that a message for us?"

He shook his head. "No. Well, yes. It is for one of your members. I was directed to only place it in the hands of Yarrik, the son of Qarl. I was told the Gods'own frequently pass through this part of the Great Coastal Road." He shrugged, "I would have waited inside Niamarlee, but it is not a free city..."

The dwarf nodded measuredly. "Yarrik, do you know this lava elf?"

Pulling away from the party, Yarrik guided his wild drakufreet closer. "I don't know many morehl," he said, studying the elf's red face. "I've never met him."

The morehl shook his head. "And we're unlikely to pass each other again." He handed over the message tube. With a short bow, the courier turned on his heel and then departed, circumventing the Great Coastal Road. The footpath he chose led him around Niamarlee, before rejoining the road and continuing south. It was a good choice, as the selumari city was off limits to his kind.

Hy'Targ flashed Yarrik a curious look, and the younger warrior fidgeted with the container. He tried a few cyphers that he'd memorized until it popped open.

Yarrik slid a piece of parchment from within, a thin-lipped expression on his face that bordered on a scowl. He scanned it once, fully, and before reading it again.

"Well, what's it say?" Jr'Orhr called out from the

wagon, hoping for an explanation. Vagha were rarely pleased to let anything delay a hot hearth and a good supper.

"My father," Yarrik stated flatly. He bit his lower lip. "He says he will have business soon in Dohan and then in Lyandrica, just south of Irontooth. He hopes to meet me when he can." Yarrik rolled up the letter and stowed it in his pack.

The rest of the Gods'own fell in line as they moved towards the city again. Eucalia, riding numbly upon Acacia's back, pulled in close to Varanthl as they rode through the curtain walls and beneath the massive, barbed portcullis.

She kept her voice low. "I don't understand," she admitted to him. "Is he not happy to hear from his father? I had no father. I'm afraid I don't quite understand…"

Varanthl drew his lip into a confused smile. "I'm afraid my experience is not much better. I only have snippets, disconnected memories of my fathers—I was created by some strange arcana and am just as confused as you are."

Eucalia grinned wryly. "We are two of a kind, then."

He bobbed his head. "I'm afraid so."

"I don't know what to make of it," Furtaevell said as he re-read the letter. King Leidergelth's head magician and chief adviser stood with his daughter, Elorall, and her betrothed prince. "Scrying reveals nothing to me, which means the author either draws from a greater magic source than I, or there is nothing significant about his or her identity."

The elf scratched his head. Not all magicians could scry, but Furtaevell was quite good at it.

After digesting the info for a few minutes, Elorall folded up the letter and kissed him on the cheek. "Thank you for trying, Father."

The cryptic letter had arrived at the castle a tenday ago and been delivered to Mantieth's father. The King kept it until it could be delivered to his son once he'd arrived back in Niamarlee.

Before Mantieth and Elorall departed, Furtaevell called out, "There is one other that you might consult. You know of the vagha sorceress living in Niamarlee?"

Mantieth nodded slightly. "By reputation, only."

"She should be easy enough to locate. She has her own following, mostly peasants and the downtrodden. Perhaps she will possess different insight. She has helped the crown before. Perhaps she could help the Gods'own?"

Mantieth raised an eyebrow. "The path spell?"

Furtaevell silently acknowledged that fact. Selumari could not cast the type of spell required to arcanely send the coral elf armies to the battlefront, where they were needed during Melkior's uprising. Furtaevell and Leidergelth knew their children would perish without help, and the rogue dwarf assisted them under a shroud of secrecy.

"It may be worth approaching her, but she is enigmatic, to say the least."

Mantieth and Elorall thanked him again and departed. A short walk brought them away from the castle and into the market square nearest the north gate.

Elorall tapped on Mantieth's arm and pointed. "She's here. We are in luck."

"We certainly are," Mantieth agreed. "Now let us hope she is willing to help."

The prince hurried over to her. "Excuse me, ma'am. Are you the dwarf they call Sh'Zzar?"

The old vaghan woman looked up at him with piercing eyes that darted out from beneath locks of silver hair. She was somehow beautiful, even in her advanced age, and that beauty startled Mantieth momentarily.

"I—I'm sorry to intrude, but we'd hoped to ask you a question and seek your services. You do contract them, yes?"

She glanced aside with a sigh. "Why don't you ask that

one's father?" Sh'Zzar bobbed her head towards Elorall.

Elorall frowned. "We already consulted him to scry anything he could about a strange letter our party received. The sender has contacted us a couple times now."

Sh'Zzar looked around nervously. "Are the rest of the Gods'own here?"

"No," Mantieth said. "But we expect them any day now. We left Xlinea a few days before them and traveled at a quicker pace."

Sh'Zzar carefully read the letter and then returned it. "I cannot help you; I'm sorry. There is much I can do which Furtaevell cannot, but not with scrying. He is likely better than I. If he can't determine your Gray Wanderer's identity, then I can do nothing else." She sighed. "You might do well to focus your fame and energy on the goblin problem plaguing the Great Coastal Road, rather than chasing after some problem developing on the far side of the world."

Mantieth cocked his head. "Come again?"

"The undead are rising in Cyrea. It's all connected—but the trogs are of more pressing concern. And this Gray Wanderer?" She glanced past the two elves and her eyes looked suddenly worried.

"What is it?" Elorall asked.

"The king's brother... He must not see me," she said with a low and raspy voice.

"But I don't have an uncle," Mantieth began saying, and then Elorall pointed to the north gate. A wagon driven by Jr'Orhr entered the market square; an unfamiliar looking dwarf rode abreast of him.

Mantieth turned back to address Sh'Zzar, but she was already gone. He glanced at Elorall. "What did she mean by, 'the undead are rising in Cyrea?'"

Elorall shrugged with a slight grimace.

"Ho, Mantieth!" Hy'Targ called out from his mammoth.

Mantieth waved and quickly forgot about the sorceress and her warning. She'd been unable to help, anyway, and all too cryptic for his liking.

Jr'Orhr stopped his wagon in front of the elves. "You gotta direct us to the nearest mead hall. Immediately!"

Mantieth grinned. "Right this way, sirs."

"We circumvented a huge segment of the Great Coastal Road and saw the damage caused by the trog army." Mantieth shook his head and glowered into a flagon of amber tinted wine. "It's devastating."

Elorall took over for him. "We found Taryl and the troops in the foothills north of the People of the Sun and the Raithlan Plains. It was only a short journey back to the Great Road; we gained several days on you and arrived half a tenday ago, where King Leidergelth accepted a letter to the Gods'own." She turned it over.

Hy'Targ quaffed a mug of ale and signaled for another. As it arrived, he read the letter drawn in the same script as the previous note sent to him at Irontooth. The dwarf passed it to Varanthl and the others as he explained the gist of it. "The Gray Wanderer says there is a man with information in Dohan. Fifty-first building, north, Fish Hook Lane in Giyrnach." He looked from face to face. "Anybody know what's there?"

Varanthl passed the letter. Neither he nor Eucalia knew a thing about that part of the world.

"I checked our records already," Mantieth said. "There is nothing on file, but that's not surprising, so I spoke with some of our tradesmen. None know it, specifically. But they told me that Fish Hook Lane is certainly in the underbelly of Dohan; it's the wrong side of town for any respectable folk."

Hy'Targ stroked his beard. Jr'Orhr was the oldest of their number and often worked abroad on behalf of Irontooth.

The prince suspected the most accurate title for him would be *spy*, but Jr'Orhr usually dodged questions that might reveal sensitive information.

Of course, he was on the other side of the ale house with Hy'Drunyr and could not be asked questions. Involving his uncle did not seem like the wisest move until they'd established a greater trust.

Yarrik read the letter. "My family is abroad, and my father is supposed to be in Dohan. I know he wants to see me. Perhaps he could help?"

"Oh yes, your family," Mantieth said. From his bag he pulled a folded envelope stamped with a wax seal. "Your uncle gave me this. He assumed I'd see you before he had a chance to catch up. Those trogs, despite their massive army, have proved quite evasive."

"I can tell already who the most popular of the Gods'own is," Hy'Targ half-cocked his mouth into a smile. "You're getting considerably more fan mail than the rest of us."

Yarrik broke the seal and read the letter quickly. He folded it and put it into a pocket, saying nothing.

"What is it?" Varanthl asked.

"Nothing. A private matter," Yarrik insisted. "I think we should make for Dohan."

Mantieth nodded. "I'm inclined to agree. If Melkior and his cultists are searching for these artifacts, then we should use all speed to beat them to the prize."

Hy'Targ scowled. "But what *are* these artifacts? Whatever they are, they are not the relics we are searching for, the Kreethaln." He raked a few stray breadcrumbs out of his whiskers and admitted, "But whatever they are, if Melkior wants them, it's a sure bet we've got to make sure he doesn't get his claws on them."

"Do think that they are related to the Kreethaln in some way, though?" Elorall asked.

Hy'Targ nodded. "At the very least, they are made from the same material and by the same crafters."

"So we are agreed, then?" Yarrik asked.

Everyone looked to Hy'Targ for an answer.

"We will make haste. But I must first return to Irontooth. Something about all this gnomish talk... It feels familiar. I want to consult Ne'Vistar and the vaghan library back home. But I agree, let's make all due haste."

The party nodded their agreements.

"I will enlist Niamarlee's fastest ship," Mantieth said. "Shall we meet you in Lyandrica?"

Hy'Targ nodded. Lyandrica was the closest port city to Irontooth. A road connected it to Irontooth, creating a crossroads at the Great Coastal Road.

"We shall make all speed and meet you there within a tenday. Those who want to accompany us to Irontooth should be ready in the morning. But at least we can grab one night's rest in a decent bed." Hy'Targ rubbed his butt. He wasn't a big fan of boat travel, but at least a ship wouldn't give him saddle sores.

Hy'Targ entered through the main gates of the Irontooth fortress's outer perimeter. The stables of the kingdom's famed mammoths were off to the side; their pens hung mostly open.

The prince had raced on ahead of the others, who opted for a slower pace and the safety of numbers. Hy'Targ knew the mammoth he rode could be counted on to outrun and outdistance any threat, short of a drake or those nefarious burned skeletons they'd escaped from during Melkior's mad search for his lover's bones. Getting to Ne'Vistar's libraries with all due haste was his top priority.

He spotted his father staring at an empty pen. Brentésion could normally be found there. King Hy'Mandr looked over the empty area with milky, wizened eyes framed by deep crows' feet.

"My son!" he turned, beaming with pride. Hy'Mandr asked, "Have you returned victorious?"

Hy'Targ scratched an itch beneath his beard. "Not exactly. The prize was a false lead. Not a Kreethaln, after all. It was something... else. But we did claim it, so I suppose so. Yes."

His father nodded his head with thoughts turned inward. The prince joined at his side.

"You know," Hy'Mandr said, addressing the empty pen. "I had always planned to give the beast to you, if Brentésion would take you. She is yours... If you can find her."

Hy'Targ nodded measuredly. "There is news on that front, in addition to my recent journey."

"Then come—you must tell me over supper."

The prince followed his father. "Certainly. But I must leave again soon. I have a day's worth of research to do, and then I must be off again."

Hy'Mandr grinned. "Then it's a good thing dwarven manners don't forbid talking with your mouth full." The vagha laughed and then went to the king's dining hall.

After updating his father on the details of his recent adventure, he dismissed himself and climbed the tower where his old mentor's library was. Ne'Vistar was close to the royal family—and the old vagha had practically raised him.

Hy'Targ grimaced as he arrived at the top of the stairs. In the last year, he'd learned that his family was larger than he ever knew. He'd always known his other uncles and his grandfather had died of plague before he'd been born, but he'd recently connected with his uncle Hy'Drynyr and not long before been informed that Ne'Vistar had been married to one of his mother's sisters.

Now, he was raiding that dwarf's library. He shined a

lamp around the room, but it was empty. Supper with his father had gone later than intended, and Ne'Vistar was long asleep by now.

Hy'Targ shrugged and sought out the books he remembered. Many of the texts had sketches and drawings of gnomish devices. Some of them had footnotes copied in the foreign script of the gremmlobahnd, even, but he'd never been able to decipher any of them before now.

He cracked a tome and flipped through it. Something clicked in Hy'Targ's brain, and he knew he'd found the book he remembered. He flipped page after page in search of a foggy memory: A hand-drawn, three-dimensional image of an object. It had always stood out to him in his mind because of how the ink drawing seemed to leap off the page; he'd first seen it when he was only a lad, but the prince had an excellent memory for such things.

Hy'Targ came to the part of the book where he'd known it to be. The next sheaf of pages fell open to reveal a rugged stump running vertical across the binding. Someone had torn the pages out long ago.

He scowled and slammed the book shut. Defiling one of Ne'Vistar's books was a grave offense. Hy'Targ spent the next several hours combing through more books, intent on verifying that his memory had not been wrong. It wasn't. And in the early morning hours, with the light of dawn burgeoning on the horizon, he departed to catch a few hours of rest.

Hy'Targ knew he only had so much time to spend here before he had to rush off to catch a boat in Lyandrica. He'd just gotten ready for bed when there was a knock at his door.

Opening it, Hy'Targ found Hy'Drunyr standing there. He raised a confused eyebrow.

"I only just arrived. Your friend Varanthl and the green elf accompanied me—we rode through the night, though I think the four-armed man might have stayed up chatting with the dryad all night had we not kept traveling. Anyway... "

Hy'Drunyr handed him the papers.

Hy'Targ unrolled them and recognized them as the missing pages.

"It occurred to me," said his uncle, "that these could be invaluable to you?"

After shaking off the dismay that his uncle had vandalized a precious book, he flipped through them. "You had these all along?"

Hy'Drunyr nodded. "I'd forgotten them entirely until only recently. I realized then what I had and knew that I possessed the only copy from Ne'Vistar's collection." He flashed a sheepish look, "He would not let me copy them many decades ago when I was still actively learning about the gremmlobahnd, and so I paid a lad to swipe them. I've not always been the most honest dwarf in my pursuit of knowledge," he confessed.

The elder vagha peeled the sheaves apart and showed Hy'Targ an ink drawing of the four interlocking blocks. They were identical to the item the Gods'own had recovered beyond Xlinea. "It appears to be a gnomish relic," he insisted, "a device of god-like potential ability."

"Potential... but for good or evil?" Hy'Targ pondered.

"Don't gods usually wish good things for their creations?" Hy'Drunyr asked.

Hy'Targ screwed up his face and thought it over. Not all the gods were as benevolent as Firiel had been to the vagha, or as protective as Eldurim had been to Ghaeial, the gods' mother.

The dwarf flipped another few pages to an old poem written in what he now knew to be the gnomish tongue. It didn't seem to have any cadence or rhythmic structure that he was familiar with, but such was often the case when translating languages absent their cultural nuance. Art was always the first casualty of science.

"It's... some kind of riddle?" Hy'Targ asked.

"Aye. And you may be just the dwarf to solve it." Hy'Drunyr set his jaw and stroked his chin as he regarded his nephew. "I... just want to warn you of the dangers. I know you've faced enemies already, but... " He took a breath. "Items like this are rare and powerful. Searching for it could put you in the path of enemies far greater than you can ever imagine... Terrible creatures that would seek to use it for their own purposes."

"More than the legendary Kreethaln?"

The old dwarf nearly laughed. *"Far worse.* There are many magic items of varying power, but I never thought to see a relic, nephew." Something about his tone turned grave. "I won't say what I suspect it is. But if it fell to an enemy—to the agents of Death? All could be lost for Esfah."

Hy'Targ chewed his lip for a moment. *And Melkior's minions are after it.*

"I just wanted to warn you to be careful. That's all."

Hy'Drunyr turned on his heel and left. Hy'Targ watched him go, knowing that sleep would be difficult to find now.

CHAPTER EIGHT

On the third day following Hy'Targ's conversation with his uncle, he found himself in Lyandrica, paying a stable hand to board his mammoth. A pony-drawn wagon had brought his other companions from Irontooth, except for Eucalia on Acacia and the farriers who followed them at a distance, ready to retrieve the mounts from the travelers' final destination.

Hy'Targ looked around the human city, famous for its bi-annual fighting competition, and smelled the salty air. He could see the stadium at the center of town, where a pair of human warriors had won the original contest. The details of their battle had become folklore and even been responsible for naming the city.

His father had fought there long ago and won the freedom for the last family of slaves under Niamarlee's chains. His mother had been part of that, as a member of the Shree clan. Hy'Targ urged his mount past the structure.

The travelers followed the roads sloping downward to the ports on the north-east side of the peninsula. It did not take them long to find their friends loitering at the docks. Mantieth and Elorall leaned against the rails of a coral ship berthed nearby.

"You could not secure the usage of an airship?" Hy'Targ nudged them.

Mantieth shrugged. "Those things are very expensive, you know. But the *Greenkiss* is almost as fast on the open water."

Most of the *Greenkiss's* crew were selumari sailors. The dwarf looked around the deck. "Where is Yarrick? I thought he was with you."

Elorall leaned against her fiancé. "He is off looking for his father in town."

Mantieth stepped slightly away to put some space between them. He thoughtfully turned his matching bracelet. He glanced at its mate on his fiancé's wrist and spoke, "He said his father might be in either Lyandrica or Dohan and thought to seek him out. He should be back soon and we'll cast off as soon as he arrives."

By the time they'd finished stowing the luggage, Yarrick approached. The dour expression on his face informed his companions how successful the search had been, and minutes later they were on open water.

Within the hold of the ship, Hy'Targ produced the documents he'd received from his uncle. Next to them he laid his copy of the gremmlobahnd lexicon. The page that lay face-up displayed the sketch of the relic's likeness that they'd claimed near Xlinea.

"I know what this thing is," he explained.

All eyes turned to Hy'Targ.

"Well, I mean, I don't know *exactly* what it is. But I know that it seems to be part of a gnomish relic." He traced a few nodules on the sketch. "It interlocks with other pieces from the same artifact."

Hy'Targ told them about what he'd learned from his uncle. "I don't know what it does, but it must be powerful. We can be certain that if Melkior's followers are looking for it, Esfah would be best served if we kept it from them."

Everyone around him murmured in assent.

"Where is it now?" Jr'Orhr asked. "I still don't trust your uncle, and if this thing is as powerful as you say... "

"It is in the vaults of Irontooth," Hy'Targ said. "It should be safe there." He ruffled the loose leaves taken from Ne'Vistar's tower. "But *this* is something I find interesting. It's a riddle. Some kind of ancient poem." He read the piece aloud:

Leguin's child from apocryphal bondage torn by fire and arcana

Close the gates and sever bond
Fling wide the godbox of eldrymetallum make
And break the road of Sabian's Circle
Close the gates—close the gates!
Break the key and quarantine
Keep Selurehl's pet at bay, the Drekloch come with Dracolem
And feast upon the gremmlobahnd kin.
Hide the pieces across Leguin's sister land
Press elemental spirit into service bound
Protection by shadow clear, obfuscation, hide
Leguin's child, the Drekloch's come in spirit, Hie
From Nekarthis's chains and Esfah's own
Keep shut the gate against further fiends
Hide Netherwold key and godbox machine
Against gnomish silence and safety break the engine of security realm
To protectors in the Netherwold lair and cursed watery grave bled from world-wound's scar
To Esfah's End and steamdancer pits where elemental guardians guide
The heart of eldrymetallum true
If gates closed must be cracked and flung
And found the cell of the gremmlobahnd

"None of that rhymes," Varanthl noted.

Hy'Targ rolled his eyes. "Yeah. Not all of them do." He glanced from face to face, searching for understanding. "You don't understand what it is?"

Mantieth shrugged. "You said it was a riddle, but not like any I've ever heard."

"It's a road map," Hy'Targ said. "It's part of gnomish history that tells what happened to them. Why they've disappeared—albeit in a rather difficult way to understand. It tells us where to find the four pieces of this... *godbox* relic."

"How do you figure?" Mantieth asked.

"It's filled with historical clues." He knocked on his own skull. "Luckily, I spotted them because of my extensive reading. The reference to 'Esfah's End' tipped me off. The islands west of Xlinea used to be called that back nearer the dawn of the Second Age. And those sigils covering everything where we found the first part? They were fresh sigils of binding. The cultists had only just bound whatever powerful presence had been enslaved to protect the artifact. I think we intruded and stole it out from under their noses."

Elorall looked intrigued by his thoughts. "Then where do you think the other four are?"

The dwarf stroked his beard. "I wish I knew. The clues are easier to spot in retrospect. But perhaps if we put our minds together..."

"Well, it'll give us something to do on the trip," Mantieth said.

Elorall squeezed his knee. "I had a few ideas of my own," she and flashed a mischievous smirk.

"This is important," Mantieth insisted. "Whatever Melkior's cultists want with this thing, he must not be allowed to claim it."

Nodhan's black eyes rolled back into their normal locations in their sockets, and he grumbled something unintelligible as he tried to shake off the fog in his mind.

The lava elf remembered himself and thrust his hands into his pockets, squeezing the items there to better focus his mind. The voice had overtaken him. "How many days have I lost *this* time?" he grumbled.

He pulled out the contents from his pockets. However long it had been, he only had the magic seed he'd stolen from that gwereste back in Charnock, and a few smooth stones that had replaced the coins in his pockets.

"You think this'll make me desperate? That you'll drive me to do what you want out of desperate poverty?" He put the seed back in his pocket and threw the stones into the gutter.

Nodhan had been poor before. It didn't scare him. It was the crucible that had made him what he was today.

You think I can't possibly do the things I've claimed? the ethereal voice whispered in his mind.

"Not while I'm in charge… You stay outta my head!" Nodhan snarled.

A dirty human chopping fish stopped momentarily to look at the morehl. She shook her head, tossed a pile of fish guts into the chum bucket, and returned to her work.

Nodhan stumbled to his feet and ignored her. *So what if they think I'm just a drunk morehl?* He took a little pleasure in the fact that his thoughts still remained somehow separate from the voice in his mind.

You are in Giyrnach for a reason. Your destiny demands you return.

"Bah! Return? To where… To *whom?* I've lived all across the Talvatic and Maris Coasts."

You know where. You have to go west.

Nodhan only laughed. "You can't make me do anything."

I think I've already proven otherwise.

The elf curled his lips into a snarl. "I'm gonna get on the first boat to Port Orric that I can find." He winced against the pain as it dug into the temple above his left eye. The voice was vying for control again.

Nodhan concentrated as he headed towards the wharf.

How long can you concentrate and keep me at bay? Once you fall asleep, I will have my chance.

Nodhan bared his teeth. "That's what tingle-leaf is for. It

can keep me awake for days."

But how will you buy any?

The disembodied voice held a smug tone. Nodhan was about to argue when he looked up and froze. He was only a block from the edge of the docks when he spotted them: *the Gods' own.*

The lava elf whirled on his heel and hurried in the other direction, trying to act casual. "Dammit! This was your plan all along, wasn't it? You somehow knew they'd be here!"

But the disembodied voice didn't speak now.

Silence? I must be right.

Risking a glance over his shoulder, Nodhan spotted his prior companions, whom he'd betrayed in Undrakull. They hadn't noticed him yet.

Nodhan slipped into a narrow alleyway and waited for them to pass, but the party remained in the road. They'd stopped for one reason or another. *Or maybe they* had *recognized me,* his mind argued.

Time for another test, he thought. He drew out a needle planted just below his skin and embedded it within the callouses he'd built up. He laid it upon a scrap of ratty cloth he swiped from a gutter.

Concentrating, he mumbled the only spell he knew, a minor transmutation. The needle melted with a flash of heat and light and returned to its true form. A stack of gold coins took its place and collapsed into the makeshift knapsack.

Nodhan stuffed a fistful into his empty pocket and twisted the remainder into a bundle.

He had three such needles left on his person for exactly this sort of occasion. Ever since his youth, he'd always kept them there for emergencies.

What are you doing? How are you doing this?

Test successful. The voice has only limited access to my memories, if any at all.

"None of your business," he cursed aloud and spotted a

group of unsavory looking fellows deeper in the alley he'd ducked into.

Nodhan whistled to the crew of thugs. He recognized the dull sheen of their eyes and the gaunt looks on their faces. *Sana junkies. They're just the right sort of ruffians I need: Both dangerous and desperate for a fix of the drug they make out on the reefs.* "You guys keen on earning a few coins?" He rattled the money in his kerchief.

"What's stopping us from killing you and just taking your money?" said a bald human, who drew a rusty blade from its sheath. It had a slight bend to it, and the man and his accomplices scratched at the body lice that afflicted them.

"You could, but you won't," Nodhan insisted. "I have a job that will let you triple your take or better." He motioned to the addict and then pointed down the road. "Around this corner is a group of people who are after me—they've been chasing me for the better part of a year now." He opened up the cloth bundle and flashed the gold at him.

The junkie's eyes dazzled.

Don't do this, Nodhan. You're better than this.

Ignoring the voice, the elf promised, "I'll pay you this much again when you come back, but I want you to attack them. Rough them up. Give em the old Giyrnach welcome!"

The ruffians nodded with toothless grins reeking of halitosis.

"Plus, they've got at least as much on their persons or more." He whispered conspiratorially, "Two of them are princes," before handing over the coins.

A greedy light blazed within the muggers' eyes. They drew weapons and charged from around the corner. In the moments that followed, Nodhan seized the opportunity to disappear.

Hy'Targ squinted and stared around the Dohanese streets, looking for whatever markers the local folk used to identify streets. He yelped as Varanthl grabbed him and yanked him backwards. The tall humanoid used his other two arms to ready his warhammer.

A ruffian's blade smashed into the ill-kept cobblestone, turning harmlessly aside. Varanthl kicked him square in the chest and sent him reeling.

The small crowd of accomplices howled nonsensical cries as they poured from the mouth of a nearby alleyway. Mantieth drew his sword and looked at the faces of his enemy. "They are sana addicts," he said, noting their sunken expressions and hollow eyes.

Elorall blasted a trio with shards of ice and Eucalia raised her palms, shaping her hands like a puppeteer. Thorny vines reached up from the ground, swallowing up ankles and snaring brigands. One of them tried to sneak up and put a blade between the dryad's shoulders, but Acacia whirled and planted his hooves into the attacker.

The unicorn's victim flew across the street and crashed into a fish vendor, destroying the man's stand.

Yarrik deftly beat his opponents with his sword, weaving between enemies as if they were children play-fighting with sticks. Those attackers in the rear watched the display of eldarim skill and stopped in their tracks.

Hy'Targ whirled back to the action and pulled his axe to bear. Glorybringer sprang into flames as he tightened his grip upon the famous axe.

Any of the attackers who still remained conscious turned and fled, howling more nonsense as they ran.

With all eyes upon them, a moment of awkward silence passed before the streets resumed their normal hustle and bustle. The Gods'own returned their weapons to their resting places.

Mantieth turned over the initial attacker with his foot. "Lives totally ruined," he mumbled. "These poor fellows would do anything for their drug. It leaves them slaves, destitute and…"

"Destitute?" Yarrik asked, pointing to the coins splayed around the unconscious bodies.

Mantieth rummaged through the first one's pockets and produced a small coral pipe, the end of which was coated in smoked sana resin. He also pulled out more coins. "There's no way they could have this much gold," he mused.

"Unless they'd just been paid to attack us," Hy'Targ understood. He looked suspiciously about the street, wondering if the addicts' benefactor was among the crowd, watching them.

The crowd paid them little further interest, except for Yarrik, who they flashed looks of leering disapproval.

Hy'Targ gathered his party. "Let's go find our destination, and quickly." He rested a hand on Yarrik's shoulder. "Perhaps you should raise your hood?"

Yarrik spotted an amazon in sailor's garb heading toward the wharf. She furrowed her brow and looked ready to spit at him. "Yeah. I think you're right."

Hy'Targ stood on the nearest intersection, staring at a guide stone. Someone had chiseled the words *Fish Hook Lane* in several common languages upon it. Buildings in heavy use, but significant disrepair, leaned a few precarious degrees on both sides of the street.

Mantieth was already counting the buildings as he moved down the road. Fewer people strolled *Fish Hook Lane*. It was the sort of place one did not wish to be noticed.

"I got it," he said. "Fifty-first building."

The Gods'own assembled in front of *Grude's Pawn and Loan*, a large, but slightly tilted building, with wrought iron bars clasped over the windows and strong wood shutters, in case a mischievous thief knew how to transmute metallic elements.

"I've seen my share of places like this," Jr'Orhr grumbled. He glanced aside at his companions. "I guess I'll lead the way." The older dwarf headed through the doors.

Racks of goods created aisles that were mostly filled with overpriced junk. Tags promised some of the items were imbued with magic, like enchanted arrows and weapons, but telltale hints indicated they were likely forgeries. The group made for the front counter, where a very bored looking trog focused on the coin he flipped from one side of his knuckles to the other. He wasn't doing a very good job of it.

"Hey, bub," Jr'Orhr caught his attention.

The trog brushed back the stringy hair that hung lankily in front of his eyes. "Master dwarf," he spoke in an exceptionally well-versed accent that indicated he'd grown up far from a swamp—likely in a free city somewhere in the northwest.

"I'm looking for something. Maybe you can help me?" Jr'Orhr asked.

The goblin's smile spread broad and toothy. "Perhaps a new set of boots? I've got some armor about, too…"

"No. I'm not looking for something so plain," Jr'Orhr interrupted.

"I can make you a great deal on a vorpal blade, or perhaps a gold sightstone attuned to Eldurim! It will increase your magic by entire magnitudes."

Mantieth scoffed. A genuine vorpal blade hung at his waist, and nothing on the floor even came close to the craftsmanship of anything in his father's armory.

The trog raised an eyebrow, assessing Mantieth's body language. "I can see I am talking to the wrong person. You are some kind of nobility… a duke, perhaps?"

Waving his blue-skinned hand, the prince said nothing.

Hy'Targ smiled. "Something like that."

Recognition glowed in the goblin's eye. "You are here for Grude, then? You are buyers?"

"Aye," Jr'Orhr insisted, a little peeved that he'd been overlooked. He suspected his mannerisms were crude compared to his royal accomplices.

The goblin waved them back and led them into the storage that dwarfed the storefront's shopping area. Artifacts on shelves and tables in this room were the real deal, not the shills and garbage peddled in the front. Several ancient tomes laid nearby, along with art pieces from early in the First Age.

Hy'Targ raised an eyebrow. It reminded him of the treasure chamber in Undrakull that he'd raided with Nodhan.

A booming voice shook him from the memory as a mangled faeli emerged from a back office. He walked with a limping gait; one leg was slightly shorter than the other and he flapped his undersized wings excitedly at the prospect of high-end customers. The ugly creature grinned to reveal his oddly angled teeth protruding from a wicked under bite. "Hello—welcome, welcome!"

He greedily rubbed his hands together as he took stock of them. "I am Grude." Grude spoke to Mantieth, but also made eye contact with Hy'Targ. The huckster was skilled at picking out the aristocrats in any group. "You keep interesting company," Grude said. "And you must be brave indeed, to bring a pure-blood eldarim to Dohan. But Grude is not one to judge—especially when it comes to my buyers."

The Gods'own kept cool faces in light of the new knowledge, but confusion was clear upon Varanthl's face.

"I think your friend does not know about Dohan's history," Grude chortled, and then continued. "Three hundred years ago, when Dohan fell to the seafaring selumari of Hiriath, the Dohanese begged the eldarim for assistance—their dragonkin would have made the difference in the war. The eldarim declined to get involved, and the war was lost and occupied by southerners, until amazons from Moothlen decided to infiltrate. Calling on an old alliance, they used magic drawn from the mystic stones to open a magic path and travel unseen to outposts around the island. They then assassinated the crew, stole their ships, and gained a navy. It's why there are so many humans around here... and explains the hate towards your friend." He winked. "I don't just collect historical artifacts. I fancy myself a privateer scholar."

Grude clapped his hands "So - what kind of artifacts do you seek?" He held Mantieth's attention.

The coral elf certainly had the appearance of wealth, and the shimmering hilt of his vorpal blade gave away his status. "We are actually here to purchase information."

"Ha! Well then, methinks I should have charged you for the lesson on Dohan's history." Grude chortled and waved away the notion. "I do broker information, in addition to all of these lovelies." He waved around the room to bring attention to the priceless artifacts.

"We were directed to you from someone called the Gray Wanderer," Hy'Targ interjected.

Grude looked at him. "The Gray Wanderer? I cannot say I know him, aside from his inclusion in the ancient epic... Say, I have an early copy of *The Soldier's Journey*, if you are in the buying mood. There is great investment value in these ancient works."

"Just the information, please," Elorall said, stepping forward. She fixed him with a cool but firm gaze, recognizing that the faeli tried to steer the conversation. The selumari enchanter was having none of it.

Grude blinked twice and then nodded. "Very well. What are you looking for?"

Hy'Targ grinned, planning to pump the informant for whatever could help them along their quest to find the Kreethaln. But he also hoped to learn more about the gnomish pieces of godbox. "Tell me, have you heard of the *Gods'own?*"

CHAPTER NINE

The Gods'own stood on the docks near where the *Greenkiss* was berthed. They mulled over Grude's map and the story he'd sold them along with it. The map was an obvious copy, but Grude had assured them that none of the others with copies were capable of actually plundering the treasure, which, by some accounts, could have been a Kreethaln.

"The other rubes who bought maps actually thought the items in the front of the store were good investments," the faeli had told them. That was enough to assure the Gods'own that the map was still viable.

Yarrik pulled his hood a little tighter around his face and spoke, "The map and rumor that the scalder told us about points to a shrine in the hill country east of Moothlen. That's just across narrows, a day's travel north. If it's all the same, I'd prefer to stay in Giyrnach to search for my father."

Hy'Targ and Mantieth traded glances. They'd each had their own struggles with parents.

"The trip is maybe four or five days at most, including the return to Dohan. Right?" Mantieth asked.

Hy'Targ twisted the ends of his beard and then nodded. "Aye. At the most. We'll be back to fetch you after half a tenday."

"Thank you," Yarrick said. "I suspect my father should not be difficult to locate, especially given the general distaste for eldarim in Dohan… He is not a quiet man. I'll stay at the Flagon's Lair." He pointed in the general direction of the inn. "I'll wait there for your return."

They began to board their ship without the eldarim. Eucalia paused in front of the gangplank and turned to address him. "Be careful," she said. Acacia snorted behind her, and then they boarded the ship and shoved off.

Nodhan's vision lurched and shifted as his head cleared. "Damn it, damn it, *damn it!*" he yelled. He swung his legs over the edge of the hammock he'd found himself in and stood on the deck boards of his cabin.

He thrust his hands into his pockets and counted the coins there. He'd spent almost half of the remnant he'd saved after hiring the sana brigands in Giyrnach.

"Did you charter a ship?"

I booked passage. I told you, we need to go west. Your former companions might have taken you...

"I don't want to go west! I just want to go to Port Orric—my home." The last thing he remembered was fleeing the alleyway. *Seed must've gotten control of me right afterward and hopped on a ship straightaway.*

Not until we are done with our mission, Nodhan. It might be the single greatest thing you ever do.

"I don't care about greatness!" he yelled into the air, thankful there were no other cabin mates to see him raving. Nodhan plucked the seed from his pocket and stared at it, fuming. "I should just throw you into the sea and be done with you!"

You cannot do that.

"The festration I can't!" He made for the door and a trio of thin tendrils shot out from the seed, wrapping themselves around the morehl's hands and binding his wrists.

I have seen your heart, lava elf. It is not as black as you think and it beats strongly with Firiel's might.

"Firiel. Ha! I'm a professional thief, little seedling. Don't talk to me of gods and ethics." He tried to work the door so he could throw his cursed relic overboard and finally be done with it.

Fair enough. But if you do not help me save all of

nature, you will have little to spend your riches upon. Everything you value will be made worthless.

Nodhan paused and stepped back from the door. He growled, "Fine," acknowledging that the seed made sense. He didn't know why, but he believed the voice in his mind. He'd seen the destruction wrought by Death's agents. The elf had heard rumors of an undead rising in the Shadowlands, north of Cyrea. It was far away, but he'd seen a similar thing happening in his region with Melkior. "What do you suggest then, *Seed*?"

Only what I've insisted on, so far.

Nodhan crooked his jaw. "No."

No?

"You know me. You've seen my mind—most of it. You know I won't take being imprisoned by you very well. There's never been a prison capable of holding me very long against my will. What do you think I'd do if you made me your slave?"

The seed did not respond.

Good. I think he believes I'd actually off myself and drag the seed to the depths of the Far Seas with me.

"Here's what I'm willing to do: We complete this gurk-jiggered mission of yours, and then I go on my merry way. We never see each other again after that, savvy?"

That would certainly be the case when...

"I'm not done. I have one condition. You cannot, under any circumstance, take control of my body again and do with it as you please. If you have a suggestion, *fine,* run it by me... but *I'm* in control. I mean, for gods' sakes, you're just a *seed.* I mean, how old can you be, even?"

I am from the youngest crop of seeds... approximately two thousand years old.

Nodhan balked, quite unsure how to respond.

I will abide by your terms, even if I do not fully agree with them.

"That's all I ask." He put the seed back into his pocket

and the tendrils retracted, fully retreating back within their woody husk. "Now let's see what kind of passage you booked, Seed. For the amount of coin you spent on it, there had better be an amazing breakfast provided."

Melkior watched the leader of the Death cult approach. The surrounding blackness of the cave would have made the man invisible to almost any other, but Melkior saw him perfectly.

"This way, my lord," said the hooded minion.

The lich nodded. He patted Rahkawmn on the side of his massive face. "You must stay. The passage will not permit for your size."

Rahkawmn snorted a displeased puff of air. A sulfuric taste hung in the humidity of the sea-side cave for some time afterwards.

Melkior followed his minion, fully aware that his dracolich friend had worried over him these last few months. He put the thought out of his mind and walked further into the depths.

The leader of the cult led him to a dug-out alcove where a crew of thirty undead stood at the ready. The mixed company of skeletons and zombies were covered in dirt and clay; they carried digging tools rather than weapons.

"We have connected the old tunnels beneath Trellan with a buried Death shrine made by my people: our people. They made it before the coming of the first races," the hooded figure said as they delved into the tunnel. "They were the first acolytes."

"Our people?" Melkior asked.

The cult leader pulled back his hood to reveal his face. The eldarim bore scars over much of it, and he licked his lips with a split tongue. "The shrine is also connected to the sea cave. Come."

Melkior followed Forktongue into a cavern of eldarim craftsmanship. "Many of us have followed Malgrimm's way since before the gods created the other Esfahn races."

At the center of the chamber rose a dais. Upon it was placed a polished throne of bone and skull. An arcane rune glowed upon the chair's wingback.

The lich sneered, understanding the trap. It would trigger for any impostor, unworthy of leading Malgrimm's army, and immolate them immediately.

Melkior ascended the steps and seated himself without a second thought. Forktongue knelt. "You are the true child and heir of your father, Malgrimm."

Other cultists seemed to melt away from the shadows and take shape. They approached, kneeling.

"We now know that you are returned, and we Melkites are yours to command," said Forktongue.

Melkior glanced around the room and noticed the iconography. A branching symbol carved into the wall told him much. "You are members of the Black Tree?"

"Something like that," Forktongue said. "We are one of its many branches."

A rumble of mirth hummed in Melkior's chest. "I was there, in the early days. We fought against the tree until… after. Then came the necralluvium. I met her, you know, after my death, when she ruled in the Crooked Spine. Sshkkryyahr the drider, one of the Tree's three founders." He leveled an amused gaze. "She had an eldarim apprentice, Nekarthis. You remind me of him, Forktongue."

"A high compliment," Forktongue said.

Melkior cocked his head. "Is it?"

Forktongue nodded stoically. "After you were interred somewhere in Charnock, the drider fell to the power of the sages. Nekarthis began his empire. He nearly broke the world during the Magestorm."

Melkior stroked his chin and nodded measuredly. "Then you must carry on a legacy of the black eldarim."

Forktongue bowed. "As you wish. With your guidance, we shall cut off all other branches and establish our dominance. No more hiding in the shadows. What is it you truly desire, my lord?"

Melkior gripped the arms of his bone chair. "I will tell you when the time is right to emerge from the shadows, Forktongue. They serve a purpose yet. As to my desires, there is only one, and it is all-consuming."

He ripped wide the shroud that concealed the inked contract between Melkior and Death. *The deed to Ailushurai's soul.* "I want what belongs to me. My beloved. Such will fulfill the prophecy and restore my full power. *Then*, and only then, will I walk the breadth of this land and strike down every mortal upon it. I and my beloved shall live in the flames of Esfah and lord over the ashes."

"My lord... " Forktongue said.

Melkior caught a note of hesitation in his voice. "Speak freely. While the mind of Malgrimm is plain to me, it has been many hundred years since I was last familiar with Esfah. There is much I still find foreign."

"Perhaps it would be wise to hedge your bets. The Melkite arm of the Black Tree has grown ever since the return of Sshkkryyahr... "

"The drider is alive?" Melkior interrupted.

"She was. Briefly. She ruled in Undrakull for a decade until Hy'Targ, prince of the Irontooth Dwarves, put an axe through her skull."

Melkior roared. He squeezed the skull that capped one arm of his throne hard enough that it broke into pieces and rattled to the floor. "I am familiar with Hy'Targ."

Forktongue stared at the busted shards of bone and continued, "She had propped up the Melkites and never gave up on your return, but with no further word on Ailushurai's location, perhaps another strategy is best."

"Ailushurai is everything. Regaining her would guarantee victory."

"We have agents within the Nekarthan branch of the Black Tree; they are more suited to subterfuge than we Melkites. They assure us that they have spies close to the Gods'own. If they ever discover the location of the bones, we will take them."

Melkior fixed him in his gaze, "What do you suggest?"

"There are many artifacts hidden in this world. Many possess immense power... Perhaps none would be as effective as exercising your covenant with the Dark One. But perhaps one of these items could be enough to tip the scales in your favor and further Malgrimm's goals for Esfah? Maybe he will grant you a boon if you have some success against the mortals—or perhaps it will lead to some clue of Ailushurai's whereabouts."

"You have an artifact in mind, Forktongue?"

The cultist nodded. "There is an item coming up for auction in Kragryn, west of Bralanthyr."

"This item will expand our power?"

Forktongue grimaced. "Our dual agents tell us that the Nekarthans desire it. If we take it, we can force them to join us and expand our numbers, unifying the two branches. We do not yet know their exact designs upon the item."

Melkior entertained the idea. Finally, he bobbed his head. "Make it so."

Hy'Targ and Varanthl led the way through the twisting corridors of the crypt, under Grude's direction. Stacked block work smelled of earth. Damp soil and roots squeezed between the old, shale-like stones of the original cairn, long since mounded over with dirt so that the barrow appeared just like every other hill in the south-east edge of the Birthlands.

The Gods'own skulked through the halls in silence. They practically held their breath as they crept around every winding corner and through each narrow alley, moving ever downward. Creatures had to be present… somewhere. They'd seen plenty of signs that the crypt had been used frequently and recently.

Hy'Targ used the haft of Glorybringer to clear a swath of cobwebs. He jumped back at the sight of a massive hellhound. The entire party stiffened and then relaxed; the beast did not move. It laid as if asleep, but drew no breath.

Varanthl reached down and stroked its head. Fur fell off in clumps and drifted to the floor in moldering clumps. The four-armed humanoid made a disgusted expression and then wiped his hands on a rag.

Mantieth whispered, "Dead?"

Varanthl nodded, and the elf squeezed in to examine it. He rolled the beast over, searching for any wounds or markings to identify its killer. The creature was nearly the size of a pony, and so Varanthl helped.

Hy'Targ wiped away another curtain of webbing and revealed the body of a giant spider that spun the silken sheaves. It, too, lay dead with its legs curled towards its thorax.

"Old age?" Mantieth suggested with a whisper.

Hy'Targ turned his head and shook it. "Unlikely. Poison is more probable."

They resumed their exploration without further incident, finally arriving in a large chamber deep below the hill. Arcane light emanated from the torches that glowed with eternal flames, the product of spells cast long ago.

Elorall cleared her mind and prepared to blast any enemies with frosty wind at a moment's notice. She nodded to her fiancé. Mantieth, Hy'Targ, and Varanthl barged into the antechamber. She followed closely on their heels with Eucalia bringing up the rear.

Nothing stirred. After a tense moment spent surveying the room, the Gods'own sheathed their weapons.

"They're all dead," Eucalia noted. All around the room, black-robed cultists laid on the floor, draped over furniture, and leaned against the walls. Whatever had killed them had done so with great violence.

"Their blood is dried, but the stains still have enough tint to reveal that they were not murdered long ago. Maybe a tenday… " Hy'Targ said. He looked over the bodies. Blood stains of red and yellow helped identify the races before they pulled back hoods to look at faces.

Mantieth stood over one, frowning. The pattern of forest green splatters indicated the blood had once been closer to a sea-foam color before it had dried. He yanked back the hood to reveal the sunken, blue-skinned face of a selumari.

Elorall joined him. "Whatever the seductive power of this cult, its snares are deep enough to hook even the defenders of nature and the races devoted to the Mother."

Varanthl stomped towards a raised plinth at the center of the room. Eucalia followed him. "Whatever the artifact was, it seems to have been taken."

The others joined them around the stand. Elorall bent toward the platform and squinted. "There is much dust here," she said.

Her companions all followed her example and eyed the flat-topped plinth. They saw it, too. A clear and perfect circle where the dust had not yet settled, and then another circle of dust.

"Some kind of cylinder?" Mantieth asked. "Like a tube, perhaps?"

"We'll likely never know," Hy'Targ said. "But at least we can tell by its shape that it's not a piece of the godbox. Nor is it one of the Kreethaln."

"Some kind of large ring," Varanthl mused over the

mystery. But his companions had already begun exiting the room, heading back towards the ship and their return to Dohan.

CHAPTER TEN

After returning to the dirty city, Hy'Targ and the Gods'own barged into Grude's showroom. Two empyrean bodyguards immediately fell into defensive positions and flanked the selumari aristocrat they protected.

"Ho!" Grude yelled. "Everyone calm down... "

The coral elf snatched his purse from a tabletop. He took a step backwards, further into the care of his guards.

"This is no robbery," the faeli assured his anonymous selumari client. "I know them." He turned his attention to the Gods'own. "But my doorkeeper should have told you I was conducting private business at the moment," his voice carried a slight edge.

"Aye. He did tell us that," Jr'Orhr said and grinned. "We ignored him. Thought it'd serve us better if we demanded satisfaction while you entertained other customers."

Grude scrunched his face in ire. "Fine... fine. Wait in the storefront; I need five minutes to complete my business with Mister Blue."

Elorall looked down her nose at Grude. "No funny business," she insisted.

The scalder shook his head. "I can sense your determination. You will have satisfaction."

Throwing distrustful glances, the party filed into the storefront and waited a few moments for Grude to call them back. The Gods'own looked around for any sign of the coral elf or his firewalker guardians, but Mr. Blue had slipped away; undoubtedly through some secret escape hatch.

"There was no artifact," Mantieth said. "Someone had already plundered the chamber and killed all its occupants roughly a tenday before we arrived."

"Hmmm," Grude hummed, rubbing his elongated chin.

"I suspect another has beaten you to it. I *did* sell the information to a number of treasure seekers, though it surprises me that any of them had the skills necessary to claim the prize."

Mantieth glared at the fence. "We paid good money for that information. Will our refund be in gold or blood?"

Grude held his hands up and chuckled. "No refunds... but I will give you something better. I'll help you find this Gray Wanderer, or whatever it was he thought I could help you find."

Mantieth was about to issue some new threat when Hy'Targ stepped in. "That will do. We are searching for one of two artifacts. Do you know the legend of the Kreethaln?" he asked, while searching for a stylus and sheet of paper. He found one and began to draw a rough, geometric sketch while Grude prattled on about what he knew of the mythic trio of devices.

Hy'Targ looked up from his drawing. "We found one of them. Lifebringer."

Grude's jaw hung slightly agape.

"We want the other two." He turned over the sketch of the first piece of the godbox they'd acquired.

"What is this?" Grude asked.

"We don't know. But it's gnomish... Probably just art or something," Hy'Targ lied.

Grude squinted as if he knew that was a lie, but he nodded. "I will make some inquiries and send word right away."

Mantieth paced back and forth in the second story room of the inn. The Flagon's Lair was not the best inn he'd ever stayed in. He wouldn't normally have called it a "good" inn, except that it overlooked both the busiest crossroads in Giyrnach and also afforded a decent view of the port.

Elorall rolled over in the bed and laid on her stomach. The naked blue flesh of her backside was open to the air, and it puckered with gooseflesh. "Come back to bed," she insisted in a playful tone.

The prince scowled; his face had scrunched tight as he tried to make sense of what bothered him. His robe hung off his shoulders, mostly open to reveal he was nude as well. He merely sighed and continued pacing, stroking his chin—a mannerism he'd picked up from his bearded companions. "It doesn't add up."

"We've been waiting for Yarrik for three days now; he has another two to show up. A lot can happen in that much time," Elorall said. Her eyes sparkled as they locked on Mantieth, her longest friend. She'd wanted him to make a move for many years until he finally acted. That and more—like proposing marriage while they were in mortal peril at the hands of Melkior. "Time is a funny thing, you know. It seems to pass ever so slowly when you're in want, and when you finally get what you desire…"

She patted the empty side of the bed.

"Again?" Mantieth flashed her a wry look. "One of our own is missing and you're horny?"

She shrugged, unabashed. "You had no complaints an hour ago."

Mantieth did not deny it and only resumed pacing. "He should have been here by now. I understand a day, or even two, but the third day since we met with Grude is almost up."

"Maybe he found his father?"

The prince shook his head slowly. "No… Yarrik would have left a message with the innkeeper."

"Would he? How long has he adventured with us? Not long. He's still young and may be prone to rash decisions. Maybe it slipped his mind or perhaps there wasn't time."

Mantieth looked at her. "And maybe he's in a desperate spot and needs our help. Meanwhile, you're rehearsing for our honeymoon."

"Just passing the time and not assuming the worst." She rolled over onto her back and locked eyes on her lover. Her hands roved slowly down her body. "And if you don't get over here, I'll be rehearsing *without you.*"

She draped one arm over her chest and her other hand moved slowly towards her hips. Elorall bit her lower lip and Mantieth broke.

"Alright. Fine!" He crawled into bed with her and Elorall wrapped her limbs around him.

The door burst open behind them. Both elves hurled expletives at the intruder.

"Sorry! Oh gods, sorry," Varanthl covered his face with two hands and fumbled for the door with his other two. "Hy'Targ sent me to fetch you both."

Mantieth rolled off his lover. "Word from Yarrik?"

Elorall pulled the blanket over herself as Varanthl blindly searched for the doorknob. "It's okay, Varanthl. I'm covered."

He lowered his hands, his face as red as a lava elf. "Oh... Oh, no." He grimaced and turned his head. Mantieth's robe hung open.

"What?" he laughed. "It's not like you haven't got one of your own." Then he caught himself and remembered the homunculus's anatomy was significantly different; he'd been stitched together from parts of dead warriors. "I mean... You *do have* one of these, don't you?" He covered himself, suddenly self-conscious.

"Yes... um... but I never expected to see one quite so blue." He turned and tried to escape out the door. "Just... just get down to the lobby as soon as possible." He flushed red again, and clicked the door shut.

Mantieth and Elorall collapsed into bed, laughing.

"See?" she said after finally catching her breath. "This is why I love you. All our shared moments like this."

The prince grinned. "There have been a lot of those

moments over the years."

She stared at him for a moment, waiting for him to acknowledge her expression of love, and then narrowed her eyes at him. "Really?" The mood suddenly shifted, and the room dropped twenty degrees colder.

Mantieth pulled the covers closer and realized his gaffe. "I mean, I love you too. I just didn't think that… "

"Whatever," she said, pulling on her clothes.

"Hey… Elorall," he tried to calm her down, throwing on whatever clothes he could find as quickly as possible. "I'm—I'm sorry," he said as the door shut on him. "Come back!"

He stared at the door for a few long seconds. It did not open.

"Ah, crap."

Mantieth hustled down the steps of the Flagon's Lair and into the lobby where many guests huddled in groups. Some folk took a light supper. Others watched the bard who played in the corner to earn his keep. A fire burned hot within the large hearth at the room's east end.

The selumari tried to hide his frown and joined the group at Elorall's side. She tried to shy away from him at first, but he flashed apologetic eyes at her. Her firmly set jaw relaxed and her posture melted slightly against his body.

Grude sat in a barrel chair in the corner, speaking with Hy'Targ. "And you've heard nothing about our missing eldarim?" the dwarf asked.

The information broker shook his head. "Not a peep. But the shara are good at disguising themselves if they have cause to visit Dohan. The smart ones do, anyway."

Varanthl tilted his head. "Shara?"

"It's what the eldarim call themselves. The purebloods, that is. *Ha.* You'll probably never hear them use the word, though. They don't talk about it with outsiders," Grude said, giving another free history lesson. "It means 'god in the making.' Whole bloody race thinks of themselves as demigods. Makes me think the Dohanese were right to drive 'em all out."

The Gods'own stared at him, unblinking.

"I've no idea of your friend's whereabouts, or any other eldarim in Giyrnach for that matter" Grude gave them the short answer. "Perhaps he had other business to attend to?"

Hy'Targ scowled but nodded slowly. "It is possible. He did have a contact he was searching for in town. Though it's strange he did not leave word for us."

Grude handed over a scrap of parchment. "Well, for his sake and yours, let's hope that he is pursuing other business. I have a lead for you that is time sensitive."

Hy'Targ passed around the paper bearing a sketch similar to his drawing of the gnomish artifact. This was slightly different and had a nodule that looked capable of interconnecting with the piece they already owned.

All eyes remained on their fence. "That piece is up for auction in Kragryn."

Mantieth's eyebrows reached high. "That's on the far side of Charnock. It will take forever to get there."

Grude turned the piece of paper over to reveal a date. "Then I suggest you hurry." He held out his hand as if for payment.

"We already paid you for this info," Hy'Targ growled.

"Yes, but not for a token." He looked at them as if they should have already known the basics of the underground black market. "You will need a token just to enter the auction. It vouches for your character and for your ability to afford the auction. It will not be cheap."

Jr'Orhr crooked his jaw. "Just give us the token."

"It's no mere trinket," Grude insisted. "They are forged from pure gold and are very expensive to craft."

Hy'Targ sighed and laid a fistful of coins onto the table.

Grude made a motion, and the dwarf rolled his eyes, adding half as many. The greedy scalder scooped them into his pocket before producing the token from his pouch.

Hy'Targ turned the marker over in his hands. It was the size of a fist and shaped like a disc. A craftsman had stamped it with a symbol on either side; one side denoted fire, the other was water. The piece was truly a fine work of art.

Grude stood and began to depart. "I suggest you leave straight away and bring all the gold you can carry."

The party broke a few seconds later, and the Gods'own hurried to gather their belongings and make for the *Greenkiss*. They'd have to leave word with the innkeeper for Yarrik. They trusted that he had located his father and took up business of his own.

A few minutes later, they hurried out the main entry of the Flagon's Lair. The door latched shut behind them and a hooded humanoid in the lobby grinned. He tugged his hood a little lower yet to conceal his smooth skin and broad-bridged nose.

Pleased that he remained undiscovered, the eldarim removed the messages in his pocket, both addressed to Yarrik of the Gods'own. He scanned them one final time, memorizing the words of warning meant for the younger eldarim.

"You should have listened to your uncle," he mumbled to nobody in particular.

The rogue shara leaned his chair back on its hind legs and stretched towards the fireplace. Reaching out, he tossed the letters into the flames. His sleeves pulled up slightly to reveal pale skin inked with the black tattoos of an acolyte of the black order: An eldarim who had chosen the Death god and forsook all others.

"Run away, little Gods'own. Your time will come soon enough."

CHAPTER ELEVEN

Mantieth leaned against the rail of the *Greenkiss* and stared out across the waves. The late-night passage of Rhaudian glimmered white against the blackness of the waves.

"I don't know what to do," he confessed to the short, hairy figure approaching him from behind. The elf knew that Elorall was already in bed, fast asleep, and recognized the sound of heavy footsteps.

Mantieth gripped the near-empty bottle of wine and took another swig. "I know everything seems fine between me and Elorall, but I'm not... Really, I'm... "

The prince finally realized the dwarf was Jr'Orhr and not Hy'Targ. He blinked twice and closed his mouth.

"Don't worry, kid," Jr'Orhr said, uncorking his own bottle. "Yer secret's safe with me." He chugged half the bottle in one long slug. Even at a distance, the smell of the potent drink made Mantieth wince.

Jr'Orhr stared out across the sea. "I know a thing or two about women."

Mantieth watched his comrade for a long moment, realizing he'd perhaps never paid much attention to the Gods'own's eldest member. Jr'Orhr obviously had history; a long scar arced from his temple to somewhere on his lower jaw, where his beard hid the cut's end. He was lucky to still have both eyes.

The blue-skinned passenger chugged the remainder of his wine and tossed the bottle into a nearby barrel. He sighed and stared at the deck boards. "Do you ever feel alone while in someone else's company?"

Jr'Orhr regarded him and sniffed. He took another swig from his bottle and then handed it to Mantieth. The elf took a long pull, made a sour face, and then turned it back.

Staring across the water, Jr'Orhr finally replied, "No." He paused a long while. "It was never like that with Sh—with *her.*"

Mantieth raised his eyebrows, suddenly intrigued. "With *whom?* Did I catch you right? She was a *Shree?* Was she related to the Queen?" He stared at the silent dwarf and got no response. *"Gods, no… did you sleep with Hy'Targ's mother?"*

Jr'Orhr gave him a sidelong look, but then shook his head. "I would'na told you even if I had." He shook his head. "I would'na *still be alive* if I had."

Mantieth felt pretty certain that it could not have been Sh'Ttil.

"We could never have been together, not all the time, anyway. That meant I cherished every moment with her." He pointed to the scar. "I'd take a second one of these if it meant I could see her again." He took another drink and stared at the moon's reflection.

Mantieth pulled the bottle away and took a drink. "What happened to her?"

"She died." Jr'Orhr did not look at the elf, and Mantieth did not press him.

Finally, the dwarf turned to Mantieth. "So. You and Elorall? The young lovers aren't so madly in love after all. The walls of these inns are paper thin, you know… All signs seem to indicate you two are wildly passionate for each other."

Mantieth's blue skin darkened with a selumari blush. "I'm not one to turn down the girl's desire." He drank again, and then the words began to flow freely. Mantieth did not think he could stop them even if he wanted to.

"I'm not sure how it happened. She was my closest friend for so many decades… I never thought of her that way—I mean, not that I overlooked her beauty, but she was never really my type. Do you remember me proposing?"

The dwarf blinked slowly and with drunk eyelids, trying

to follow along with Mantieth's stream-of-consciousness complaints.

"And it's been one thing after another. If it's not attacking goblin hordes, it's lich problems. It's never a good time to bring up my reservations with her—she's just... always so happy. How can I say no to her?"

"Paper-thin walls, mate," Jr'Orhr reminded him. "Way I hear it, it don't seem like you've said no very often."

Mantieth grimaced. Jr'Orhr was right, of course. The elf sighed. "And now, with all the traveling, I dare not bring it up. The mission is important, but we've spent *so much time together*. I don't think I could bear it if we were fighting the whole time."

Jr'Orhr swished the liquid around in the bottle. Its contents had nearly been emptied. "Word of advice, kid." He put the stopper in the bottle. "Keep it all corked up. Your problems can only hurt the rest of us. And coping with it is easy." He bit the cork and spat it over the *Greenkiss's* edge. "That's what booze is for. Just ditch that sissy selumari stuff and get a real drink." He took out another drink, nearly cross-eyed by now.

Mantieth took the bottle from him. "I would hate to lose my best friend. But I also don't want to lose myself." The blue-skinned elf turned slightly green as he put the bottle to his lips.

He finished the bottle with a cringe and then handed it back to the dwarf. "A couple a' sorry, drunk asses up far beyond reasonable hours. What are we to do?" Mantieth asked.

Jr'Orhr leaned over the rail, bleary eyed, and looked at the elf wistfully. "We could just jump. It'd all be over in a few minutes."

Mantieth shook his head and pointed to the skin behind his ear. "I have all the best coral elf genes," he said. "Gills. I'd just watch you sink to the bottom."

The dwarf chuckled. "Bed then. We'll just hafta settle fer knowing that every hero suffers. Remember the final years of Davian Whisperwynd? Poor sod was a wreck, an' he was one of the greatest elf heroes. I must be feeling mighty heroic tonight." He tried to shake the last few drops onto his lips, but there weren't any. "Mighty heroic indeed."

He tossed the bottle aside, and the two drunk adventurers returned to their cabins.

Nodhan realized he was clutching the seed. He opened his eyes and emerged from a hazy-like sleep. "Not this again," he muttered angrily. "You did it, after I told you not to !"

I did nothing.

The elf rubbed his temples; his head was pounding. The fog had only dissipated a little. It proved to be actual fog hanging above ground level: A peaty, cloy odor permeated the dank air of the fen.

Nodhan remembered. Since arriving in Charnock, he'd traveled with a few other morehl he'd met along the road. They were taking the Great Coastal Road to Undrakull, and he thought it safest to travel past Irontooth and Niamarlee in their company.

Your companions abandoned you.

Nodhan staggered to his feet and looked around, uncertain even of the direction of the road. He assumed his companions had moved off the road to sleep out of sight.

He checked his pockets, but already knew his more precious items had been stolen. He almost laughed. "I should have known better."

Known better than to travel with your own kind, or known that they planned to get you drunk and rob you?

He shrugged. "Probably both." He sighed. "Seed, do you know which way is the road? I want to get back to Undrakull. I have contacts there who can help me."

But our mission…

"Our mission will never succeed if I'm dead."

Very well. It is some distance. Travel forward.

Nodhan hung his head and walked into the morning mists. Almost an hour had passed before Nodhan realized Seed had lied to him. "I'm going to starve out here and die," he lamented.

You will not starve, Seed said.

"Hah. But dying is still on the table, eh?"

A group of bushes nearby a fetid pool seemed to shudder as they produced berries and nuts before the morehl's eyes. A stump near it blossomed with mushrooms bigger than he'd ever seen. The lava elf tore off a section of cloth from his tunic to replace the pouches that had been taken by his traveling companions. He harvested as much as he could fit and then tied it to his belt before filling his stomach.

As soon as he finished, his ears twitched. Some kind of rumbling vibrated the surrounding air.

Nodhan spotted a sheaf of hanging moss draped over a fallen and rotting oak. He scrambled beneath it and pulled the shroud tighter to camouflage himself.

A goblin scout ran into view and passed him by, followed by another. Their feet slapped against the mud patches like grim portents, promising more would soon follow. They paused by the swamp as more trogs came, thousands of them. Trolls stomped past with other such monsters.

Hungry swamp dwellers devoured what was left of the bushes and fungus before abandoning them to scoop handfuls of scum from the pool. Nodhan watched with disgust as the trogs consumed whatever they could find to provide nutrition.

More of the army came, including a large-wheeled sled the size of a carriage house. It came to a rest directly in front of Nodhan's hiding spot, and he silently cursed.

A scrawny goblin with an over-sized signal horn put it to his lips and gave an extended blow. The trogs made camp there with the elf stuck in the middle of it.

Nodhan sighed with ironic bemusement. It appeared the trogs planned to stay for a while.

Grinding his teeth, the lava elf squeezed the seed, hoping it could feel some kind of pain from it, but Nodhan had no indication such a thing was possible. Nodhan hunkered lower yet and tried to flatten himself into the dirt when someone dumped an armload of dried wood into a heap on the other side of the wheeled sled.

More and more were piled atop the mound, one of the trogs working the tinder and kindling until flames took hold. A terrible shriek arose as two more trogs yanked the ropes and practically dragged a captured horse near the fire. With a sickening *thwack,* they tried to behead the steed. The thing cried out in terrified pain; the first blow failed to kill the beast. *Thwack! Thwack!* It finally fell silent and collapsed to the ground. Heavy footfalls approached.

Gruntch. Gruntch. Gruntch. Beyond the wheels, Nodhan could barely see what it was. The creature's stumps looked like mossy elephant feet. They certainly did not belong to a trog.

"Get that meat on the fire," a low voice boomed.

"Yes, Ratargul," one of the trogs barked, using an extremely sharp obsidian blade to divide joints and quarter the horse until its flesh steamed in the swamp air.

Nodhan's breath caught. Ratargul the Smotherer was the shambling mound that had chased the Gods'own through the Black Glades after their flight from Undrakull. The morehl knew the trogs had been amassing a force to harass travelers, but this was no mere gang. The Smotherer had cultivated an army.

He watched with rapt interest, momentarily wondering how someone could even kill a shambling mound. As far as he knew, they were living masses of animated bog. Did they have a weakness? Could one plunge a dagger into its heart and expect it to die?

Nodhan turned his eyes up and arched his back slightly to see over the top of the sled and examine the monster. He couldn't see more of Ratargul; some kind of drakufreet had been strapped to the wagon with tight chains that kept its body and wings bound. It was nearly the size of a dragon, and its scales looked like copper plates. A muzzle covered its mouth; only its eyes were capable of moving, and they locked on Nodhan.

The elf's breath caught in his throat.

Do you understand our mission yet?

Nodhan said nothing. He already knew Seed could not read his mind.

"Make way!" someone cried out nearby. "Make way for Heshgillick the Dread!"

Someone dropped a bunch of tree stumps beyond the sled, and the largest trog feet Nodhan had ever seen carried Heshgillick to his seat. A pair of tiny goblin legs, Heshgillick's majordomo, accompanied him along with half a dozen sets of avian feet that surely belonged to human-sized ravens.

Harpies, Nodhan thought to himself.

"When do we eat?" one of them asked in a sultry voice. "Horse flesh doesn't need to be cooked," she insisted.

"All in good time, my sweet," Heshgillick growled. "Soon, we will eat like this for every meal. Already a dozen villages have fallen across the Moorlech. Once we regather the rest of the bands raiding across the Raithlan Plains, we make our presence known in earnest. Soon we will wage war upon the coast. Even Niamarlee and the dwarves of the mountain will fall."

The goblin scullions dragged the central carcass of the horse into the cluster of harpies. They squealed like greedy crows and tore at the fresh meat.

"Ratargul," Heshgillick commanded. "Are our forces ready and prepared for the next step in the invasion?"

"I still don't see the point of your stratagem. We should

strike in large numbers and take the castle by sheer force," the shambling mound argued. His voice dripped with derision.

"You don't understand the genius of his plan," the small voice of the majordomo piped up.

"Shut your mouth, Tsut. Let Heshgillick defend his own plan. He is in charge, not you."

Heshgillick rose to his feet. "Know your place, Ratargul. Unless you are challenging me for control of the army?"

A tense silence hung in the air. Nodhan held his breath. He'd seen Ratargul in action before. He could scarcely believe a mere trog could back the monster down, but Ratargul wilted.

"No. I mean, *yes,*" Ratargul said. "The army has been properly blooded. They are prepared for a large-scale invasion. First Niamarlee, and then the rest of Charnock."

The last time Nodhan had seen the goblins, they were young and bumbling fools. But they were now organized. Here was the force behind that—and with such overwhelming numbers. If a strategic mind directed them, then they could wreak havoc across the entire continent.

I've got to stop them, he thought. Nodhan caught himself. *No, I don't... Why would I even think that?* The elf clutched hands into fists and set his jaw. *Seed. He's been messing with my mind—his emotions must be somehow rubbing off on me.*

Nodhan thought of a few instances where he'd acted quite differently than his nature had been previously. *What I need is to get out of here as soon as possible and return to Port Orric.*

Heshgillick's voice boomed, "And now I will attempt to train the dragonkin again. I want to ride it into battle and knock King Leidergelth's head clean from his body."

Good luck with that, thought Nodhan. *I won't be around to see it.* He looked up and locked eyes again with the entrapped dragonkin. Something in its look pleaded with Nodhan. Deep down, the elf knew he wasn't leaving any time soon.

The *Greenkiss* arrived in Niamarlee ahead of an oncoming squall. With rain on their heels, the travelers left the sailors to batten the hatches against the storm and hurried towards the castle.

Shortly after the Gods'own got within the tiled roofs of Leidergelth's castle, rain fell in sheets. Rivulets rolled across the coral architecture and washed the dried salt off the construction.

The adventurers gladly accepted the respite from the rocking ship and took the opportunity of a hot meal and a warm bed. Beads of condensation clung to every surface as the humidity increased. It made Hy'Targ's beard itch. Even the silken armor he wore, spun by a captive and evil drider, chaffed beneath his breastplate.

Hy'Targ thought that even the fine sheets and blankets of Niamarlee felt uncomfortable and wet, thanks to the storm. Instead of sleeping, he stretched his legs in the long corridors of the castle. The dwarf only passed an occasional selumari sentry until he spotted Mantieth leaning against a railing. Overlooking the outpost, a view of the bay spread out beyond them.

He meandered over and leaned against the same rail, shoulder to shoulder with the elf. The rain did not reach them, only the spray moistened their cheeks as drops splashed off the roofs.

"Can't sleep, Mantieth?" Hy'Targ had sensed some earlier tension between his selumari companions. "Women trouble?"

"Something like that," Mantieth admitted. He turned. "Tell me about your mother."

The request took Hy'Targ aback. "I don't remember much of her, to be honest... just that she was beautiful. I remember her face, I think."

"You think?"

"Memories are weird. They aren't always as true as we believe them to be," Hy'Targ explained. "I remember what she looks like and the feeling of holding her hand as we walked through the halls of the Irontooth kingdom. I was only a whelp—less than ten years old, maybe only half that. But I remember her differently; in my mind she looked one way, but after so many years, my mind filled in blanks with paintings of her image. I remember being young and thinking, 'but that's not how I remember her.' I was pretty young when I had that thought, young twenties perhaps... still an adolescent by dwarven reckoning."

Mantieth stroked his jaw. "Interesting," he said.

"Is it the same for you?"

Mantieth shook his head. "No. Well, yes. My problem is far different, but I do wonder how many of my memories are real and how much of everything is just my own perception of things."

Hy'Targ shrugged. "I know the paintings filled in the gaps, but I can hardly remember that face from my earliest reckonings."

The elf nodded. "I remember my mother, Queen Naemyar, pretty well. I was also around twenty when things changed. She and my father were close. About the time Elorall's mother died, something changed between them. I know that Elorall's mother, Raeyalla, always thought she would marry my father, but I don't know if that had anything to do with my mother's change. I only know that they fought a lot around the time Raeyalla died and shortly after the funeral, she simply left." He sighed. "I always blamed my father, though he's never said an unkind word about her. In retrospect, I think he may be as confused by her departure as I am."

Hy'Targ cocked his head. "And what has changed?"

"I don't know if I can trust my memories," Mantieth admitted. "What ever happened to your mother. She died?"

The vagha sighed. "She must be dead after all these years. Nobody really knows. Her traveling party simply disappeared without a trace. Finding her became my father's mad obsession for decades."

After a long silence, Mantieth pulled a letter from his pocket and unfolded it. "This arrived from Cyrea. It's from my mother. She hasn't contacted me in years, but she heard about the wedding. She wrote, 'Hopefully I can arrange to be in Niamarlee for the ceremony,'" He folded the letter and stuffed it back into his pocket. "She says I must only name the date." Mantieth shook his head.

Side by side, they stared out into the stormy night. Hy'Targ said, "Having lost my mother, I would be thrilled to suddenly discover her alive and well. It might be different for you... but my mother *is* gone. Maybe it's not too late for you."

Mantieth grimaced, nodding in silence. Together,, they watched the storm.

CHAPTER TWELVE

After dispatching letters to the gate guards of Niamarlee and Irontooth, the Gods'own headed east with full provisions. They'd hoped Yarrik might still arrive at one or the other location and provided instructions on how to find them in Kragryn.

Coral sky ships were too valuable to rent out, even for a prince. Especially with some unknown threat harassing the skies. Until King Leidergelth knew what was behind the disappearances of his eagle scouts, he wouldn't have loaned out a sky ship even if they were cheap. Besides, Mantieth had already raided the royal treasury to secure funds for the auction. All those factors limited the Gods'own to their saddles.

None of the travelers could guess what the item they sought might sell for, but if even one other party knew the origin of the godbox, or who was after it, then the price would increase tenfold or more. The adventurers had to suspect that all other buyers knew more about the artifact than they did.

Hopefully, the gold would win them the next piece of the relic. If it could not, the Gods'own were prepared for a fight. Hopefully they would not be too exhausted from their trip, if it came to that.

Kragyrn, their destination, was near the west coast of Charnock, which made boat travel an option. But the distance around the continent's perimeter forced them to travel through Great Wash, a series of winding bodies of water containing Ender's Gulf, Hadden Bay, and Delmarra Bay. After the Wash looped around the horn and met the Tarvenish Ocean, they would have to travel another seven hundred leagues. Just the trip along the Tarvenish coast would take up to thirty days, and that was only forty percent of the distance.

Trudging through the northern edge of the Moorlech,

dangerous as that was, cutting through the hill country where Varanthl's people lived, and then down through the Raithlan plains would take only a little longer than a couple tendays. The countryside would prove more difficult to travel than the Great Coastal Road, but cutting across the continent was the fastest route to Kragryn.

The Gods'own had already traveled three hard days from Niamarlee. Eucalia, perched atop her unicorn, paused at the front of their group. A valley sloped down before them.

"What is it?" Elorall asked her.

Eucalia stroked Acacia's neck while staring into the valley. "Something is wrong in the village," she said. "I can't put my finger on it."

The rest of the party joined her and observed for a moment.

"There's no smoke," Mantieth recognized, squinting against the high sun. "We've been riding hard since morning, and it's nearly midday. No cooking fires, no movement in the streets, but also there's no damage."

Jr'Orhr nodded atop his mammoth. "Ought to be one or the other. Why else would a village be deserted unless something chased 'em out?"

Hy'Targ glanced at Varanthl. The homunculus tightened his grip on the haft of his battle hammer.

"Well, let's go find out, then," Hy'Targ said.

"Do we have time for any delays?" Mantieth asked.

The vagha scratched at his beard. "No... but the trail does lead directly through. We've more time to investigate down there than to wait on a hillside debating a course of action."

Looking around to each other, the Gods'own traded nods and began the descent into the valley. It did not take them long to arrive at the center of the village. It was only large enough to host a few hundred folk.

A hand-painted sign at the edge of the community

identified it as a free town. A collection of mixed races were welcome, so long as the laws were followed.

At the village square, with no faces to greet them, it was impossible to tell the makeup of the community. They took that moment to water their mounts. After a few minutes spent in silence, Jr'Orhr spotted movement.

"There." He pointed. "I saw someone peeking out from behind a curtain."

Mantieth turned on his heels and made for the door. He didn't like the idea that they could be walking into an ambush. Some of the more intelligent trogs had been known to set such traps.

Before he could turn the handle, the door opened. A frightened selumari held up his hands in surrender. He was very old, and a number of other residents huddled inside the house behind him.

"My lord?" the elf said, finally recognizing the prince.

As the village elder emerged into the square, so did others, mostly human and selumari, but a few gwereste as well. The remaining houses within eyesight took it as a signal that they, too, should come out.

"What happened here?" Mantieth asked.

"We had a report that the trogs were on the move—but you've come to save us!" The elder looked optimistically at the Gods'own. "Is the rest of the army nearby?"

"The army?" Elorall asked, drawing closer.

"Yes," said the elder. "The force of soldiers dispatched by Niamarlee and Irontooth. They have been trying to clean up the outliers ever since the alliance was formalized."

"He means the crew Taryl is a part of," Hy'Targ said, turning to the leader. "He is a friend eldarim."

"Ah, yes," the older elf confirmed. "They say that one of the leaders is a dragonlord, or a dragonslayer, or some such title. We'd just heard last night that a massive snarl of goblins had emerged nearby and were headed this way."

"Your information must have been wrong," Jr'Orhr stated flatly.

The elder set his jaw and shook his head ruefully. "More likely, they turned aside to one of the other villages. We are small here in the outliers, but there are many other such towns dotting the countryside, typically a half day's travel from each other, more or less. We may not possess the strength of numbers or trade available in larger cities, but our proximity helps mitigate some of our lack."

As soon as he'd finished speaking, a young human burst into view down the road, running at a full sprint. The boy slid to a stop before the elder and doubled over to his knees, panting for breath. He was perhaps in his middle teens, dirty and weathered, with small cuts and raised welts where bracken had whipped him across the face during his run.

"What news, boy?" the village elder asked.

Between gasps of air, the lad reported, "They are moving towards Graeyhaiven. We are spared... today, at least."

Hy'Targ looked around at the somber crowd. The news did not brighten their mood.

"Graeyhaiven is the next village down the westerly road," the elder commented for the benefit of the Gods'own.

"Ah," said Hy'targ. He understood. These people were spared, but at the expense of an attack on close friends and extended family members. The dwarf took fistfuls of course fur and clambered up the side of his mammoth. "We're likely to run into trouble then. If we can help, we will."

"Thank you," said the elder, watching them move out. "Gods' speed to you—to all of you!"

Nodhan trailed after the trogs on foot. He'd followed them for several days now. The goblins sent forward scouts out in advance of their positions, but never maintained a rearguard of any significance. Occasionally, other bands of trogs or contingents of scouts sent out by Heshgillick or Tsut joined them from abroad. The elf reasoned that Tsut was some kind of secretary. Ratargul always remained at the front of the army. The Smotherer was mere muscle for the real leader.

"I don't know why I'm still doing this, Seed," Nodhan spoke in hushed tones as he crept around the back side of the encampment.

Because it's the right thing to do. You will see things my way, eventually.

"Right. Ha." He spotted the copper-colored dragonkin in the distance.

A dozen burly trogs held thick ropes attached to the odd drakufreet. Holes had been made through tender bits of wings to tie the lanyards to her.

Heshgillick stood nearby as his minions suppressed the beast. Tsut watched from a distance as the trog chief climbed on. He tried to ride the creature—to break it.

Eventually the thing tried to rear back and throw him, but the trogs managed to drag it back towards the dirt. Refusing to obey a new master, the draconic mount dropped to the ground and refused any movement at all.

"I *will* ride you into battle, some day," Heshgillick roared at the creature, striking it repeatedly with a thick prod. The creature did not move, and Heshgillick beat it with a stick until the lumber snapped.

Nodhan felt a twinge of indignation for the restrained beast. *I wonder if Seed is able to manipulate my emotions. Since when has this sort of thing ever bothered me before?*

This was the second attempt to break the beast that Nodhan had seen since Seed forced him into the Moorlech swamps. Still, the lava elf felt more and more uncertain that even Seed knew what this "mission" was about.

Like before, after Heshgillick finished administering a beating, the trogs loaded the dragonkin onto the wagon and bound it.

I think we should rescue that creature.

"Are you crazy?" But Nodhan felt an impulse to do exactly that, unsure if that motivation was genuine or manipulation. He bit his lip and watched them move back towards the main trog camp.

But these goblins must be stopped. Remember the mission...

"Tell me the mission. Right now. Spell it out for me. I don't believe in all the mumbo jumbo you're trying to push on me."

Seed did not respond for a long while.

"You know, I have ways of being rid of you. Even if it costs me a hand, it's better than losing my life. Which is, apparently, what you're trying to get me to do. Besides—I've got that book I stole from the drider. With the right buyer, that could purchase an entire *kingdom*. I wouldn't need to ever work again."

I could just take control of you and rescue that beast.

"I've got ways around that, too. Now tell me the mission; I won't let you manipulate me. I'm done with being your restrained dragonkin."

Seed somehow sounded recalcitrant as it spoke, though only in the elf's mind. *Fine. The creature may be important, or not. There is an evil I must stop. A growing root that festers beneath the soil.*

"And how will you do that?"

Exist. Manifest my destiny.

Nodhan rubbed his face. "I don't know what that even means."

I must fulfill my purpose.

"But what *is* your purpose?"

Seed was silent. Nodhan suspected that it didn't really

know, and that concerned him. He might never be free of the thing if had no end game in mind.

Nodhan looked up and watched the wagon disappear among the throng of goblin soldiers. Only the creature's height crested above the lumbering trolls that wandered around it.

The pang echoed in his heart again as he empathized with the dragonkin.

"Fine," Nodhan hissed. "I will rescue the beast. But you'd better start listening to my advice about things from here on out."

He spotted a trog pelter, the close equivalent of a goblin marksman, wandering in the fen. He searched for the right sized stones to use with his sling during the next battle. Creeping up on the wayward goblin, the morehl slit his throat from behind and dragged the body into the marshes.

Mixing the trog's yellowish blood with mud, he wiped the concoction over his skin to try shifting the hue as much as possible.

Nodhan stole whatever troggish gear he could find to help disguise himself and then entered the crowd of enemies. With a thumb, he tested the keen edge of his blade and hoped it would make short work of the drakufreet's bonds. *Hopefully I can just cut one, and the thing will free itself, casting the army into disarray so I can escape amid the chaos.*

He slipped his red-skinned hands beneath the sleeves of his garments and kept his head down. The sled was close, and Nodhan grumbled slightly when he saw the ropes had been shored up with additional chains. He wondered how quickly he could pick the locks.

Casting a glance to the side, he spotted Heshgillick and his harem of harpies. They stared into the sky and Nodhan spotted what they searched for. A trio of shadows moved quickly across the ground, and the harpies sprang into the sky so they could tear the coral elf scouts to pieces.

Heshgillick was on his feet in an instant. "Eagle riders!" he shouted. "Selumari scouts know our position—you know the drill! We move out immediately."

Seconds later, Nodhan found himself on the move and jogging shoulder to shoulder with the trog army, trying his best to blend in and keep up. He had no idea where they headed, but he was about to find out.

Graeyhaiven was in flames. The Gods'own could smell the burning village before they could see it. Acrid odors of burning pitch and wood that usually dried before being placed on a pyre. It almost overpowered the stench of the trogs. Almost.

As soon as the goblins were in full view of the Gods'own, the heroes threw caution to the wind and charged. The trogs backs were turned as they faced an enemy in the opposite direction.

Acacia was the first in. The unicorn gored a massive troll, driving his keen horn into the base of the monster's spine. He ripped his horn back as he reared up and tore it free, busting two ragged ends of bone that hung just above the pelvis.

The troll shrieked and collapsed, and the trogs surrounding him whirled to face the new enemies. Hy'Targ trampled a score of them beneath his mammoth as he slid to the ground. Glorybringer burst to life in a halo of flames and he severed the troll's head, cauterizing the wounds so that it could not rise again.

Eucalia used her nature-magic and called upon the vines of the ground to entangle feet of Graeyhaiven's invaders. Mantieth, Varanthl, and Jr'Orhr hacked down the surprised trogs as if they were splitting firewood and Elorall called down lightning on their nearby flank, incinerating swaths of goblins and leaving a trail of blackened corpses in her wake.

Whatever goblins could still move fled for the cover of the trees. In a gap made between the enemy forces, Elorall spotted the troggish captain directing his invasion force: A goblin glistening in red and white war-paint. A death-magic wielder next to him summoned black magic. The wizard snatched invisible shards of pure death force and flung them at his victims, a force of selumari on the far side of town.

Those fingers of death struck down with unerring accuracy, and Elorall growled. She'd been the recipient of such a spell before, and it took much of her stamina to hold such an attack at bay.

The elven enchanter howled her challenge, and the enemy wizard turned to face her from the raised perch he and the commander had taken. Elorall threw a blast of arcane cold at them so severe that the goblin's feet froze to the ground.

As he tried to counter back, the goblin spell-caster's foot snapped off above the ankle. He roared and tried to call upon the Death God, but he suddenly broke apart.

Shouting an order to charge, an eldarim warrior smashed through the frozen death mage and busted him to pieces. He landed, burying his sword deep in the torso of the surprised goblin captain beside him.

The remaining force harassing Graeyhaiven turned and fled into the trees. No sooner did they disappear, Eucalia and Acacia entered into a kind of trance. They put their heads together, cautious not to cut the dryad.

Moments later, the trees rustled and shook. Those observing heard the crunching of bones and cracking of branches. Goblins shrieked with groans and gurgles as the flora itself turned on them. And then everything fell suddenly quiet.

"Taryl!" Hy'Targ called, spotting the eldarim at the front of the Graeyhaiven army.

The dragonlord embraced the vaghan prince. "You didn't leave any for us," he laughed as they separated. He looked over the Gods'own. "Where is Yarrik?"

"We assumed something came up. He had some family business and left us during our travels to attend to it."

Taryl looked concerned, but a looming shadow directly overhead grew rapidly as a wounded selumari riding an eagle dropped down next to them. The coral elf stumbled from his mount.

"They—they're all dead," the elf stammered.

Mantieth and Elorall hurried over with the rest of the party in pursuit.

"Who are you talking about?" Taryl asked.

"The other riders. The scouts." He swallowed hard. "King Leidergelth has been sending us out in groups after the single fliers kept disappearing," the scout said. "Too many scouts disappeared without a trace. Now I know why."

The eagle nearby gave a sort of hop and then stumbled, falling to its side and revealing a nasty, open wound. With a horrific, groaning screech, it groaned its last and then collapsed.

"I'll never make it back in time to report to Niamarlee," the scout moaned.

"Who did this?" Mantieth asked.

"Trogs. So many trogs. I saw this army and recognized the banners. I'd be falling to my death now if I hadn't… The army—a massive army—it has a force of harpies. Maybe six, maybe fifteen. I don't know, but they came out of nowhere and slashed our birds to pieces."

"Where?" Taryl insisted. "How far away?"

"Twenty-five, maybe thirty leagues southwest, hidden in the Moorlech."

Taryl nodded grimly. "Then it's as I thought. A large army *does* exist. Forces like this horde that attacked Graeyhaiven are just a distraction, probably supply raiders. How big do you estimate the force is?"

The selumari balked at the question and needed a reference.

"Graeyhaiven's attackers were probably eight-hundred or so."

Blanching slightly, the scout admitted, "Near fifty times that size."

Taryl stiffened and stepped aside with the Gods'own. "None of this is going according to plan. I thought we'd put together an adequate force with nearly three thousand soldiers. I'm not sure what we can do..."

"There was one other thing," the scout interrupted. "They had a dragonkin chained to a wagon. Biggest one I'd ever seen, metallic bronze in color—I thought it was a statue or some kind of goblin idol at first."

"Brentésion," Hy'Targ said, looking south and weighing his options.

The scout turned his eyes to the Gods'own. "You've got to ride for Niamarlee. The king must know of the goblin threat. And Irontooth, too! If either kingdom is caught unprepared, they will only know doom!"

Mantieth made to agree, but Taryl grabbed him by the arm and turned the adventurers away from the town. "You have your own mission."

The elven prince shot the eldarim a confused look. "But the fate of Niamarlee might well rest on getting a message to my father."

Taryl nodded soberly. "Yes, and I will try to send him word." He looked Hy'Targ in the eye. "And I'll see what can be done for Brentésion in the meanwhile, but you are the Gods'own."

Elorall looked confused. She was obviously ready to back her fiancé's call and abandon their current aims to ride for Niamarlee. "What does that even mean, though? How can someone chosen for greatness by the gods just abandon people to possible death?"

"The Gods'own are champions chosen by the gods to

protect *all of Esfah*," Taryl insisted. "Not just your homes. Like it or not, whatever course the gods have set you upon, you must see it through until the end. I don't even know what brought you out this way, but you cannot change course now if you doubt the gods' will. Do not trade your corner of Charnock for the whole continent... or even the world. You serve a higher calling."

Hy'Targ looked hesitatingly to the south again. "We are on a tight timeline. I'm not sure we'll even make it to Kragryn in time."

Taryl put a hand on the dwarf's shoulder. "Then best not to delay. You can put the drakufreet's fate in my hands, just as I am leaving the fate of Esfah in *yours*."

Hy'Targ swallowed, nodded, and then walked to his mammoth. "Gods'own... Let's mount up. We still have a few hours to ride before dark."

Mantieth wanted to argue and advocate for considering Niamarlee—sending even just one of them back, but the pained look in Hy'Targ's eyes said it all. To have come so close to a chance at reclaiming Brentésion, only to be forced to continue onward, cut the dwarf deeply. They all must make sacrifices.

The selumari prince nodded measuredly and then climbed aboard his horse.

CHAPTER THIRTEEN

A tenday's span of travel brought the Gods'own to the People of the Sun, Varanthl's kin. At a steady pace, their mounts could travel eight to ten leagues per day, leaving a forty to fifty-day journey still ahead just to reach Kragryn.

They rode upon the human village an hour after sundown. The late-night reflection of the moon, Rhaudian, glinted off the amazon's spears as they guarded against the approach of invaders. They were typically a peaceful people: welcoming to all. But peaceful did not mean undefended.

Varanthl greeted them as he rode at the head of their party. The warriors lowered their weapons. They'd come to recognize their fellow warrior, who they'd tried to kill at their first meeting, thinking Varanthl a legendary monster.

The Gods'own came to a stop before Chief Geru's hut. Geru came out to greet them. "Cousin," the chief greeted Varanthl. "What brings you by?"

"A mission of some urgency, Chief Geru." Varanthl looked at him askew. "Changes to your security to protect our secret?" He implied of the bones. The night watch was far heavier than he remembered.

Varanthl and Hy'Targ had left the remains of Ailushurai, the lich Melkior's mad obsession, right where it all began, and in the least likely place any would suspect. They hoped that the residual "odor" from the old crypt would mask the bones' presence from the sniffing of even Melkior's black skeleton trackers.

Geru shook his head. "No. The trog attacks from the Moorlech have increased as of late, and even we have had straggling goblins invade a time or two. Shall I call for your uncle, Murthak?"

"No. There is not time. We must leave in the morning

but had hoped to acquire some last-minute provisions. Stim root would also be wonderful to keep our animals on their feet." Varanthl lowered his voice to reinforce the seriousness of their situation. "We must reach Kragryn as soon as possible. We have only twenty-eight days to reach the city."

Geru shot him a flabbergasted look. And then he looked at the traveling party. "That's what the stim root is for? It's more than four hundred leagues to Kragryn; I visited there once, and it was a two-month journey to reach it."

Varanthl nodded slowly. "We understand the situation. We might very well ride our mounts to death in order to arrive by our deadline."

Acacia snorted behind the four-armed man, and Eucalia rubbed his neck to calm the unicorn.

"You will arrive only *if* your mounts survive the trip," Geru insisted. "Stim root can only keep person or beast going for a few days at most. After that, it takes a toll."

Varanthl tightened his jaw. "We have no other options."

"I have one, I think." Chief Geru looked at the members of the Gods'own. The travelers' faces were already weary from the road, and they'd barely made it one third of the distance. The chief waved over a few sentries and directed them to find supplies and lodging for their road-weary friends.

"Don't kill the horses and mammoths yet," Geru insisted, drawing another complaint from the unicorn. "I must rouse Murthak. Leave everything to me," he said, against the Gods'own's warning that he might be overly optimistic.

"There will be no harm in letting me try," Geru said. "You just get a good night's rest. If my plan proves fool-hardy, you'll have lost nothing. You can still ride your animals to death, if you wish."

Varanthl and the others nodded and then retired for some much-needed rest.

In the morning, the travelers rose with the sun. Varanthl left his lodging to find Chief Geru standing opposite his uncle,

Murthak the Skald.

"Good morning," Murthak said. He and Geru both had tired lines drawn on their faces, but the skald's eyes twinkled brightly.

"You have good news?" Hy'Targ yawned behind Varanthl.

"I think we do," Murthak said. His eyes locked immediately upon Eucalia. "You have a dryad among you, a rare sight. If she is willing to participate, this trip will be all that much easier."

Chief Geru interrupted. "You should know, if my plan fails, it would make reaching your destination nearly impossible. You are already timed enough as it is."

Hy'Targ squinted at the ambitious chief. "I don't much like taking risks if I can help it. What is your plan?"

Geru explained, "I propose that, instead of traveling southwest, we head north..."

Nodhan trudged through the fetid landscape. The convoy had paused for only brief moments, and the morehl was not certain that the trog leaders had any actual plan for the army's movements.

Eventually, with the invader elf on the brink of collapse, the goblin horde finally stopped to make camp. Tall cypresses with hanging vines and sheaves of moss curtained the area for a league in any given direction. Heshgillick and his troops were safe from prying eyes here.

The elf caught his breath and foraged for food. There was none to be had and Nodhan's stomach twisted in despair. He slumped against a fallen log. He'd already exhausted the supply he'd gathered earlier. Other members of the foul company were also in search of nourishment.

I can provide you some respite, Seed promised.

He watched as a root grew in the soil and a shelf fungus the size of his head elongated from the dank wood of the log. Nodhan dug up the root and took a bite. It crunched wetly and had a bland and starchy flavor. It was not tasty, but it would provide some well-needed nutrition.

He was just taking another bite when a voice yelled.

"Don't eat that!" Footsteps rushed towards him. "It's toxic, ya stupid gurk—spit it out. Quick!"

The trog interloper smacked the shelf fungus from Nodhan's hand and tried to shake him. "I said spit it out—them death plates will poison anything except vermin and morehl."

Nodhan had already swallowed the mouthful.

The shaking suddenly stopped, and the elf could feel the goblin's eyes upon him. Nodhan glanced down to see the red backs of his hand. Spending nigh two days sprinting through the humid swamps had made him sweat off much of his camouflage. He didn't check, but he knew it would be the same with his face.

"Hey... Wait a minute," the goblin said, putting two and two together.

Nodhan glanced at the ground and spotted a forked stick next to the shelf fungus. Quick as a striking snake, he snatched both. The morehl jammed the stick into the enemy's eyes, putting them both out. He screeched as Nodhan whirled to escape.

The blind trog's companions jumped to attention. Fights breaking out in the ranks were not uncommon, but they usually ended with both parties being gutted.

With the wounded goblin shouting to his friends, Nodhan realized he could not get by them, and so he plunged deeper into the goblin ranks. Trogs pursued him relentlessly, and the elf did his best to keep his hood pulled down. If his true identity were discovered by everyone, he'd never get out alive.

Goblins laughed as Nodhan bounced off him. They shouted half-heartedly when they realized a crew gave chase, intent on revenge. Vengeance was sport for trogs.

Nodhan took a hard turn around the corner of the giant sled and paused momentarily in the shadow cast by the dragonkin. Finally, he spotted his opening and leapt beneath the creature's wing. Climbing deeper into the gap between the creature's girth and the edge of the sled, he held his breath and made himself as small as possible. He felt certain none had seen him hide. Moments later, he heard the wet slaps of goblin feet dashing past in search of him, and then finally, nothing but the distant sounds of muted conversations and crowd noises.

He waited for an opening, but it never seemed to come. Hours passed, and then the sled began to move. Heshgillick bellowed, "Not here, boys. We're on the move again!"

Nodhan's heart sank. He broke off a tiny piece of the fungus and ate it. At least he had that.

Chief Geru's wagon paused at the top of the hill of the north country, where mounds rose and fell like moguls dotting the flatlands. The Gods'own stopped near him. The human stood and pointed.

"There is our destination."

A stony bowl laid in the distance, nestled between hillocks. Petrified trees rose and broke off in stumps tipped at askew angles.

When they finally arrived and stopped at the edge, they felt an eerie stillness radiating from the land.

"What do they call this place?" Varanthl asked his uncle.

"They call it the vortex," Murthak said, snapping the reins and urging the horses forward. They crossed the threshold, and the winds began to churn, seeming to come from the ground itself. They kicked up dust in a circular whirlwind. Ground lightning crackled and reached skyward, lacing the winds with ominous blue and white light.

The travelers pushed through, and after a few moments, passed the windy screen. Within the eye of the whirling storm, they found a serene calm.

Pushing ahead to the center, they felt the stark contrast between the whirlwind and the peace of its middle. A petrified forest of branchless trees reached high, like fingers of some buried stone behemoth.

Finally, Chief Geru stopped his wagon at the edge of a clearing. The party disembarked their mounts and the crew of humans from the People of the Sun exited the wagon. Four humans besides Geru and Murthak began setting up tents.

Elorall and Mantieth traded glances. The distant winds churned and rumbled only slightly in the distance, vibrating the air at a molecular level. Even still, it raised gooseflesh on their arms and gave a static-like property to the otherwise still air.

"There is something about this place," Murthak explained. "It amplifies a person's concentration. That property greatly helps a wizard connect with the source of their arcane abilities."

"So you can cast a path spell big enough to send us all the way to Kragryn?" Hy'Targ noted.

Elorall and Mantieth looked from face to face with eagerness. It was normally a spell that was impossible for selumari to cast and had not entered their mind to attempt. Typically thought of as a vagha spell, Mantieth's father had employed a great deal of effort to send aid to them during their raid on Melkior's keep.

Mantieth watched the four human spell casters take a yellowed stone from each of their pockets. *Sightstones*. He'd forgotten how humans were a kind of universal caster; they were creations of Tarvanehl, the Father and creator god, rather than Mother Ghaeial, known commonly as Nature. The humans could manipulate whatever kinds of magic were available in the elements that were attuned to their surroundings. To them, every element was a possibility.

Murthak bobbed his head towards the tents; their wagon was provisioned with food and drink enough to last for days. "Our oracles will be able to concentrate their energies over and over. At some point, the magic will be enough for the casting."

The old skald motioned to the circle where the humans sat around a young fire. "It may be many hours... days, even. I invite any of you who can draw a spark of magic from Eldurim's domain to join us. It will make our chances of success all the more likely."

Varanthl and Eucalia took a seat among them. Hy'Targ and Jr'Orhr joined them as well.

The blue-skinned elves watched their peers in unnerving silence as they meditated. They connected to their arcane sources while focusing those energies together, intertwining the cumulative magic energy. They glowed with a slight, golden shimmer, like the halos some claimed to have seen in visions of the divine.

Elorall whispered, "I suspect it won't be long now."

At the edge of Kragryn, four stone bubbles emerged from the soil and waited for a moment before stabilizing. Mammoth tusks broke through the first, and then the second, as if the stone were the thickness of eggshell. Hy'Targ and Jr'Orhr busted free.

The other two broke shortly after. Acacia tore through the next; Eucalia emerged abreast of Varanthl on his horse. Elorall blasted the other two pieces with a gust of wind, releasing her and Mantieth.

Their delay had lasted fourteen days, but it had finally produced the necessary magic. Such a spell typically had a range of less than half the distance. Sending the Gods'own all the way to Kragryn took every ounce of arcane ability that they could muster.

Hy'Targ brushed the stone fragments and dusted off his shoulders. He urged his mount forward and into the town. The rest of the Gods'own followed suit.

The buildings of Kragryn looked like sleek, uniform towers of gray and black. West of Kragryn, across a land-bridge that led into the ocean, a volcano belched fumes that dusted anything east in dark ash and sulfuric odors. Many of the buildings were built from baked clay tiles or molded of obsidian, much how the structures at Niamarlee had been shaped out of coral.

Elorall pulled her hood up to hide her face. "It's a sure bet there are many morehl here."

Mantieth nodded as he identified the races who walked the city streets. Humans with sooty faces strolled about. A few trogs also watched to and fro, as did a handful of other races who made up the minority. The largest percentage of pedestrians, however, were lava elves.

Hy'Targ guided his beast alongside Jr'Orhr who had their map and the token. "Have you been to Kragryn before?"

He shook his head, wagging his beard. "No. But I've heard some things about it."

"Any recommendations on lodging?"

The older dwarf shrugged.

Hy'Targ braced himself in the stirrups and lifted himself as tall as possible to scout out the best inn. His eyes zeroed in on one figure in the distance. "It can't be... " He kicked his mammoth into action with a *"Hie!"*

The Gods'own watched, confused, as Hy'Targ suddenly bolted down the road. Pedestrians dashed out of the way, hurling curses at the mammoth rider who had almost trampled them.

Hy'Targ deftly piloted his mount to a T-stop in front of a dwarf casually walking down the street. "Hello, Uncle," Hy'Targ said. "Funny that we should find you here, given the great lengths we went through to arrive here in time."

Hy'Drunyr looked up at his nephew and gave him a sheepish wave. "Greetings, nephew." He jerked his head to the side. "I really think we should talk in private.

CHAPTER FOURTEEN

"Alright." Hy'Targ stared at his uncle. *"Talk."*

Hy'Drunyr made a motion to try and shush him. The Kragryn crowds bustled around them as the remainder of the Gods'own caught up to them. "Not here. Follow me to my lodging. I've rented a house."

The adventurers followed Hy'Drunyr, who walked wordlessly through the streets until they arrived at a large estate protected by a tall stone and steel fence. A company of mixed humans and lava elves patrolled the grounds. "I've rented both the home and the protective detail," the dwarf explained. He flashed a wink. "I am not without my own resources here in Kragryn. Your father has his history and connections and I have my own."

Hy'Drunyr led the Gods'own into the home, where a gray elf served them drinks and a spread of midday snacks. The frehlasuhl half-breed bowed and backed out of the room as if he'd never been there to begin with.

Jr'Orhr's posture appeared tense, hostile even. "And why are you in Kragryn?" He made no effort to mask the suspicion in his voice.

Hy'Drunyr looked embarrassed. "Likely the same as you." He held up another letter with the intended recipient's name written in a familiar scrawl: *Gods'own*. The seal was broken.

Jr'Orhr snatched the letter from the dwarf's hand. He scanned it and handed it to Hy'Targ. "You're here for the auction," he accused.

Hy'Drunyr nodded slowly.

Hy'Targ looked up from the letter with the rest of his companions, trying to get a glance at it. "It's from the Gray Wanderer. How long have you had it? We could have been saved months of travel!" He tossed it to Mantieth and briefly summarized, "the Wanderer knew of the plan to sell the item."

His uncle grimaced. "I *am* sorry," he insisted. "But I had to leave Irontooth prior to your return. I took the letter, but knew you would never make it in time since you hadn't gotten back to Irontooth. I assumed you had to be made aware of it… that you're here at all is quite surprising."

Understanding washed over Hy'targ's face. The timing sounded right. Maybe he *had* been looking out for their interests. His posture relaxed slightly, and he glanced aside to Jr'Orhr, who remained stoic.

"I will admit to an ulterior motive," Hy'Drunyr said. "There is a secondary item being offered along with the artifact. A gnomish map which I have long searched Esfah for."

"A map?" Mantieth pushed his way forward. "A map to what?"

Hy'Drunyr looked at him. "To the secrets of Gnomehome."

It took a couple days, but Hy'Drunyr arranged a preview tour of the auction items for his nephew and the rest of his companions. The fact that the Gods'own held a bidding marker acquired from Grude permitted them entry, even without Hy'Drunyr's assistance, but they hadn't told him about it yet.

The party stayed in the rented house, still unsure if they could fully trust Hy'Targ's uncle. Jr'Orhr insisted the best way to determine if they could was sticking close, especially since Hy'Drunyr had not expected their arrival in Kragryn.

Hy'Drunyr led the party to a low building in the residential district south east of the city's center. Pebble lawns raked into mosaic patterns reflected different styles in the neighborhood, and fences made bold statements about the community. The rich who lived here were serious about security.

A tall and bulky lava elf greeted them at the gate. Contrary to morehl fashion, he had short hair. An ornate falchion hung at his side, suggesting the guard was somehow more than he seemed. The weight of the blade was far beyond the light, precision blades preferred by most morehl; it dealt wounds by the sheer brute strength of its wielder.

Hy'Targ eyed its owner suspiciously. He was the largest morehl he'd ever seen, and he suspected the elf to be half eldarim. He'd styled his shortened coif so that it made his pointed ears seem that much longer, appearing to intentionally obscure the stumpy nature of a hybrid elf's ears. The prince also noticed that the guard deferred to Hy'Drunyr.

"My name is Pftheng," the large half-elf said, bowing. He flashed a wink to the old dwarf before turning his eyes to the Gods'own. "Welcome to the Fire and Flood Club. Do you have a token?"

Hy'Drunyr took an identical token to the one they had acquired in Dohan and showed it to Pftheng. The imprinted sigils made sense in light of the name.

Pftheng opened the gates and escorted them towards the house. "Do not touch any of the artifacts. All items are property of the owners and they *will* take offense. Further, it could harm the high reputation of the auctioneering company and destroy the club itself. What are we besides our reputations?"

Only after the Gods'own agreed did Pftheng move to open the door. "A final note. Please do not make eye contact with the hosts. They can sometimes prove... problematic." He turned the knob and opened the door. A sprawling mansion stretched before them and they followed Pftheng.

As large as it was, the walls and furnishing proved sparse. Morehl sentries were stationed at random locations. The company's steps echoed through the halls.

"The grounds are likely rented by the hosts, who are just here to sell their rarities," Hy'Drunyr pointed out.

"And what is the Fire and Flood Club?" Mantieth asked.

"A private organization of wealthy antiquities collectors. Most are interested in preservation of art and antiquities..."

"And sometimes power?" Hy'Targ interrupted his uncle.

The old vagha nodded his head. "Sometimes."

"Sounds like the highest-end kind of customer that Grude served." Jr'Orhr watched Hy'Drunyr for any sign that he recognized the name, but couldn't find any.

Pftheng led them towards the center chamber of the mansion. Hoots and howls spilled from a nearby door that hung open. "Remember my warning," Pftheng commented as they approached.

As the Gods'own walked past the door and towards the central room, they allowed themselves to glance sidelong at the ruckus. A throng of faeli cavorted in the room with reckless abandon. Cases of empty liquor bottles lay busted open and empty, and the remains of multiple feasts littered the floor as the scalder hosts engaged in some kind of unknown, violent game.

They passed beyond the door without incident, and Pftheng led them into an atrium. Here, security was at its stiffest. The guards were not lava elf, but hired empyreans: The firewalker race known for their battle prowess and signature trident weapons.

Pftheng led the crew past a few different exhibits. Hy'Targ was interested in them from a historical perspective, but Mantieth interjected, "We're really only interested in one piece..."

"Two pieces," Hy'Drunyr insisted. "You know the ones."

Pftheng half-bowed with a slight grin and showed them to the artifact. It was identical to the one that they'd claimed beyond Xlinea, except that the connection ports were reversed. The artifact appeared capable of interlinking with Hy'Targ's to create a larger item. A scroll case laid next to it.

"The scalder hosts are an adventuring and artifact liberation crew who discovered these in Faeleise," Pftheng informed them.

"Artifact liberation crew?" Eucalia asked.

"I think that means thieves," Varanthl kept his voice low.

Pftheng shrugged, which confirmed the humanoid's suspicion.

"The item is one part of the famed Malfus Necrosis: The item the Gremmlobahnd had created on behalf of Nekarthis the World Breaker in the heart of the Netherwold. Had the gnomes not somehow rigged it to explode, the Magestorm Wars might have ended quite differently."

Hy'Targ was tempted to reach out and take it, if only for examination. He remembered Pftheng's warnings and resisted. "What does it do; how does it work?"

"I'm afraid that information has been lost to antiquity. Only legends remain. Mostly children's tales and many of them are contradictory." Pftheng pointed to the scroll case. "The faeli claim the contents of those writings may hold the key to the location of another of these artifacts and also to the secrets of the Malfus Necrosis. Of course, this cannot be validated as they are written in gnomish and so its secrets may be lost forever."

Hy'Targ and Hy'Drunyr traded a conspiratorial glance. The vaghan prince bowed. "Thank you, Pftheng. We will see you in a few days when the auction begins."

A morehl wearing the symbols of the Fire and Flood Club validated their token and opened the door. The Gods'own took their places within the atrium they'd visited just a few days prior. Overhead, the faeli hosts hung from perches they'd fashioned and watched the bidding.

Over his upper shoulder, Varanthl carried Mantieth's saddlebags filled with gold coins. Together, they meandered through the crowd.

Most of the members wore some kind of mask or low hood to disguise their identity. These high-end clients kept items of immense value or power stored for their personal pleasure; it could be dangerous to reveal an identity in such scheming company.

Mantieth tapped Hy'Targ and pointed to Hy'Drunyr's position. The older dwarf had gone in earlier to make sure that he was present for every item. They snaked their way toward him while the lava elf auctioneer stepped onto a stool in front of the next artifact.

"Uncle," greeted Hy'Targ.

The old vagha barely noticed them. Finally, he snapped out of it, but he seemed weak, looking as if all the color had gone out of him and been replaced by only grays. He reached into his pocket and withdrew a glass jar filled with vapors of burnt dragons' weed incense. Some kind of rubber mouthpiece with a flexible check valve was installed on the vial, and Hy'Drunyr inhaled deeply.

His color immediately returned and his face brightened with a smile. Hy'Drunyr returned the greeting, "Nephew."

Hy'Targ scanned the other occupants of the room. There were at least fifteen other parties. One cloaked creature towered above the rest: an areosa. His identity was impossible to ascertain with the cloak, but his midnight fur at the haunches and tail identified his species, at least. Frostwings were rare enough as it was, but this one's cloak and accessories seemed to suggest it had come from the Shadowlands in the far north.

Other wealthy persons made sure to look away and avoid eye contact. A selumari kept her mask close. A human and his cadre wearing matching cloaks caught the dwarf's eye.

"I believe they are the competition looking to buy our

item," Hy'Drunyr noted. "They looked over all the items except the gnomish ones. It's a sure bet those're what they want."

The auctioneer soon planted his stump before the artifacts. As the opposing bidders Hy'Drunyr had identified leaned forward with sudden interest, Elorall's keen eyes spotted a marking.

She whispered to the rest, "It's those same cultists we identified beyond Last Rock."

"I see it, too," Mantieth said, just as a cultist raised his sleeve to bid on the gnomish scroll case. "She's got a tattoo on her wrist. It's the same as the ones who tried to kill us."

The woman did not try to hide it and locked eyes with the Gods'own. When she realized what they were looking at, she sneered.

Hy'Drunyr leaned in. "I recognize the woman. She is the Demarch of Southwaym on the Mertide Sea."

The Gods'own only returned blank stares.

Rummaging his hands through his silvery hair, the old dwarf cursed. "By Sha'la'dinan... Her family controls the largest banking network south of the equator." He pulled them closer and gave them a very serious look. "How much gold did you bring?"

Mantieth answered, "Five hundred thousand, standard gold weight."

Hy'Drunyr cast a suspicious eye at Varanthl.

"Most of it is in platinum," Mantieth explained the smaller size. "It takes a tenth of the space."

The old vagha relaxed. "I think we should pool our resources. I have almost a fifth of what you brought. Together, it may be enough."

Bidding on the scroll case stalled out around seventy-five thousand gold. The Demarch of Southwaym was in the lead and she wore a smug look, having backed down the blue-furred, areosan bidder.

"Are there any other bids?" the auctioneer called.

"Ninety thousand," Hy'Drunyr called.

The cultists scowled at him.

"One hundred," replied the Demarch of Southwaym.

"One ten."

"One fifteen," Hy'Drunyr fired back.

"I thought you had less than a hundred," Hy'Targ whispered insistently.

"I may need a small loan, but trust me. I know what I'm doing."

Hy'Targ exhaled nervously as Mantieth gave him a worried look.

The demarch called out, "One twenty."

"One hundred twenty-five thousand gold!" Hy'Drunyr said.

"The bid is to you," the morehl auctioneer looked back at the lady.

She waved her hand, almost smiling. "Let the vagha have it. Show us the next item."

The crowd shifted as the sellers moved positions. Overhead, the scalder hosts had turned their attention to the items. "These are some of the highest bids we've seen in quite some time," the auctioneer stated gleefully. "Don't miss your chance to get in on this historic opportunity. We expect a high price for this genuine piece of the Malfus Necrosis. Shall we open the bid at two hundred thousand?"

Bidding took off right away, increasing in small amounts.

Mantieth curled his lip, upset at losing some of his funds before the bidding had even started. Hy'Drunyr noticed. "Don't worry so much. I have a few other loans I can call in to pay you back."

Bidding petered out around two hundred-fifty. Finally, Mantieth began bidding against the demarch and the price shot above three hundred.

"Three seventy-five," the demarch hissed.

"Four hundred."

"Four fifty."

Mantieth shot an angry look at Hy'Drunyr. "F-four sixty."

"Four seventy."

"Seventy-five," Mantieth said. Nervousness lodged in his gut.

The woman grinned, suspecting she must have closed in on the selumari's maximum bid. "Four hundred and ninety thousand gold."

Mantieth scowled when the auctioneer looked back at him. The elf hissed to Hy'Drunyr. "What if we back out of the letter and put it all to the piece we know is in front of us?"

Hy'Drunyr gulped. "The Flame and Flood Club is no place to fool around. They will kill me for reneging on a pledge!"

"We cannot let those cultists deliver that part of the godbox to their master," Hy'Targ said.

"What do you mean?" Hy'Drunyr asked. He hadn't yet been told of the Gods'own's true mission.

"The demarch wears the mark of a cult devoted to Melkior, the risen lich who has some wicked purpose for it," explained Mantieth.

Hy'Drunyr looked shocked. "No. No, we mustn't let that happen, indeed!" He flashed them a wink. "But trust me. Let them win the bid."

The auctioneer had Mantieth firmly in his sights. The cultists and also the faeli hosts watched the coral elf with intense scrutiny.

Mantieth sighed and shook his head. "I yield."

"The item is won for four hundred and ninety thousand gold." A murmur rippled through the crowd at the vast amount.

"Come on," Hy'Drunyr tapped Varanthl. "Let's go pay for this letter. We'll want to beat the demarch to the bursar."

Mantieth kept a watch over the item they'd lost. Firewalker guards stood post by it to prevent any mischief.

At a booth near the side of the room, they found Pftheng. He had a scale and an open book to log entries. A mineral test kit lay open and off to the side.

Hy'Drunyr handed him a sack of coin, which the lava elf promptly weighed. He made some notes in the book and bit a gold piece. Finally, he tested a gold coin with a blotter from the kit; it did not change color, and so he tested a second random coin the same way before nodding.

"You owe another thirty thousand," Pftheng said.

The scalders had joined near them, along with two of their mercenaries.

Hy'Drunyr looked to Mantieth. His eyes pleaded for the assistance and the elf took a few pre-sorted bundles of coin in that amount and handed them over.

Pftheng repeated the same treatment and then nodded, dismissing them. He removed the bundles of coin from the scale upon the floor and moved them off to the side.

The demarch stood a little way off and scoffed at them while her minions removed their coin belts and laid sack after sack of coin upon the scales in a mound that towered far above what the Gods'own had brought.

Hy'Drunyr squinted at the demarch. He lied, "Wait a minute. I recognize her—she's that counterfeit coin smelter from over in Sheikarah."

The guards immediately took an offensive posture. "I am not!" she screeched even as Pftheng reached for a coin.

From his position, only Mantieth could see Pftheng palm a coin as he reached into a random sack. Pftheng bit it and scowled. The coin had no bend to it. He dabbed it with the blotter and it turned a horrid ochre-green. Pftheng shook his head at the faeli.

Palming another coin, he reached in and feigned taking

another sample. He tossed it to the scalder.

The faeli leader bit the coin and yelped as he snatched his blunt weapon. He glared at her and bared his teeth.

"I don't know what he's talking about—and I was guaranteed of my anonymity by the Fire and Flood... "

The faeli knocked the demarch's head clean from her shoulders with his cudgel even while she tried to argue. His scalder minions cackled and threw her body atop the sacks of coin that the cultists had brought. The corpse spurted blood all over the payment.

"Dispose of that trash," the scalder growled. As Pftheng nodded vigorously and got to work, he turned to Mantieth. "Does your offer still stand? Four hundred seventy-five thousand?"

Still in shock, Mantieth nodded shortly.

"You may pay the master of coin and take the item."

Cultists in the background complained. One made a move for the artifact. The scalders shrieked angrily and the empyrean guards moved in, stabbing and slashing with their tridents. They quickly dispersed the cultists while dealing with only minor wounds.

Mantieth looked at their faeli host and then at Varanthl, who held the remainder of their money. Still piecing it all together, he responded, "Th-thank you."

Hy'Drunyr practically spilled out of the doorway as he stowed the gnomish scroll case in his robes. The Gods'own quickly caught up with him in time to see the dwarf whistle and signal to someone in the distance. The old vagha darted for the side of the house.

"I think your uncle is going to get us all killed," Elorall said.

"I've been trying to warn you all," Jr'Orhr said as the

party hurried after him. They rounded a corner and caught up on the other side of the estate.

The wagon Hy'Drunyr had signaled pulled up to a rear servant access. Stopping, the driver lashed the reins of the two horses to a post before hopping down to help.

"Come on... Quickly!" Hy'Drunyr yelped at his companions.

"I don't even know what's happening right now," Mantieth complained, throwing his emptied money sacks into the open wagon. The portion of the Malfus Necrosis hung in a satchel over his shoulder where it could be easily defended.

The door opened to reveal Pftheng. He flashed a wink to the driver and tossed the human a small sack of coins before unceremoniously kicking the decapitated body of the demarch into the streets. "Drop this one on the beach for the giant crabs to clean up."

Pftheng nodded to Hy'Drunyr. "You know the deal. Here's your half." He dropped one of the sacks that the demarch cultist had brought in front of the door to prop it open.

Hy'Drunyr nodded and then the half-morehl disappeared, returning to his duties. "Quickly now," the dwarf said, starting a fire-line to haul the bags into the back of the wagon. As soon as they'd stowed the riches, they all clambered aboard.

"What about the body?" Eucalia asked.

"I'll get it later," the driver told her. "Pftheng was quite insistent on the job. A speedy getaway, he said." He cracked the reigns and they sped off.

The wagon jostled and bumped.

"Did all of that really just happen?" Mantieth asked. "Did we really just remotely rob the Coinery of Southwaym?"

Hy'Drunyr grinned broadly. "Something like that. I've been planning that for months... since Xlinea, actually. Pftheng and I have worked a few jobs together over the years."

His nephew gave him a disappointed look. "That's what all this was? A bank robbery?"

Hy'Drunyr's look turned grave, and he took out the scroll case. "No." He cleared his throat. "It's about *this*." He dug out a map and spread it before them. It showed an overlay of several levels of a labyrinth. "I have a portion of this map, but it was a copy and had only the top-most level shown." He grabbed the seat of the wagon to prevent being jostled clear out of the vehicle. "I was always coming to Kragryn for it, since before your letter… Since before you met me in Xlinea, in fact."

Varanthl cocked his head. "But what is it a map of?" He'd had some experiences already with labyrinths.

"It's the underbarrows of Gnomehome. The lost city of the gremmlobahnd." Hy'Drunyr looked at them. "I need to find out what happened to them. It's the mystery I've been trying to solve for centuries. And you're going to go there."

Hy'Targ looked at him. "Why is that?"

"Because it's where the next piece of the Malfus Necrosis is… or at least, that's the rumor. And you're taking me with you," Hy'Drunyr insisted.

Mantieth cringed. "I don't think that's such a good idea."

Jr'Orhr quickly jumped in to agree with that assertion.

"Though the upper level is well explored, the lower levels are incredibly dangerous. You are going to need an expert on the gremmlobahnd if you hope to survive." Hy'Drunyr shoved the map into the case. "Besides, the map is mine. If you want it, I'm coming with it."

Hy'Targ crooked his jaw and looked at everyone in his party. They looked back at him, reluctant but defeated. "Fine. But you'll have to pull your weight."

The old vagha nodded vigorously. "This may well be my last adventure, and I'm determined to see it through."

"Just so you know," Mantieth said. "I'm keeping half of

what you stole, on behalf of Niamarlee. Almost a hundred and fifty thousand."

Hy'Drunyr shrugged and looked around. He only suddenly realized something. "Say, didn't you have an eldarim with your crew the last time we met?"

Yarrik groaned. He could feel the gentle shifting of the floorboards beneath his rump and heard their rhythmic creaks. He could tell he was on a ship, but that's all he knew.

His arms were bound behind him, making his shoulders burn and the skin ache beneath the tight lashes around his wrists.

He couldn't see. A knit bag had been pulled over his head, stifling the eldarim's warm breath and forcing him to inhale only shallowly.

Through the rest of his senses, only faded voices and familiar boat sounds reached him. Whoever had taken him—whatever they wanted—he would have to wait until they decided it was time to meet.

CHAPTER FIFTEEN

"Do you feel it, Aerie?" Kaine asked as he rubbed the smooth skin of his head. He'd finally gotten around to shaving his pate and revealed his tattoos of devotion. They clearly identified him as a sage. He was one of the elders in the tiny community that had grown within a hidden dale at the Feylands. But Kaine had never been comfortable declaring himself with any rank and refused to take the tattoo which would have identified him as a master. His devotion was selfless, even to the point of sacrificing his personal honor.

The sprite, Aerie, tinkled at the old human with a kind of worried chime. Kaine, and what passed for his eidolon companion, had come across the Delmarra bay after booking passage with a ship out of Dehnlee.

He and his two sprites continued plunging south and into the Raithlan Plains. "I fear that, however mobile we are, the voice that compels our mission moves too erratically and with more speed than we can muster." Kaine bit his lip and continued walking.

They would find the thing, eventually. Kaine was driven to identify the child as the answer to an ancient prophecy of the eldarim sages, or else not. Either way, they might be able to return to the Feylands in peace afterward.

"Heh. Peace," Kaine scoffed. They'd passed by a few burned out villages along the road. He knew that Esfah did not come by peace easily, and he wondered if such a notion was only little more than a clever fiction. Certainly, peace was never more than a season, like summer before a long winter. A cold winter always came after every spell of goodly warm weather.

Kaine shook his head, pointed his nose south towards Bralanthyr, and began ambling along the long and winding path. He would find the voice that had dragged him from the

Feylands, eventually.

Eucalia rode abreast of Elorall as they traveled south from Kragryn. Two days had already passed since their departure from the city. She scowled, and Acacia did not look altogether happy, either.

"What is it?" Elorall asked her.

"Something is not right," she noted. "It has felt off since we left the town."

Elorall rubbed her eyes, which had become strangely irritated from the wind blowing off the Tarvenish Ocean. She glanced ahead to where Mantieth was chatting with Varanthl. "I know what you mean. Maybe we've all been a little on edge since we first set out and encountered you on the road... but that's got nothing to do with it, I'm sure. Mantieth has been acting... I dunno..."

"That's not what I meant," Eucalia blushed a deeper shade of green at Elorall's admission. "I meant the environment. Few green things grow here."

"Yeah," Elorall said, trying to save face. "That's what I meant." She rubbed her irritated eyes. "Usually salt doesn't bother me at all."

Eucalia sniffed the air. "It's not salt. That's soot... and sulfur."

The party continued for another day before the volcano came into view in the west. Cliffs boxed them in on the east. Jr'Orhr examined the maps and the writings from the scroll case Hy'Drunyr had purchased while the other dwarf took over riding atop his mammoth. Hy'Targ had also taken a turn examining the documents.

"You helped make a copy of the lexicon in Xlinea. Perhaps we ought to make a copy of these writings and the maps," Jr'Orhr suggested.

Hy'Drunyr scowled. "I'd rather not." The tone of his voice indicated there was no arguing with him. "It's not just that I paid a great sum of money for them..."

"More than you had," Mantieth reminded him.

Hy'Drunyr rolled his eyes. "These maps are the culmination of my life's pursuit. I'd rather they remained special and unique. At least until after I am dead and gone. Then I hope they are reprinted for all Esfah, should my life have amounted to anything worth reading by scholars."

The others shrugged. Hy'Drunyr wasn't going anywhere, as far as they were concerned.

After a short while, Hy'Drunyr stopped and dismounted. He pulled them together to warn them. "The morehl near Skarfeildhem used to be the scourge of Bralanthyr in the east. Now, they mainly raid the roads south of Kragryn. We live in an age that attempts to look more civilized as a method of self-preservation."

"Not very civilized if they're going to raid us," Hy'Targ said.

His uncle shrugged. "They call it a 'toll for safe passage.' It's just another name for banditry."

"You fear they will take your gold?" Mantieth asked, "And I still claim half of that for Niamarlee."

"I don't fear losing the gold near as much as them claiming this new portion of the godbox."

The party nodded their agreement. "You have a suggestion?" Varanthl asked.

"I do," said their elder dwarf. "There is a dwarven elevator up ahead, maybe a quarter league." He pointed. "You see the shadow of the mountain?"

They nodded.

"Buhlruch is ahead. It's a dwarven mountain. Everything atop the ridge here, above the cliff, is vaghan territory and they patrol it against the lava elves. There's bad blood in Buhlruch between them."

"Aye," Jr'Orhr said. "They've got a saying, 'Never piss off the Buhlruchs.' Those gurks'll hold a grudge forever."

Hy'Drunyr nodded measuredly. "The long memory is due in part to how much they suffered in the wars of the first age. They practically gutted the Bralanthyr region."

"Perhaps we can go to them for assistance," Elorall sounded hopeful. "They are your kin, are they not?"

All eyes turned to Hy'Drunyr, who knew the region best. "Dwarven kin is a funny thing. We have our clans and families and ancient ties, but we also keep to our own mountains and kingdoms unless special circumstances arise. I may belong to the Hydrak clan, just as my nephew and brother, and even have a few cousins in Buhlruch—but that don't make 'em beholden to me for any purpose."

Mantieth cocked his head. "From my diplomacy lessons, that's maybe half-true. A blood relation should still hold significance, unless there has been some kind of... "

"Shut your damned mouth, boy, and let it alone," Hy'Drunyr snapped.

All eyebrows rose. Jr'Orhr guffawed in a heavy, meaty laugh. "What in the festration did you do in Buhlruch to earn their eternal ire?"

"Never mind," Hy'Drunyr was already climbing into the back of the wagon. He piled blankets and other items over himself. "It's none of your business." He threw the flap of fabric over himself like a petulant child. "Don't let them find me or we're all in for a heap of trouble *before* we ever make it to Gnomehome."

Jr'Orhr, still chuckling, snapped the reins and urged the ponies forward. He glanced sidelong at the other Gods'own. "Don't worry. I have a cousin in Buhlruch. I'll write him when this is all over with and ask him all the sordid details."

Hy'Targ laughed as he heard his uncle sigh defeatedly beneath the blankets.

A hollow in the cliff side opened to reveal a cable-driven platform on a pulley system. Roller wheels lay positioned within the cliff side that had been melded by stone crafters to create a steep ramp. A small crew of vagha emerged from a cave near the elevator's entrance.

The vagha sentries looked over the Gods'own for a few minutes. "Not many of your kind around here," they commented to the selumari. "They usually pass around by way of the Tarvenish."

Elorall shrugged. "We're just traveling through."

The guards finally shrugged and ushered them into the elevator. Because of the weight, the mammoths had to go up separately, but everyone made the trip, eventually.

"Where are you headed?" asked the curious vagha at the top of the cliff side. He operated the dumbwaiter system that controlled the cable pulls. It dropped the massive stone weights into vertical shafts nearby.

"Gnomehome," said Hy'Targ.

His answer elicited a hearty chuckle from the operator. "Chasing treasure, eh? Well, good luck. I ne'er seen a dwarf return with anything to show for his efforts. If they return at all."

Nodhan squeezed tighter against the metallic-hued body of the draconic prisoner. He'd been hiding for days now and was eternally grateful that his canteen had been full when he'd been forced to take refuge from his pursuers.

The lava elf nibbled on a bit of the shelf fungus and silently thanked Firiel that the trogs had stayed consistently on the move. Had the goblin chief decided to try to ride the beast again, Nodhan would be discovered immediately. Of course, much to his misfortune, after his presence had been initially reported, Heshgillick's generals instituted an internal patrol of the camp. They suspected that someone may have hired an assassin to kill their leader. Heshgillick suspected some jealous goblin captain from another region—perhaps even the famous King Garnash in Dereh'Liandor, who Heshgillick hoped to some day rival in fame. Goblin subterfuge typically involved assassination by jealous ilk.

Nodhan couldn't make a break for it in the night because of the patrols, and they never ventured far beyond the dragonkin because of its proximity to their leader's tent. Heshgillick usually remained insulated near the center of the army, and that was where the captive creature's wagon remained.

Sighing, the morehl realized his hiding spot was both the best and worst place to be. He looked ahead and saw the poor creature staring at him.

The beast's mouth was muzzled to prevent any casualties. Its piercing gaze unnerved Nodhan. It had been watching him with some curiosity now for several days.

At least Seed has been quiet. Because he couldn't talk aloud, he'd been unable to respond to the pesky thorn in his plans. After the first day of non-responsiveness, Seed had quit trying to motivate Nodhan. *Seed's got enough sense of self-preservation to hibernate for a while.*

Heshgillick stomped nearby with his minion Tsut in tow. Nodhan heard the distinct *sluntch, sluntch* sounds of the shambling mound's footsteps as he trailed the goblin chief.

"We have not amassed our horde in order to remain cowering in the fens," Heshgillick snarled.

"But you are so close," insisted Tsut. "Keeping mobile for the past ten years, striking from the shadows until the time is right…"

"It is right *now,*" Heshgillick roared.

Ratargul laughed nearby. "Finally, you listen to wise council instead of that runt. There is another village not far… and then the mountain pass."

"That will take us beyond the Moorlech again," Tsut warned, "and into the greater body of Bralanthyr. Once we leave the mountain pass, we will have tipped our hand. There is no going back to the safety of the swamp."

"I know that!" Heshgillick growled. "I say when it is time to attack. I say it is now."

Ratargul chuffed his approval with some wordless grunt.

Nodhan could sense the tension between the shambler and Tsut. Each vied to influence the de facto king.

"Once we flood across Bralanthyr, more trogs will come. We'll grow bigger and stronger with every village we take. And then— even King Garnash will notice that King Heshgillick is greatest."

Heshgillick's minions continued to mutter at each other, despite their leader's sudden absence. He'd entered his nearby tent where his harem of harpies remained at his disposal.

Nodhan blanched at the violent sounds of goblin intimacy. It was disgusting enough that he was tempted to make a run for freedom, even in broad daylight. He looked up again and saw the metallic creature looking down at him, observing him still.

The dragonkin cocked its head.

Nodhan felt a moment of compassion for the creature. He'd been a slave before, both literally and figuratively, having grown up as a street urchin near Emmira. He put a hand on the creature's flank and rubbed along the beast's smooth scales. *It'll be alright. These creatures won't be able to hold you forever. I've seen you fight them.*

I know, the dragonkin's raspy voice startled Nodhan. It echoed in the lava elf's mind.

The elf looked back at the creature and maintained his gaze. *You—you hear my mind?*

So long as you are in contact with me, yes. I have been named by a former friend, though I never bonded with him in this manner. I am desperate enough to initiate the bonding now, and that is no small matter. King Hy'Mandr, my friend, called me Brentésion.

CHAPTER SIXTEEN

The road seemed to stretch into an endless gray waste. Heather and grasses rose in the east where the plains of Bralanthyr stretched across the horizon.

What made the road feel eternal was less the mundanity of it and more the sheer amount of it. The Gods'own regularly passed through village and vale, each relatively similar to the last, but the drive seemed to sap the energy from the crew. South, ever south they rode.

Noticing the sleepiness of the party, Hy'Drunyr finally crawled out from his hiding spot, having cleared the jurisdiction of Buhlruch and the shadow of Skarfeildhem's bandits. "It's not that the road is so incredibly boring," he commented. "It's all a matter of comparison. Our destination is exciting enough that the journey pales by contrast."

Mantieth glanced from side to side, scanning the expanse of the landscape. He spotted fawns in the distance. Beyond them roamed a trio of wild drakufreet. "It just goes to show the size of Charnock."

Hy'Targ nodded slowly from atop his mount. "And it's only half as tall as the Birthlands are wide," he compared their continent to the next one north of them.

"And yet travelers explore them often," Hy'Drunyr said. "It seems that not any force in all of Esfah could keep those with adventurous spirits from traveling abroad." He fixed his gaze on his nephew. "You know your mother's clan is supposedly from the Birthlands"

Hy'Targ cocked his head. His father rarely talked of Queen Sh'Ttil and his old mentor, Ne'Vistar, never spoke of his wife, Sh'Ttil's sister Sh'Mmarra. She had perished in a plague long before the prince could ever remember. It felt like a forbidden topic of discussion: One filled with information no tutor would ever teach.

"You knew my mother?"

Hy'Drunyr chuckled. "Aye. That was in the days before your father took such a keen dislike to me."

"What caused the rift?" Hy'Targ asked. "Did it have something to do with my mother?"

The tension in his uncle's voice was palpable. "Aye." Hy'Drunyr paused for a long moment. "We used to be close, he and I. We even adventured together in our early years before that damned tournament in Lyandrica."

"Tournament?"

"It's unimportant. That was long before your parents had even met."

They traveled a little way in silence. "What happened to her... my mother?" Hy'Targ finally asked.

"She went missing."

The prince glared at his uncle. "Don't patronize me, Uncle. If I wanted the same old answer, I would've asked the same old vagha. But if you can't, or won't, give me an answer, then..."

Hy'Drunyr waved off his nephew's anger. "I suppose you are owed an explanation."

Hy'Targ glanced aside and found Mantieth and Elorall also listened in, thin-lipped. They looked for a sign that they should fall back and give them some privacy. The dwarf didn't give them one. He'd never been ashamed of his past before, and he didn't plan to start now—he simply did not have any information on his family's past. He lacked the same closure that Mantieth had regarding his mother.

"Your father blames me, of course. I had a hand in it. You see, after they married, she discovered her own adventurous spirit. She took my place on your father's crew. I think Hy'Mandr thinks I was jealous. And I may have been, but I did not kill her."

"What happened?"

Hy'Drunyr sighed. "I gave her the details of a resurgent death cult that was forming on the western slopes of the Stonejaw range, near the hills of Bralanthyr. She rode off with a small band right away, before your father could even get word. She was never heard from again. They never found any trace of the cultists aside from the one who had delivered me the initial message.

"She had been a distant cousin, it seemed. The Shree clan is often considered one of the most factious and contentious of the tribes. They span the highest of dwarven courts and the lowest dregs of the bottom castes. They're known for their beauty and have often married kings in Gundakhor... or worked dwarven brothels in Shen la'Terl."

"Why would she go off on her own after some crazed cult?" Hy'Targ wondered aloud.

"She sometimes did that. Sh'Ttil often led her own expeditions and conducted her own business. Hy'Mandr could not have kept her, even if he'd wanted to."

"That's odd."

"Odd?" Hy'Drunyr raised a brow. He spoke with a kind of admiration, "Not odd for a vagha warrior queen."

"No. Not that she adventured herself—I suspect that would have been the only sort of woman who could tame my father. But my memories are odd... I remember her often visiting. I remember my mother much as she looked in the portraits, but somehow different. And she was regularly with me as a child... " He stroked his beard in deep thought. "Perhaps my childhood memories were somehow jumbled."

Hy'Drunyr shrugged. "Maybe a nanny of some sort? They could have found one who looked similar, so you didn't feel abandoned as a whelp."

"Perhaps," Hy'Targ mumbled, and he left it at that.

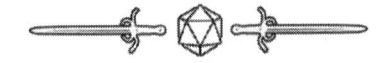

What we are has no word in your tongue, Brentēsion spoke into Nodhan's mind. *You would not comprehend our language, anyway. Perhaps the best amalgamation of terms might be dracolem.*

Nodhan peeked out from his hiding spot. The trog forces had slowed noticeably. He grimaced. Between Brentēsion and Seed, the poor morehl couldn't get a moment's peace.

What did you mean when you said we were bonded? Nodhan sent her a thought.

It means we can communicate like this. We are now linked, you and I. Dangerous is such bonding. We dracolem can only do so with one Esfahn. Doing so makes us... Brentēsion paused as she searched for the proper word ... *mortal.*

Are you saying you could not die otherwise?

I am saying that I am more vulnerable than ever before, Brentēsion said. *Our languages are not perfectly compatible.*

And you did not bond this way with King Hy'Mandr?

Brentēsion stared into the lava elf's eyes. *I have never been in such need before.*

Nodhan frowned. He only had more questions every time either Brentēsion or Seed tried to answer them. *So I should just free you and be on my way?*

No. We must remain together. I sense something in you. Some kind of pull on the threads of destiny. I feel it: You are touched by the goddesses of fate.

Fate? Nodhan mocked. *I make my own fate. Besides, whatever the foreign gods of another planet might have to do with me would have little to do with our meeting.*

Brentēsion laughed. *Surely? The goddesses may be the heirs and children of Turambar—tied to Esfah's sister planet Leguin, but the dracolem once called Leguin home before the dark times... before the Drekloch came. We called Esfah home for a time... but now, my family is gone. And yet I still do my duty.*

Duty? Even in his mind, Nodhan's words were tainted by resentment. *I like to jettison any such obligations.*

Perhaps you should not! Brentésion chastised him. *If more folk attempted to thwart evil and make Esfah better, then Malgrimm's forces would not be growing so rampant. Then again, the fates might not have brought us together.*

There you go again with that, Nodhan said. *I still don't know what you're talking about.*

I cannot know the specifics, but myself and other dracolem champions have been preserved to protect Esfah. Some dark force strikes at her heart. I only know that you are now bound up in that because of what you carry in your pocket.

The morehl reached down and touched his last remaining piece of shelf fungus. He felt momentary confusion, and then his other hand touched the bulge in his clothing: Seed.

Nodhan risked being discovered and muttered a verbal curse upon the interloping plant life. "Festrations take you, Seed. I wish I'd never stolen the damned thing in the first place."

"Heshgillick is a fool, Grackyll" Ratargul hissed. He stood just beyond the edge of the army, which trickled past like a lava flow. The horde moved at a slow pace and mimicked an inchworm. When one part stopped to rest, the others continued past; so large was it, that the rearguard was able to meander through to the front and break camp as those resting picked up and moved again. Tsut had not blown the signal horn in days.

Ratargul's companion, a goblin death mage, shrugged. "Look at what he has accomplished so far," Grackyll said. "But that may be more Tsut's doing than Heshgillick's." He pointed to the far distance.

Scouts from an enemy army spied them from a distance. They were not the first to watch and keep their distance. Both Ratargul and Grackyll turned to stare at them. The distance was great, but they could tell the scouts were probably human—certainly taller than dwarves, but their exact race couldn't be determined.

"Our army is so great that they don't dare attack us," Grackyll mocked. "Let them pray to their gods that we pass by *their* towns and villages."

Ratargul towered over the mage. "Regardless, Heshgillick does not have what it takes to lead us into battle. You know this. We have spoken of it already. He is strong, but too often remains out of battle—it has been *I* who led the troops, blooded them, and earned their trust. Meanwhile, Heshgillick remains with his harpy whores upon the leash of Tsut."

Grackyll cocked his head. "Still, Heshgillick is strong. Stronger than any other trog. Perhaps stronger than *you*—that is what will make him king. It is why all the varied tribes have flocked to him."

"And you will follow him if he is king?"

The goblin mage nodded apprehensively. "I will follow whoever is king; whoever the Death god grants favor to return Bralanthyr to a trogland. Goblins will rule all... I will serve whoever that king is."

"Then we shall see," said Ratargul. The animated mound of living swamp sludge bent low to look into the chief spell caster's face. "Do you suppose that Heshgillick even knows *how* to kill a shambling mound?"

"No. I don't suppose he does," answered Grackyll.

"Heh. None know—and that is why Ratargul the Smotherer will be king."

Grackyll dutifully followed the monstrous warrior, but behind him he mumbled, "Only *I* know how."

CHAPTER SEVENTEEN

"Do you have what I asked for?" Melkior asked.

Forktongue nodded. "Your loyal servants have collected them these last few weeks." He dumped a sack onto the table at the edge of the room. Hundreds of dead crows tumbled across the platform.

"Excellent." Melkior grinned. He took a vial of the inky black necralluvium from his robes and removed the stopper. As his servant spoke, he worked to pour a drop onto each dead animal.

"We do not believe the Nekarthans knew of the auction for the Malfus Necrosis..."

Melkior interrupted him. "The Nekarthans operate chiefly through subterfuge. Do you really think the item went unnoticed by the other branch of the Black Forest?"

Forktongue scowled and shook his head. "I meant to say that they were making no play for it. Whatever their intentions and method for increasing their power, the godbox did not factor into it, according to our spies."

"Perhaps the other faction does not respect the Melkites?"

"Perhaps," admitted Forktongue. "But they will... When we use the Malfus Necrosis to access the Netherwold and unleash the armies of the dead waiting within the Abyss. It will allow us to crack open the portals to Selurehl's realm and then flood across Esfah. The raw might of such an army will wipe clean every surface with the power of entropy and decay—hasn't that been Malgrimm's command since the beginning?"

Melkior finished with his vial and turned to his minion. "Yes. But his promise must be fulfilled. Reclaiming Ailushurai is a chief mandate."

"But we can overthrow our enemies without her, my lord—both the living, and also our Nekarthan brothers. We do not need…"

"Securing *her* is an ultimatum for me. I will not raze this planet until her bones are secured." Melkior's voice was stern and sharp as the iron of a winnowing blade.

Forktongue bobbed his head. He suggested, "As you wish. But with such a massive force, there is no way her remains can elude you for long."

Melkior nodded slowly, thoughtfully. "Yes. You may be right. And I *do* require access to Selurehl's realm to enforce my bargain." He traced a finger across his tattooed collarbone where Malgrimm had written the contract for Ailushurai's soul upon the lich's skin.

A human male burst through the door, carrying the head of a human female. It had turned ashen and festered days ago. It emitted a pungent odor.

The cultist bowed and set the head down upon the ground. He swallowed audibly.

"Did you acquire the item from the auction in Kragryn?" Forktongue hissed.

The messenger shook his head. "A dwarf and his companions tricked our faeli hosts and absconded with the piece of the godbox."

Melkior seethed. His lip curled.

Forktongue remained emotionless. And then he exploded with rage, producing a dagger from his robes and knifing the envoy repeatedly until he lay dead in a pool of his own warm blood.

Finally, Forktongue composed himself. He smoothed his robes and turned back to Melkior. "We must devise a new plan."

Melkior approached. "There is nothing wrong with the

plan," he said. "And there is another way. If we cannot secure the Malfus Necrosis, there is always *Drakyntatsu's Sphere*."

"The scribblings of the mad dwarf Sabian?" Forktongue scoffed.

"Not all madmen are wrong," he stated coolly. "It was his writings in my mind when I struck my dark bargain with my father, Malgrimm. It was his map of spheres that I planned to use once I was ready to enforce my contract against Selurehl. A back door into the Abyss, if you will."

Forktongue nodded thoughtfully. "But all copies were sought out and destroyed by zealots long before Nekarthis revealed himself in the Netherwold."

"A pity," Melkior sighed. "But perhaps Sshkkryyahr has kept her word; she knew of my need and had agreed to preserve one for me."

Summoning the magic coursing through his body, the undead lord flicked his finger across the tip of Forktongue's blade. When he was sapped of his energy or had gone too long without sustenance, the lich would bleed dust—but he was still strong from ingesting the necralluvium. A black drop pooled at the wound and he touched it to the corpse of the messenger, who soon crawled to his feet jerkily.

"He will continue to serve." Melkior turned to his birds. "What we need is information. Before we raise the first wave of our new army, we will need to place our eyes across the world. Spies I can control and commune with."

The lich waved his arms and the cluster of crows exploded into a cloud of flapping wings and beaks as they abandoned their roost and raced through halls, tunnels, and whatever openings they could find until they escaped into the sky, and then spread abroad to fulfill their master's purpose.

Nodhan watched all the happenings in the goblin army.

There was little else to hold his interest. The tow-sled moved at an incredibly slow pace.

He could tell something was different in how Ratargul approached the center of the camp. The *sluntch skruntch* of his gait had quickened and the angle of his shoulders seemed straighter.

What is this? Nodhan wondered.

A possible opportunity, Brentésion responded.

The lava elf grimaced. He'd still not grown familiar with the lack of mental privacy. *You may be right.*

Ratargul punched Brentésion in the nose as he walked past, stomping through the slough. A host of mud men sprang up from the ground with an otherworldly groan. Slightly larger than humans, and twisted in grotesque ways, they dripped sludge and looked like distorted caricatures of humans made from runny clay.

The shambling mound nodded to them, and the pack of monstrous minions followed. Ratargul stomped towards Tsut and bowled him over before snatching the horn. He snapped the leather thong that tethered it to the scrawny trog and then blew it, signaling a stop to their forces.

Heshgillick stomped towards the presumptuous monster and roared. He unfurled a massive, double-side blade that looked more like a giant hunk of scrap than a sword. It terminated in jagged points at either side of its tip.

Ratargul growled, "I lead now!"

Heshgillick snarled something unintelligible and rushed towards his enemy, muscles bulging. Still, the monster dwarfed him—but size made little difference to the combatants.

The shambling mound pulled an oak log from his own girth and wielded it as a club. They locked weapons. Letting the slow wagon that held the bound dracolem come to a stop, the trolls towing it turned to watch their leader.

Ratargul's mud men interfered and blocked them from

going to Heshgillick's aid.

"Say it!" roared the shambling mound. "Say Ratargul leads."

"Never!" a chorus of shrieking echoed all around them as the harpies landed at the edge of the fight.

Before they could spring in to help their master, Grackyll emerged from the crowd of onlooking goblins with his fingers splayed, and then he snapped them shut. Hands of dirt resembling mud men snatched their ankles and then hardened like stone, pinning the front line of onlookers in place to prevent interference.

Now! Brentésion urged. *This is your opportunity—seize it and live.*

Nodhan peeked out of the crook beneath the dracolem's arm and realized any trog nearby was engrossed in the combat. The winner would lead the goblin army.

Placing the palm of his hand on Brentésion's side, he thought, *Do not move until I say so.*

He pulled a needle from the callous skin at his arm and cast his minor spell, turning the simple sliver of metal into a set of lock picks. Nodhan slinked from seal to seal and worked the mechanisms. Finally, he crawled back onto the sled and tried turning the tumblers on the contraption that held Brentésion's muzzle in place.

To the side, Ratargul swung his club at the trog champion who chopped at it with his heavy blade. Heshgillick hacked the log in two pieces. He grinned smugly, but failed to see the follow-up blow from the monster. It knocked him off his feet and sent him reeling to the ground.

A trog yelped, "Hey! You're not supposed to be here," and pointed a finger at Nodhan. The goblin soldiers nearby drew axes and tried to grab him.

The morehl scrambled up Brentésion's back and kicked the bonds free. Chains and ropes slid away as the dracolem stretched his wings wide. *Let's go—we've got to get out of here!*

But the muzzle, Brentésion argued. *I may need to open my mouth for defense—I could need it in the air—they have fliers.*

"I'll get it later!" Nodhan yelled, glancing down. "I don't think the harpies will be a problem."

A sleepy kind of voice trilled in the back of his brain. **Oh. I just realized we are moving again... I hope you're not doing anything rash.**

"You're late to the party, Seed!" Nodhan howled as Brentésion beat his wings and leapt into the sky.

All the nearby trogs and even Ratargul stood stiff and straight, watching the metallic beast's scales shimmer in the light as it crawled further skyward. All except Heshgillick.

The massive goblin swung his blade with everyone distracted. It fully cleaved through the shambling mound's midsection and Ratargul slid into two even pieces and collapsed, leaking fetid sludge from the cut.

Heshgillick raised his sword high and roared in victory, searching the skies for his escaped prize. Before he was finished, his battle-cry turned to confused yelping.

Ratargul's hands dragged Heshgillick to the soil. The monster's lower half seemed to liquefy, and the muddy effluence and rotted leaves crawled over the restrained goblin. The most fluid parts of the shambling mound forced their way down Heshgillick's throat and into his nostrils, turning his cries to gurgling, fearful screams.

And then they stopped altogether.

Days had passed, blending from one to the next like chalk smeared across a slate. Finally, the Gods'own arrived at the edge of a sloped mound. Grass fleeced it with blue-tinged greens. The rise was gentle, but the expansive piling went on for leagues. After a full day's ride, Hy'Drunyr pointed to the great stone ring of the gremmlobahnd.

The caravan halted and Hy'Drunyr clambered stiffly from his wagon and stretched. "There they are. The warding pillars of the gnomish underbarrows."

Varanthl approached and stared at the circular stumps of stone. "They look more like hewn stumps."

Hy'Drunyr nodded. "That they do. They were toppled long ago. Once the guards had disappeared, there were none to grant access to the Gnomehome. Raiders and adventurers eventually toppled the towers in order to break in and attempt to plunder the gremmlobahnd's riches." The old dwarf turned in a circle as the Gods'own joined at his side. "They say that the towers shot some kind of lightning at them, killing all intruders. They were expert crafters and excelled at devising traps."

He led the others around the stone ring. It was smooth and polished, although weathered and pitted from age. "What was it for?" asked Eucalia.

Hy'Drunyr shrugged.

A massive stone sat a short distance away from the ring. Hy'Drunyr led the way. "This way," he said. He pushed against the stone and moved it easily. It opened to a descending stairway, which wound downward into the dark, where they could not see.

Eucalia rubbed Acacia's flanks down while the travelers loaded up their spelunking supplies. "We may be in the caverns for up to a tenday. You can mind the mounts and keep them safe, right? Like before?"

Acacia snorted with approval, but also some ire.

They lit their torches, cinched their packs, and walked into the depths. After a considerable distance, the stairs ended, and a cavern yawned open before them. Old dust, soot, and rubbish littered the grounds. Debris from old structures and machines long since decayed or destroyed cast ominous shadows off the flickering lights.

"It's a dead city," Elorall's whispered words echoed

starkly in the dust-choked air.

A rodent stirred somewhere in the distance.

"Dead?" asked Hy'Drunyr. "Or merely abandoned?"

Hunched over, Hy'Targ lowered Glorybringer's flames to the floor and scanned a section beyond them; while the others burned torches, his father's magic axe blazed like an everburning brand. Old footprints showed in the dust like knead marks on dough. "Other explorers?"

His uncle half-shrugged and half nodded. "Many come and go. The gremmlobahnd dig deep, much like the vagha. Well actually, 'dig' is too generic a term. This whole structure is actually built rather than tunneled. Except for maybe the lowest levels."

They paused while Hy'Drunyr oriented himself. He used the maps they'd acquired from the Fire and Flood Club. Once he was done, the party was on the move. Mantieth's ears perked up as the old dwarf mumbled something about, *"the last time I was here."* But he let it slide as he often did for Jr'Orhr, the next eldest in their party.

Tunnels opened to them the longer they traveled. They appeared both archaic and sophisticated. Silken draperies woven by generations of spiders hung in semi-transparent sheaves.

Thick dust muffled all sounds, as if blanketed in a layer of snow. Varanthl touched a randomly abandoned piece of undersized furniture and the moldered item crumbled under its own weight. He ushered it into the final state of decay with a simple poke.

They continued into another atrium and found it much the same. Overhead atriums built up into domes where the gremmlobahnd had lived. The larger galleries seemed to be old marketplaces and public areas. Little was left of them, but the booths and structures inside the interconnected vaults appeared to be shops, or perhaps even dwellings for creatures slightly smaller than dwarves.

The Gods'own had been exploring mostly in silence. Varanthl used the light of his torch to turn in a slow arc.. He peered into the darkness that stretched well beyond the range of his light.

"Guys… Where is Hy'Drunyr?"

CHAPTER EIGHTEEN

"I've got some fresh footprints over here," Mantieth's voice echoed in the dark. The Gods'own hurried over to his side. He was easy to find in the subterranean cavern. Any light source stood out like a beacon in the black.

Varanthl, who spent his fair share of time trapped in underground labyrinths, waved his torch high overhead and noticed the myriad of jewel-like orbs. They were placed all around, as if they might have been sunstones, only no one knew how to activate them. "I wonder what it must have looked like in its glory?"

"Pretty spectacular, I assume," Hy'Targ muttered. "It's already given me ideas to suggest for Irontooth."

Eucalia scowled and shook her head. "I don't like it. I loathe any place without regular access to the sun."

"He went this way," Jr'Orhr stated, crouching near the dust and pointing where the footprints went. It looked like a kind of tunnel connecting through several structures and that had been built of hewn lumber. It had long since turned ashen gray. Broken cobwebs dangled from age-weakened reinforcement braces where Hy'Drunyr had passed. The hallway did not look stable.

Jr'Orhr sighed. "Next time, we put your uncle on a leash."

Hy'Targ grunted an agreement and then ducked into the shaft. The others followed him, keeping low to prevent from bumping the horizontal braces that kept the walls from collapsing upon themselves.

One of Varanthl's torches licked too greedily at the air, as if something in its fuel source popped. The flames fluctuated slightly. The burp of fire splashed against the overhead webbing and caught hold.

Elorall gasped and began to summon a water-based spell to quench it, but too late. Varanthl tried to pat the flames down and smother them. He slapped the smoldering bits into submission with the rest of his peers howling for him to stop.

It had only taken mere seconds, but the rotted boards creaked and groaned. An untouched support beam shifted and fell.

"Everybody back!" Jr'Orhr yelped, and the Gods'own retreated to the mouth of the tunnel. A moment later it collapsed in on itself. The landslide the thin wall had held back for centuries broke the silence as scattered rubble across the floor.

The others grumbled about their options and finally opted to venture back to the spot where they'd first realized that Hy'Drunyr had gone missing. It was the logical place for the old vagha to come searching for them.

"I just wish we knew if Hy'Drunyr was caught in the cave-in," Hy'Targ lamented. "The adventure may be futile without him. He had the maps."

Mantieth growled. He'd invested a significant sum of wealth in the journey. "Geriatric dwarven desires be damned. Why didn't we make a copy of the maps?" He mumbled a bevy of elven profanity beneath his breath.

Elorall put a hand on his arm to comfort him, but he shook her off. She crossed her arms instead.

"Maybe *you all* didn't," Jr'Orhr said. "But if Hy'Drunyr is dead, we can make another attempt."

"Without the maps?" Hy'Targ asked. "My uncle said he'd been trying to access the lower levels for years and wasn't able to figure it out. I've learned quite a bit about the gremmlobahnd recently, but it's no comparison to what Hy'Drunyr knows, or even knew back then."

Before despair could set in, Jr'Orhr sighed. "I am certain your father never explained how I came to be one of his adventurers or why he sends me to do… what it is that I do for him behind the scenes. Or about this." He motioned to the long scar that ran from forehead to chin.

All eyes turned to the dwarf.

"Why would your scar matter?" Mantieth asked. "I know *my father* could sometimes be vain and remove courtesans for aesthetic reasons, but the vagha?"

Jr'Orhr shook his head and glanced sidelong at Hy'Targ. "Your mentor gave this to me."

"Ne'Vistar?" Incredulity seeped into Hy'Targ's voice.

"He may be a bookish scholar, but his heart is vagha." He swallowed his shame. "Many years ago, mind you, I fell in love with a married lass. I was younger than you by a few years. It was foolish, but I wooed her and stole her away whenever her husband wasn't around." He swallowed again. "The Shree sisters had such overwhelming beauty. It was overpowering. I knew I could have pursued the third sister. She was unmarried, but there were other rumors about Sh'Zzar that discouraged it."

"Wait," Mantieth interjected. His education had taught him enough to connect the dots. "You had an affair with the Queen's sister?" Their prior conversation aboard the *Greenkiss* was finally making sense.

Jr'Orhr fingered his scar and nodded. "Maybe it was an affair *for her*. For me, it was love. And then her husband discovered it..."

"Ne'Vistar attacked you?" Hy'Targ asked.

"And I had it coming," Jr'Orhr stated. "I have always been the better fighter, but not on that day. A husband's pride will always surpass skill."

Hy'Targ asked, "But how did you remain in the Adventurer King's company with such an intimate betrayal so close to him?"

"And how is this connected to the maps?" Elorall asked.

"Hy'Mandr knew my secret. And I ask that the Gods'own keep it: I cannot forget. The physician said my mind was special. Everything I see and commit to memory I can recall perfectly. They called it eidetic."

"You never forget?" Elorall clarified. "That sounds like a curse."

Jr'Orhr shrugged. "I *can*... booze helps. But if I intend to keep a memory alive... It will always remain with me. The sights. The smells. The *feel* of someone." He touched his scar again and then self-consciously put his hand away. "It is a skill your father has employed of me for many years... and that reason is why Hy'Mandr and Ne'Vistar had grown somewhat colder. Especially after Sh'Ttil disappeared and then Sh'Mmarra died." He choked on the words. "I remember every moment of the plague that took her when you were just a whelp."

They all shared Jr'Orhr's pain for a silent moment. And then a voice broke through distant darkness. "I found you!" Hy'Drunyr called out, waving his torch in the distance. "Somehow the tunnel I'd ventured into collapsed and I had to go all the way around."

The Gods'own traded glances, knowing they would keep Jr'Orhr's secret. Hy'Drunyr had proved himself useful, but he was not Gods'own.

"It's all so very familiar to me," Hy'Drunyr muttered while he led the party this way and that. Finally, they arrived at a terminating passageway and paused.

The adventurers huddled in the dark near a vault-like door. Despite being sealed ages ago, the metal of its craftsmanship still gleamed in the torchlight. Chains and other metal nearby had rusted, but the barrier remained as strong as ever.

"This symbol is what has eluded me," Hy'Drunyr pointed to a frame where it seemed etched in the hatch. "There are a few areas where others have forced their way down below, but those folk have never returned. I've never been able to make it beyond this point, and I feel the designated method downward is likely the safest."

Hy'Targ dragged a finger over the symbol and the chiseled lines took new shape where he had touched it. His finger tracks kept their form for a few moments. Then, the odd shapes took their original form. "What does the symbol mean?"

"It's gnomish," Hy'Drunyr told him.

The prince grimaced while focusing on it, trying to remember. "It means, 'locked?'"

Hy'Drunyr nodded. "The maps have since revealed much to me." He used a finger to trace the symbol in reverse. The door clicked with a deep *thud*.

"Handy trick," Mantieth quipped. "I knew there was a reason we brought him along."

A turning stairwell brought them to the next sub level. This passage felt far more utilitarian. Block walls made straight paths. Few stations dotted the promenade, opening up into antechambers. The contents in each of them lay in ruins. No one had plundered them, but age and humidity had done their worst and vermin had destroyed anything useful.

"I think this was a transit level," Hy'Targ stated. "It looks like the gnomes lived above but used these halls to move about more freely."

"Hold!" Hy'Drunyr yelped before Eucalia could walk around a corner and scout ahead. He brought his torch down to her ankles. A thin, metal cable crossed the hall, still drawn tight with tension.

"Some kind of trap?" Varanthl wondered aloud.

Hy'Drunyr nodded, pointing ahead to a curving wall with protruding spikes the length of short swords. "It might be the gnomish equivalent to blade golems. They called them *razorcrests.*"

Hy'Targ stepped nimbly over the tripwire and

approached it. The others followed suit.

They could not see the body of the machine, only the curving side which appeared to be a roller wheel with serrated spikes: Ready to decimate any living enemy near it.

In the distance from where they'd come from, an ominous, otherworldly noise echoed. All the Gods'own stiffened.

"Perhaps we should keep moving?" Mantieth suggested, and they resumed their trek through the main passage where Hy'Drunyr had been leading them.

They walked another hour in the dark.

"Uncle," Hy'Targ asked. "Where are we headed?"

He grumbled in the shadows. "I'm still looking for the next door. There should be another way down around here, somewhere." Hy'Drunyr drummed his fingers on his chin as he scanned the walls they walked past.

The eerie sound echoed down the corridor behind them again. Together they paused to look back as it increased in volume before clarifying into a sort of chittering sound.

Finally, the blackness turned a charcoal gray and then became a dim, false kind of light. Sprite-like orbs flitted in and out as if dust motes in a moonbeam.

"What is it?" Varanthl asked nervously, keeping his voice low.

"Unsure," Hy'Drunyr whispered back. "These halls are littered with traps. So is the upper level, but I led us on the safest path—and most of those dangers have been long-since deactivated."

Eucalia suddenly shrieked. She turned and fled through the gathering and rushed away. And then the others saw *it* emerging from the dark. Varanthl whirled and ran, his blood running cold. "Teeth and eyes! All hunger!"

The others fled on his heels. Ghastly shrieks and noises gave pursuit.

"And a song of flame and withering," Eucalia wheezed.

"What is it?" Elorall shouted? "I saw none of that."

They'd slowed to communicate and the creature pursuing them grew louder as it approached.

"The song played by the bone man—the Death Bard of Dereh'Liandor. He is coming for us to ferry our souls to the Abyss," Eucalia insisted.

"No." Varanthl argued. "It is the b'yandhar returned to health: A legend from my people of a tunnel-dwelling monster. *It is a beholder*. They can create powerful illusions and reshape reality!"

"It's none of those things," Hy'Targ argued as they picked up their pace. "But whatever it really is, it can use our fears against us. It takes their shapes."

"What did you see?" Hy'Drunyr asked, nursing a cramp in his side as they ran.

Hy'Targ barked, "I'm not sharing."

An ear-splitting roar deafened them as the fear monster surged ahead in a cloud of smoke and screeching hellscape. Its presence splashed near them like a rushing tide. Within the smoke, each one saw their loved ones being dismembered by other loved ones, twisting knives gleeful and twitching with joy as they inflicted agony upon one another.

The party shrieked and bolted ahead, invigorated by terror-induced endorphins. They turned a corner and heard a loud *sprang-whick!* as they activated a tripwire.

A red light lit in the inky darkness, and then the halls began to rumble. Whatever the illusory creature was, it suddenly disappeared when a razorcrest roared to life.

Above them, and on the walls and floor surrounding them, some foreign magic none of them understood flared into effect. The razorcrest belched a horrible metal on metal blare and long-frozen gears suddenly unstuck.

Surrounding each intruder were glowing sigils that lit up the halls before and behind them. They glowed, each with their elemental colors to identify them. Red and gold shined for the dwarves; the elves glowed green and blue. Eucalia's green and gold intermingled with the silvery white of Varanthl as he took her hand. They fled back the way they'd come, running from the new threat.

"We've got to get out of here!" Mantieth shouted. "At least until we know how to beat these things."

"Full agreement," Hy'Targ yelled in hasty retreat.

Elorall and Eucalia stood their ground ahead of them, while the others slid to a stop.

They summoned their best restraining magic. Eucalia gripped at the razorcrest with a snarl of roots and vines that wormed through the gears and wheels that drove it. Elorall froze a wall of ice on either side of it.

Several seconds stretched out into what felt like forever. And then the razorcrest belched another growl and roared into action again. It shattered the ice wall and gave chase, with vines still dangling from the blades and spikes threatening the party.

The Gods'own fled before it, only able to match pace with the villainous wheels. Even if they could have hidden, the glowing marks would have identified them in the dark at least a hundred paces away.

"There!" yelled Mantieth, pointing ahead. "The floor!"

Jr'Orhr slid to his knees where the floor hatch was marked with the *locked* sigil etched. He traced the *unlock* symbol over it and the aperture fell open. The vagha threw himself through the opening and each of the others followed suit after him, plunging into the dark, just before the razorcrest closed the gap and rolled over the top of the hole.

Hy'Targ groaned and then rubbed his aching back. He'd landed atop Mantieth, who had already drawn his sword, even though it would've proved useless against a threat like a gnomish razorcrest. Luckily, his magic armor had protected him, even if the vorpal blade had torn through the outer layer of armor he wore.

Jr'Orhr landed atop him with a stiff *whumpfh!* that knocked the air from both the vaghas' lungs and drove Hy'Targ back into the sharp edge of the sword. The light-spun armor woven by the drider held, though it pinched dreadfully.

The Gods'own grumbled and groaned in the dark as they rolled off each other. They held their breaths in the blackness. Only after the silence returned and indicated that their pursuit had been lost did Hy'Targ re-light Glorybringer. The others lit their torches off its flames.

Flickering torchlight revealed familiar shapes. The hollow sounds of old bones clattering against one another echoed with a sick emptiness as the Gods'own untangled from each other. The pile of skeletal remains revealed desiccated bodies that were shorter than dwarves. There were too many of them to count.

"It's some kind of catacomb?" Hy'Targ wondered aloud as the party spread out and explored. They remained within eyesight and earshot of each other.

"Not catacombs," said Hy'Drunyr, pointing to a faded word imprinted upon a sign.

Hy'Targ squinted and did his best to recall the obscure language. "'Health?'"

Hy'Targ nodded. "That's the literal translation. In gnomish, this would have been a hospital."

"So maybe that pile of bones was not from some predator's leftovers?" Mantieth asked hopefully. He knew he could not hope for such luck.

Hy'Targ shook his head. "Why would a hospital throw remains in the middle of a room and heap them up like that?"

Mantieth gulped, knowing his friend spoke the truth.

"Look at this," Varanthl said in the adjacent room.

The others joined him in the chamber, where tarnished metal beds remained in relatively straight lines on both sides of the room. "What is interesting about it?" Elorall asked.

"You have a keen interest in triage wards?" Hy'Drunyr asked.

Varanthl grimaced. "I've not seen many hospitals. I likely never will." He shrugged. "Not since the Kreethaln's regenerative powers seemed to have been absorbed into me. I've seen one in Niamarlee and in Irontooth. Is it common that they are this empty? That's not been my experience."

"Mine either," said Hy'Targ with a certain level of intrigue. He wandered through, guessing that the pile of bones in the previous room were the remnants of whatever poor gremmlobahnd had awaited their death within the infirmary, too sick or injured to flee with the rest of their kin. Wherever they had gone.

He searched between the beds while his uncle unfurled his map. "We're wasting time," he muttered. "The map says we're on the correct level. There is some kind of shrine and it's not far from here, provided we don't bump into any more *trouble*." He glanced back at the heaping pile of bones. Whatever had chased them, had already dined here on the weak and indisposed... It had access to this level, too.

Hy'Targ sifted through the crumbling threads of hospital sheets and pillows. They disintegrated under his touch. He began to turn back to the party and abandon the search when his toe tapped something hard and metallic. It skittered a cubit away and caught his eye.

The dwarf picked it up and examined it in the dim light.

"What is it?" Varanthl asked.

Hy'Drunyr answered before he could, "It's a gnomish puzzlebox. They were famous for making them, but so few remain in existence..."

Hy'Targ had already begun fidgeting with it before his uncle could warn him against it.

A light flashed around it, momentarily blinding them. As the Gods'own and Hy'Drunyr squinted to adjust their eyes, they spotted a short figure on his hands and knees looking up at them. An elderly gnome gasped.

He spoke the common tongue. "Please... Please, sirs... Tell me how many years have passed since the Magestorm ended?"

CHAPTER NINETEEN

"My name is Gryeslan," the gnome said after drinking from Mantieth's canteen. He groaned slightly as he tried to move. He sighed and relaxed in the bed, though the mattress and bedding were long since destroyed. "I won't have long."

As if pained, the elderly creature lowered the goggles that he wore around his forehead. Gnomes' eyes worked on a different spectrum and without them, they were nearly blind... *with them* they saw far more than any Esfahn creatures.

"What do you mean?" Hy'Targ asked.

"I am dying," Gryeslan said. He grimaced as he tried to bend back towards the water. The gnome scowled at them all; the gremmlobahnd looked much like square-jawed human children, but with beards that could rival the vaghas'. Though they did not always let them grow, Gryeslan's was long and white. The most unsettling difference was in the hands: They were slightly larger than even Varanthl's.

"Of course, that's nothing new," Gryeslan explained. "I was dying in this hospital when the chaos broke out... I've been dying for centuries. Word reached us that our kind had broken Nekarthis's hold and divided the Malfus Necrosis." He trailed off; time was limited, and he only had so many words before his end came—he had to choose them wisely. "We made a weapon to protect us, long before we ever came to Esfah... but it never produced the desired effect. It protected us rather than hunt our enemy as we'd hoped."

"The end of the Magestorm Wars," Hy'Drunyr stated enthusiastically.

Gryeslan nodded slowly, as if it pained him. "I was already quite old, and according to you, it ended over eleven hundred years ago." His eyes turned down to the box in Hy'Targ's hands. He chuckled while he looked around the despair of the room. "I escaped the mad eldarim's contingency plan, only to have Death find me, anyway."

"What do you mean?" Hy'Targ asked.

"That cube. It's a simple storage pocket, not meant to store a body. I crawled in when the warlord's minion came for us, feeding on the helpless in the hospital."

"The drekloch?" Hy'Drunyr asked.

Gryeslan nodded. "Nekarthis had imprisoned it for his own means, but his defeat must have released it. Its threat was how he prevented his minions from simply killing him and dividing up his kingdom… fear of it kept them in line. His removal would have meant the drekloch's release and that beast would feast upon every last gremmlobahnd, not stopping until everyone was consumed. Without the gnomes, their stolen power would not be sustainable."

"But how did you live an entire millennium in there?" asked Elorall.

"Time does not pass the same way inside," Gryeslan tried to explain. "For me, only a few minutes had passed. But this kind of box could only be opened from the outside. It is a very basic model. Most have a failsafe meant to open them from within… If one knows where to look." The gnome used his nimble fingers to make a few minor adjustments to the box, and it broke apart into six pieces. "I have disabled it so that nobody else will make that same error."

"So the gremmlobahnd fled Esfah because of the drekloch?" Varanthl asked.

"More or less."

"You mentioned a weapon," Mantieth asked. "What was it?"

With a shaky hand, Gryeslan handed the blue elf a scroll. "Visit this location. I am sure that you will find answers. That is, unless the castle has been plundered, or the drekloch has already intervened."

Hy'Drunyr seemed impatient. As interesting as Gryeslan was to his research, he had little time for absolving dying gnomish consciences. They had come with a purpose. He turned the map to face Gryeslan. "We are here to collect this piece of the Malfus Necrosis. It is of grave importance. The fate of whole societies might very well rest on securing it. If you only knew our enemies..."

Gryeslan waved off the old vagha. "I've been alive for over two millennia now, thanks to that *cube,*" he spat the last word. "Let me die in peace. What you seek is down that hallway. Orient yourself and the map will follow you." He coughed and touched the bloody expectorant. "I don't have much time left."

Hy'Drunyr's eyes twinkled. He bowed curtly. "Thank you, kind gnome." The dwarf turned to leave.

"I'll stay with him," Hy'Targ said. "I'll catch up. None should be left alone in their final moments."

The rest of the Gods'own nodded and then chased after Hy'Drunyr. At the very least, they didn't want him getting lost and stranding them in the center of an unexplored labyrinth with no map.

A few moments later, Gryeslan and Hy'Targ were left alone. The gnome stared at the darkness of the doorway. He spoke with a life-wearied kind of pain. "I'm not sure I trust the old one."

"He is my uncle," Hy'Targ said.

Gryeslan stared at him and then shrugged. "We cannot choose our family, they say. I had a brother who..." a coughing fit interrupted Gryeslan. He wiped away the blood that passed his lips. "It's not relevant anymore." He took another gnomish puzzlecube hidden among his robes and pressed it into Hy'Targ's hand.

"What's this?"

"*It's the weapon.* I'm certain that it will someday be needed, even if the gremmlobahnd are no longer a part of Esfah.

You may yet have need of it—especially since the drekloch still stalk these halls. I can smell their stink."

"Th-thank you," he insisted.

"Don't thank me yet, vagha. The drekloch can be defeated if you release the weapons from their eternal prisons where they were sealed by Nekarthis long ago."

"So Nekarthis put them there. But why?"

Gryeslan grinned. A bead of blood pooled at the corner of his lips. "He had to. To keep his contingency plan active. What I fear is not my race's mortal enemy. The drekloch has never been a mastermind. It lacks the nuance of subterfuge for that. Someone, or some *thing* could be directing it; its chief power is fear, and it victimizes all but the sturdiest of hearts. Ever has the drekloch played lackey to viler enemies who want to wield its terror." He looked Hy'Targ in the eye. "Be cautious, young vagha. I should know; being trapped within a puzzle cube is a fate worse than death."

The gnome looked down at the metallic, geometric object. "You must be prepared to pass a great test in order to use what lies within."

Hy'targ gulped. "The others, my friends, they are heading towards the piece of the godbox. Will they be safe?"

"Safe enough," Gryeslan said. "They will still require some information which I will give you." His voice trailed off as if cut short. The gnome had trouble breathing. He locked eyes with the dwarf. "I can give you what you seek… but use it for *good.* Advance life rather than your own goals… Protect the gods, for their will is good… forsake Malgrimm… "

Gryeslan's pronouncement of the cursed name of the Death god seemed to suck the air out of the room.

"I will," Hy'Targ promised. He clutched the secret cube. Gryeslan also held it tight. The old gnome nodded as if he pinned all his personal hope on the dwarf.

"Do you intend to use the godbox, then?"

"Only if it will prevent the purposes of evil," Hy'targ said. "We hope to take it and prevent its use by Death's minions."

Gryeslan bowed his head. "You will need more than just the four pieces of the Malfus Necrosis and the key to operate it. You will also need great heart."

"A key?" Hy'Targ had not heard of a key before now.

Gryeslan's eyelids slowly closed as if he were dozing off. He muttered a line from a poem in his native tongue. "Dedymon pyllus... amplo-kthroi; Obfys Netherwold Kreethaln et'thaypyx mahkin."

Hy'Targ shook him gently. "Kreethaln?"

Gryeslan half opened his eyes. "Yes. It translates to 'key' in the common tongue." He returned to a state of partial wakefulness, though pain sparked in his eyes while the rest of his body seemed to wilt. Whatever illness plagued him, it was worsening rapidly.

Gryeslan translated, "Keep shut the gate against further fiends; Hide Netherwold key and godbox machine."

"I know that piece," the dwarf insisted. He repeated the last lines of it. "'If gates closed must be cracked and flung; and found the cell of the gremmlobahnd.'"

"Then you know it will lead you to the remaining pieces, but not the *key*." He glanced down to Hy'Targ's wrist and his eyes locked on the dwarf's bracelet. "Are you a son of Gundakhor?"

"Not exactly." Hy'Targ suspected the gnome's mind was slipping.

"Oh. You carry on his legacy, then."

The dwarf shrugged, not understanding.

"I do not know where the three keys are. I only know that the piece of the Malfus Necrosis in the heart of gnome home was taken from the Netherwold. It was foolish, I know." Gryeslan sighed. "But I thought it would be safer here in our possession than left where the agents of evil could recover it."

Pain bled into the gnome's voice. "I defied the council's wishes when I recovered it and the drekloch found its way in. Because of me."

Hy'Targ squeezed the dying gnome's hand. "You cannot blame yourself. You did what you thought was right."

"That is nice to say, even if it's not true," Gryeslan said. "I will tell you what you must know. Keep it hidden and keep it safe."

———⚔︎⬢⚔︎———

Hy'Targ abandoned the hospital after Gryeslan finally fell still; he'd let the old gnome slip away peacefully first. He closed his eyes with his hands before pocketing the old gremmlobahnd's goggles.

Outside the doors he found Mantieth, crouching along the wall, waiting for him. "Gryeslan is dead," Hy'Targ told him.

The selumari nodded solemnly. "I thought it likely."

"I think whatever chased us into that trap may have been a drekloch," said the dwarf. "Greyslan practically said as much."

"I had been thinking the same thing," Mantieth said. He absentmindedly twisted the bracelet that hung on his wrist. Varanthl had given it to him as a sign of friendship, and Mantieth had given one to Elorall prior to that. She'd mistaken it for a proposal. "I stayed back in case you needed any assistance."

The vagha bobbed his head thankfully and stood near the blue elf who hadn't made any rush to climb to his feet. "Something on your mind, Mantieth?"

He grimaced, stretching his blue lips taut. He twisted the bangle again. "I'm feeling... *anxious.*" Mantieth stared away and into the darkness of the halls. "What did you see in the visions as the monster chased us?"

Hy'Targ sighed. "Burdens. The expectations of

leadership and the crown, much as I assume my father's fears might be. I saw myself chained to the lonely throne beneath the mountain, never able to leave and besieged by the problems of rule."

Mantieth swallowed. "I saw something similar. Only not so lonely. I was swallowed, drowned out, squeezed of all my color so that I was practically frehlasuhl gray. I was surrounded by family and children... Each had forks and they all took and devoured pieces of me. It felt suffocating." The elf sighed. "I am not sure who I really am... or who I was. Not in the vision, anyway."

Hy'Targ did not know how to respond. He merely stood by until Mantieth shook his head.

"We'd better find the others. They went that way," Mantieth pointed down a tunnel. "Did the gnome give up anything else?"

"The password needed to claim the next piece of the Malfus Necrosis," Hy'Targ said, "and a warning." He began trekking through the dark and made no mention of the puzzle cube in his pocket.

Hy'Targ and Mantieth entered the chamber at the end of the hall. The Gods'own's torches lit the circular chamber and revealed the domed roof of the undercroft. Bent metal sheets lined the ceiling and reflected the light from their sources, allowing them all to see well.

A series of eight pillars rose from the floor. They stretched fifteen cubits tall, almost reaching the ceiling. Thick crystal spread from each one and connected to the next, hemming in all sides of the octagon with transparent, but impenetrable walls.

The dwarf stared through the crystalline structure. "What's that inside?"

"You remember the ring on the hillock when we arrived outside the entry to Gnomehome?" Varanthl said.

Hy'Targ nodded and began walking around the enclosure.

"We think it's another device like that," the homunculus said.

Mantieth walked the opposite direction around it. Both stared at the ring inside the octagon with a sense of wonder. It stood vertically on one edge, firmly rooted to the floor and covered in runes that seemed to glow with a faint sheen. Almost like a full moon's shimmer.

The center of the ring held their attention. All was dark except for an ominous red line that seeped like lava through a crag. It moved with their gaze as they circumnavigated the prismatic cage and determined what it was.

"It's a portal," Hy'Targ stated breathlessly. "And it's open."

"Where does it lead?" Elorall asked, joining his side.

"Gryeslan told me he came here from the Netherwold… and he brought trouble on his heels. He retrieved the part of the godbox left there since the Magestorm Wars. Something followed him through. These walls must have been meant to contain the drekloch that Nekarthis kept."

Hy'Drunyr chuffed, "Well, it failed."

Nobody responded. They'd all experienced the monster's pursuit differently, and none wished to revisit those thoughts.

"But where is the durned thing?" Jr'Orhr asked. "We've already been round and round this whole room while we waited for ya."

Hy'Targ made a circuit of his own. He stopped at a flat panel where some kind of stump protruded. He pushed and pulled at it, but it felt firm. "It's too short to be a lever and too solid for a button."

The others joined him. "It looks like the door lock from these last few levels," Eucalia noticed.

Hy'Targ touched the parts of the wall around the stump and finally heard something hum. "It's that otherworldly, gnomish magic," he mumbled.

A panel opened around the stump and something inside clicked, releasing the item. Mantieth pulled on the protruding bit and blanched as he removed it.

The stump was a forearm and hand. Its skeletal form was unmistakable, and as he removed it, the skin disintegrated into tiny shards of metal, like sequins, or drops of molten lead. They bounced across the floor and scattered like beads.

All the adventurers stared into the hole where the arm had come from. A kind of lever crossed inside and the party members traded nervous glances.

"Someone needs to open the door," Hy'Drunyr broke the silence. The old dwarf looked at Varanthl. "You've got a couple extra arms, lad. Maybe you should be the first to attempt it?"

The Gods'own argued with each other over how to proceed. With the severed limb lying amongst them, they all agreed that sticking a hand inside was a poor decision.

Finally, without any warning, Varanthl frowned and plunged one arm into the hole, drawing surprised shouts from his friends.

A loud click echoed in the chamber and Varanthl yelped.

"What's wrong?" asked Elorall.

"Something's got me," he said. "Pinched me good. I can't let go and I can't pull my arm free."

"Well, hold on," Hy'Drunyr said. "Gnomes were known for their trickery at times and... "

"Hold on? What else can I do? And besides—you're the one who told me to put an arm in here."

Hy'Drunyr ignored him and began looking around the

trapped homunculus for clues. He furrowed his brow as he read something etched on the flat wall. "Something appeared here, just like on the door."

"Actually, this thing moves," Varanthl said. "I think I can turn it."

"Wait a moment," the dwarf cautioned.

Varanthl suddenly screamed and reeled backwards.

A nasty *shlitch* sound pierced the air at the same time, severing Varanthl's arm with surprising speed. He landed on his back, blood spilling from the wound and drenching the ground.

Varanthl howled in shock and in pain.

His friends knelt by his side immediately. Mantieth yanked a belt free and tied off the bloody stump, applying pressure to the tourniquet.

Hy'Drunyr turned and stared at him curiously. "I said to *hold on.*"

Hy'Targ scowled at his uncle and hurried to the wall. "Where is this writing?"

They searched for it together, but it had disappeared. Hy'Targ tapped around the area where Varanthl's fleshy stump hung from the wall, trickling blood in thick rivulets. The panel seemed to come alive again, and the wall released the arm.

Hy'Targ retrieved the severed limb and returned it to Varanthl while his uncle looked on curiously. He held it up to his friend's wound while Mantieth released his hold on the belt.

Varanthl growled, clearly in great pain, but the flesh began to slowly stitch itself back together across the cut line. After a few minutes, he could flex his fingers again.

"How is that even possible?" Hy'Drunyr asked. "Magic can restore the spark of life and promote healing… but restoring severed limbs? I have never seen that, not in all my days."

"Ever since what happened with the first Kreethaln—with Life-Bringer—I've healed really fast," the homunculus said.

Hy'Targ tapped his friend. "I hate to ask this of you, but we need to try this again."

Varanthl sighed through his nose and remembered the pain, but he still nodded. "Let's just get it right this time."

Hy'Targ nodded.

The homunculus reached in and grabbed the handle. He grimaced as the contraption pinched his arm into place.

"Here it is," Hy'Targ said, examining the etched words. "Hold in place." He retrieved the gnomish lexicon from his backpack and began to consult it with his uncle looking over his shoulder.

"It is a riddle," they agreed, looking at a bank of numbers below a text string.

"It wants to know when Arrival Day was?" Hy'Drunyr asked. "Did Gryeslan tell you when he deposited the item?"

"I don't think that's what it means," Hy'Targ said. "Wasn't Arrival Day a gnomish celebration?"

His uncle cocked his head. "Yes, it was the day the gnomes suddenly arrived at Esfah." He began flicking the numbers etched in the wall and they disappeared one by one until only a few remained. "The first day of the fourth month," he said.

Hy'Targ looked to his friend and nodded.

CHAPTER TWENTY

Squeezing the handle in his grip, Varanthl grit his teeth and turned the lever again. It creaked with an old, metallic sound until it clicked and released. He pulled a long tube from the wall and revealed another piece of the godbox to match the other two they'd already claimed.

Varanthl scooped it out and released the tray. It retracted back into the wall and the homunculus rubbed the sore spot on his forearm as it slowly disappeared into a thin, red line. "Let's not do that again."

Hy'Targ took the piece of the Malfus Necrosis and examined it. "This was it. This is what we came for.

An ominous rumble sounded in the deep, vibrating the floor, and it seemed, the darkness.

"Then let's get out of here unless there is further reason to stay?" asked Eucalia.

"I'm with her," said Elorall.

They huddled together and consulted Hy'Drunyr's maps. They could reach a stairwell leading vertically without too great of travel.

The Gods'own and Hy'Drunyr plunged into the tunnels. Having already set off one trap, they moved slowly to avoid further surprises. They eventually arrived without incident.

A massive stairwell opened on a circular, vertical shaft that terminated in alternating, flat landings as the broad steps rotated through the well.

Varanthl looked over the edge and peered into the black. "How far down do you suppose it goes?"

Hy'Drunyr tossed a stone into the depths, but they could not hear it land. The old dwarf looked at the humanoid. "Shall we delve the dark and explore a little?"

Mantieth leaned between them. "You guys can come

back and explore another day. Our mission is to claim and protect the godbox so that Melkior's cultists cannot claim it. Also, I've left a great sum of gold above ground with the pack animals. Let's not delay and risk its fate to bandits."

Hy'Drunyr shrugged. "As you wish."

They ascended the vertical shaft in a cautious manner, fearful of both the traps and the drekloch who they suspected still prowled. The adventurers bypassed the second level and followed the path to the top-most level, where they found the door. They drew the open sign to activate it and exited on the familiar upper level of Gnomehome that had been the safest. Still, they moved with relative speed and silence until they returned to the original dome where they'd first accessed the labyrinth. They ascended through the secret door that returned them to the surface and where they'd left their mounts.

Evening was already drawing to a close, and the sky had darkened to deep reds and oranges. The illumination felt blindingly bright after so much time spent below the surface.

Acacia snorted a greeting. He'd kept the other mounts herded relatively close and Eucalia yipped with concern. "There's blood all over his horn."

The others followed her and rushed to the unicorn. Thick, muddy yellow blood had congealed in splatters across Acacia's face. There was more gore strewn across the horses and matted into the fur of the mammoths, making heavy clumps.

"What happened here?" Hy'Targ wondered incredulously, while his uncle examined the ripped canopy upholstery that had previously covered the wagon.

"We'll likely never know the exact details," Mantieth said, "but it was definitely goblins." Nearby, they found a trampled patch of dirt with torn clods. Yellow trog blood mixed with the mud, while bodies of dead wolves and war dogs lay still nearby. Severed limbs, torsos, and heads of goblins lay intermixed among the carnage, and stone axes lay abandoned in the grass.

Eucalia stroked Acacia's neck. "It's a good thing we left you here to mind after things."

Elorall rubbed the viscous blood between her fingertips. "They must have attacked last night while we were still wandering the darkness. The trog invasions have certainly gotten worse. And it's no longer just confined to the Moorlech. All of Charnock seems overrun."

Varanthl retrieved camp supplies and set them up for the evening. Especially with the presence of goblins, they did not want to risk traveling in the dark.

Mantieth stopped him from building a fire or building camp. He shook his head with a shudder. The memory of the drekloch still turned through his mind and stomach. "We can ride for at least an hour before we need to make camp." He watched as Hy'Drunyr and Jr'Orhr pushed the stone back over the secret entrance, but it did little to ease his nerves. "I suggest we get as much distance between us and this place as possible."

Yarrick could hear the faint rattle of chains as his fellow prisoners shifted in the blackness. He knew that he was not alone, but he assumed that the others were bound as he had been. A thick rope looped through his teeth, gagging him to silence.

The last thing he remembered was being dragged into the room and put in shackles.

A splatter of cold wetness smacked the back of his head when he leaned too far forward. The steady drip from overhead had proved useful the last couple days when he'd used it to saturate the rope between his jaws and suck the moisture, to keep from dying of dehydration.

He blinked when a sliver of light split in a vertical shaft. *No, not quite silver... More like gold.* Yarrick didn't know how long he'd been here, but it had been several days, and the pangs in the pit of his gut reminded him that it had been a long while since he'd last had a meal.

Whoever his captors were, they often moved their prisoners. Yarrick hoped they were transporting him again. At least they had fed him during each journey prior to... wherever he found himself, now.

The eldarim blinked against the harsh light. Beyond the door, the hall connecting to the stone chamber must have had a window and dusk was drawing in, coloring the light with oranges and reds. The daylight was fading; it was only intensely brilliant by comparison.

He glanced sidelong through the room and spotted half a dozen other eldarim. They also squinted against the illumination, and drips of water fell in front of each of them as well. The prison ran efficiently. Far more so than Yarrick assumed the Dohanese were capable of operating. His stomach turned. Whatever motivation his captors had to abduct him, it was more than lingering racial tensions from old wars.

By their look, the other eldarim had been here much longer than Yarrick. Each one's forehead had been marked with a dweomernull, an anti-magic sigil that prevented its wearer from accessing the source of Esfah's intrinsic arcana.

A greater look of understanding painted their faces, however, when a line of folk entered the room. They wore hooded robes and carried fine silver trays. They looked exactly as Yarrick assumed a cultist would. He'd heard about clusters of acolytes who pledged fealty to Death.

Yarrick flattened his back against the wall as the smell of food wafted over to him. The cultists outnumbered the captives by one. The robed leader at the center of the room oversaw operations. At his or her direction, the acolytes placed a tray of food before each of them and then untied the bonds behind their heads.

The eldarim greedily ate with their fingers. Their captors

had not provided them with cutlery. Yarrick tried to get the attention of the person adjacent him, but the nameless eldarim shushed him and looked fearfully at the cultist overseer, as if afraid of some unknown repercussion.

As they finished their meal, another cultist entered the room. Her hood was down around her neck and Yarrick could smell her perfume. Her eyes twinkled with hope and enthusiasm. He might have considered her beautiful were it not for the profane tattoos that displayed her loyalty to the Death God, Malgrimm.

The beautiful woman looked at each in turn and smiled as if taking measurement of them. Her smile revealed broken teeth blackened her gums.

"That one," she pointed a finger to the person who had been seated next to Yarrick. The other cultists mobbed him so that he could not resist, and then dragged him away. He howled.

A few lower-ranked cultists entered the room to clear away trays, close shackles, and re-tie their prisoners' gags. And then they closed the door behind them, plunging their captive eldarim back into darkness.

Little happened on the trek through the heart of Charnock. Most of the land ahead of the Gods'own went through flatland. Villages and the occasional small city dotted the region. There were enough that the travelers did not worry about provisions and were able to spend every third night or so in the comfort of commercial lodging.

A direct route from Irontooth to the Gnomehome gate would take them directly through the city of Bralanthyr. There, they planned to head east through a mountain pass and take dwarven roads to return to Hy'Mandr's castle.

Bralanthyr's surrounding lands were as varied as any region, but the fertile area had the knack to turn each one to profit. Their swamps grew tart fenberries for both eating and wine making. Their plains bloomed with broomcorn and other crops, while pollinators produced an abundance of honey that they traded to Irontooth and Buhlruch for mead production. With eldarim guidance long ago, they'd practiced replanting of forests, and which they harvested on a schedule. They milled so that their resources did not deplete.

Because of its industrious wealth, Bralanthyr had a long and bloody history of wars as many kingdoms vied for its control. Since the dawn of the second age, though, large-scale conflicts had practically ceased. It became a wiser option to trade and negotiate with Bralanthyr than to disrupt the market of goods which flowed through it.

Hy'Targ had read much of the details on the war for Bralanthyr and gave his companions a days' long analysis of it, until they'd tired and fallen into a relative silence. The endless droll of feet slogging along the roads became an apathetic cadence in the background of their lives.

The trip would take thirty-five days to reach the main city of Bralanthyr and that again to reach Irontooth.

They grew eager for a return to civilization after their travels across Charnock.

With midday approaching, Jr'Orhr's gut rumbled, though it was still nearly two hours prior to their scheduled break for lunch. Riding abreast of Hy'Targ, he'd listed off all the things he planned to eat before the moment they arrived in Bralanthyr, which was known for terrific restaurants. "Mutton fritters. Roast pork dumplings. Stewed pumpkin chowder with smoked hen and ground mustard seed..."

Mantieth clambered up the backside of Hy'Targ's mammoth, leaping silently from the back of his horse to the next mount over with skill unheard of in vaghan circles. "Don't mind me," he commented when Jr'Orhr paused. "I don't intend to interrupt."

The selumari used the added elevation and stared off

into the distance.

"What is it?" asked Hy'Targ.

"The better question is what food will be left over for the rest of us after Jr'Orhr devours the city?" Mantieth jested.

The dwarf looked back to where Elorall and Eucalia rode abreast each other and chatted. "I think the more interesting question is to what is happening between you and the young lady... or what *isn't* happening?"

Mantieth raised an eyebrow.

"Seems like you've been avoiding the future princess as of late. Almost since we left Dohan, in fact. Maybe she hasn't noticed yet, but I've certainly got a sense for it... and she'll catch on if you don't fix it." Jr'Orhr looked back one more time and nodded. "I'd say sooner rather than later."

The elf ignored him and scanned the horizon. "And why are you so eager to eat?"

"Just sick of the road and gnawing on preserved rations, I suppose."

Mantieth shook his head and drew in a sharp breath. He gave the other two a serious look. "You don't smell it? It's faint, but I noticed it. The smell of smoke on the wind."

The vagha screwed up their faces and looked to the horizon.

"The smells of smoke are making you hungry for a hearth and a meal without even knowing why." Mantieth pointed ahead. "Smoke. You might not be able to see it yet, but it will be evident within the next day or so."

"What do you mean?" Hy'Targ asked.

Mantieth frowned. "Bralanthyr is burning. I've not seen the city for over a decade, so I cannot guess to the size of the fire, but it is certainly in flames."

"And something else," Jr'Orhr noted. "Did you catch that flash of light?" He pointed due north.

Mantieth turned and looked. "I see it. Spyglass?"

"I think so. Seen enough of 'em to recognize it. Can you tell who is watching the road?"

The elf twisted his mouth. "They are a long way off, but it looks like trogs. That would remain consistent with what we've experienced since before we even left Irontooth for Xlinea."

"Is there danger?" Hy'Targ asked.

"Not for more than a day," Mantieth said. "I'd guess they are mere scouts reporting back to a larger battle group. It may be half a tenday before they could even gather reinforcements and give chase. But we ought to keep our guard up anyway, just in case."

Hy'Targ crooked his jaw and raked out his beard with his sturdy fingers. "The larger goblin battle-group worries me far more than the ones killing your father's scouts. How likely do you think it is that they are behind the fires ahead of us?"

His two peers traded nervous glances.

"Probably high," admitted Jr'Orhr.

Hy'Targ tightened his lips and continued driving his mammoth onward.

An hour later they stopped to rest for lunch. Varanthl built a quick fire and brought a pot to boil over the flames. He'd purchased a stock of jarred meats and broths in the last village, which helped improve their speed. It reduced the time it took for meals.

The four-armed man finished assembling the meal as the others discussed the potential dangers ahead. Elorall brought Mantieth the first bowl from the pot. "I brought you this, Mantieth."

"No, thank you," he mumbled. "I can get my own." The elf glanced sidelong at Jr'Orhr and caught the old vagha's grin. He ignored him and then retrieved his lunch.

Mantieth returned and took his seat with the group listening to Hy'Drunyr speak.

"... trogs are everywhere. I'm telling you, let me cut

across by myself. I can take the pieces of the godbox back to Irontooth for you, and keep safe Niamarlee's coin, as well."

Mantieth narrowed his gaze. He was still unsure what to think of his friend's uncle. He turned to gauge Hy'Targ's reaction. The dwarf also looked skeptical.

"I'm sure that my reputation must remain suspect. Perhaps I haven't done enough yet to demonstrate that I am not the dwarf that your father has long said I am." Hy'Drunyr flashed a disappointed look at his companions. Some appeared like they were swayed by his words, but Jr'Orhr would not be. Never Jr'Orhr.

"Regardless, let me return alone, then, to Irontooth. You might insist on riding through the flames of war, but I am not a warrior," Hy'Drunyr requested.

"Wait," Hy'Targ said. "Perhaps there is some wisdom to that. We should consider that the trogs might have been manipulated by Melkior, or by Death on his behalf."

"Are you really prepared to place this much trust in him?" Jr'Orhr cautioned. "Your father would not be pleased."

Hy'Targ shrugged. "We can put it on the list with my other flaws, but the fact that I did not stay in Ne'Vistar's tower two years ago when the option presented itself ought to earn me a lot of grace." He turned to his uncle. "We should split up the pair of Malfus Necrosis pieces. Get it into the safe as soon as possible and tell no one except my father, if you must. Hopefully it will prevent even an overwhelming force from collecting them."

A collection of scowls circulated the ring of faces as they ate. With a lack of good options, this felt the safest, but Varanthl stared into his stew with certain disdain."

The selumari prince sighed through his nose. "And take my half of the gold as well; it must get back to Niamarlee." He did not wish to endorse the plan, but he also saw a certain logic to it.

"You have an opinion on the plan?" Elorall asked Varanthl.

The four-armed homunculus looked up and dropped his spoon. "Not really. I just think that this stew needs salt. Badly."

A human woman scooped up her child when she saw the smoke rising in ominous wisps above the edge of Bralanthyr. They had been traveling east from a stint in the fenberry marshes, where she worked for a tenday at a time with half of that off to rest between shifts. Her family had been berry collectors going back three generations.

"Come on, Baba!" she hugged her child tightly. "We can't go back to the marshes… We must flee. Maybe we'll even go as far as Buhlruch. The dwarves can defend us."

The child squirmed and fussed. She did not understand what her mother saw: Bralanthyr was under attack. They could not return.

Hastily, the woman passed a bald, elderly human who angled his path towards the chaos in the distance. "You should not go that way, mister," she said. "Unless the army arrives, you'll only find death in the city."

"Kaine," said the old man. White locks fell around his shoulders and mirrored the two long streams of silver hair that began on his lips and fell to his chest.

"Excuse me?"

"Kaine. It is my name. And I will be quite safe. These fiends cannot harm me, though you are certainly wise to run away."

The berry collector's eyes brightened when she heard the horns from an army's approach. "Perhaps all is not lost. "

Kaine shook his head. "Your first instinct was right. Hide your child, at least until this battle is won."

She watched the old man continue towards the battle

that brewed at Bralanthyr's edges. "But they'll kill you! There are so many trogs. I've seen them. Come with us."

He shook his head. "No, they won't. It is not my war and I do not plan to fight in it." He stared in the distance. A massive trog army looked like a black line, festering on the horizon where the air was marred by clouds of soot. The immense horde stood far in the distance, waiting between Kaine and the city. "Something *else* draws me to it." Kaine resumed his steady gait. "It's not something goblins can interfere with… and not something they can stop."

The woman watched him go.

CHAPTER TWENTY-ONE

The Gods'own plunged onward towards the fight they knew lay ahead. Smoke rolled steadily towards them like a morning haze rising off a lake, and the odor of wildfire hung heavily in the air.

In the distance, Hy'Drunyr and his wagon were a barely visible dot on the horizon. He'd long since peeled off and made for the eastern pass that would bring him back to Irontooth.

Hy'Targ slowed his mammoth before it could trample the cluster of poorly constructed tents made of winter quilts, bed sheets, and whatever bulk cloth their owners could assemble in a hurry. Somber faces of human citizens, and a sparse few other races, emerged.

They moved more slowly to avoid injuring those displaced by war. With nowhere to turn, Bralanthyr's refugees camped at the furthest reaches of the battlefield.

Elorall spurred her horse towards Hy'Targ, who rode in the lead. "What can we do to help these people?"

The dwarf bit his lower lip and shook his head. "I'm afraid we can do nothing."

"Except help them win back their home?" Mantieth called.

Hy'Targ shook his head. "We are just passing through. We will collect a report so we can try to summon aid at Irontooth or Niamarlee."

"The army, and all these people, could be massacred by that time," Jr'Orhr said flatly. "Weren't our people once in a similar state before we claimed Irontooth for a refuge?"

Hy'Targ bobbed his head and then halted his mount. Balancing on the beast, he stood and hollered at those who waited despairingly within the tent city. "Head east through the mountain passes! Perhaps some folk in the towns nearby will provide enough support for you to travel to Irontooth. The vagha will protect you until Bralanthyr's fate is determined."

Grubby, soot-lined faces looked up at him. A glimmer of hope dared to shine in their eyes.

"Tell the gatekeepers that Prince Hy'Targ promised asylum and they will let you pass," he added.

The dwarf took his seat and resumed their trek. A corona glowed around the silhouette of the city that had begun to loom. Before they'd reached the edge of it, the tent city had already broken down and begun to move.

"I don't like the looks of this," Jr'Orhr noted.

Hy'Targ cast a sidelong glance at him.

"The trogs have scouts south and west of Bralanthyr," he explained. "*And* they have an army more than adequate to siege the city. This goes well beyond their normal pattern of destroy, devour, and depart." Jr'Orhr drummed his fingers on his chin. "This is more methodical."

"A goblin with a plan?" Hy'Targ guessed.

"It has been our working theory for some time, has it not? I think this proves it."

Together, the Gods'own entered the city limits. Troops stationed in the rear motioned them past and pointed the way to the command center. Bralanthyr was not a walled city, not anymore. In the past it had once boasted a stone exterior barrier, but the city had outgrown it since their emphasis on trade caused a boom. They'd expanded well past their old borders.

Many of the walls had been torn down to make way for infrastructure improvements and ease local travel. Those remaining walls were inside the central area of the city now. The Gods'own passed them by and found the bulk of the army kept within them. They used the old boundary for additional protection and a way to increase their security.

Pressing ahead, they passed quiet buildings and occasional bodies. Conscripted soldiers clutched old weapons and wore whatever ill-fitting armor they could find.

An odd, gray silence cast a pall over the city. Something they could not quite put their finger on until Eucalia mentioned it.

"Not even the birds are chirping... In fact, I haven't seen one since we crossed the plains."

They traveled deeper into the starkly muted city and noted faces peeking out from windows and doorways. Many of the civilians had not been able to leave for lack of resources or out of sheer stubbornness.

Finally, Hy'Targ noted, "We must be getting close." He bobbed his head towards a company of mixed vagha and selumari who mingled with a cluster of female amazons. "Their gear is in better condition here."

They didn't travel much further before they found what they assumed was the command center for the battle. Hy'Targ gave their names to a female lieutenant who pointed them to a large, pillared building. A stable hand promptly hurried over to refresh and care for the travelers' mounts.

"It feels like a human library," Hy'Targ mentioned to his companions as they ascended the exterior stairs.

"You and your libraries," Mantieth mumbled.

They passed the doors and found a stacked block of books in the center of the open building. "I told you," Hy'Targ said. He grabbed an amazon officer and asked her, "Why are all the books off the shelves?"

She flashed a confused look at first and then realized they were newcomers to the battle. "Trogs firebombed the north side of the building to drive out many when the battle started a tenday ago. This building is stone, but its contents are not. We moved the books to the center where they won't catch fire quite so easily."

Mantieth stepped forward, eager for information. "I see the uniforms of soldiers from Niamarlee and Irontooth. Are they part of the trog hunters that both kingdoms commissioned?"

Understanding spread across her face. "You are Prince Mantieth." She looked to the dwarves, finally settling on the younger one's face. "And Prince Hy'Targ... You are the Gods'own?"

"Yes. At your service," Elorall interjected. "We are just passing through, but we hoped to bring word to Irontooth and Niamarlee. Perhaps we can convince them to bring a greater force to bear."

"It would take all due speed to reach us in time," the amazon spoke with a hint of arrogance. Amazons were known across Esfah for their speed across land.

"We have a few coral airships," Mantieth said. Few could rival the speed of the wind.

The amazon nodded. "Yes. Of course. We would welcome whatever help we can get. But to answer your initial question, yes, many of the vagha and selumari are from the army you speak. We might have lost the city already were it not for them." She paused thoughtfully. "There is someone here who guessed that your party might pass through. He would very much like to speak with the Gods'own."

Ratargul the Smotherer emerged from the house he'd claimed for himself on the north side of a Bralanthyr estate. The other homes nearby had all been burned out, leaving only charred husks behind.

He heard his harpy lookouts squawking terribly about some new incoming threat. Their cry had been enough to pull him away from feasting upon the home's previous owner, a wealthy selumari who proved severely unprepared for invasion.

"What is the meaning of… " Ratargul looked up where the harpy pointed. A trio of dark shapes circled high overhead and grew in size as they descended.

"Eagles? Have the coral elves come to parley? We will

take and eat them as soon as they land."

The harpy shook her head. "No, Lord Smotherer. Winged Drakufreet. Agamids with riders."

The harpy cocked her head at the curious turn. Never had the Moorlech formed any formal alliance in the past with dragonkin or their eldarim masters.

Ratargul nodded at their approach; he had half expected their arrival. The Moorlech was independent, but the shambling mound had long ago made promises to many of Death's followers. It did not surprise him that some would come to call.

The shambler shooed the harpy away, hoping for more privacy than was likely. A crowd of onlookers gathered in a broad circle to watch as the three obsidian drakufreet touched down upon Bralanthyr soil. Their riders slid down the scaly mounts and adjusted their hoods against the midday sun.

Ratargul could not see all their faces behind the hood, only their broad noses and strong jaws. It was enough to identify them as eldarim acolytes. He glanced sidelong and saw the harpy lookout scampering away. *No doubt the bitch is going to find that traitorous Tsut and tattle. The runt has been deeper with the harem than any realize. His usefulness is almost at an end.*

The trio of black clad riders approached Ratargul. "Show us the proof, shambler," one demanded.

"The proof? I am Ratargul the Smotherer!"

"Any shambling mound could make that same claim. Your kind all look the same to us, and we know what you are… We know the one who made you," a dark eldarim hissed. "Show us the mark you made in covenant with us or you die here and now."

Ratargul ignored the insult made against his pride and peeled aside a patch of slimy vines and moss to reveal a patch of ochre skin much like a trog's. A raised welt made the mark of Nekarthis where the sigil had been branded. "I am Ratargul the Smotherer who swore allegiance to the Dark Forest." He looked at the gathering goblin faces. "Let us go inside to discuss business."

The eldarim nodded. They whistled and their mounts leapt into the sky, where they climbed into the clouds and then circled overhead.

Ratargul escorted his guests into the house.

Before the Gods'own could get settled, Taryl entered the building. The eldarim dragonlord reached in for a hug and embraced Hy'targ. "You are a sight for sore eyes," he exclaimed. "As you can see, princes, we found your trogs."

"I think the problem is larger than Niamarlee ever expected," Mantieth said, "or Irontooth, for that matter."

Taryl nodded. "How they grew from a minor nuisance plaguing the road to... *this,* and right under our noses, confounds me."

Hy'targ grimaced. "Unless it was done on purpose."

Taryl nodded knowingly. The Gods'own knew he shared the opinion that either some goblin savant or another intelligent force guided the trogs' strategy. But now, the goblins threatened to destabilize the economy of nearly half the continent by taking down Bralanthyr. There was no way the affected kingdoms wouldn't take notice.

The eldarim quietly took stock of who had arrived in the city. He frowned. "So my nephew is still not among you? I knew it was foolish, but I had hoped for a turn-about."

Elorall said, "He did not show up in Kragryn. We left him several messages... " she trailed off, understanding that his failure to connect with either the Gods'own or his uncle meant some ill fate must have found him.

Taryl's face turned ashen; he'd had much time to think on the topic since first learning of his nephew's disappearance. "He was last with you in Dohan?"

Mantieth's face turned to concern as well. He hadn't yet made the same connections as Elorall. "He stayed behind when we went on a short trip across the Talvat for a quick trek near Moothlen... Nothing came of it and the brief foray took only a few days. Yarrick had hoped to connect with his father while we were away from Giyrnach."

"I did learn my brother, Qarl, might have been there." The eldarim ground his teeth. "You delivered my letter to him before you left, correct?"

"Yes," said Elorall, "but he did not share its contents with us."

Taryl exhaled through his nose. "Time was so short at our last crossing that we did not have a chance to discuss it. I'd still hoped Yarrick might be in transit... " he trailed off. Finally, he said, "In my letter I told him not to trust his father."

A somber moment passed between them. Hy'targ interrupted it. "Tell us how the battle goes here. We cannot stay long. We'd hoped to take stock of the situation so we knew best how to travel safely home. We can pledge to report back to Irontooth and Niamarlee. Hopefully, that means we can provide reinforcements."

"Good. You may have noticed that there are no birds anywhere in this gods-cursed city. We've been unable to send any messages by carrier bird to any of our allies. Something's got every airborne creature in the region terrified. All the birds fled the city a day before the trogs attacked."

"We'll get a message delivered as soon as possible," Hy'Targ promised.

Taryl bobbed his head as if he'd actually hoped they would stay and lend support. "Your mission to Kragryn was successful then?"

Hy'targ nodded.

"There should be enough vagha skilled with magic that we can summon a Path spell and let Eldurim guide you home without goblin intervention," Taryl said. He shrugged. "Maybe we can't get you all home at once, but we ought to be able to send you all to Irontooth over a day or two." He waved to an aide, sent him to gather the dwarven wizards, and any followers of Eldurim who had apprenticed in mystic disciplines.

"Thank you for the help, my friend," Hy'targ said. "And with any luck, we're both wrong and Yarrick is in Irontooth, waiting for us to return."

Taryl nodded. "In the meanwhile, I will show you the damage." His voice grew severe, "Your father will want to send help straight away. Yours, too, Mantieth." He looked at Hy'targ again. "Irontooth has a storage supply for now, but more than half the kingdom's food comes from trade of ore with Bralanthyr. No Bralanthyr can only mean…"

"Very hungry dwarves," Hy'targ finished for him.

Kaine grinned as he approached Bralanthyr. He grabbed the talisman around his neck and removed it. To the uneducated eye it was little more than a rock engraved with a decorative symbol and bound to a lanyard.

None of the goblins had noticed him yet. The human sage wandered into the goblin camp. Trogs who spotted him turned and snarled. They sprinted towards him, reaching for their weapons.

Holding a stone high so his enemies could see it, the goblins stopped in their tracks. Try as they might, they could not draw axe or sword.

They wrenched at their weapons and cursed their arms and hands that failed them. By the time they pulled a weapon free, the goblins quite forgot why they had drawn it in the first place. More than one goblin looked across suspiciously at his neighbor, who suddenly brandished a weapon, and small skirmishes broke out in their ranks.

Some who gave up trying to attack the man snarled at

his back side, watching him walk with the calm demeanor of an apex predator, strolling through a shepherd's flock. They tried not to look at the stone he held aloft, but it drew their eyes.

Try as they wanted, the goblins could not attack Kaine. Whatever his strange magic was, it insulated him well, and the human left a trail of confusion in his wake.

Tsut sucked in a breath of air and headed for the door of Ratargul's base of operations. Internally, he wondered if he was making a foolish choice. The goblin had not gotten this far, engineering the unprecedented rise of the Moorlech trogs, by making reactionary or emotional decisions.

But this time, fools threatened to destabilize everything he had worked for, and his hackles got the better of Tsut. He barged through the door and found the shambling mound accompanied by three eldarim in black cloaks. Their hoods were pulled down to reveal pale skin and silvery hair that fell in locks around their shoulders. Scarred marks identified them as devotees to the Black Forest and the strongest of the Death cults.

"What is the meaning of this?" Ratargul growled.

"I should ask you the same thing," Tsut accused. "You demanded to lead and murdered Heshgillick for control so that you could have a war on your personal time-line—*before* we were ready..."

"And we are winning that war, you tiny gurk. Don't make me smash you to paste!" Ratargul loomed large. "And your harpy spy, too."

Tsut almost laughed at Ratargul's posturing. The three intruders watched them curiously. "Of course I have my own spies, you oaf... I am the heart of the Moorlech! You may have strength enough to claim a crown, but without the heart of the trogs, they'll have no will to fight."

The Smotherer began to melt into a liquid-like form, hurling threats of murder. "I should kill you for your insolent…"

"If you kill me, more than half your army will simply walk away. Immediately. I've already left instructions with my loyal minions, should I not return."

Ratargul's form solidified and Tsut continued. "I demand to know what's going on, or my decision will be the same and the army breaks here and now, despite the fact that we're winning your war against Bralanthyr. You need me, and you need me alive."

One of the eldarim stepped forward. He seemed to seethe darkness.

"I will tell the Heart what it needs so that it does not fail," he hissed. "For if the Moorlech falters, the Black Forest will eradicate every crawling thing that draws breath within that swamp. They will raise up their charred remains as an undead army of loyal minions who will be more adept to serve."

The creature fixed Tsut with a hard stare that raised the hair on the goblin's flesh.

"You are part of a larger plan. Our cult's resources in Undrakull are again under the power of the Nekarthans now that the Melkite influence has waned since the drider's death," he continued.

"Nekarthans and Melkites?" Tsut asked. He dared not interrupt, but knowledge was power, and he had to know what dangers were at play.

"Two branches of the Black Forest. Different arms often locked in cold war—we want the same thing for our black god, but our end paths are quite different… and you have your part to play in it. Your siege on Bralanthyr will raise the interests of those with trade alliances in the city. Did you not notice the arrival of the Gods'own, the so-called heroes of Charnock?"

Tsut nodded. "Yes, but our scouts determined that they

were simply passing through..."

"And we want that," the eldarim said. "They are merely a handful of adventurers and could not shift the tide of war on their own. But their allies in Irontooth and Niamarlee could have a significant impact."

"Y-you want them to send *help?*"

The cultist nodded firmly. "Especially the selumari forces. The fastest way for them to render aid is to send their coral airships. Once they've been drawn off, the Black Forest strikes like a stranglevine in the darkness. Our agents in Undrakull have sued for peace on the coast ever since Sshkkryyahr died, lulling them into a greater sense of security."

"The dwarves..."

"Forget the vagha, they will be dealt with later. Niamarlee is the true target. Our allies will take the elven city... and the standing stones nearest it will allow our sorcerers to cast the kinds of magic we require to easily topple the dwarves and take whatever relics are in their possession. Then, we can establish our own leaders as we see fit. The goblins can keep whatever spoils they earn at Bralanthyr."

Tsut's hackles raised at the thought that they'd been manipulated this whole time. "We trogs are some mere distraction? This is the greatest army of goblins to have been raised in Charnock during the second age!"

Before Tsut could get too excited, the eldarim stepped uncomfortably close. His peers flanked precariously close as well, amplifying the evil aura that seemed to roll off him. "Are you not an agent of the Death God, our lord Malgrimm?" The dark eldarim towered over Tsut, who gulped.

The trog had never been scared of the mighty Heshgillick. Ratargul did not particularly frighten him and had proved easily predictable. But these agents of the Nekarthis cult?

Tsut swallowed hard. "I serve the dark one, as does all the Moorlech."

The trio of eldarim stepped back slightly to allow some breathing space. Their point had been taken. *The Moorlech served the Dark One and broke their oaths only at grave peril.*

"Good," Ratargul roared to save face before the cultists. "Then get out there and *serve*."

"By doing what?" the bewildered Tsut asked for direction, happy for any way out of the command center.

"I don't care," Ratargul snapped, as eager for Tsut to leave as the goblin was to go. "Go burn a new section of city or something."

Tsut hung his head and then scampered away.

The eldarim cultists traded looks with each other. One spoke, "I will observe the efforts and make sure the goblins continue to find success… but not too much of it that the selumari will give up on their ally."

CHAPTER TWENTY-TWO

"Straight ahead, sir!" a vagha soldier yelled, tightening his grip on his axe while also cinching his armor tighter. He pointed with his weapon, but Taryl and the Gods'own could hear the crashing of ceramic pots and the *whoosh* of flames as the trogs hurled caissons across the Broadstreet kill-zone. Their fragile pots smashed and spilled firebrands that spread flames to any opportune source.

Taryl crept towards the edge of the buildings and nodded to the wide lane ahead. "Broadstreet is the city's central traffic corridor: The busiest merchant district that separates the two halves of the city. It is made from a natural division, where we could dig in and hold the line. Trogs control the northwest; we have the southeast." He ducked back as goblin pelters hurled bullet-sized stones at him from their slings. The missiles cracked loudly as they lodged in the stucco shell the eldarim used as cover.

Bodies littered Broadstreet. Unsuspecting vendors, travelers, and workers lay sprawled in unflattering repose with bullet wounds torn through cloth and flesh. Ghastly axe wounds rent open to the sky. Random arrows with swampy black fletchings protruded from corpses like tiny flags that marked the edge of the goblins' territory.

"They caught Bralanthyr off guard," Taryl explained. "The city's army tried to respond swiftly and decisively, but they had no idea how big the Moorlech's army was. None of us did, until it mobilized. They knocked out more than half of Bralanthyr's amazons in the first encounter."

Hy'Targ peeked around the corner. Broadstreet lived up to its name. It was more than fifty cubits across, triple the size of a standard road in most cities.

Goblins cheered as buildings ignited.

Taryl grinned and shook his head. "I wonder at their tactics," he growled. "Perhaps whatever genius had earned them half the city of Bralanthyr has suddenly quit on them. They'd used the cover of the buildings to their advantage up until now. Burning Broadstreet acts against their interests, unless that interest is pure chaos."

The eldarim tapped the adventurers on the shoulder and then led them away to help the crews fight the fires. From nearby wells, lines of bucketeers passed water towards the buildings even as the blaze intensified.

Many locations around the city had large cisterns that collected rainwater, runoff, refuse, and the like. It wasn't clean, but it could douse flames all the same.

A firefighter howled back, "We need more water—lots of it!" She wiped soot and sweat from her face. Hy'Targ could see where the blaze had melted hair at her brows and eyelids.

"Right away, Captain Halle," someone shouted. The water brigade grew busier. More buckets passed and more quickly, though with less water in each. They'd reached their terminal limit.

Elorall rushed forward. "I am a spell caster," she yelled over the din. "I can summon the waters of Aguarehl."

Halle motioned her forward and pointed to the nearest building, where the worst of the fires had taken root. The coral elf extended her hands and blasted the conflagration with a torrent of rain. Eucalia joined by her side and intensified it.

Near the base of the building, flames lit brighter and with a blue tint. They intensified and pushed back, minimizing the spell casters' efforts.

"It's almost like they are pumping sewer gas through the subterranean vents to feed the blaze," Halle growled.

Grunting through her efforts, Elorall asked, "Are there no other selumari magicians in the army?"

Halle turned from her and flashed a sign to a corps of

dwarves, behind her before turning back to the enchanter. "We've barely got any in the company. The rumor is that King Leidergelth kept most of them close to Niamarlee because of some foreign, undead threat. I've only seen one other coral elf magician with Taryl's crew—but I don't see her here." She waved the spell casters off so they could conserve their energy. "This is no good. We've come too late to combat the fire with magic."

The dwarves from Halle's company charged through the streets on mammoths and draught horses. They dragged chains and ropes that yanked free support beams on the structures, one row behind the blaze. Buildings collapsed to rubble, creating a manageable barrier behind the fire line.

Taryl whistled to Elorall and Eucalia. They were moving behind the break to let the fire burn itself out as the goblins increased their hold on the city.

None were happy for the willful demolition, but it proved necessary. "At least it widens the gap," Hy'Targ mumbled at the rubble zone. "It'll be easier to see the trogs coming."

Taryl nodded measuredly. "And come they will."

Eucalia walked with uneasy steps, trying to keep up with the Gods'own while also extending her senses. Something did not feel right in the city... Many things were wrong, in fact.

Firstly, a hollow spot of black grew in her sixth sense, like an obscuring after-image left by looking into the sun. She felt the blind spot somewhere on the far side of the city, and it had increased in strength. Secondly, the dryad's connection to the earth and water stirred uneasily, especially when she tried to sense the equilibrium of their magics. Things disturbed their balance: dirty things. Things she could not quite discern.

Ahead of them, the team of dwarven spell casters had gathered, which Taryl earlier requested. They would send at least a few others back to Irontooth.

Eucalia stumbled and Varanthl paused near her.

He asked, "Are you okay?"

She nodded and released her grip on the mystic connections. They reached the border of the skirmish line, behind the flaming structures heaving their final gasps. Floors and roofs cracked and snapped as the freshly razed buildings collapsed in upon themselves.

A foul stench suddenly overwhelmed the dryad. She wondered aloud, "Is that the gas Halle was talking about?"

Somewhere nearby, a voice screamed and goblins poured out of buildings, flashing their axes with guttural snarls. Varanthl snatched his hammer and rushed towards the fray, as did the other Gods'own.

Vagha and selumari fell to the surprise attacks.

More and more trogs continued to come. They pressed against the city's defenders fiercely enough that the new boundary might be shoved backwards yet again.

"The sewers!" Taryl hollered. "They're tunneling up from below."

A trog snarled and leapt for the eldarim, who leapt back into the arms of another goblin. Moments later, a trio of fiery red drakufreet blitzed towards Taryl, scrambling on all four. The saurons tore through his flankers and then stood to their hind legs, guarded him.

They were as tall as he was upon their hind legs, and they brandished their claws and snarled at the enemy. Saurons, as a sub-breed, looked more like draconic crocodile-folk. The hulking beasts used claws and teeth, but were also capable of wielding simple weapons, despite an intelligence slightly lower than required for sentience.

Hy'Targ and Jr'Orhr swung their axes and hacked down

the enemy like firewood. But they could chop them down forever; the trogs kept coming.

Elorall sprinted towards the dwarven casters who were supposed to be in the safety of Irontooth right about now. Eucalia ran hot on her heels. She grabbed the thaumaturgists with the flashiest looking head-dress, assuming he was their leader. "When I tell you, I need you to summon fire, as much fire as you can!"

"W-where?" he stammered.

"Below ground. We'll clean these sewers out once and for all."

Eucalia glanced sidelong at Elorall and understood the plan. The selumari's eyes turned milky white as a storm head began to brew in a ring far around the southern sides of Bralanthyr.

The dryad grabbed a handful of the wizards and linked hands with them. "Summon your magic with me! We must make sure Elorall's spell is as effective as possible. Summon the power of Eldurim, the earth god, when I tell you."

Taryl, brandishing eldarim steel, fell back so that he and his companion berserkers guarded the vulnerable crafters while they wove their magics together.

The sky suddenly split with a peal of thunder and winds rushed, forcing their way towards the ground below. They poured into the sewers and swept any gases possible towards the center of the city, crushing the fumes into a pressurized zone.

"Now," Eucalia insisted, squeezing the hands of the vagha on either side of her. Their earth craft sealed the vents and grates of the sewer lines that crossed below Broadstreet, bottling up the passages and sealing in the noxious vapors of both trog and free methane.

"Give me fire!" Elorall roared, and the dwarves complied, sparking Firiel's kiss into the sealed sewers below.

The ground bucked and jerked, collapsing a full cubit as

cerulean flames shot skyward wherever the subterranean shafts cracked first. The faltering ground belched a puff of flame as the heave settled, both burning and burying the enemies below them while knocking those above ground onto their backs.

Bralanthyr's defenders scrambled back to their feet while a new wave of trogs charged their line from across Broadstreet. More forces arrived behind Taryl and the Gods'own to reinforce the new battlefront.

Guiding the spell casters behind a wall of their infantry, Taryl regrouped with his friends. He looked from Hy'Targ to Mantieth. "You can tell your fathers that we are keeping things interesting. But you can also inform Hy'Mandr that Brentésion has not yet been found, though it's been confirmed that this is the group that took her." Taryl began making plans with the dwarven wizards to open a path, even as the hordes approached.

"What is that?" Elorall interrupted, staring across the skirmish.

The others looked in the same direction. "The goblin vanguard?" Mantieth asked with a hint of sarcasm.

"No. I feel it, too," Eucalia insisted.

Hy'Targ locked eyes on the thing. A black form hid near the rubble of a collapsed building. Smoke and flames concealed much of it: A massive, black dragonkin watched the battle. It was an agamid, a winged drakufreet, and Hy'Targ's stomach did a flip. He thought it a small dragon at first.

Taryl spotted it, too. "A winged sukie… A flying dragonkin mount," he explained.

Below the obsidian drakufreet they spotted its rider. A black clad cultist whose robe was opened to reveal the pale skin of his chest. His hood covered his face, but even so they felt his eyes upon them.

Mantieth squinted. "The marks upon his skin are different from the other cultists," he said. The elf had the best eyesight among them, and none doubted his information.

"These are not the same as those on Melkior's worshipers in Xlinea. They are similar, but different."

Taryl growled. "Nekarthans. A sect of the Black Forest. If they are here, I fear there is more at stake than just the fate of Bralanthyr."

Hy'Targ crooked his jaw. "So, not the same cultists we've been fighting to keep from acquiring the godbox pieces?"

Mantieth shook his head.

"The Nekarthans and Melkites both serve Death, but they are often at odds with each other," Taryl explained.

The dwarf relaxed his jaw and turned to Jr'Orhr and the dwarven spell casters. He slung the satchel, which contained their remaining piece of the Malfus Necrosis, over Jr'Orhr's shoulder. "There is a change of plans," Hy'Targ said. "Get this into the safe as soon as possible, Jr'Orhr. The rest of the Gods'own will stay to help defend Bralanthyr."

Before Jr'Orhr could argue, Eucalia and the vaghan thaumaturge nearest her linked arms and summoned a Path through the earth. A bubble of stone wrapped around the bewildered dwarf and sucked him into the soil. He was suddenly gone.

"I know, I know," Kaine groused at the two diminutive sprites who clung to his hat. They spoke in their native language, a kind of tinkling that sounded like tiny wind-chimes. The duo were all that remained of the once powerful sprite swarm that had been the eidolon of his master, Wehge. "I feel it."

The human looked around uneasily and clutched his mystic stone tighter to him. Trogs surrounded him on every side as he crossed through Bralanthyr. Ahead of him was a dark presence that he knew had to be a powerful acolyte of Death. Most races of Esfah were born to serve a specific god: The one who had created them. But acolytes forsook one or both of their allegiances to focus their devotion on only one deity.

What he felt before him was overwhelmingly strong, and Kaine suspected it came from an eldarim. Like humans, the eldarim were not created by the five primary gods of Esfah. That meant that almost all eldarim were acolytes; only what the eldarim called the "white shara" did not devote themselves to a specific god. Most families and clans formed obligations or reverence for a particular god. Humans, made by Tarvanehl the All-Father, were made with ties to none of the elemental properties of Esfah, but the eldarim, who came to life independent of the Creators, contained all the elements, which made them very powerful indeed. The white shara especially. Most of the eldarim had become acolytes through the ages, as had many humans.

Kaine clutched the totem as he held it aloft. He crossed through the boundary of Broadstreet and into the open; he could feel every set of eyes upon him, and the sprites tinkled nervously.

"Don't worry so much," he whispered to them. "Ghaeial the Mother Goddess put this rune upon the rock. We'll be safe." He strode forward, wishing that was the exact truth of the matter. The magic of the Feylands had granted him an extremely long life, and he'd learned the ways of the sages since he was young; many hundred years before the Magestorm Wars. He'd encountered a few clever enemies, who had found cleverer ways to circumvent the magic of his totem. The presence of an eldari Death acolyte made him nervous.

He heard the sounds of battle ahead and quickened his pace. A roar sounded, extremely close, and a black dragonkin flared its wings. The beast hissed and Kaine's sprites squeaked in terror, so shrill it sounded like tinnitus in his ears.

The beast's rider flung back his hood to reveal scars and tattoo markings devoting himself to Death. He growled, "I know what you are, sage, and I understand the sign that you carry." Hatred seemed to roll off the cultist with a palpable, oily feel.

Kaine noticed the eldarim's hand stayed upon the hilt of his blade. He had not, and could not, draw it.

With a sneer, he tore a bolt of black cloth from his robe and held out the strip of fabric with a sneer. "And I know how to defeat it!" The acolyte blinded himself with the cloth and yanked his sword free.

Without the ability to see the sign, it had no effect. The fiend rushed towards the sage and hacked at the air.

Kaine ducked and side-stepped each slash of the eldarim's blade. Every stroke came uncannily close.

"We Nekarthans train in the secret of the shadows. We do not need sight to attack our prey!" He whirled and swung his blade. Had Kaine not ducked, it would have taken his head off.

Suddenly, a blast of frigid air bit the cultist, slowing him enough that the sage was able to put some distance between them. The acolyte stumbled as vines entangled his feet, making him pause to cut them away.

He roared with frustration and ripped the blinders free to find the Gods'own taking positions against him. The acolyte sneered and then whistled. His winged mount rushed to his side and the black rider took to the air as Bralanthry's defenders finished eliminating the rest of the goblin raiders who had surged across Broadstreet to attack.

Nodhan hooked an arm out to catch the morehl child who bounded into the backyard of his estate in Port Orric. He had only just returned home after the long journey. "Whoa, Oren!" he yelped. "What have I told you about rushing up to creatures who do not know you?"

"It's dangerous," the child said, obviously more

enthralled with the sight of the massive bronze beast perched in their back yard than the return of his guardian.

Brentésion laid as low as possible and looked more like a giant napping pet than a powerful beast of war.

"Now let me look at you," Nodhan said. "It's been too long since I've been back. And believe me, I tried to get here sooner." He scowled at the bulge in his pocket.

Oren had grown nearly as tall as Nodhan's chest. His ears were long and pointed, and his skin shone a deep red. "You were barely waist high when I was last home."

"The neighbors will talk," called Laelysh from the house. Oren's mother stood in the doorway with her arms folded; she nodded towards the brassy dracolem. The backyard was fenced with a tall, stone barrier, but Brentésion was taller than that if she stood.

Laelysh was Nodhan's oldest friend, and he'd found enough success to put her up in his home. She cared for the place while he was away on his expeditions. Their home was in the nicest part of Port Orric. Not a typical hive of thievery, but he'd stored a wealth of ill-begotten treasures within, and he knew Laelysh could care for it. She'd grown up picking pockets alongside Nodhan in the gutters of Emmira.

She disappeared within the house momentarily while Nodhan introduced the child to Brentésion. The child had been a surprise to Nodhan when they'd reconnected a few years ago. She claimed Oren was named after his father; Nodhan had known Oren Senior well. The older Oren possessed devilishly handsome good looks and poor skills at grifting. It did not surprise him to hear that the senior Oren had been murdered in a deal gone awry, prompting Nodhan to put up Laelysh and her child.

Laelysh returned with an armload of blankets. She tried to throw as many over Brentésion as possible to hide him. "This isn't working. I think we'll need a boat sail."

Nodhan waved away her concern. "Let the neighbors prattle."

"They already think you're up to no good when you're away on business..."

He shrugged. "Well, that's mostly true."

"But this? A mount like this would cost a fortune. Only a king, or his top knight, would have access to something like this," Laelysh said.

"Or *had* something like this," Nodhan flashed her a grin. He felt invigorated now that he was finally home, where he could rest and enjoy the company of something other than those meddlesome voices in his head.

"Ha. Ha," Laelysh gave a slow, sarcastic laugh. "Seriously, though. You don't stay around long enough to hear their gossiping."

"Well, maybe we should urge some other lava elves to move into the neighborhood."

She flashed him a look which he well understood. There were not many affluent morehl in the neighborhood who would tolerate the snooty neighbors. "What am I supposed to tell them?"

Nodhan shrugged. "This one is easy. You can tell them the truth of it: I liberated Brentésion from a group of trogs who had captured him. As to the original owner, whether king, knight, or eldarim, who can say?"

She sighed and melted into a resentful hug. They embraced platonically for a few moments. They were friends, and nothing more, though their local cover was as a traditional family unit. "I'm glad you're back. We'll call someone about boarding your... *new pet*... in the morning."

He squeezed her shoulders and then released her. "I hope to stay for a while. This last one was a long journey... Did you sell some items when I was gone?"

Laelysh nodded. "Coffers are up. I sold one of your maps for a small fortune."

"Oh? Which one?"

"Some treasure map written in ancient eldari. The Cyrean Sage's cypher. Sold it to some fop who claimed to be from there, but it could've been a lie," she said. "He didn't sweat enough. If he came from up north, he should've been much too warm here, especially since I keep the fires going full time." She smiled at how easy it had been to read him. "It was a human male... smelled like salt. A sailor, I'd reckon. *Chariot's Wake* was in harbor about that time, and I suspect he was part of Ry'ober's crew."

Nodhan grinned, recognizing her keen insight. Morehl preferred much warmer temperatures when possible. "I'm glad I missed it, then. She's probably procuring it as a buyer's agent; the wealthy do prefer their anonymity." He looked through the door, but did not smell any food; she hadn't known when she could expect him home again. "Perhaps we should go out to eat? Maybe that little bistro in the lower district?"

His companion didn't seem to hear him. Her child was playing near a strange creature that she did not yet trust, and so she only half-heard.

"What does it even eat?" Laelysh asked, watching Brentésion skeptically as Oren patted the creature's snout gently.

"It eats, um, obviously it would need... " He furrowed his brow. "Come to think of it, I've been with her for weeks now and I've never seen Brentésion eat."

CHAPTER TWENTY-THREE

The Gods'own sat around a campfire in the command area of Bralanthyr's defenders, wondering about the arrival of the black eldarim.

"Well, they're definitely cultists," Varanthl said. "Just not the same kind that have been dogging us."

Using a stick, Elorall drew a new mark in the dirt and then dragged a line from that to a symbol representing the adventurers. Several signs crisscrossed in a web of lines.

"Perhaps it all just *seems* interconnected," Mantieth suggested. "Maybe there is no rhyme or reason to any of it. We *have* traveled all across the continent these last many months. Might be that we just stumbled through the plans of several, independent intrigues."

Hy'Targ stroked his beard. "I hope you're right. But what if you aren't? Best to prepare for the worst possible contingency and then be pleasantly surprised, as my father always says."

The old library door closed behind them. Turning, they spotted someone they hoped might carry some clues.

The sage whom they had rescued at Broadstreet departed the old library where Taryl and the other commanders had interrogated him, trying to ascertain a reason for his presence. With no answers relevant to the battle for Bralanthyr, they pumped him for whatever details they could about the trogs' army strength and placement.

Kaine descended the steps and walked towards the Gods'own.

They said nothing to him, knowing that the sage had already been bombarded with questions. Kaine took a seat at the fire and relaxed in the silence, evaluating each with his keen eyes.

Sages were better known as enlightened sorcerer-scholars. They were friends of spirits, the elemental sub-deities often found in the world—except for those created by Death, whom the goblins often worshiped as a pantheon of minor gods.

The order of sages traced their roots back to pre-history, as eldarim scholars began to preserve the knowledge of what occurred before *the making:* The creation of the first races by the gods. Most of that knowledge had been lost in the destruction of Daur-Bor-Nin. Few sages had escaped, and even fewer remained upon Esfah now.

There was a saying that, should you ever meet a sage, they likely possessed more knowledge than all in the room combined. The Gods'own would have to see if that were true.

"Thank you," Kaine said. "That acolyte nearly ended me." He scanned the circle another time. "I recognize your descriptions and have heard a few tales in my travels. They call you the Gods'own, after the Champions of the Gods?"

Mantieth nodded. "The Champions stopped the rise of Melkior in the old stories. Some creative bards hailed us as reincarnated heroes. Audiences took up the name."

Kaine chuffed a short laugh. "Of course. That makes a wonderful story, though there is no such thing as reincarnation. Just a remaking of new things in old patterns."

Hy'Targ cocked his head. "You mentioned your travels. What brought you to Bralanthyr, or are you passing through, as are we?"

Kaine grinned. "Are you just passing through?"

"We intended to," the dwarf said. "Lucky for you we did not."

"Luck and the will of the gods are often confused, and rarely can we ever know one from the other. Only Mitta knows," Kaine referred to the neutral goddess of fate most revered by the firewalker race in Empyreanoral, northeast of Dohan.

The sage continued, "I was driven south some time ago. Drawn by something like the cry of a child: A child of destiny I have long sought after. It came to me in a dream that pulled me from my home in the Feylands."

Hy'Targ raised his brows. "You must have been traveling for more than a year?"

Kaine's eyes glossed over as he counted the time. "Yes. That sounds accurate. It is my mandate. A child will be born, the first new child since the dawning of the first age... but a root of evil grows stronger each day, spreading below the surface like blight within the soil."

Confused faces watched the sage, searching for more details, but he provided none. However, Kaine's demeanor changed.

"Do you truly believe you are Gods'own?"

"The people certainly believe it," Mantieth said.

"But do *you* believe it?" the sage asked. "Personal belief is a powerful thing. Even more powerful than those four items you carry. You may need the strength of faith before you reach the trails' end."

Hy'Targ tried to play coy. "What do you mean by our four items? Many are aware we've quested for powerful artifacts, but we currently have none in our possession."

Kaine smiled like one who had just won a game. "You think you are telling the truth." He pointed to his wrist. "You have not discovered the power of your bracelets yet? They represent a family, yet incomplete. But I believe you will discover their nature before all is done. Again, I say, belief is a powerful thing."

Varanthl perked up. "Bracelets?"

The sage rose to his feet. "If you believe that is all they are, then that is all they will ever be." Kaine smirked. "Now, I must be off. Whatever feeling has driven me this direction has moved on. I sense it again, far off and away." He turned without excuse and began walking, mumbling something about an irresponsible badger folk losing his way.

Kaine turned and called back to them, "There are far greater evils than trogs and harpies brewing below the surface. If there was ever any doubt, I sense that at least one of your party truly *is Gods'own*." He turned and then disappeared behind the buildings of Bralanthyr.

The adventurers traded uncertain looks with each other. Those wearing one of the bracelets collected by Varanthl turned them about on their wrists.

"What did all of that mean?" Eucalia finally spoke up.

"That Mantieth is probably wrong," Hy'Targ spoke softly. "It *is* all connected... and that our actions may affect the wills and outcomes of the gods, and the plans of all creatures great and small." He turned and looked back towards the goblins' vanguard. "It means that the battle for Bralanthyr is far more important than any of us expect."

Varanthl twisted the band around his wrist. "Jordyll only told me that they were fireproof... " he trailed off and looked at it. He had gotten them from a band of outcast, gray elves who had accepted him into their family after the People of the Sun, his blood relations, drove him out thinking him a monster. "She said that they meant *family*."

Mantieth squinted at his bracelet, given to him by the homunculus. He swallowed hard, remembering that he'd taken one from the giant finger of a friend who had been burned to death by dragon's fire: Rhyll, the treefolk. He cast a sidelong look at Elorall, who wore it as a token of their engagement. The prince shut his eyes and exhaled morosely through his nose.

"But what *are they*, exactly?" Hy'Targ wondered aloud. "Certainly, they must be some kind of *relic*... But what kind? There are many kinds of magic items. Those made by the gods, those imbued by spirits, and those crafted by the gremmlobahnd…"

"And maybe more importantly," Elorall asked, "how do they work?"

They sat back and watched as everyone tried various methods of activating the powers the sage claimed they had. Nothing seemed to work.

"Do you ever wonder that you seem to be attracted by relics?" Eucalia asked. "I mean, that you have been drawn by them? Most folk never see one in their lives and the Gods'own have acquired many in so short a time."

Hy'Targ squeezed his hands and bobbed his head. "I have given that some thought, indeed." The others looked at him. They knew he was an avid student of history. Hy'Targ had proven himself skilled with an axe, but his true heart belonged to a stack of books.

"It seems to me," the dwarf continued, "as if something is changing in this world. There have been many cataclysms, events that brought about new eras. The Making triggered the First Age. Steering Esfah's destiny away from the eldarim, monsters, and dragons marked a period of the First Age. The time of the Champions was another; when the dead rose for the first time. Then came the Dragoncrusades and the Magestorm Wars. The Second Age arrived when Ghaeial walked the land and created anew, calling new species to walk the lands."

Elorall's face sparkled with wonder at the thought. "I wonder if we are on the precipice of such a change. Kaine the sage seemed to think so."

Mantieth turned to hide his scowl and the burgeoning, foul mood that had begun growing in him since before Hy'Targ had received the first letter from the Gray Wanderer.

———⚔︎◈⚔︎———

Forktongue entered the chamber where Melkior often brooded upon his throne. He tried to summon a deeper connection to Malgrimm and beg for aid when he was not staring through the eyes of his undead crows that obsessively scoured the planet for Ailushurai's bones. The lich stood at the far edge of the room and whirled when the eldarim minion entered.

Melkior's face, chin, and chest were slicked with black slop. Tendrils of necralluvium wriggled like clumps of maggots.

"Our enemies have moved against the Gods'own," Forktongue exclaimed.

Melkior cocked his head. "Enemies?"

"The Nekarthans -"

"Are not our enemies," Melkior insisted.

Forktongue pressed his lips together and bowed.

"I do not care about petty rivalries between the sparring arms of the Black Forest. If we all serve Lord Death, then our goals are the same. Let them destroy the sons of Hy'Mandr and Leidergelth if they can." Melkior shifted a bandage on his arm to discover that it still leaked fine sand, despite devouring fresh necralluvium.

He tightened the wrappings. "I may still be crippled from the wound given by the Kreethaln, but the necralluvium has sustained me until now."

Forktongue drew closer and looked at the deadly black fluid.

Melkior scowled. "It has reinvigorated my power; however, it is not a permanent solution. I must find some way to reconnect to Death."

A shadow seemed to meld away from one of the tunnels leading into the throne. The skeleton, burned black by arcane fire, entered and moved with a lithe grace that communicated its deadly efficiency.

Forktongue raised a wary brow. He understood this was far deadlier variety than any common skeleton.

"My hunter has returned," Melkior said.

The black skeleton screeched.

"So long as I stay fat on necralluvium, I can maintain one of these... and he has made an interesting discovery."

With a hiss, the skeleton collapsed into a heap like a charred structure succumbing to gravity. Melkior checked his bandage again, and it no longer leaked without the continued assertion of power. "He has located the resting place of my beloved's bones."

Forktongue looked from the pile of blackened bones on the floor, to the sand leakage behind his master's cloth wraps. "Do you wish her to see you like this? Falling apart?"

Melkior shook his head. "That would not be an issue; her resurrection should give me the power to heal myself. Except that my father Malgrimm might leave me cursed to this eternally shameful state. I will not take such a chance." He relaxed his posture. "No. For now, it is enough for me to know where she resides. My attention is no longer divided, and it is time to plan."

"So whatever the Nekarthans do between now and your next plan is moot?"

The lich nodded slowly. "I must heal this wound," Melkior insisted. "Then, I will be worthy to reclaim my bride. I will not resurrect her to endure my shame—I will conquer my enemies with power, and then I will have my satisfaction and the blessings of Malgrimm both."

His minion paused. "I may know a way," he suggested. "I shall dispatch an agent to Dohan immediately. Allow me to send Nesma, the local cultist who first stumbled onto your presence here. He is well suited to the task."

Melkior cocked his head and stared at Forktongue with blazing eyes.

"Let me verify my suspicions. I dare not present false hope, but I do believe I know of an artifact that can stabilize your power, even in Ailushurai's absence."

Melkior grinned and nodded, permitting Nesma's

appointment. "Soon she will again be in my arms. Let the gods' heroes believe I think she's been lost to me... Until it is too late."

Human, dwarven, and coral elf soldiers moved through the command center, scuttling past the camp erected by the Gods'own. Murmurs rippled through the army that the trogs mustered together on the far side of Broadstreet. Already, many sling pelters had taken positions in the tallest buildings, where they traded occasional missiles with selumari, human, and vaghan opponents.

Their campfire lapped at the air like a thirsty dog. Soll's light waned as the fiery orb crept towards the horizon. The army was on edge, expecting an attack in the dark, but Mantieth remained oblivious to anything but his personal frustrations.

Hy'Targ took a seat upon a stool nearby and glanced around. None of the others were nearby to hear. "Something on your mind, Mantieth?"

The blue elf frowned and sighed. "I... don't know."

Hy'Targ raised his eyebrows. "It's got to do with Elorall." He wasn't asking.

Mantieth's frown set into a tight-jawed grimace. "How do you?"

"Everybody knows," he interrupted. "Something is bothering you, and everyone sees it but you two elves. Whatever it is, it's starting to affect the rest of us—especially now that we are on the dangerous verge of battle."

The elf shrugged. "We've been through wars. It's not like we can't handle trogs."

Hy'Targ seethed hot air from his nose. *"Of course* we can handle goblins... Right up until we can't. We're not invincible, Mantieth. Remember Rhyll?"

Mantieth nodded slowly. He let out a breath. "The

drekloch's vision, what I saw, was an unhappy marriage. My father's and mother's marriage fell apart. Those last few years were just shades of gray. Total apathy. There was no spark, no color between them."

Hy'Targ's face softened. "You're afraid of repeating the same mistakes?"

"I'm *doomed to repeat them!*" he shouted. He ran his fingers through his hair and pulled on his scalp. "It is inescapable. I am cursed by Avanna, the cruel goddess of ill fates."

"Rubbish," Hy'Targ insisted. "Elloral's been your friend since you two were children. You told me how you used to play on the shoals together. She's been your advocate and biggest supporter since before your parents even split. That elf girl has loved you since she the first day she knew you."

"That's just it," Mantieth said. "Things have changed since then."

"Have they? She is still adventuring by your side. She is still your closest friend." Hy'Targ's eyes might have bored a hole through him. "She hasn't changed one bit—only *you* have—bent out of shape by some nightmare that's likely to never happen." He paused. "I only wish I had what you've found with her."

The elf sighed. "Perhaps you're right. We have had our fair share of adventures… and she's always been my escape. But it's so risky to trade a friend for a lover; does it really work? I confess I have great fear of it. Can I really marry her?"

"Well, you'd better. Your proposal was already made and accepted."

Mantieth twisted the mysterious bracelet upon his wrist. "You asked if I remembered Rhyll? Of course I do—I can't shake thoughts of the moment I took the band off his finger and put it on Elorall's wrist."

Hy'Targ cocked his head.

The elf continued. "The proposal was quite accidental. I

was trying to inspire Elorall: We were overwhelmed by the undead at Melkior's keep and I thought we were going to die..."

"So you proposed?" Hy'Targ jested.

"No—*I didn't*—and that's the thing. I said something like, 'You and me against the world and all the odds?' Yes, I put jewelry on her when I asked her to follow me, *but that was into battle*. I was not asking her to marry me... She misunderstood. And now it would be much too embarrassing to tell her..."

They both whirled when they heard movement nearby. Elorall stood there, shock and embarrassment plastered to her face. Their eyes met, and it quickly turned to a look of hurt and betrayal.

Elorall spun on her heels and dashed away.

Mantieth's heart sank like a stone. "Elorall? Elorall! Come back—I didn't mean it like that!" he shouted, but she was gone, and the sun had already dipped below the horizon, resulting in darkness.

Mantieth turned to his dwarven friend, hoping for some kind of absolution. "I—I didn't mean it like that..."

Hy'Targ clenched his jaw. "I don't know if you can undo this damage."

The elf stared after her, searching for her. "This isn't my fault. She can't feel hurt over a misunderstanding."

Hy'Targ slowly shook his head. "That might have been the case except for one thing."

Mantieth stared at him.

"You have been letting your little fish swim around in her coral reef all this time, even though you knew your proposal wasn't real. That made it very real to her, and she's gonna take this real personal."

The elf scowled. He knew Hy'Targ was right—but he had no idea how to fix it. "How do I... ?"

The air split with a war-horn, not letting Mantieth finish. Immediately after, gongs and bells rang out from Bralanthyr's defenders. Whoever led the goblin army had decided to press the attack.

CHAPTER TWENTY-FOUR

"The Gods'own have not yet departed," one of the cultists hissed. "Are they so foolish they think they can defeat us without calling upon foreign aid?"

Three Nekarthans, the black riders upon winged dragonkin, stood in a circle. Tsut watched from a distance, and Grackyll, the trog wizard, stood by his side. The shrunken goblin couldn't help but notice the absence of any leaders from the Moorlech.

"Mark my words, Grackyll," Tsut whispered, "Ratargul has lost control of his army. He made a deal with the Dark Lord and it will cost him everything to claim a prize he will never hold."

Grackyll merely nodded. He'd cast a simple incantation that allowed them to eavesdrop and hear what the black eldarim were saying.

"Our plan cannot begin in earnest until they have sought help from Bralanthyr's neighbors—so long as the coral airships hang above Niamarlee," one cultist said, "it remains too risky for our servants in Undrakull to reveal themselves."

One of his peers nodded. "Strike from the shadows and never reveal our hand until the enemy's neck is exposed. It is the Nekarthan way." He shook his head at one of the three. "You exposed our presence and may have jeopardized our plans."

The chastised one put his hands up in defense. "We needed information we could trust; we needed certainty that the Gods'own remained in Bralanthyr. I could not know that a wandering sage would pop up in the middle of a skirmish."

"Not just *any* sage," said another. He appeared to be the leader since he talked the most. "That was the sage who has sought to undo what we have worked towards for decades—

longer, in fact. If he is successful... "

Trying to save face, the admonished one said, "We need an aerial threat. Such that demands Niamarlee bring their sky-borne forces to bear." He waved to Grackyll and Tsut. "You two, bring your harpies to us and blow the horns for battle. We attack at dusk! The sky will become a storm of death and from on high we shall reign down attrition with impunity."

Tsut and the wizard nodded and began moving away to comply. "I do not like Ratargul being in charge, but at least he belonged to the same fen as us," he whispered to Grackyll.

The spell caster nodded.

With the spell still active, it would only fade away once the goblins were out of range. The leader spoke again. "That plan sounds reasonable. But if it does not work, there may not be one that does. And where is Ratargul? Someone tell that useless lump of sludge to blow the signal horn."

Tsut shook his head and then scampered off into the harem.

Only a thin ribbon of light from below the door provided any illumination. It was not much, but it was something to give Yarrick some hope.

He stared through the dark and recognized the shiny eyes of a fellow prisoner. Light was almost nonexistent as Yarrick's eyes traced the lines of the dweomernull sign. He had to assume he'd been marked with one as well; his connection to the magic of Esfah felt severed.

Yarrick was not particularly adept at spell craft, but he was competent enough. Reaching out with his senses, he felt nothing. No connection to the elements that fueled arcane abilities.

In the dark, his fellow prisoners were shadowy blurs, but he could ascertain some things about them. One wore garb that identified him as a fisherman. Another was dressed like a herdsman. Still another, like an artisan. Pureblooded eldarim were the least populous race of Esfah, but they were incredibly varied. The fact that they were each shara meant that there must have been some kind of link between them; something that held them each in common with one another. And the reason they had been taken.

Try as he could, Yarrick could not find any commonality between them. Nothing outward at least. Then, it dawned on him. It was the lack of a link that was significant. It was too dark to be sure, but he could find no identifying marks upon his fellow captives. Their clothes had no ceremonial stitching, no patches or marks to indicate allegiances. None had visible tattoos or ritual scars. He assumed that they, like he, bore none under their clothes.

They're white shara, like my clan. Yarrick and his uncle, and presumably the rest of their clan-mates, were not acolytes. They served all the gods without preference, which was unlike the eldarim. Their allegiance was not to any specific god of Esfah, but to Esfah herself: to Mother Ghaeial. If they all came from clans who had intentionally remained neutral or were individuals who had failed to follow clan traditions and make pledges to household gods, he could not tell. As long as the damp rope gagged their mouths, his knowledge would remain limited, but he at least had a theory.

So far, there had been two prisoners taken since the feeding ritual. Neither of them had returned. It had been ten days between the two, judging by the passage of Soll's light at the bottom of the door.

Yarrick sucked hard on the rope between his teeth and pulled as much moisture from it as he could. The last captive was taken nine days ago. He clenched his jaw and bit the rope, irked by having such little information to go on. But still, it was enough to form a plan.

Mantieth scrambled through the pandemonium. Sounds of weapons impacting shields and ripping flesh sang through the air. Bowstrings twanged and sling stones smashed nearby. He ducked an incoming enemy, then parried to one side to avoid being crushed by an amazon. She rode past on her chariot, charging through the fray. The woman beside the driver threw javelins to clear a path.

"Elorall? Elorall!" he screamed and spotted a flash of blue skin up ahead, where the trogs swarmed thickest. Mantieth glanced behind him and saw Varanthl's towering frame as he swung his hammer. Below that, Hy'Targ's axe, Glorybringer, blazed like a brand. He couldn't spot Eucalia through all the commotion, but he thought he saw a glimpse of Acacia, her unicorn comrade.

His heart quickened. *Yarrick, Jr'Orhr, Nodhan, Elorall... So many of the Gods' own are not with us—fracturing and reducing our strength.* He realized that his subconscious had somehow slipped the lava elf into his account of their numbers, but despite all the trouble he'd caused, Mantieth had never quite given up hope on the red elf. *He had been in our first band of travelers... but Elorall? Maybe I can fix that relationship, at least.* Mantieth was reluctant to give up on someone so long as the other party drew breath. *I should write to my mother.*

Mantieth turned back towards his target and slashed with his vorpal sword. The magic blade, given to him by his father on his name day, was keen and thirsty for blood. Its need parched the coral elf's throat and with a flick of his wrist, troggish heads flew off from their shoulders.

He pushed his way through the crowd of enemies, cutting them down as he pressed forward. A human screamed and fled from the defensive line before them, although he didn't find any selumari.

The line had held, but barely. Bralanthyr's Broadstreet was now firmly in the possession of the enemy, unless they could successfully repel them.

Standing on his toes, Mantieth tried to spot his fiancé over that line, but he could not. Sounds like smashing pots echoed behind and around him, followed by the *whoosh* of flames. Someone high in the night sky hurled firepots at the defenders below.

He saw that flash of blue again as a small company of defenders hurried to engage with the enemies that circumvented the front lines. "Elorall!" There were too many. Every few moments, the defensive line faltered somewhere and goblins poured through the breaches.

Overhead, the stars twinkled as whatever aerial creatures attacked them momentarily blotted out the heavenly lights. The elf cursed to himself. *If only Bralanthyr had some sort of airborne navy.*

Mantieth dashed towards Elorall's last position. She'd moved, but he did see cerulean flashes of light bursting on the far side of a nearby crowd, the telltale aura of selumari magic granted by the wind Goddess, Ailuril.

He rushed forward and was nearly bowled over by a crew of routing humans. A massive pair of feet stomped on one, breaking the man open at his midsection as the troll landed on top of him. A fetid odor rolled off the beast in waves and the troll kicked the next slowest straggler, sending him flying.

Mantieth ducked the troll's blow. The monster was extremely fast for its size. It tried to score a cheap shot against the elf while pretending to chase the faltering amazons. But Mantieth had expected it and the unwieldy club passed harmlessly above him.

The coral elf scrambled closer towards the monster who stood more than twice his height. His closeness took away much of the beast's ability to strike by keeping inside its range. Roaring in frustration, the troll flailed, trying to get an angle on the speedy elf. Finally, it opted to try stomping on Mantieth and smashed all around with its clunky feet like some kind of fiendish dance.

Mantieth slashed at his enemy's legs. On the second attempt, his blade found tendons, and the troll collapsed into a screeching heap. Before it could right itself and continue its attempt on the elf's life, Mantieth brought his vorpal blade to bear and hacked cleanly through the monster's neck.

The body twitched slightly as the troll lay dead and Mantieth caught his breath. He noticed the wounds on the troll's legs had already begun to close. The monster's famed regenerative powers could even regrow severed heads if the body wasn't burned.

Mantieth looked around in a scramble, trying to find a dwarven caster or a torch. A danger sense buzzed in his mind and he looked up just in time to see a firepot hurled his way. The elf dodged, somersaulting away. He looked up just in time to see the harpy who had tried to end him snarl and then fly back into the night.

Looking back, Mantieth saw that the firepot had broken near the troll and the flames had already spread to the monster's body. He silently praised Mitta, the goddess of luck, and then sprinted towards the flashes of blue light.

A shadow darkened the ground momentarily and a massive, winged dragonkin swooped down through the sky; the black-clad eldarim rode upon its back. The agamid tore through the crew of defenders with jagged talons. It snatched the selumari sorcerer into the air and then dashed her to the ground before she could summon Ailuril's winds to cushion her fall.

Her elven body smashed into the broken soil with a sickening thud, like dropped eggs. The drakufreet and rider soared back into the sky, where it roared in victory at having killed the spell caster.

Mantieth sprinted towards her and fell to his knees beside her. Her face was ruined and her limbs contorted into odd, broken angles. He took her hand and squeezed it. Hot, salty tears tumbled down his cheeks, and he caressed her bare arm. *Wait—there is no bracelet! Her clothes are different.*

Terror gripped his heart as much as relief when he realized it had not been Elorall, but the other selumari spell crafter from Niamarlee, who Halle had mentioned earlier. He leapt back to his feet and howled, "Elorall?"

More goblins poured through a faltering section of the defenders' line, and Mantieth pulled out his sword. He hacked at them, holding back a dozen of them by himself. Every few seconds, there were less and less of the enemy as he methodically cut them to pieces. Muscle memory took over: All those years of training at the hands of his father's hired had forged him into the best swordsman Niamarlee had ever seen.

He'd always resented Leidergelth's rigid training regimen - until now. The trogs were barely enough to hold his full attention, and he risked looking back over his shoulder in between blows. He spotted Varanthl and Hy'Targ making their way towards him to shore up that part of the line. Eucalia and Acacia were only a little way beyond them.

And then he saw her. Elorall.

Beside her, a duo of amazon warriors fell to smoking trails of black magic as a cluster of goblin wizards hurled death magic at them. Her guards dropped their blood splattered kukris and collapsed dead, clutching their chest and throats.

Elorall brushed aside the deadly, ethereal darts and blasted the cadre of death crafters with a bolt of lightning. Three of them collapsed in smoking heaps of charred flesh; their lack of adorning talismans and baubles indicated they were lower-level casters, initiates only. Their leader glanced up at the sky and then fled, leaving Elorall alone, surrounded by her dead companions.

Mantieth saw the shadow flash across the ground again. "Elorall! Get down!"

They locked eyes only briefly, and Mantieth's gut sank. He saw genuine panic in them.

The ebony dragonkin flared its wings wide and as it hovered directly above the selumari sorcerer. It belched a lung full of black flame at her.

Elorall held her hand aloft and caught the deadly flames with a watery shield. It rippled and verged on breaking against the intense, black fire. The beast, rider, and magician were locked together, like three clashing swordsmen; neither could yield nor press ahead without disastrous consequences.

The acolyte upon the back of the winged mount snarled. He reached for his sword, ready to tip the scales of the combat.

Mantieth yelled and clutched the handle of his vorpal blade as he rushed towards the enemy. Firepots smashed to the ground around him and flames sprang to life, blocking him.

The harpies who had thrown them cackled overhead. One still held a blazing firepot. She sneered, ready to use it at the first opportune moment.

Elorall dropped one hand back. Sweat beaded her brow as she split her concentration; faltering here would have deadly consequences. She summoned unseen winds with her spare hand, and the pressure in the air seemed to change at barely perceptible levels.

The eldarim slowly dragged his blade from his sheath as the flying fen-borne creature provided interference.

"Leave him alone, you harpy bitch!" Elorall screamed.

The winged creature snarled and hurled the remaining canister of fire at *her* feet, sparing Mantieth.

It broke open just as she used her command of the air to push more of the subterranean sewer gases to the surface. They ignited in a cloud of fire and fury, scattering charred harpies like leaves to the wind.

The blast rocked the battlefield and knocked Mantieth

off his feet. The other Gods'own had reached him only in time to be blown to the dirt, too late to affect the outcome.

Hunks of charred dragonkin fell around them and the damaged eldarim cultist who rode the beast landed upon Mantieth, knocked back by the concussive wave. The elf's blade impaled the rider, severing spine and piercing vital organs, killing the fiend instantly.

Mantieth pulled the blade from his enemy's corpse with a horrific *schlurking* sound. He ignored the odor of burned hair and flesh as he stumbled to his feet. Mantieth tried to shake off the shock ringing fresh in his ears as the rest of his crew scrambled to his side.

"Elorall?" Mantieth managed weakly. Then he sank to his knees and screamed, "Elorall!" But only a crater remained where she'd made her last stand.

And just beyond, a new wave of goblins rushed toward them.

CHAPTER TWENTY-FIVE

Yarrick stared at the door. That plank hovering above the thin beam of light was his only link to the outside world.

Today was the tenth day. Today, the cultists would feed them and make another selection. The sliver of light gradually turned an orange hue as the sun headed towards dusk.

As it had done in the last two encounters, the door opened and the procession of cultists entered carrying trays of food. This time, they'd brought another prisoner.

A robed cultist forced him into the place of the last prisoner. He clapped him in shackles and withdrew a key from his pocket.

Yarrick watched the figure place the meal before the newcomer and then slipped his key back into the pocket. Cocking his head, Yarrick spotted a ripped edge on the pocket. Textile fibers frayed at its edges, making him the only one who could identify it, even if by such a subtle detail.

Just as it had been during previous feedings, the profanely beautiful cultist came into the room for the selection process. Her pungent perfume made Yarrick's nostrils flare. The woman seemed to notice, and she smirked.

"Him," she said, pointing to the prisoner who had been chained across from Yarrick. They dragged him away screaming and the woman bent low to Yarrick. "Do not worry. I shall choose you soon enough… Unless that one proves to be from the bloodline we seek."

She reveled in the look on her prisoners' faces. "And if that should be the case, we'll simply stop coming to feed you." With a devious grin, she turned to make her exit, commenting to two of the lowest ranking cultists, "This place smells revolting. When you are done clearing away their trays, splash them each with a bucket of lavender water."

They bowed and then watched her leave before turning to begin their work in obscurity. First, they tied each of the gags through their prisoner's teeth, and then hauled away their trays while whispering to each other.

"Haven't you seen it, though?"

"No. And I doubt *you* have either. They don't let just anybody examine the Horn of Hielosch."

"I *have* seen it. It's at the center of the castle... " he turned a wry look towards the prisoners. "We shouldn't discuss any details in front of them."

"What are they going to do? Tattle on us?"

The other cultist shrugged and looked Yarrick dead in the eye. When he looked away, the eldarim tightened his jaw and began to grind his teeth on the rope gag.

"No," said the cultist, "I suppose not."

Outside the main door, the sun dropped into the horizon and the sky took on ominous red hues. Other cultists began depositing the scented buckets of water outside the doors for cleansing.

"You don't suppose they'll ever find one, do you?"

"One of the living heirs to the Death Bard of Dereh'Liandor? Yeah, right."

"You think him a myth?"

"Maybe. He certainly existed, but I think his infamy is greatly exaggerated. I doubt they'll ever find an heir—they've been at this for decades."

They retreated momentarily and then returned carrying a bucket each. They splashed a prisoner each in turn and then retrieved another bucket.

"I still say you're a liar. They wouldn't let just anybody have access to such a powerful artifact."

The other cultist chuffed. "Well, what good is it in the wrong person's hand? No one else can use it."

His companion stood stiffly, halting. His bucket was still

full. "What do you mean?"

The cultist smirked. "Surely you'll have a turn cleaning up the mess it makes of these." He nodded towards the prisoners. "Only the blood of Hielosch's descendants can use it. Everyone else... " He trailed off in silence.

"Everyone else what?" He didn't get an answer. "Tell me what it does."

"They just sort of... melt."

They splashed the last two captives with their buckets. The person Yarrick assumed was the senior cultist took the key again from his pocket. The frayed edges of it lodged in Yarrick's mind. He closed the door behind them, inserted the key, and clicked it locked.

Yarrick began to chew.

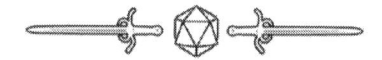

Javelins whistled over Mantieth's head as reinforcements came from the amazons. The spears hailed down upon the trogs, lancing them and leaving them dead upon the smoldering battlefield, or pinning them to the dirt. Humans rushed in to defend the elven prince from the onslaught of advancing goblins.

"Come on," Hy'Targ insisted, barely able to pull his friend to his feet. "They're buying us time so we can retreat."

Mantieth's priceless sword fell to the dirt and his arms hung limp. He stood there, listless, as if he planned to simply let Death take him. "They... they killed her."

"I know. I watched it happen," Hy'Targ said, tugging on his friend's arm to lead him away. "Now come on. She didn't die so you could stand here gawking like a fool while some swamp dwelling gurk cuts your throat."

Mantieth looked at him with vacant eyes. "She's... dead, Hy'Targ. They killed her."

Hy'Targ looked at Varanthl, and the big homunculus

scooped him up. The dwarf grabbed his vorpal sword and wiped it clean of blood, using the body of the dead cultist to strop the blade, and then Hy'Targ hurried after him.

Eucalia took up the rear upon Acacia. She carried a spike sword she'd grown from the ground and turned as hard as any morehl poniard. Both her weapon and Acacia's horn were splattered with the ochre and yellow hues of trog blood.

Mantieth continued rambling as his friends carried him away from the crater and the oncoming horde. "I, I broke her heart... I didn't tell her how I felt... not really... "

Both Taryl and the amazon leader, Halle, approached Varanthl and the elf he carried. "We need your father's help," Halle cried. "Between the firebombs and the winged eldarim riders, they're tearing us apart out here. We have vagha spell crafters; let us send you to Niamarlee and beg your father's assistance. If he'd send his coral ships and eagle riders, we could end it a couple days... We just need these durngamed skies cleared so we can mount an offensive."

"She's dead... *dead,* and I didn't get to tell her," Mantieth said, staring at Halle blankly.

Hy'Targ shook his head when he met Taryl's gaze. "Elorall... "

Taryl tightened his jaw and raked his fingers through his hair. "Damn it," he mumbled reverently.

"She took out an eldarim and the dragonkin he rode. Even scattered the harpies... At great cost," the dwarf spoke solemnly.

Halle scowled. "All the better reason to summon a Path and send him back home for support. She's dead, but we still need help, or we'll all join her."

"Give him some time," Hy'Targ said. "He's suffering deeply. He's going to need a moment."

Halle frowned and looked him over with stern eyes. "We don't have as many moments as he needs."

Mantieth slumped in Varanthl's arms and continued to mumble, asking himself rhetorical questions, "Why did I say that? If I hadn't said that, she wouldn't have stormed off..."

A runner approached and whispered a report to the commanders.

Taryl stated, "I'm not sure we have any vagha left with strength enough to cast a spell that sends him all the way to Niamarlee... Even if we did, I'm not sure Mantieth will remember why we sent him there in the first place. Perhaps things will be better in the morning for him—at least I have the confidence we could summon enough magic after a night's rest."

Halle rubbed her chin and mulled over the scout's report. "We've heard reports that the trogs are backing off, so that may be possible."

The eldarim nodded and turned back to the Gods'own. "We're retreating a couple blocks to increase the buffer between us and the battle lines—even if the trogs are mostly retreating for the night." Taryl pointed the way. "If they really wanted the city, they'd have held the line and dug in."

"If not the city, then what did they want with this last attack?" Eucalia asked.

Taryl grimaced. "To show us that they are strong enough to hit us whenever they want."

Halle nodded at the assertion and pointed to Mantieth. "We can do nothing until tomorrow. In the meanwhile, prop him up by the fire and get him some ale, and lots of it. Unless you can find anything stronger?"

"Will that help?" Varanthl asked.

Halle shook her head and answered honestly. "No. He won't recover from *this* anytime soon."

Nodhan strolled through the upper streets of Port Orric.

He wore the same finery common of the selumari in his neighborhood, and he moved with a slight swagger in his step.

He flashed Laelysh a grin as they walked along the road with Oren in tow. The boy dragged a stick as he walked, watching it dig a furrow in the soil behind him as he followed.

The morehl reveled in the fact that his neighbors boasted a deep and innate disapproval of him, despite the tenants of a free city, complete with its progressive thinking. That ideology, popular in many urban areas, mandated that those same neighbors *had* to accept him, regardless of old racial prejudice. Upsetting their status quo gave him a sense of perverse glee— the same kind he felt when he plundered priceless treasure troves.

Nodhan glanced at the boy and smiled. So long as everyone kept up the ruse for a generation or two, those old animosities could finally die, as long as no one stirred up too much dissension regarding the issues.

"I miss Brentésion," Oren said out of nowhere.

Nodhan and Laelysh paused to let the child keep up. He had been playing with the dracolem quite often. Which was good for him. It kept the creature entertained while the morehl laid low and focused his attention on placating the seed that still frequently argued with him.

"Remember what we talked about?" Laelysh spoke with her son. "We must not mention Brentésion. He is our secret. Not everyone can afford to have such a fine pet. We do not want those around us to resent us, do we?"

Nodhan's jaw tightened. Keeping the secret was the boy's one real job. Nothing could sour their residence in Port Orric like the sudden discovery of the morehl's true trade. His fancy, foppish clothes were all part of that cover… That, and he truly enjoyed a finely tailored suit.

The boy shrugged. "But Brentésion said she would miss me whenever she has to leave. And now, I miss her too."

"That's cute," Laelysh turned to Nodhan and whispered. "He thinks the drakufreet talks to him like he is an eldarim. Children have a special way."

Nodhan bobbed his head, but secretly ground his teeth. He didn't know the dracolem could talk with anyone else, and he'd kept much of the creature's secrets from even Laelysh.

He scooped up the boy. "Come now, Sir Oren," he said. "Let us walk to the square and visit the confectionarium," he winked.

"The confectionarium?" Oren said with a kind of reverence.

Nodhan nodded and led the way. The shop sold all manner of sweets, including a hot and sticky loaf filled with custards, spices, and creams. Sticky Loaf agreed with folk of every species, it seemed, albeit for different reasons.

Oren raced on ahead, practically dragging his mother and guardian along. He put his hands up to indicate a size. "I'm going to eat a sticky loaf *this big*."

Nodhan laughed as they entered the commercial part of town that catered to a high-end clientele. Shops here sold finer clothing and goods, while the more utilitarian shops were located a few blocks below. Levels of the city grew more focused on industry the closer one got to sea level, and the wharfs that had inspired the name of the city.

The lava elf smiled and carried on with Laelysh, putting up the charade that he was nothing more than a happy and successful trader out for a stroll. Deep down, something buzzed in his gut. He knew something was wrong; he could feel it in his bones.

Nodhan purchased treats for each of them at the confectionarium and sat at the high-top table.

"So Brentésion thinks she may have to leave soon?" Nodhan asked the boy.

"She says you would go with her," Oren replied, "But we're not supposed to talk about Brentésion." He sopped a forkful of his sticky loaf in the warm cream it came with and took a huge bite.

Fire and death, Nodhan silently cursed. He glanced back and then saw the thing that had bothered him. His keen eyes had noticed it before, but only in his peripheral vision. A tall, cloaked figure had been stalking them since their walk down from the residential level where they lived.

Nodhan scratched an itch on his forearm and fingered the weapon he'd kept there by way of his needle spell. Nodhan turned back casually, hoping to get another glance at the stalker and learn something about them, but the figure had already slipped beyond out of sight.

Fire and death, he repeated, knowing he would have to keep an eye out for whoever this mysterious fiend was and tread cautiously until he knew what powers, and allegiances, they represented.

Mantieth stared into the fire, borderline catatonic. His friends surrounded him, also watching the flames. They shared in his pain.

Silence reigned over the night. For the most part, anyway. Occasional clamor arose as minor skirmishes punctuated the night. Small goblin raiding parties tested the new defensive perimeter set by Bralanthyr's army. The trogs refused to give them any respite and sent the defenders a clear message: *We've got goblin lives we can throw away. There are more of us than of you.*

The Gods'own passed a bottle of *Old Groakh* around the circle. Varanthl had found it in a liquor stash when they sat Mantieth by the fire. The homunculus hadn't understood the rarity of the dwarven whiskey, but Hy'Targ had nabbed it straight away as they searched for something to medicate their selumari friend.

Hy'Targ poured a cup and set it before Mantieth. The elf's eyes flitted to it, at least, before returning to the fire. That was some progress, he supposed.

The dwarf took a pull off the bottle and swished the smoky liquid around his mouth before handing it over to Varanthl. He swallowed. "This bottle could purchase half a fleet of mammoths," he said. "Maybe even a small coral airship. A worthy memorial for her... for Elorall."

Varanthl sniffed the bottle and winced. He took a hesitant swig and coughed as if his lungs had just been frozen. Shaking his head, he handed the bottle to Eucalia.

The dryad tipped her head back and guzzled several glugs. Acacia laid with legs curled under him, and Eucalia set the bottle in front of the unicorn.

Hy'Targ stared at her in bewilderment for a moment. "How's he supposed to..."

The unicorn bit the bottle by the neck and tossed it back to take a swig before setting it down.

"He's a unicorn, not some mere animal," Eucalia explained. "Not everybody understands that they are as intelligent as you or I." She tossed the bottle back to the dwarf.

Hy'Targ nodded and then wiped the equestrian slobber from the *Old Groakh* before taking another swallow.

"It was all a misunderstanding," Mantieth said heavily. "She thought I had asked for her hand... proclaimed my love, even. But I didn't. I *never* did." He threw back the cup of whiskey and then motioned for the bottle. The elf mumbled, "But I should have."

Hy'Targ handed it to him and Mantieth poured another cup. He passed the glass to the dwarf and kept the bottle.

"I just wish I would've known sooner," the elf lamented.

"Known what?" Varanthl asked.

"That I *did* love her." Mantieth took another drink. "I always have. She was always the one for me, but I was never able to see it until now... *We were always meant to be*. She's the only one I ever loved—maybe the only one I ever *could*... I just wish I'd have realized it sooner... I wish I would have told her that I loved her... made it real."

The others sat in silence with him for a long while, saying nothing. Mantieth continued to drink. He told a few stories of their exploits and mischief as young selumari, now with the added clarity of his revelation: A love unprofessed and which could never be.

Deep into the night, the *Old Groakh* ran dry, and the Gods'own nodded off into fitful sleep filled with dreams that replayed those horrific events over and over in their minds.

CHAPTER TWENTY-SIX

The two remaining eldarim cultists remained inside the building where Ratargul had established his base of operations. A handful of goblins ran to and fro, relaying orders and news to the Nekarthans. Their special goblins had been marked on their foreheads with black tattoos of the Nekarthan sigil. These with a secret affinity or long connection to the Black Forest pledged fealty to the cultists and their cause.

"I hate him," Tsut told Grackyll, the goblin wizard. He pointed to the next scout with a tattoo. "And him. And him."

"Are there any you hate who do not bear the mark?" Grackyll asked.

Tsut shrugged. "Does Ratargul have the tattoo?"

Grackyll nodded.

"Then no." The influential goblin watched them pass between the two black dragonkin who guarded the door.

"They issue commands as if they command the Moorlech," Grackyll observed.

"Because they do," Tsut said.

Ratargul's massive girth towered over the other goblins as he emerged from a band of raiders who had just returned. He headed for the door as Tsut and the spell caster watched. The drakufreet growled and closed ranks, denying him entry.

The shambling mound growled back at them, but they did not let him pass. Shouting, the monster raised enough noise that the eldarim finally opened the door.

They did not let him pass and spoke from the porch. "Your services are not currently needed, shambling mound. We shall summon you when we need you."

"You cannot cut me out! I lead the army!" Ratargul howled.

The eldarim raised their eyebrows, amused by the

premise.

"You need me. Now let me in," he continued to argue.

"You overestimate your place," a cultist said. "Your actions and orders have been rash. The branch of Nekarthis has not grown so long by committing to headstrong action or by rushing into battles needlessly."

"I've done everything you wanted..." he argued.

"And then some," an eldarim hissed. "You rushed into a needless battle to save face with a lesser goblin and that conflict revealed our presence—only that can explain how the Gods'own anticipated us and now one of our own was killed." His voice struck like hammer blows. It was stern enough that Ratargul knew he could not argue his way back into the fold.

He spat several curses as a marked goblin ran towards the headquarters. Ratargul lashed out in a rage and dismembered the trog.

The two eldarim stared at the shambling mound who turned and left, still spouting curses while the goblin corpse bled out at the feet of the acolytes.

Tsut turned to Grackyll. "His fall makes me happy, but he can fall further yet. In the meantime, we've got to do something about those cultists."

Grackyll nodded. "They certainly don't represent the Moorlech's best interest."

Tsut bobbed his head with agreement and watched Ratargul storm off into the distance. "I swear, I'll kill that shambling mound before all of this is done."

"There's more coming in!" shouted a selumari archer on the rooftop of an adjacent building. He stood four stories higher than the Gods'own's position on the street.

By morning, Halle and Taryl had convinced Mantieth to plead their case for Leidergelth's help. Before they'd had a chance to open a path with the vaghan thaumaturgists, the horns of war had called again, scrambling the defenders for action.

Hy'Targ looked up and saw where the archer pointed. The dwarf called back, "Got it! You keep 'em thinned and we'll hack 'em down."

The Gods'own's remnant tagged along with a contingent that guarded a campus of large structures. One was Bralanthyr's orphanage. Two other buildings, apartments both, surrounded the dormitory. The cluster of structures housed those who had been displaced from their homes north of Broadstreet and had nowhere else to go.

These people had no other options but to perish if the city fell. Halle's forces had crammed them in tightly. Thousands of souls occupied those three buildings and the smaller ones surrounding them. She wanted to keep them as close as possible so they could alert them of any emergency and move them in time.

Hy'Targ scowled. He'd looked into a few faces of the residents there. Halle's logic was moot. They would not move if the order came up. For these folks, this was their last stand.

"Gimme a boost, would ya?" the dwarf asked Varanthl.

The homunculus nodded and helped his friend up to the ladder hanging many cubits above the ground. Hy'Targ began climbing; he could hear the oncoming horde of goblin soldiers. The noise of their uncontested parade through the streets echoed through the corridors between urban buildings. "I gotta see what we're dealing with."

Varanthl leapt up after him and grabbed the ladder, following him to the rooftop.

Hy'Targ glanced back. Mantieth paced back and forth. He was still stuck in his own head, and the dwarf wondered if the elf was more of a liability than an asset at this point. He shook his head. *No. We'll need every sword to defend against this army.*

Acacia turned his head and watched the elf while the

dryad summoned a platform of green beneath her feet. It rose upon thick cords of vine, lifting her more quickly than the others could climb.

Hy'Targ and Varanthl crested the top and found her waiting with the coral elf archer. The selumari had four others with him. They dragged a full bale of arrows and set barricades to cover them while they aimed at their targets.

"It's bad," the archer said.

Hy'Targ crept to the edge of the building and looked down at the streets below. The enemy filled the streets like he'd never seen before, except during parades on Turambar's day.

"We'll never stop that," Varanthl said despairingly.

"We must," said Eucalia. "The people here are defenseless."

Hy'Targ growled to the archers. "I want every one of these arrows in a goblin neck, and for the love of the gods, don't shoot me."

The selumari cocked his head, nodding.

Hy'Targ swung a leg over the ledge and scrambled down the ladder as quickly as possible. The others followed him.

Eucalia was already on the ground by the time Hy'Targ reached it. "What do you have in mind?"

"Killbox," he said and winked. "Make some thorny walls or something and keep 'em all in a straight line. You'll know what I mean when I get back."

She looked down the long road and saw where the side streets opened and nodded, suddenly understanding his plan.

"Varanthl." Hy'Targ jerked his head towards the dozen or so amazons who had come to defend this zone with him. "Hold the fort. I'll be right back and make sure Mantieth and the others duck when they see me coming!"

Hy'Targ turned to run in the direction of the command center, but the unicorn barred his way. Acacia's snort sounded almost like a growl.

"Um, what does he want?" Hy'Targ turned his gaze to Eucalia.

"He says to climb up." She watched the dwarf as he struggled to mount him bareback. "I'd suggest you hold on tight."

Hy'Targ grabbed a fistful of mane and then yelped as the horned beast dashed away with his vaghan passenger clinging on for all he was worth. Patches of green sprouted from every hoof print leading a trail back towards the center of their muster.

Varanthl readied his hammer and took his place alongside the amazons. One of them nodded to him respectfully, recognizing their human bond. Eucalia returned to the rooftop, and Mantieth curled his lip as he drew his vorpal blade. His face tightened into a mask of rage and emotion. The elf was sure to burst at any moment.

The army's sounds grew louder and louder as their stomping feet grew closer. Many trogs fell as the arrows rained down from overhead. Goblins held their shields over the top of their heads to provide some protection—but their chief asset was their numbers. The archers could not possibly dispatch them all.

"Hold this line!" Varanthl howled to his companions as the goblins drew close.

Mantieth paced back and forth until he finally broke. He shouted, pouring out all his rage and sorrow. His cracking voice didn't even produce words, just raw emotion. He leapt forward and charged into the enemy like an elf possessed.

His vorpal sword sang as it bit goblin flesh and he turned like a vortex: hacking, blocking, parrying, stabbing. Trog after trog fell to his sword and the disposition of the goblin vanguard suddenly shifted. This lone elf became their only target.

Driven by his rage, they could not touch him. He was

fueled by it, and not even Mantieth knew if that supply would ever ebb.

Varanthl and the humans used the distraction to their advantage. They engaged before the crushing onslaught of enemies. They yielded only a few steps at a time, but stayed alive, though for how long, none could tell. An amazon fell to a goblin's stone axe.

The homunculus's stomach sank as he heard the screeches of a troll in the enemy ranks. He scanned the army for it and noticed the side streets had begun to fill with greenery. A wall of thorns had been built up, funneling all the enemies directly towards the orphanage and its doomed rooftop defenders.

The troll screeched again, enabling Varanthl's eyes to lock onto it. Another noise responded, trumpets blasting behind them.

Varanthl whirled as soon as he felt the tremors of the stampede behind him. "Everybody down!"

The amazons fled, leaping within alcoves on buildings or crashing through nearby doors and allies for cover. Mantieth remained on his feet, driven by his bloodlust. He was deaf to anything but the blood pounding in his ears and the drive to kill... *kill... kill!*

Varanthl glanced back and saw Hy'Targ storming through on the mammoth he'd stabled since their arrival. Someone else rode atop another mammoth, Jr'Orhr's beast, and a chain stretched between the interior tusks of each of them as the trampling mounts hugged the edges of the street, forming a killbox.

They stampeded closer, and Varanthl launched himself at Mantieth. The elf snarled, blind with rage, and he turned to face his friend who he could not discern from his foes.

Varanthl tried to tackle him as the coral elf plunged his blade into the homunculus's midsection. He wrapped all four arms around him and dragged him to the cobblestone street just as the two mammoths stormed past. Their chain stretched tight between them like a razor-wire; it zipped overhead, dismembering unwary goblins who had nowhere to go. Those not caught in the chain's path were likely trampled.

A draconic roar echoed as well. A small pack of drakufreet charged behind the mammoths, cleaning up any stragglers. Their scales shimmered in a variety of colors.

Varanthl groaned and shifted as the sword bit deeply. He gasped and used one hand to pull the sword free. The other three hands still held tightly to Mantieth, but the elf no longer resisted his grapple.

"I'm sorry. I'm so sorry," Mantieth bawled. Tears rolled down his cheeks. "I didn't mean to… I just… she's dead…"

"I know," said Varanthl. "I'll miss her too… not like you. But I've had my own, similar losses." He grimaced and tossed the vorpal blade aside, sucking air through his teeth to mitigate the pain.

"I just… I wonder if it would have been better had I been the one who died."

Varanthl sighed and released the coral elf, who sobbed for a few moments. "If you stab me again, you just might be. Fast healing aside."

Mantieth wiped his cheeks and nodded.

Varanthl returned the selumari's weapon to him.

They both turned and looked back to find the goblins fleeing. The enemy had relinquished this street, at least. Taryl turned and flashed them a grin from atop Jr'Orhr's mount.

Eucalia climbed back to the ground. "I certainly hope that sends the trogs back to the fens."

Varanthl nodded. "Likewise… but I fear reclaiming one street won't have so great an impact."

Upon their woolly mounts, Taryl and Hy'Targ returned with a small horde of wild dragonkin following their eldarim. They arrived just in time to catch the conversation. "I hope the other streets have had the success that we've been able to find."

Taryl set his jaw. "I'm guessing that may not be likely."

The two eldarim cultists stood on either side of the rough map they'd constructed of Bralanthyr and placed upon a table to visualize the battle's progression. A distant shriek caught their attention. They exited the building and then turned their eyes skyward.

A winged drakufreet champion descended in a controlled glide. It was another agamid suchia, exactly like theirs. Sukies made ideal mounts, and the agamids, the winged type, were perfect for their purposes, though few but eldarim could ever master them. The largest size drakufreet, the champions, were nearly the size of dragons, but were less intelligent. Full drakes and wyrms were at least as intelligent as any other creature, and far more than some, especially the Elder Dragons who first tumbled to Esfah long before any race thought to measure the passage of time. The Elder Dragons who had birthed the drakufreet race had even mastered the common language.

The beast landed with a thud. A hooded eldarim pulled back his cowl to show them the mark upon his forehead.

"Welcome, brother," said the one.

"News from the Black Forest, I presume? Have the airships departed Niamarlee?" asked the other.

The newcomer shook his head. "Gather your things. There has been a change of plans. Niamarlee will not fall by conflict. Ever in motion is the swaying of the Forest's branches upon the winds of change."

One of the first eldarim cocked his head. "We've invested much in this gambit. Who issued that order?"

"One of the four Masked Ones." His words seemed to suck the air out of any argument. "They desire something else for Niamarlee."

He continued, "Our other agents are so close to their targets that another plan for establishing our dominion has become optimal." He chortled. "For once, the Melkites may have been on the right track. Though they may not know the scope of the pieces they have in play; our hidden side of the board is poised to react. We shall do what we do best: Manipulate the game and drag all plunder into the shadows. More will be explained when we reach Cyrea."

"Cyrea? You mean that we go to meet -"

"Yes," the newcomer snapped. "We go to meet *her*. The Mistress, head of the Masked Ones."

CHAPTER TWENTY-SEVEN

A horde of goblins followed Ratargul the Smotherer as he stormed towards the central base of the trog forces. They screeched and yelped as they huddled near him, bolstering the monstrous leader of the Moorlech.

Ratargul pointed at the trio of eldarim as they secured saddle bags and straps for their flying mounts' bardings. "You! Eldarim of the Black Forest! You cannot push Ratargul the Smotherer from the command of the trogs..."

"You can have it," one of the cultists fired back, barely paying him any mind.

The shambling mound stood erect with surprise. "What?"

"It's yours. We are leaving," he said, bowing with mock humility.

"You... you're just going?"

"Indeed. Take Bralanthyr. Burn it. Leave it alone. We do not care. The winds have changed and so have our orders; a new wind blows in the north and our masters call us home."

Ratargul shuffled from foot to foot. Their new course took him by total surprise. "No. Wait, you must help us take the city first. We can take Bralanthyr and you will have gained a powerful ally."

The eldarim scoffed. "You do not know what true power is. You could have already taken this city, but if we had, you would not have gained what you most seek. Power."

As one, the trio clambered aboard their agamids and took to the sky. In less than a minute, they disappeared, no more than specks on the horizon.

Ratargul worked his jaw, still reeling from the shock. Then he twisted the situation to his advantage. He'd already pulled the strongest trogs to his side in order to leverage the

Nekarthans into seeing things his way.

"The Eldarim knew we could take the city!" he declared. "And also, I have rid us of them—and good riddance! We could have sacked Bralanthyr a night ago, but the eldarim stalled us, purposefully holding back... like they were waiting for something."

"Orders, King Ratargul?" one of the misshapen trogs asked. His voice whined through his twisted, bent nose.

"We take the city now!" Ratargul howled. "It is ours—the Black Forest knew it, we knew it, none can stop us. All forces, attack! Show those squinchy gurks who's lords of Bralanthyr."

The army shouted in response. They began to move towards the city with frenzied fervor, increasing their pace with every step.

Tsut and Grackyll pushed their way towards the front, shouting down the legion's commanders and trying to be heard, but none would listen to them. The trog leaders were already dispersing towards their command sections to rally their minions.

"This is how it ends," Tsut spat to the sorcerer. "An orgy of spilled blood, much of it goblin. Nobody controls the trog army, not even Ratargul—not truly."

Grackyll nodded measuredly. "And it is on the move... but this is not how it ends."

"No?" Tsut raised an eyebrow.

"No. It ends with us killing The Smotherer and reclaiming what belongs to us: control of the horde."

The trogs poured into Bralanthyr like frenzied sharks with blood in the water. They clutched weapons and howled battle cries as they sprinted across Broadstreet and into the defensive line formed by the mixed company of humans, vagha, and selumari.

Bells rang as the defenders scrambled all forces to the battlefront. The wave of goblin bodies gathered and surged forward like a tsunami, crashing against the breakers with stone axes and slings.

A wave of swampy stench rolled off the marauders and hit the defenders just before the frenzied horde smashed into the shield wall and barricade. The sound of their impact echoed like hammers upon anvils.

Goblin spell casters flung their dark arcana as their vanguard pushed forward and weakened the defenses like acid against limestone. "For the Moorlech!" some cried out. Others screeched, "For Ratargul!"

Holding nothing back, the Smotherer's forces outnumbered the defenders at least four to one. They'd had the numbers to easily win from the conflict's beginning, and now they knew it. Unlike vaghan cities, most citizens of human cities were not prepared to fight invaders—and every defender who had to split his or her attention between defending the helpless or hacking down invaders pulled double-duty, further skewing the odds in favor of the trogs.

The Gods'own, Taryl, and a small fleet of drakufreet he had summoned from the wilds rushed to the front. Just before hitting the front, Taryl lamented, "This looks to be a massacre…"

A trio of sorcerers stood with the amazon general. "If the end has arrived, let us burn them all. We can summon a dragon—if we're all to die here, today, let us take the trogs with us."

"No! I will not entertain such a notion," Halle howled. Several of her commanders stood nearby. Taryl and the others veered towards her.

"I will kill any sorcerer who begins to conjure wyrmcraft—further, I will execute his or her family at the end of this war. Do I make myself clear?" she demanded.

They gulped and nodded their understanding.

Taryl did not bother asking about the conflict. She met his eyes and explained anyway, "I will not summon a dragon to annihilate these trogs. Such a creature would lay waste to Bralanthyr. The future must hold more than cinder and ash, regardless of the victors."

The eldarim nodded and continued past. He knew as well as any that she made the best choice. Even he, a dragonlord who could take control of a rampaging wyrm or drake, knew that dragon magic was not an exact science. More often than not, the odds were stacked against even him—and a dragon could easily melt Bralanthyr, and all its inhabitants.

Taryl arrived with the Gods'own at the second line of defense. The first verged on the overwhelming numbers of the Moorlech, and there was no third line of defense. All those citizens hiding in their homes on the south side, and those displaced in the orphanage and the refuge facilities, would die if they faltered.

The Gods'own filled in gaps. From their vantage, they could see the wreckage where Elorall fell near the ruins of Broadstreet. Below them, the front line wavered under the ferocity of the trogs who fell by the score, but continued the relentless crush of superior numbers. The sight sucked the air from the defender's ranks, undercutting their resolve.

Something caught in Mantieth's throat. He took a step forward. "Friends, we must protect this city," he yelled to his fellow defenders. Bralanthyr is not the buildings and the houses—it is the people. Ten blocks that way," he pointed in the direction of the orphanage, "is the heart of the matter. Defenseless folk wait for our success. Those people *need* us... even if we sacrifice our own lives here to give them another day, we *must* carry the day. We've all known friends and lovers who did the same for us... perhaps this is the way of things? Sorrow and..."

Taryl stepped forward and put a hand on Mantieth's chest to interrupt him before the elf could spiral. "Protect the city! Protect the people," Taryl yelled, salvaging the coral elf's speech. "Save Bralanthyr!"

"Save Bralanthyr!" the army shouted in unison and then began beating weapon against shield, bolstering their failing hearts.

Harpies flew overhead, fewer than before, but carrying double clay pots. They were lashed together by strands of twine. One hurled her payload into the front line where it broke open. The firepot ignited the second jar containing lantern oil, and the bomb exploded, scattering amazon warriors in its wake.

Ranks broke as the humans fled the flames. A cluster of vagha on the second line rushed for the faltering front, knowing they were sterner than their human counterparts. They could fight with flames dancing around their feet, provided they did not intensify too greatly.

At the sight of fighters rushing to battle, the defenders' war cry intensified and others also charged ahead, reinforcing the front. In a matter of seconds, all the defenders of Bralanthyr surged forward. They crashed into the overwhelming tide of trogs, who yielded dozens of cubits as the counter attackers hacked and slashed, culling their ranks.

But it was not the route they desperately needed. The trogs had committed to Ratargul's madness, and they knew their numbers were superior.

Mantieth and his friends fought with reckless abandon, killing as many enemy combatants as they encountered. Varanthl swung his hammer in wide, high arcs overtop of Hy'Targ's head and the dwarf slashed Glorybringer against any threats the homunculus's hammer did not smash.

Eucalia fought alongside Acacia. Yellowish goblin blood slicked the unicorn's face and neck. His rear legs were splattered with the gory stuff and he whirled to kick, planting both hooves into the face of a charging trog. He crumpled to the dirt, his head a ruined mess of liquid yellow and chunky gray.

Mantieth spun and slashed in a wide arc. His vorpal sword sliced through all assailants who rushed him, and their corpses fell to the cracked and ruined soil, clearing the elf's field of vision momentarily.

The pitched battle had a definite trajectory; he could sense it more than he could see it. Bralanthyr's defenders were superior fighters, but they could not hold out against the hordes. Doom would find every one of them. That thought lodged in his gut and poisoned his resolve.

His eyes caught the busted cobblestone at his feet and he looked down at the scorched tile. He stood directly adjacent to the crater where Elorall had made her final stand.

"So be it!" he howled with despair. "I will see Elorall again before the day is through," he declared like an apocalyptic prophet. Mantieth flung himself at the swelling wave of goblins who moved his way.

Behind him, Eucalia screamed as a trog's axe hacked and sundered her blade of hardened wood. It erupted in splinters and she fell. Six trogs had overwhelmed Varanthl and grappled with him so he could not bring his hammer to bear.

The elf screamed with rage and began chopping limb from joint as the wall of enemies pressed for him, finally making the elf retreat one step at a time.

A swampy stench from the horde nearly overwhelmed Mantieth, thickening the air like a hot, wet wind rolling off a smoldering trash heap. He felt his rear foot plant uneasily at the edge of the crater's lip.

Enemies continued to crush against him, threatening to send him careening into the black pit.

And then, his sensitive selumari ears caught it; a kind of whooshing sound. It rumbled in the chasm behind him.

A geyser of water shot from the ground where an old cistern had been long buried. A screaming elf enchanter rode the jet of water into the air.

"Elorall!" Mantieth howled as his enemies shied back two steps.

Her eyes blazed with blue fury. Bruises and cuts marked her body, and much of her outfit and hair had been burned and torn away from yesterday's explosion.

The geyser turned into a tornado, whipping a torrent of water and wind across the battlefield as the funnel of air took shape around her. Elorall's bracelet glowed with a brilliant cerulean aura that blazed clear, even through the churning gray vortex.

Trogs forgot the rest of the defenders and targeted this new threat, marked by the blue fire within. They aimed for the source and launched a hail of stone bullets, javelins, and any other projectiles they found.

She batted them aside effortlessly. Elorall channeled the very power of the goddess Ailuril through her mystic bracelet. The elf caught and turned the enemy missiles around on their wide, looping arcs and then fired them back at the enemy, finding the soft targets of troggish bellies and throats.

Elorall turned her attention to the harpies flapping around her and waved a gust of wind at them, scattering the flying monsters. They dropped their fire and oil pots and the enchanter scooped them up before they could break on the ground below. Elorall flung them in a straight line, driving them through the heart of the trogs' army and dashing them against goblin feet, where they erupted with the fire of godly wrath.

The Moorlech's morale snapped and the rear of the goblin army broke ranks, fleeing. With nothing to hold them in the battle, the front line followed suit, joining the total route. Within seconds, the pitch of the battle had flipped entirely.

Defenders chased after the fleeing trogs, lodging sword and javelin in their backs and repelling them fully from the city. The Gods'own remained at the crater as Elorall rode the swiftly dispelling tornado to the ground.

Her bracelet's shine diminished, but her arm seemed to flicker between solid existence and not being there at all. Mantieth watched it with worry on his face, as did Elorall. Finally, the involuntary phasing subsided like a twitching and cramping muscle that had finally calmed.

Exhaustion played across the wounded coral elf's face and she tried to speak. Taking two steps, her knees buckled. Mantieth rushed to her side, but she pushed him away. She leaned instead on Eucalia's shoulder and let the dryad help her to her feet.

Wearily, the Gods'own began their trek back towards camp. The absence of battle sounds hung over Bralanthyr; a stark contrast to the last many days.

Mantieth followed Hy'Targ, who limped at the rear of the party. He wiped away a tear from both eyes and caught up with the vaghan prince.

"She—she's alive," Mantieth said with a warbling voice.

"Aye," Hy'targ said, grimacing at the pain in his body. "But something tells me she's no longer yours."

The retreating goblins began to slow their withdrawal a few leagues beyond the edge of the city. Even the dimwitted trogs reassessed recent events once they'd gotten beyond the urban setting and reestablished their state of mind.

Whatever that air goddess had been, it had not followed them past the city, and they still possessed superior numbers. Since the defenders had pushed them beyond the city borders, they would be spread too thin to keep the Moorlech's forces out.

"Muster!" Ratargul shouted, calling his forces to surround him. "Muster, muster!"

His hordes formed up around him, giving him the

chance to issue orders so they might retake the city. The shambling mound gave his minions a chance to catch their breath. Before he could open his mouth to speak, a voice cried out.

"Ratargul is weak!" it echoed above the assembly.

"A challenge?" Ratargul roared. "Reveal yourself, coward!"

"The shambler is not the strongest—his strength is a fraud."

Ratargul snapped his head towards the sound of the voice. The crowd parted, creating a long tunnel with a solitary goblin at the end of it. Tsut stood there, a runt with no fear on his face.

"I said, Ratargul is weak," he stated defiantly. "Ratargul knew it, too, and so he gave over control of the army to the Nekarthan eldarim."

A murmur rippled through the forces. The shambling mound scanned the crowd; his scrawny enemy had poisoned his devotees with the truth and he roared, "Face me, then—I'll tear you to pieces!"

"Ratargul has a weak mind. They exploited him like any other simpleton," Tsut yelled, and then reeled as the monstrous warrior charged for him.

Ratargul reached out with strong hands, hoping to wring Tsut's neck.

Tsut ducked beneath him, using his diminutive size to his advantage.

The crowd's center dilated and formed a circle where the two squared off against each other. From within his body, the swamp creature drew the wicked blade that had once been Heshgillick's.

Ratargul charged again, clutching the sword menacingly. This time, he stumbled, staggering to a slow lope before stopping entirely.

Grackyll stood on the far side of the circle. He'd emerged from the crowd and hurled an invisible ball of magic at Ratargul, sapping the monster's strength.

The warrior roared, pivoted, and hurled his weapon at the spell caster. It flew just clumsily enough for Grackyll to sidestep it; the jagged blade whipped past him and lodged in the chest of a nearby trog, breaking his clavicle. Yellow blood spurted from the fatal wound. With Grackyll's concentration broken, Ratargul whirled back towards Tsut.

But it was too late. Tsut had already dashed forward and readied his dagger. Before Ratargul could react, or even locate the small goblin, Tsut had wiped aside the hoary fronds and stringy vines to expose the patch of flesh where the shambling mound's mark of Nekarthan allegiance had been made.

Tsut shrieked as he plunged the dagger deep into his enemy's body.

Ratargul howled, sounding like the watery gasps of a drowning man. He staggered two steps and tried to assume a fluid like-form to drown Tsut, as he'd done to Heshgillick before him. The Smotherer instead poured out muddy brown liquid and collapsed like a cut water skin. He gasped one final time, and then lay dead, resembling a pile of waterlogged leaves and other swamp detritus.

The goblin runt scooped up the sack-like skin that was the shambler's secret heart and hung it over his head to signify his victory. It dangled like the skin of a flayed goblin imp, barely the size of a stillborn.

All around him, goblins bent their knee and bowed their head, swearing fealty to King Tsut. The last to take a knee was Grackyll, who held the new king's gaze as he did so. "Long live King Tsut of the Moorlech," Grackyll said, tipping his head.

A short silence followed as the horde expected him to issue some kind of statement. Finally, Tsut declared, "Goblins will rule, but this is not the right time, and this is not the best way. We must not overextend ourselves like this." He cast his eyes across the army. It was still impressive by any measurement.

"Bralanthyr was never the goblin dream. It belonged to those who would manipulate us, and we could never keep it. We wouldn't want it. Let us return to the Moorlech and to the Black Glades." He turned his eyes to the ruined city. "Let the other folk keep their smelly city. Our time will come, and then all races will work for us. But until then, go home. Find all your wives and make babies. Breed us an army for the future," he growled.

Hy'Targ crawled up the ladder and reached the top of the building. It afforded a long view across the reaches of the city. When they'd first arrived in Bralanthyr, the view had been much different, but many structures that blocked the skyline had been burned or demolished since, changing the visible lanes dramatically.

Despite the limp, the vaghan prince meandered over to where Taryl stood, gazing into the distance. "There they are," Hy'Targ said, locking eyes on the distant goblin army where it regrouped.

Taryl shook his head and then turned to watch the same thing, shaking away the distraction of his thoughts. He'd been somewhere else, with someone else.

Hy'Targ grimaced. He assumed he was wondering after his nephew's fate. "Yes. And I certainly hope they do not come to their senses and launch another assault. I'm quite certain we cannot replicate our previous success."

They both stared at the distant enemy for some time. And then the trog army broke apart into smaller clusters and dispersed.

Hy'Targ and Taryl traded surprised looks with each other. Goblins were known to be full of surprises, but this had caught them both off-guard. Clusters of goblins wandered away, heading further into the distance and moving without any real sense of urgency.

"Did... did we just win this war?" Hy'Targ asked.

"It appears that way," Taryl said. He allowed a grin to spread across his face. "It looks that way indeed." He handed Hy'Targ a spyglass and the dwarf raised it to his eye.

From their current vantage, they could see the entirety of the defeated Moorlech horde. But he could not find Brentésion among them.

CHAPTER TWENTY-EIGHT

Mounts carried Taryl and the Gods'own towards the sloping path that cut through the Stonejaw mountain range. The army that had been originally tasked with hunting down the elusive trog army and securing Brentésion had been converted into a goblin taskforce. Now, their role had shifted again. Taryl left a portion of the mixed army at Bralanthyr to defend them while they rebuilt.

Taryl rode his dragonkin between Hy'Targ's mammoth and Mantieth's horse. "I'm sorry we were unable to locate Brentésion," he said.

Talk had been largely muted in the wake of so many loses. The trip back to Irontooth was nearly three hundred and fifty leagues and would take at least thirty days. They'd only ticked off a few of them so far, and Taryl expected spirits to lift somewhat as they drew closer to home.

Hy'Targ shrugged. "I know my father loved riding her, but if Ratargul's army did not have Brentésion, then she must be gone."

Mantieth turned in his saddle to look back at Elorall. She hadn't looked him in the eyes since the miracle that brought her back. "I don't know, Hy'Targ. I don't think one should ever give up hope."

They rode a few more minutes in silence. Only the crunching of gravel beneath feet and turning wheels sounded around them. That, and the regular sounds of what remained of Taryl's corps of fighters.

"Tell your father it has been an honor working for him," Taryl said.

"Tell him yourself," Hy'Targ fired back.

Taryl shook his head. "I can't stay and don't plan to return to Irontooth. I worry for my nephew. Yarrick is out there somewhere, alive or dead, and I plan to find him."

"We'll go with you," Mantieth insisted, but Taryl shook his head.

"This is not your burden. You accepted him into the Gods'own, but I fear this may be an eldari family matter."

The two nodded slowly, accepting the answer, even if they did not like it.

"But you will send word if you locate him or require help?" Hy'Targ asked.

Taryl nodded. He spurred his sukie mount to a little extra speed, and then peeled off from the larger company, riding through a mountain road and out of sight.

Yarrick had been chewing for days. His teeth hurt and his jaw muscles burned as he ground the rope between his mandibles.

He shivered and recalled the count. *Ten.* Today was the tenth day since the cultist's last visit. They would come again in the evening with food, and then they would make their next selection.

The last fraying strip of woven rope finally snapped between his teeth. The gag fell to his shoulders and then slid to the stony floor.

Yarrick winced and worked his jaw open and closed. Finally, he looked around the room again. The motley collection of white shara looked back at him with wonder in their eyes. Yarrick was still far from free; he was still bound in shackles like the rest, only he could now speak.

He needed information, and he had to act fast, but his peers could not speak. *That leaves only yes and no questions*, he told himself.

Yarrick spoke in barely more than a whisper, but it felt as if he shouted his words, the way they broke the silence of the chamber. "My name is Yarrick," he said, and explained his assumptions about their predicament. "I am a warrior. Have any of you been trained to fight?"

All heads shook no.

"As I suspected." He still needed many more details. "I know little about my clan history, but that we migrated from Dereh'Liandor long ago, like so many others. I was born in Sontarra, but spent much of my life in Charnock. Are you also from Charnock?"

One nodded yes and the others no.

"The Birthlands?"

All of them shook their heads.

"Hiriath? Dohan?"

Two yeses. And then one more.

So our continent of origin has nothing in common.

"My family has taken no oaths to any gods. We are universalists, belonging to the line of the white shara. Are any of you acolytes and have taken allegiance to specific gods?"

All shook their heads no.

I was right. We are all of the white.

"I did not see when I was brought here, but it feels like we are in a tower keep somewhere. Do any of you know about this place or where we are held?"

Only one nodded. The newest prisoner who had been chained here ten days ago.

Yarrick bit his lip, irked that he'd asked two questions instead of one. "You know where we are?"

No.

"About the building then... We are in some kind of castle tower?"

He nodded yes.

"How many levels high are we? Perhaps we can get free and escape over the wall... two levels?"

The prisoner confirmed the height at three levels, and

also that there were many armed guards in the castle.

Yarrick could see the hope failing in the prisoners' eyes at the revelation. "Do not despair. It is good that there are guards with weapons. It means I have the chance to disarm one and take a sword. Then, we might escape."

The line of light below the door deepened to a ruddy orange. Yarrick scrambled to snatch the gag rope from the floor and twisted it around his head, biting on the frayed ends to keep the rope's break hidden.

Footsteps shuffled in the hall beyond the door, and Yarrick's gut twisted into a knot. He formed a desperate plan in his mind. *I've only got one shot at this...*

Road-weary, the army containing the Gods'own trekked north towards the Irontooth castle. Built into the side of the mountain, the outer walls jutted out from the monolith where they sat on the sloping bastions. Already, those with keen eyes could spot vagha stationed atop the ramparts.

Within sight of the dwarven home, the mammoths, ponies, and horses quickened their gait. An hour later, the forces began passing inside through the broad gates of the vaghan city.

Hy'Targ and his companions were among the first to enter. He flashed an exhausted grin to his father, who stood high above the main courtyard.

The Adventurer King welcomed them in dwarven fashion. He held aloft Earthfang, the battleaxe he now carried and which had once belonged to his wife, Queen Sh'Ttil. Hy'Mandr winked at his son and Hy'Targ nodded in return.

As the king returned to his hall, surely to preside over a feast that honored the return of the Gods'own, the prince's eyes scanned the parapets for his uncle. He failed to locate him and when the stable master came to take his mammoth's reins, Hy'Targ asked, "Is Hy'Drunyr in the city?"

The dwarf raised his bushy eyebrows, slightly taken aback. Hy'Targ knew his uncle was not a popular figure, at least in these parts, and assumed he had insulted the stable master with the question.

"I don't mean to insinuate you and he have dealings. I'm simply asking after a fact," he clarified.

The stable master shrugged. "I can't say with full certainty, but I heard a credible rumor a tenday ago that the King's brother was headed out of town on some business venture or another, as he often does. But there are far more interesting persons in the castle walls."

Hy'Targ cocked his head.

The stable master informed him, "King Leidergelth and some of his selumari have come. They expected the return of the Gods'own and assumed you would take the southern pass, making Irontooth your first logical destination."

Hy'Targ nodded and thanked the dwarf, letting him return to his duties. He turned to locate his friends. Mantieth hurried his gait to catch up to Elorall, but her body language indicated she still had no desire to speak with him.

The prince paused and scratched his beard while Varanthl walked closer. All four of his arms were full of bundled supplies. "You know," Hy'Targ told him, "there are servants who can carry that for you. You are Gods'own and a friend of the crown."

Varanthl shrugged. "I'm fine. I prefer to do it myself, actually. The small tasks help fill the otherwise silent time."

Hy'Targ shot him a screwy look.

Varanthl grinned. "Actually, before all of this, my life was felt in the minutia. Little chores like laundry and scrubbing dishes reminds me of those days… routines I learned alongside my father."

Hy'Targ nodded. It was as good a reason as any. He looked up as a scarred dwarf approached through the crowds in the courtyard.

Jr'Orhr took a few big steps and hugged the vaghan prince. "Glad to see yer alive. Both of you. I heard the fighting was nasty at Bralanthyr."

Hy'Targ nodded and scanned his friend. "Well, you look fat and clean. And I'd take that any day over glorious battles and the long road."

Jr'Orhr smiled, half agreeing. "Come along. The King's got a feast in the works, but we can grab a few mugs of ale before then." He handed over a rolled sheaf of fresh parchments.

"What's this?" the prince asked. He unrolled them.

Jr'Orhr tapped his head, reminding him of his eidetic memory. "I made you a copy of your uncle's materials. Had to find some way to occupy myself ever since those sorcerers sent me away from Bralanthyr."

Hy'Targ looked at the familiar language of the gremmlobahnd. It was a perfect copy of the scrolls Hy'Drunyr had purchased in Kragryn.

Jr'Orhr nodded to answer the next question before Hy'Targ could ask. "All three pieces of the Malfus Necrosis artifacts are safely locked away in the vault. I took the one from Hy'Drunyr as soon as he stepped through the portcullis.."

Elorall walked ahead of the others as she entered the halls of the Irontooth keep. She'd been here enough that she knew the way. The royal family had quarters set aside for the Gods'own. She stopped in her tracks.

The coral elf King Leidergelth stood in front of her. Elorall's father, Leidergelth's high enchanter, stood beside him. Virakh, the king's creepy majordomo, hovered some distance behind them, observing as he always did.

Furtaevell and the king looked surprised to see her so

soon, thinking she would have been in the group nearest the princes. Elorall leaned into her father's arms. "Oh, daughter, I'm so glad to see you safe and sound," he said. "We were just visiting, diplomatic duties and all," Furtaevell said, trying to make it seem as if the two worried fathers were not checking up on their children.

"I don't even care," Elorall said, overlooking a clear lie, but figuring a parent was entitled to those little indiscretions. She squeezed him tighter.

Mantieth hurried into the passage behind her, clearly looking for her. "Let's go away, father. I will tell you about my trip… just you and I." Her eyes glanced at the selumari prince and practically frosted over.

Furtaevell nodded and took his daughter by the hand. He nodded to King Leidergelth and then sidestepped the ever-watchful Virakh.

Leidergelth cocked his head, but nodded in acknowledgment as his son hurried closer. Once Elorall and Furtaevell were gone, he embraced his son briefly and stiffly. He'd never been overly warm, and so his observation of Elorall was keen. "She seemed very cold. Towards you, that is."

Mantieth nodded. He still watched the hallway where she'd departed rather than looking his father in the eye. He opened his mouth to tell him everything, but his father spoke first.

"Your mother and I have been communicating again, I'm happy to report." His eye twinkled slightly. "Thanks to your fiancé, that is. She started it by sending word of your engagement all the way to her in Cyrea."

Leidergelth turned and began strolling the expansive vaghan passageways, knowing that the travelers badly needed a bath. There was feast prepared for them after. "That girl has always loved you, you know? Both her father and I have known it for decades." He smiled at Mantieth. "I had feared you might never show her any interest, despite how she pined for you. But I am glad that is over now and there has been a change of heart."

Mantieth grumbled, "There certainly has been." He turned to catch his father's curious glance. "I really, truly and deeply, love her... If something were to happen to her, I don't know how I could go on."

They took another few steps in silence. "She seemed a little distant... aloof. Your mother and I began our estrangement that way. I'm glad to hear how much you love her I and trust that, whatever happened out there, your love will promptly overshadow it."

Mantieth gulped. He certainly hoped so. "I'm sure she's just rattled from the last battle. She was at the center of a massive explosion that would have killed her had the Goddess Ailuril not intervened... or perhaps it was the Luck Goddess, Mitta," he said. "She was flung into a cistern and left there for a full day before we discovered her." His voice ached with the memory. "We'd thought her dead... "

"Well," the king said, still feeling chipper from the news of his rekindled marriage. "She is alive now. Come, there is a feast! Go and woo her there," he said and clapped Mantieth on the shoulder. He coughed slightly. "But first, perhaps a bath."

CHAPTER TWENTY-NINE

Dining and merrymaking in King Hy'Mandr's feast hall began winding down as revelers meandered back and forth from the keg table where ales and bottles of wines were stocked. Many mingled in the room, standing to keep their full bellies from complaining.

Elorall remained at her seat. She'd been well trained in diplomatic decorum and knew how to impress at formal events. This feast did not qualify as that, but habits were hard to break, and she was in the presence of two kings.

Eucalia came and sat next to her. The dryad had no formal training and had spent most of her life in the forest among gentler folk. She insistently tapped the coral elf on the thigh.

"What is it?" Elorall asked.

The dryad pointed to a door with her head. It led to a balcony that overlooked the city. "Mantieth wants to talk. He says its important."

With unprecedented calm and composure, Elorall nodded and plucked the napkin from her lap. She set it on the table and then excused herself.

Stepping out and into the late evening air, she found her former lover standing there. Mantieth held a small bouquet of watercrest lilies, her favorite flower.

"What?" Elorall crossed her arms and took several paces forward, but remained just out of arm's reach of him. "You summoned me, Prince Mantieth?"

"I... I hoped we could talk," he stammered, taken aback by such formal use of his title.

"So talk, then."

"Listen, Elorall. I'm sorry for what I said, for the doubts that I had. I was too blind to the fact that I genuinely loved you.

I still do, now more than ever."

Elorall cocked her head. Her body language did not soften. "And I am sorry. I too was blind. However, mine was at least excusable."

"Elorall... " he took a step towards her and she took one step back to keep a distance between them.

She shook her head and put up one finger of warning. Mantieth set the flowers on the railing overlooking the city. It was obvious she would not accept them.

"We have so much history together that we... "

Elorall interrupted him. "That is in the past. This thing—how you betrayed me with your dishonesty—that is our present."

Mantieth hung his head. "And the future?"

"I can see no future here," she said stonily.

The prince looked up, hoping to search her eyes for hope, but Elorall had already turned and retreated to the party.

He turned his eyes aside and looked at the flowers he'd gathered for her. The gentle wind rolled them off the balcony and scattered them across the top of the city.

Mantieth felt more alone than ever upon the balcony, unsure if the breeze was natural, or a result of Elorall's command of the winds.

Nodhan laid in his comfortable bed at his Port Orric home. Laelysh slept in the next room over.

He'd tried to drift off, but Seed had continued prattling on about their great mission.

"Give me a few more weeks, Seed," he begged, exhausted and ready for bed. The morehl squeezed his pillow tight, twisting it under his head.

We are out of position. Your trip east took us far from the action we needed to take.

"I'm not sure you really know where this great thing is supposed to happen—so, until then, I say we wait in the comfort of my home and..."

I could make you.

"Don't act like a child. You gave me your word. Besides, we've had this conversation already."

I have someone I must meet. Even now, he searches for me.

"Well, I'll gladly hand you over," Nodhan mumbled. "Tell me their name and I'll make the arrangements in the morning." He could feel himself beginning to drool on the pillow.

Well... I don't know his name...

"What's he look like?"

I... don't...

"I'm gonna go to sleep now."

The faint sound of a bottle rolling on the home's hardwoods reached Nodhan's ears. He went from verging on slumber to armed and at his feet in less than a second.

Silently, he charged through the dark of his house with sword in hand. The intruder barely had time to react to the bottle, and the lava elf found him before he could flee.

"State your business," Nodhan barked with his blade a finger's breadth from the stranger's throat. His eyes glanced to the simple alarm he'd set up each night since spotting the spy outside the confectionarium.

"I wondered if you had spotted me," the figure said, pulling his hood back and opening his cloak slightly. He was eldarim, and the tattoos on his chest revealed him as a Melkite follower and an acolyte of the Death god.

"I spotted you a mile away... I know you've spied me well enough to discover my big beasty pet in the rear yard. In five seconds, I'm going to feed you to her, so you'd better make those seconds count."

"My name is Grick, and we have met before. I first saw you in the lair of that faeli pawn broker, the one in Dohan."

Nodhan cocked his head and squinted. "I sold you a map." He shrugged slightly. "I sell many maps. Most of them I have confidence in. This one... this one I remember *you* had great confidence in, though its treasure was unknown to me. If this is because there was nothing buried at the end of its trail..."

Grick shook his head slowly. He grinned wickedly. "Oh, no. It contained exactly what it promised."

Something about the evil glimmer in Grick's eye made Seed begin to panic. It sounded like a dull buzzing in Nodhan's mind, as if a swarm of high summer cicadas chirping through the air.

"Before I left, you told Grude about a big score. Rumor has it that you raided the vault at Undrakull nearly two years ago. An ancient book was taken from the Melkite leader there... The *Book of the Void*. I want it."

Grick rubbed his wrists anxiously. Nodhan caught a glimmer of jewelry. It seemed to chafe the pale skin around the eldarim's joint, which almost looked diseased.

"The book is already in Grude's possession," Nodhan lied. "Besides, there's no way I'd be stupid enough to keep something that valuable *here*." He looked Grick in the face. "I was raised as a thief in the slums of Emmira and learned an important lesson as a child: Don't shit where you eat."

The intruder scanned his face.

Nodhan was glad he was so skilled a liar. He pressed his point. "If you struggled to outbid competitors for that map I first sold you, you won't have any chance at purchasing the book. It's worth could fetch an entire island."

Grick sneered. "Money is no longer an issue for me. And competitors would be wise not to bid against me."

"Yeah, well, good luck with that. The Fire and Flood Club's clients have deep pockets." Nodhan nodded towards the door. "The next ship to Dohan leaves in the morning. I'm sure you'll want to be on it."

"I am prepared to pay handsomely for it," Grick hissed. "You could cut out Grude's commission entirely. I will pay any price."

"The deal is already done," Nodhan said. "If you know Grude, then you know Grude's rules about this kind of double dealing."

Grick curled his lip in a wicked smile that bared his teeth in a rictus grin. "Dohan it is, then." The Death cultist backed away slowly before exiting the home.

A few moments after Nodhan felt certain he was gone, the elf sprang into action. "Quiet down, now, Seed," he insisted. "I've got too much to do without you screaming through all the recesses of my brain."

You could not feel what I felt. You must not sell him that book.

"Don't worry. He could never afford it," Nodhan said, as he gathered his traveling gear.

He snatched a sack filled with gold coins and entered Laelysh's room. He shook her gently, and she rolled to face him. "Nodhan? What's wrong?"

"Trouble. A past client has found me and wants something I possess. I'm going to leave for a while so he can't take it, and so you'll be out of danger." He put the heavy purse in her hands. "This is to pay for guards. I am hiring mercenaries for security. This should be more than enough to pay wages for a full year, at least. Hopefully I'll be back before then."

He leaned in to kiss her goodbye. His hot lips met hers and she leaned into it, but Nodhan pulled away rather than meet her passion equally.

Seed tried to question his actions, but Nodhan knew his own lifestyle. He could afford no romantic entanglements, especially with such a long-time and respected friend.

Especially now.

"I must leave. Tell Oren goodbye for me... and from Brentésion." He slipped out of the room and hurried towards his buried vault, where he kept the invaluable items.

The *Book of the Void* seemed to suck the very light from the room. On the table next to it sat a second copy. He grinned, remembering that Laelysh had been an expert forgery artist when they'd first met. Her replica was so good that Nodhan couldn't even tell which was which without the label to identify them.

Nodhan suspected Grude may be able to tell, however. He scooped up the ancient book and wrapped it in cloth, binding it tightly for travel, and then headed for the rear of his home where Brentésion waited. She snorted at Nodhan's late-night appearance.

The elf only needed to place one hand upon the dracolem's scaled snout, and Brentésion knew everything in the span of a heartbeat. With a flap of her wings, she dismantled the canopy of tarps that Nodhan's family had erected over her as camouflage.

Before the sun could rise, they were airborne and heading south.

Rahkawmn snorted his displeasure when Melkior entered the sea-side cave from the rear tunnel. That passageway led to the Melkites' hidden lair in the bowels of Trellan.

"I know, I know," Melkior mumbled as he placed a hand gently upon his old friend. "I have been away too long." The lich glanced back at the blackness of the cave, and then at his bandages. "The grievous wound inflicted by the homunculus will not heal, though the cult's collection of necralluvium sustains me for a short while." He swallowed and admitted, "However, its healing effects seem to last shorter each time."

Melkior leaned against his oldest companion's bulky girth. "Forktongue knows many things about the world that passed us by while we waited in our tombs. There are strange new artifacts forged in our absence, including the ancient ones hidden before The Making. We can harness them to our benefit. Forktongue sent a minion after one of them. It should help sustain me. The others will help me have my revenge."

Rahkawmn tightened his massive jaw. He did not like Forktongue and he did not like the path his eldarim friend was taking. Melkior was only growing further in debt to Lord Death, rather than mustering power to rid himself of the bonds the Bastard God had over him.

The dracolich wanted little more than for him and his dragonlord friend to ride away from the conflict and corruption. Were it not for Death's curse, perhaps they could have done that in the afterlife? Rahkawmn mused that he might ever know. *How far does Melkior's dark deal extend?*

"Remember those days when you and I rode over the coasts, circling Hadden Bay and Ender's Gulf with Ailushurai clutching tightly?" Melkior smiled warmly, sounding almost like his old self... before Death took him.

He locked eyes with his draconic companion. "It will be like that again. We can restore order, make things like they were... before..."

Rahkawmn looked into his friend's face. *Before you killed her,* the white dragon remembered. *How deep does his madness extend?*

He sighed and his throaty rumble startled a clutch of gulls outside the cave upon the beach. They yelled and took flight. Rahkawmn wondered again, and not for the last time, if there was redemption available for him and Melkior. And if not, was abandoning him now better than the torments of the Abyss?

"Soon," Melkior insisted, oblivious to his companion's philosophical musings. "Soon, all will be made right again."

CHAPTER THIRTY

Mantieth sulked in Hy'Targ's doorway. "My life is over," the elf whined.

Varanthl turned and cocked his head alongside his vaghan friend. "You do not look deceased," Varanthl said.

Hy'Targ raised an eyebrow, not certain if Varanthl was joking or if he didn't understand the euphemism. He turned back to the elf. "She's not taking you back, eh?"

Mantieth wandered in with crooked steps. He clung to a fresh bottle of wine, and his friends could tell this was not his first of the evening. "Remember that time I drank with Nodhan in prison?"

"We were not there for that," Varanthl said, taking the bottle from him.

"Good. Drink with me," the elf slurred. "I could use a friend."

"Where is the cork?" Varanthl asked.

Mantieth shrugged sheepishly. "I guess we'll just have to finish it."

Varanthl looked sideways at the dwarf.

"Don't look at me. That's sound logic, even if wine isn't my particular flavor." Hy'Targ got up from his desk where he'd been pouring over the documents copied for him by Jr'Orhr. They still had much to learn in their search for the remaining relics, but that mystery would not be solved this night—his selumari friend had a pressing need.

Varanthl handed Hy'Targ the bottle as Mantieth slumped into a seat. "I will get some glasses, then." The homunculus returned a few moments later and poured them all a round. He took a sip of his own and looked up to see both his friends holding out empty glasses for a refill.

"Seriously?" Varanthl asked.

Hy'Targ nodded. "I know you're still new to being alive, or whatever, but this is a real thing. I don't know a lot about love, I've yet to have a lass catch my eye, but what I *do know* is the rules of a broken heart. When your friend's heart is broken, it's his friends' duty to get drunk with him."

The dwarf shook his glass to demand the refill. Varanthl shrugged and filled it. He drained his own and caught up quickly.

Soon, their wine had run dry, and they were chasing down another bottle. Or three.

The sun was already high in the sky by the time Hy'Targ awoke. Blinking hurt his face, and his pulse pounded in his ears. Hy'Targ glanced across the room. Mantieth was passed out, still in a painful looking pose, sprawled over a chair. By the sound of his snores, the coral elf wouldn't be rising any time soon.

Varanthl was already gone, likely running about the castle already, doing his laundry or other kinds of chores. His regenerative capabilities came in handy at times like this.

Hy'Targ chugged down a pitcher of water that he'd been wise enough to fill last night and sat at his desk. Luckily, the silence of his apartment allowed him to resume what he'd been doing the previous night. He looked over the maps of Gnomehome and at the other sheets Jr'Orhr had produced.

His mind was still somewhat hazy, though, and he blinked away the fog. Hy'Targ instead picked up the gnomish puzzlecube that Gryeslan had given him: The old gremmlobahnd they'd met in Gnomehome.

He played with it absentmindedly. "Gryeslan said it contained a weapon."

Hy'targ fumbled with the device and it activated. The thing seemed to unravel all at once, like a coiled spring released. It unlinked into a circle-like a chain that opened up and lassoed him, dropping him into the middle of it.

He looked up just in time to see the gate shimmer and then blink closed, like some kind of eye made out of pure lightning.

For a long moment, Hy'targ simply sat there, dumped into the pocket dimension that Gryeslan had described to him. Panic momentarily overwhelmed him—the gnome had been trapped inside one of these for over a thousand years!

He calmed slightly once he remembered that there was supposed to be a failsafe, some kind of way to open the portal from within. Hy'targ looked around. The floors were made of burnished metal, and it looked more like some kind of compartment.

A familiar creature loomed in the distance.

"Brentésion?" he asked cautiously, spotting the metal dragonkin ahead of him in the shadows. He rushed forward and bumped into a thick pane of glass, a similar kind of unbreakable crystal to what the Gods'own had discovered in the heart of Gnomehome. It had meant to trap the drekloch.

He squinted in the dim light. This was not Brentésion. It appeared identical in every way, except it was silver in color. He bent over and examined an engraved nameplate that read Hárgyros.

Hy'targ stood and checked his surroundings. The room was shaped like a wedge and the back wall curved in an arc, suggesting he stood in one third of a circular enclosure. The two sides angled towards a terminal point where Hárgyros slumbered behind a pane of impenetrable glass and a steel plinth protruded from the ground. Light was low in each of those, too.

The dwarf touched the metallic post, and it activated. An apparition of a gnome appeared in the air. It spoke in the native tongue of the gremmlobahnd and then paused for an answer. Hearing none, the ghostly gnome disappeared in a flash of dim light.

Hy'targ activated it again, but the result was the same. He listened to the gnome speak, and felt certain he asked a question, but could not translate it quick enough without his lexicon present.

Within the compartment beside him, the lights suddenly turned on, illuminating the entire chamber. Hy'targ wondered only momentarily why his area had not done so and assumed there was some kind of defect or damage to his side of the cubicle.

And then he saw her and stopped wondering about everything else. On the other side of the glass stood a red-haired dwarven woman about his age. She was the most beautiful vagha he'd ever laid eyes on.

Hy'targ silently cursed Mantieth for even making him think about love. Surely this was all part of some kind of wine-fueled fever dream? He bit his lip and knew it was not.

She wore clothes built for a colder climate, styled of a kind he did not know, except for the steel boots of a warrior. Hy'targ could only assume she hailed from a far north tribe, since the southern pole of Esfah hosted no civilized life.

He stared through the glass, knowing she could not see him. The light on her side would turn the glass to a mirror finish.

Hy'targ could only watch, unsure how far removed he actually was from her, and he wondered if—despite all the artifacts they'd recently claimed—this gnomish puzzle cube might have led to the truest treasure?

Epilogue

The cultist behind Yarrick untied his gag and let the two ends fall before bending over to set his food before him. Yarrick slipped his gag beneath him to hide it. As the cultist bent over to position the meal tray, Yarrick spotted the frayed edge of his pocket, exactly as he'd hoped.

Yarrick took a chance and slipped his chained hands into the pocket, quickly and silently. Just as quietly as he put his hands in, he pulled them out. None of the other cultists saw.

He sneakily unlocked the fetters around his ankle and then palmed the key, bending forward and keeping low to scoop food into his mouth as if he were a dog.

The cultists paid their prisoners little mind, and Yarrick worked the key into the shackle holes around his wrists. The latches released, just as the beautiful woman with the black mouth entered.

Yarrick sprang into action and snatched the tray they'd brought his food upon. He smacked the lady across the face and spun her to the ground, dazing her. He did not relish striking a woman, but took no chance in case she was a spell caster.

The eldarim warrior dashed down the hallway, sparing a glance out the window. A vertical wall spilled downward and onto a cliff-side that ended at the tumultuous seawater. Whitecaps crashed against the rocks below.

He rounded a corner and sprinted ahead, hoping to find a guard station, a soldier he could disarm, anything that could help aid Yarrick's escape.

The prisoner rattled a shut door made of wrought iron; it was locked. He ran forward, the next door was also closed. Finally, the last door at the end of the hall opened into a galley where the meals had been prepared.

Yarrick ran to the other door leading from the kitchens

and found it locked, also. He whirled around, hoping to double back, but found his beautiful captor standing in the doorway, nursing a flush cheek. A crew of her minions flooded in around her and the gang tackled him.

"You nearly embarrassed me and in front of our leader. He has finally returned to us and intends to watch the ceremony. We had closed off the hallways for his security."

The cultists managed to restrain Yarrick and forced him back into his chains before shoving him back into the halls. Another of his fellow shara stood there. Defeat darkened the captive's eyes.

"Now, go," said the woman, prodding her prisoners forward and guiding them to a large chamber at the center of the castle.

Yarrick looked up and spotted a balcony walkway. A short, cloaked figure wearing a hood stood on the upper level, watching. Yarrick assumed that was the woman's master.

The eldarim peered closer, trying to see a face, and saw only a glint of stone. He wore some kind of mask.

At a central pedestal, a silvery ocarina rested upon a velvet pillow. It was smooth and exquisitely crafted except for a jagged, cast line that crisscrossed the instrument. It appeared to be made of pure eldrymetallum.

The woman whispered to him, "You will have your turn right afterward, trouble-maker." She picked up the ocarina and put it into the hands of the other captive. "Blow. Make something that passes for music."

The captive's eyes met Yarrick's. There was somehow both panic and resignation in them. He pressed the instrument to his dry and cracked lips and then blew into it. The ocarina made no sound, but the eldarim slave dropped the relic. His skin suddenly peeled back from his face, and the flesh and blood beneath boiled and dissolved.

He shrieked and collapsed to his knees as his flesh split

like aged paper and his organs fell out, steaming upon the stone floor beneath him. Muscles and tendons shriveled, snapping like acorn husks in a fire. The cult's victim collapsed in a quivering heap that pulsated and leaked strangely liquefied proteins in a wide and chunky puddle.

High above, the cult leader stood resolute, unmoved by the gruesome scene. The female cultist retrieved the instrument and wiped it clean.

She slowly spun to Yarrick. "Your turn."

Evaquar narrowed her eyes to slits as her sister moved a piece upon the game board. "You are cheating again, Avanna," the goddess hissed.

"You cannot prove that." Avanna signaled to her consort, the bone man who guided souls to the afterlife. "You may begin your song, Hielosch."

The Deathbard set the point of his rabab and dragged the bow across its strings. It emitted a sound like rosin upon a flexing saw blade. He set his fingers and turned it into a musical tune.

Mitta scanned the game board. "She is set to take a valuable piece, Evaquar."

Avanna shrugged. "It is just a game, sister."

Evaquar set her jaw. "But for the pieces, it is life and death. This is just a game of fate."

Avanna reached for a piece and repeated. "Just a game."

The End

Appendices

Glossary of Terms

Abyss – the home of the Void, a realm where silence reigns aside from pockets of terror and chaos where unknown gods reign. This is a similar concept to Greek myths of an underworld.

Ailuril – the second born of the Esfahan gods. She is represented by the color blue and has power over the air elements.

Agamid – a winged type Drakufreet

Aguarehl – the fourth born of the Esfahan gods. He is represented by the color green and has power over the water elements.

Amazon – the race of mankind said to have been deposited whole upon Esfah as one of the few races created by Tarvanehl himself. Amazons are the warrior caste of human race.

Areosa – commonly known as the frostwings, a frigid felinoid, winged race with magic resistance.

Bloodless – another common name for the undead.

Deadzone – synonym for the Abyss, except from the point of view of the trogs or morehl. Within their respective religions, versions of the afterlife differ wildly and as often as they align in geopolitical goals, neither could imagine spending an eternal afterlife in the company of the other.

Death – the half-brother god who is the child of Nature and Void.

Dragons – these beasts come in two forms: Drake and Wyrm. Drakes have wings, and wyrms do not. Though the dragonkin are a kind of subspecies, they are not the same thing, no matter how similar they are. They used to live hidden across Esfah, but were nearly eradicated in the Dragoncrusades. Dragons have eternal spirits and when they die, they return to the plane where they now dwell. Dragonmagic came in two forms and it summons them from this realm or from nearby (the older form of this magic which has now been forgotten since these mythic beasts have largely gone out from Esfah.)

Drakufreet – the dragonkin come from the same realm as dragons and appear as a type of draconic hybrid race. They come in multiple types and subspecies. Agamids are a flying type of the subspecies which include Saurons (a gator-like humanoid variant,) Mokole (a rideable dragonfolk that is something of a mix between Sauron and Suchia,) Suchia (a buffalo-sized drakufreet that can make an excellent mount). Of these, the Champion sized are the largest and most fearsome, ranging up to three quarters in size of a dragon's size.

Eldarim – a human-like race that emerged over eons from Esfah's primordial soup and predated the gods-made races. The eldarim are versatile and have proven the capacity to breed with many of Esfah's races. They are called eldarim, meaning "from the earth."

Eldurim – the firstborn of the Esfahan gods. He is represented by the color gold and has power over the earth elements.

Efflorah – the race of treefolk.

Esfah – the world and one of two planets revolving around Soll.

Empyrea – known commonly as the firewalkers, a war-loving mercenary race.

Faeli – commonly known as scalders or steam dancers. These creatures are fickle and capricious and were once captured and tormented by Death.

Festration – a kind of location so tainted by evil activity that the very land itself has become corrupt and avails itself to wickedness.

Firiel – the third born of the Esfahan gods. She is represented by the color red and has power over the fire elements.

First Age – everything from the beginning of creation to the year 863.

Frehlasuhl – also called the Forsaken or Mudbloods. They are the offspring of selumari and morehl unions. They cannot breed with each other to have children, only with one or the other race, but they are rejected wholesale by both.

Ghaeial – the mother goddess known more commonly as Nature.

Ghwereste – called the "feral folk." These are a hybrid of animal and man created at the dawn of the Second Age.

Kreethaln – there are three of these mystical artifacts made of an unknown metal. Little is known about them except that they each possess some kind of arcane power. Their names are Life-bringer, Wisdom-giver, and Spell-crafter.

Leguin – a sister planet to Esfah that also orbits Sol; it can often be seen in the night sky appearing above the horizon like a bright star.

Lich – a powerful undead spell caster. Lichs often possess necromantic capabilities, though their created undead are maintained by force of will, rather than by other means, such as the Necralluvium.

Mokole – see Drakufreet

Morehl – commonly called lava elves. They have red skin in addition to their elf-like features and their blood is said to smoke when exposed to air.

Necralluvium - a kind of magical potion with a seeming life of its own. This black filth can kill the living. The dead that are exposed to it become animated.

Rhaudian – the name of the moon. It circulates Esfah twice in a daily cycle.

Sarslayan – commonly known as swamp stalkers. These snake-men emerged in the Second Age as a result of Death using magic to twist the creations of his half-brother Aguarehl. They create more of their kind through magic conversion rather than by reproduction.

Sauron – see Drakufreet

Second Age – everything after year 863 of the First Age. This began when Ghaeial walked the face of Esfah and surveyed the damages of the myriad of wars. The 864th year is year 1 of the Second Age.

Selurehl – the name of the second god to emerge after Tarvanehl, usually known as Void.

Selumari – commonly called coral elves. They have blue skin in addition to their elf-like features.

Shara – what the eldarim people refer to themselves as when they communicate with each other. It means "little god-in-the-making."

Soll – the sun.

Suchia – see Drakufreet

Sukie – nickname for Suchia

Tarvanehl – the creator god who came first, according to all mythology and story; he is often known as Father Time, or simply The Father.

Teldrim – a race of extinct horse lords that bore many similarities to the Amazons. A creation of Tarvanehl, these were remarkable because the race could intermix with any other. They were eradicated by Melkior shortly after their emergence.

Trog – a synonym for goblin. trogs much prefer to live in boggy areas and tend to pollute the land.

Vagha – commonly known as dwarves.

Void – sometimes used interchangeably with the Abyss or, the power or person of Selurehl who is frequently referred to as Void just as his son Malgrimm is more widely regarded as Death. Context determines the meaning.

Warchief – a title of rank among the vagha. Below the king is a Warchief who leads Warlords and Warcommanders under them. It might commonly be understood as a sort of general.

Timeline

Included is the general timeline of major world events in Esfah. Please note that, during the time before the Mother, Ghaeial, became a goddess and the First Age began, Prehistory spanned a scope of time measuring eons. In that time, verily, only *Time* existed. Despite the sage's attempts to capture much data and ancient knowledge, they did not begin tracking time and dates until the first passing of the Daybringer. The first three years of history might very well have been hundreds or even a thousand years as the gods (and the earliest race of eldarim) kept time differently.

Prehistory N.D.

Tarvanehl exists and creates within the realm of Void/Abyss and Esfah and Leguin are born; Ghaeial realizes she is a goddess and falls in love with Tarvanehl.

Turambar courts Leguin.

Selurehl, third of the brother gods grows angry.

Eldurim, the firstborn (earth) god-son of Ghaeial and Tarvanehl is born.

Ailuril, the second born (wind) god-daughter of Ghaeial and Tarvanehl is born.

Firiel, third born (fire) god-daughter of Ghaeial and Tarvanehl is born

Aguarehl, fourth born god-son (water) of Ghaeial and Tarvanehl is born

Malgrimm, the cursed bastard son (Death) is conceived and birthed after Selurehl's violence upon Ghaeial

Eldarim are birthed by Esfah and slowly emerge from the mire of her lands and water, evolving over long periods of time. They call themselves the Shara in their own tongue.

The First Age

03FA the Daybringer Comet passes Esfah for the First Time, the Sisters of Fate are birthed of Turambar and Leguin, Dragons and the Drakufreet are created during the schism of the god-children.

04FA Earliest creations of the gods: "monsters" are formed

15FA selumari are created

16FA vagha are created, trogs are created

17FA morehl are created

19FA The Dawn of War. morehl invaders overthrow the first selumari

22FA Humans arrive on Esfah via Tarvanehl's intervention

28FA Davian Whisperwynd leaves Maris-ta-Sehlim

32FA The proto-empyreans are birthed in the whirlwind

42FA Gundraokh Shatterfist finds the Bands of Turambar and renames the city of Orelod to Gundakhor

96FA Sshkkryyahr the Dread rises to power

103FA Malgrimm attempts to create a new powerful, destructive force within the Shadowlands, but the Areosan's magic resistance helps them maintain mild independence from the Death god and he abandons them to the frost plains.

143FA Undead created, Melkior is defeated upon the Raithlan Plains by the gods' chosen Champions

167FA Dilution of the eldarim race and the reduction of the Dragon population via the Dragoncrusades that eliminated nearly all the natural dragons of Esfah; the spells that compelled natural dragons that still remained in the realm became forgotten after this date in favor of those drawing eternal dragons through the interplanar rifts

341FA Existence of the empyreans is discovered when they aid the elder races in the first major Undead uprising.

447FA *Book of the Land, 1st Ed.* is published and immediately begins revisions

520FA morehl city of Karakto falls to the selumari

532FA morehl discover cursed bullets and retake Karakto

544FA Large load of Eldrymetallum discovered on the Karakto slopes

562FA Final version of *The Book of the Land* completed after 23 quintennial installments

836FA The Magestorm Wars erupt with the tectonic cataclysm that opens the Netherwold and nearly splits Dereh'Liandor in two; the Arcana Veil stiffens

842FA Disappearance of the gremmlobahnd and the genocide of the drakufreet

863FA Final battle of the Magestorm Wars ends the first age, the faeli are birthed in the Firequags and captured by the forces of Death and subjected to torments in the pits of the World Wound.

The Second Age

01SA Ghaeial walks the earth and surveys the damage of the elder races.

03SA Ghaeial creates the ghwereste

79SA The plagues of the World Wound and its evils continue and the first of the sarslayan emerge from the nearby Snekdenn Bayou

153SA The areosa race emerges from the Shadowlands. They are known mostly as rumors, but their existence is verified to the outside world.

209SA Whether the faeli escaped the torments of the World Wound or were released, none know, but they were so twisted by the centuries of abuse that they have become more children of Malgrimm than Ghaeial

233SA Under Ghaeial's wishes, the sylvan efflorah, existing as trees since even before the humans came to Esfah, picked up their roots and first emerged from forest and grove

829SA Zephras "Thunderfist" dies in Cyrea defending Balgavarr Reaches from a dragon

967SA Geril sa'Ghuren "Dragonsbane" born

1021SA Geril sa'Ghuren rules in Balgavarr

1082SA Coryn Sa'Geril is born

1119SA Daybringer Comet makes its pass by Esfah

1122SA Kholkoro Wicebrow writes her commentary *Kholkoro's commentary on Book of the Land*

1127SA The famed "Adventurer King" Hy'Mandr sa'Meril is blinded

1139SA Melkior is revived

1142SA Daybringer Comet makes its circuit

Christopher D. Schmitz

The Birthlands
Oxforge
Daur-Bor-Nin
Hagrond Mount
New Emmira
Far Seas
Great Coastal Road
Tenebrakth
Barad's Spire
Tumult Straights
Diriath's Tower
The Broken Crown

Christopher D. Schmitz

Books in the Dragon Dice Universe of Esfah

Rise and Fall of the Obsidian Grotto
Cast of Fate
Tome of Tarvanehl*
Heart of Stone and Flame*
Ashes of Ailushurai
Rise of the Champions
Drakuwar
Chill Wind
Eye of the Storm
Secrets of the Shadowlands
Army of the Dead**

*These two short books were the first produced by TSR and are included inside the re-released (2020) version of Cast of Fate, which was originally produced in 1996.

**This book was scheduled for release by TSR in the late 1990s but never published. A version of this book was released in 2003 but should not necessarily be considered Esfah canon and unless it is rereleased should not be considered part of *the Esfah Sagas*.

About the author:

Christopher D. Schmitz is author of both Sci-Fi/Fantasy Fiction and Nonfiction books and has been published in both traditional and independent outlets. If you've investigated indie writers of the upper Midwest, you may have heard his name whispered in dark alleys with an equal mix of respect and disdain. He has been featured on television broadcasts, podcasts, and runs a blog for indie authors... but you've still probably never heard of him.

As an avid consumer of comic books, movies, cartoons, and books (especially sci-fi and fantasy) this child of the 80s basically lived out Stranger Things, but shadowy government agencies won't let him say more than that. He lives in rural Minnesota with his family where he drinks unsafe amounts of coffee; the caffeine shakes keep the cold from killing him. In his off-time he plays haunted bagpipes in places of low repute, but that's a story for another time.

He has a special offer for readers on the following page.

You can connect with him via the following links:
http://www.authorchristopherdschmitz.com

Follow me on Twitter:
https://twitter.com/cylonbagpiper
Follow me on Goodreads:
www.goodreads.com/author/show/129258.Christopher_Schmitz
Like/Follow me on Facebook:
https://www.facebook.com/authorchristopherdschmitz
Subscribe to my blog:
https://authorchristopherdschmitz.wordpress.com
Favorite me at Smashwords:
www.smashwords.com/profile/view/authorchristopherdschmitz
My Amazon Author Profile:
amazon.com/author/christopherdschmitz
Follow me at Bookbub:
www.bookbub.com/authors/christopher-d-schmitz

SPECIAL OFFER:

As a special bonus for you, I'd like to invite you download FIVE ebooks for free as a part of my Starter Library.

To get your free Starter Library, simply visit this link:

https://www.subscribepage.com/p1o9c9

Enter your email address and then collect your books as they are sent to you. It's that simple!

FREE STARTER BOOK LIBRARY

If you like Sci-Fi and Fantasy, you'll love these books, subscribe now to have them delivered right away.

Dragon Dice

Dragon Dice™ is SFR Inc.'s core product. We are constantly working to create a quality game that everyone can enjoy. Dragon Dice™ was originally created by Lester Smith and produced by TSR© in 1995. After several years, TSR, now owned by Wizards of the Coast, had put Dragon Dice™ on hold to work on other projects. In October of 2000, SFR Inc. purchased the rights to Dragon Dice™ and now will continue to support and create NEW! products for the game.

Dragon Dice™ is strategy game where players create mythical armies using dice to represent each troop. The game combines strategy and skill as well as a little luck. Each person tries to win the game by outmaneuvering the opponent and capture 2 terrains. Of course, eliminating your opponent completely is another acceptable way of winning.

Get online today and "Roll your way to victory!"

http://www.sfr-inc.com